David Daniel Shaw was born in Leeds. He studied Law, completing his degree in 1984 and, after sampling work in banking, decided to join the Police Force. He is currently a Sergeant working in Leeds and has fulfilled his life's ambition by writing this, his first science fiction novel.

David is married and has two young children. An avid football fan, he also enjoys tennis and riding with his daughter. Whilst beavering away on his second book he jokes, 'I may eventually be able to replace the rigours of police work with the greater rigours of writing.'

Cruel
Intervention

David Daniel Shaw

Cruel
Intervention

Vanguard Press

A CIP catalogue record for this title is
available from the British Library

ISBN 1 84386 108 9

*Vanguard Press is an imprint of
Pegasus Elliot MacKenzie Publishers Ltd.*
www.pegasuspublishers.com

First Published in 2004

**Vanguard Press
Sheraton House Castle Park
Cambridge England**

Printed & Bound in Great Britain

THE DEED

In defiance of death, the woman's eyes stared skyward.

She laid half on the road, half on the grass verge, a small red dot slightly off centre on her forehead, like a married Indian woman who had applied her bindi whilst distracted. Her left arm was beneath her body while the right lay across her chest, her fingers still clawed, indicating a vain attempt to fight off her killer.

'Don't touch her,' DC Todd barked from his car to the young uniformed officer who had arrived at the scene before him. 'Don't go any closer.'

PC Harris stood, his mouth slightly open, as he looked at the dead woman. Below her head a patch of grass the size of a large plate had turned a dirty brown colour, relinquishing its verdant green to thick red blood. Her car, only metres away, was still running, the cooler fan impatiently whirring, unaware that its owner was not coming back.

'She's been shot,' PC Harris said, pointing out the obvious. 'But her face and head are hardly marked.'

'Just make sure you stand well back, sonny,' the seasoned detective said, empathising with the young officer's naivety whilst ensuring that the crime scene was not compromised. 'The bullet does most of its damage on the way through,' he explained. 'The point of entry is usually small, but the back of her head, well, there's probably not a lot of that left.'

'Hey, what if she's still alive...? we have to check,' the new boy said in a panicky voice, and stepped forward.

The detective extended his shovel-like hand and pulled back the rookie. 'I said no closer, do you hear me?' Harris nodded. 'Look, you see her legs?' The woman wore a short white summer skirt and white sandals. 'See where they're near to the ground? Purple shadowing. That's what we call settling. After someone dies, the blood stops circulating around the body and not long after it settles at the lowest points. She's not still alive, I can

11

assure you of that... DC Todd to control.'

'DC Todd, go ahead.'

'I want CID supervision, the Force Medical Officer and Scenes of Crime here as soon as possible. There's been a fatal shooting, a young woman in her twenties, about two miles east of Barwick-in-Elmet on the country road near to Garforth golf club. I'm gonna seal off the area as best I can.'

'Received,John, I'll get the circus on the road.'

THE CONSEQUENCE

Chapter 1

21st July 2001

Rick laid half asleep on the sofa, enjoying the serenity that fills the mind at the moment when consciousness gives way to sleep. The TV ads no longer persuaded him now, as images of his recent honeymoon in the Maldives filled him with a sense of well-being and produced a contented half-smile on his face.

As his slumber deepened, he became aware of a tapping sound. He awoke with a start as the determined knock on the door was repeated. A quick rub of his eyes and a glance at the clock and he was on his feet. KNOCK-KNOCK-KNOCK.

'OK, OK, I'm coming,' he called. 'Where's your key?'

Rick visibly flinched as he opened the door. Instead of his new wife, Ellie, being there to reprimand him about leaving his key in the door, there stood two well-dressed men.

'Are you Richard Sheldon?' one of them asked in a low voice.

'Well, yes,' Rick said, his brow forming a furrow. 'Who are you, it's almost midnight?'

'I'm Detective Chief Inspector Fenton, and this is Detective Sergeant Moore,' said the taller of the two men looking at his colleague. 'Could we come in, please?' He held up a police warrant card to show his authenticity.

'What's happened?' Rick said, as he looked from one man to the other.

'It would be better if we went inside, Mr Sheldon,' said the taller detective.

The short walk from the door to the lounge seemed to take an eternity. What could be so important at this time of the night that two CID officers had to come knocking at his door, he thought. Oh, God, he hadn't paid that speeding fine from two months ago. But even that, surely, didn't merit this.

'Sir, I'm afraid we've got some disturbing news for you, would you like to take a seat?'

Rick sat, as if obeying the officer would lessen the impact of the forthcoming news, or persuade the messenger to relate the bombshell in a more soothing way. It did neither.

'There's no easy way of telling you this, I'm afraid,' said the DCI, 'Your wife… she's been killed!'

Nothing could have prepared Rick for this. He looked at the man who'd told him. The detective looked back at him. The first emotion that the officer recognised in Rick's eyes was that of utter disbelief. Please, no, was the invisible appeal that passed from Rick to the messenger. Then he read acceptance in Rick's eyes; that moment when, despite not wanting to accept a given situation, the fact that it must be true strikes home with a stab to the heart. The detective, himself, felt a deep sadness. In his twenty-four years in the Force he'd had to give similar news to many people, and this time was no easier than the last, or the first. He saw despair, fear and pain grip Rick in a vice, and he turned his gaze from the unfortunate soul. The next words would have to be from the man he had just destroyed, because nothing he said now would be heard.

The two policemen looked respectfully down at the floor, giving Rick time to comprehend the news and to compose himself.

'How? Where? What the hell's happened?' stuttered Rick, his eyes filling with unwanted tears.

The detective's difficult task was not complete.

'You may have trouble taking this in at the moment, Richard,' he said as softly as he could. 'She's been murdered.'

***

The morgue lived up to its reputation. Cold floors and walls. Stark, uninviting décor. That was how it was designed to be, though. Clinical. Factual. And the fact was that Ellie was dead. Only hours earlier she had been a free spirit filled with excitement at the thought of visiting her mum and dad and telling them about all the fun she'd had on her honeymoon, and of the things she would have loved to have done, but daren't, for fear of harming the growing life inside her. Her son or daughter to be, that would never be.

An immaculately clean and shiny tray slid open, holding its client.

The regular morgue attendant carefully removed the white sheet from the face of the woman laid on the slab, and Rick answered 'Yes' to the question put to him. Legal process required a formal identification of *the body*, and Rick despised the rule.

He glanced at the soulless mass under the sheet and saw the slightly enlarged abdominal region, where his child lay. It too, was lifeless now.

Chapter 2

22nd July 2001

Despite Rick being only thirty years old, both of his parents had passed away. But this was different, he thought. This was not how things were supposed to be. This defied the expected and as such left him feeling numb. It was as if the natural rules of life had been changed for him. Why, when his life was so wonderful and full, had some force intervened to deprive him of everything?

Rick lay awake all that night. To have allowed sleep to take over would have been to risk another visit to the Maldives and then, on waking, reach the realisation of his loss all over again. He would not allow that to happen.

***

Without eating or changing Rick took the short car journey to his friend's house. It was 8.35 on Sunday morning when he knocked at the door. A woolly head appeared at the bedroom window.

'Rick, what are you doing here at this time? Hang on a minute.'

Thomas Newton, adorned only in boxer shorts and scratching his head in bemusement, opened the door. Before he could ask again why Rick was bothering him at this hour, the unwelcome visitor barged passed him and made for the lounge.

'Hey, steady on mate,' Tom protested, as he closed the door behind him. 'What's the matter with you?'

As Tom entered the living room he saw Rick sitting on the edge of a chair, his head in his hands. He laughed out loud, 'Now this has got to be a record. Back from the romantic honeymoon in the romantic Indian Ocean and a row the very next day. It doesn't look good, kid, I mean you've just agreed to love and cherish...'

'Ellie's dead,' Rick interrupted, still hiding his face fully.

'Yeah, right. Hey, I don't think that's funny. Look, it's early pal, I just want to get a bit more sleep, so grab a coffee and...'

'Are you deaf?' Rick said rudely. 'She's been killed by some fucking nutcase on the way to her mum's last night.'

He looked up at Tom with a red face.

The two men had known each other since high school. They had shared secrets, played jokes and told of loves and losses over the years. They knew each other like twin brothers.

Tom studied his friend's face. He saw no signs of a trick, no hidden agenda. The realisation that Rick was telling the truth overwhelmed him. He sank into a chair without averting his gaze, not knowing what to say or what to do next.

Tom's girlfriend, Josie Hinds, breezed into the room. 'Rick. This is a bit early, isn't it? You really could be more considerate.'

'Josie, shut up,' scolded Tom.

'Look, you, I was fast asleep.' She glanced at Rick, ready to give him a dressing-down, but saw his face. 'What's happened? Are you all right?'

Rick looked away from her. He really didn't want to tell the news again.

'Ellie's been killed,' Tom said in a low voice, as if to keep the news a secret between the two of them.

'What...what...killed?' stammered Josie.

Tom stood and walked over to her, gesturing for her to keep her voice down. 'Let him tell us what's happened in his own time. Christ, killed, I can hardly believe it. Who'd want to kill Ellie?'

'Sorry to bother you two with this,' Rick said, wiping tears from his eyes with the backs of his hands. 'I just want to tell you what the police told me. I can't make any sense of it at the moment, and I just want to talk about it, to you.' He sounded disoriented.

'Ellie, dead,' Josie muttered, staring at the floor.

'Look, we'll make a coffee,' Tom said. 'You just sit there and relax for a minute.'

Tom and Josie went into the kitchen, leaving Rick to compose himself.

'She didn't turn up at her mum's last night,' Josie recalled. 'I'd been over there earlier in the week and Mary said she'd had a phone call from her and was expecting her to visit around nine o'clock the day after they came back, so I got there about quarter to. I was going to surprise her, but she didn't show. To be honest, Mary and John weren't concerned. I wasn't really, I mean, just back off the honeymoon. Mary said it would be best to leave them alone and let Ellie ring when she was ready. None of us thought anything of it. I stayed for a couple of hours and then came home.'

'Listen, you're good friends with her mum and dad. Do you think they know?'

'How do I know? We'd better ask Rick.'

Rick looked more calm on their return to the lounge.

'Do John and Mary know?' Tom asked.

'Yeah. John rang me about three this morning. The police told me first, and I couldn't face telling them so I asked the two detectives if they'd do it.'

'Go at your own pace,' Tom said to reassure his friend. 'We're here for you for as long as you need.'

'The police say she's been shot. Shot, for God's sake. Terrorists and drug-pushers get bloody shot, not...' Rick swallowed hard and took a deep breath. 'It was on that country road between Garforth and Barwick. Her car was parked and she was found half on the road, half on the grass verge, near to the car. A passing motorist came across her but she was already dead, it was too late. She was on her way to her mum's. I didn't even want her to go. Why didn't she listen to me? Why did she have to go out? Why?'

'Listen, blame doesn't come into this,' said Tom. 'And no-one can see into the future, either.'

'I know, but if only she'd stayed at home, she'd still be with me.'

Josie began to cry, and left the room as inconspicuously as possible.

'Or would she?' he continued, 'What if it wasn't a madman? It might have been someone who hated her, someone with a grudge, or somebody who had a reason. They say you never know a person one hundred per cent. Maybe…'

'Talking like this won't do you any good,' Tom stopped him in his tracks. 'No-one knows who killed her or why. No-one. Leave it to the police; their job is to find out what happened, and they will.'

'They'd better. If they don't, I will.' Rick's voice was raised. 'The bastard's gonna pay…you mark my words… he'll pay for this.' As he shouted uncontrollably, Rick hammered his fist into the table, breaking it clean in two.

Chapter 3

Physical fatigue and mental exhaustion took their toll, and Rick slept his way through the next two days, waking only to visit the bathroom. He slept deeply, a kindness afforded him by the Sandman who had clearly decided that to sprinkle his unconsciousness with recent happy times, or harsh reality, would serve only to tip the sleeper over the edge.

Sleep gave Rick's body the rest it needed, but did nothing to soothe his inner pain.

He awoke with an almighty headache. Trudging down the stairs Rick saw the two oil paintings of beach scenes chosen by Ellie only three or four weeks before. As he opened the cupboard to get some pain-killers he remembered the disagreement he had had with her over whether the kitchen utensils and appliances should be blue or silver. He felt that silver would best suit the décor. As he looked around the silent kitchen, blue appliances everywhere, he gave a wry grin. Then he saw the shopping list that she'd made out before setting off for her parent's house. He touched the words on the scrap paper as though it would bring him closer to her.

Rick thought of the many tragic tales he had seen on the news over the years; a person's child being abducted and murdered, a train crash that wiped out a wife and two children, leaving dad to face life alone, cancer taking a young father of three, and he began to understand the depth of emotions experienced by those people who, through no fault of their own, were the ones whose names appeared on the News at Ten. The ones left behind following the calamity, the ones who had to cope, the ones who were soon forgotten because their story was no longer current. Yes, there would be families all over the country tonight yawning as they watch the late story about the young woman in Leeds, six months pregnant, found shot without a motive on a country lane.

How did those left behind cope? Rick wondered not only how he would cope, but whether he would cope.

As he quenched his thirst with the remainder of the water from taking the Aspirin he heard the letter-box click. His interest in the post was minimal, but sat on top of various colourful fliers was a bright red envelope, visible even amongst the junk mail. He opened it with mild intrigue, and gasped at the contents.

SO – SHE'S DEAD. YOU POOR THING. HOW DO YOU FEEL?
NEVER FORGET, THOUGH, THERE'S ALWAYS SOMEONE WORSE OFF THAN YOU. BUT WHAT GOES AROUND COMES
AROUND. BYE FOR NOW.

The words were arranged using letters from magazines and newspapers, as he had seen many times on murder mystery films. Rick looked at the postmark on the envelope. Nottingham. But he'd never known anyone in Nottingham. He read the sadistic script over and over again, but it gave no clues as to the author's identity or the reason for its existence. He sat on the bottom stair for almost two hours, gazing at the four lines of uneven text. SO – SHE'S DEAD: someone who knows Ellie's dead. Oh, come on, the whole country knows, he thought. HOW DO YOU FEEL? Why would anybody want to know, or ask, how he feels? Possibly someone who has suffered themselves and justice was not done, but what could that be to do with him, and how could he be blamed for their plight? It was true, there was always someone worse off than you, but WHAT GOES AROUND COMES AROUND. Was that a threat? There was certainly a suggestion in that statement that something he had done in the past had resulted in Ellie's death. But what? He hadn't lived the life of a saint, but neither had he committed an act so terrible as to bring about retribution on this scale. And BYE FOR NOW:

did this mean he could expect more of the same, or worse?

One thing was certain, he would have to take this letter to the police. It was possible that some sick crank had written it, but who in Nottingham would know his address? No, this had to be the work of the killer, Rick thought. The one who killed Ellie had created this and posted it in Nottingham as a red herring. And whoever it was, they hated him with a vengeance.

***

'Can I speak to Chief Inspector Fenton?' Rick said to the young police woman on the desk, 'It's very urgent.'

'And you are?' the officer asked.

'Rick...Richard Sheldon,' he replied hurriedly.

'Please take a seat a moment,' she said, smiling at him.

Rick didn't want to smile, nor did he want to sit and wait. He wanted to give this wretched letter to whoever would use it to find the killer of his wife and child.

Five minutes passed. Rick became agitated, but then he saw the CID boss emerge from the office.

'Mr Sheldon, please come through,' said the detective in a matter of fact tone.

He was shown to Mr Fenton's office, which he found surprisingly plush, though not large.

'Sit down,' said the Chief Inspector, his open hand indicating a blue swivel chair. 'And call me Doug, please.'

Reaching inside his jacket, Rick said, 'This came in the post this morning,' and he tossed the red envelope onto the desk. Doug looked puzzled momentarily, and asked Rick what was in it. 'It's a "communication" from some sick coward,' he replied. 'Take a look.'

Doug opened the envelope cautiously, taking great care to touch only the very corners and edges of both the envelope itself and the single sheet within. He read the message and then read it again. Rick scrutinised the detective's face. Much to his surprise, and mild annoyance, Doug gave none of his feelings away through facial expressions, in fact he maintained a poker face throughout. Rick had to remind himself firstly that the letter was not aimed at the reader, and secondly that Doug was looking at it with a trained professional eye, whereas when he had read it earlier he'd felt anger and revulsion.

'Mm,' Doug uttered unconsciously as he read it a third time. Had he gleaned a clue from the page? 'It could be the killer who put this together, or some nut who wants to make you feel even worse than you do already. There's definitely an element of jealousy in there, though, that's a fact.'

Well, Rick thought, that's pure genius! He had reached this and many other conclusions himself this morning. Was that all the high-ranking detective could offer?

'What about fingerprints?' Rick asked in a dejected voice.

'Yes. There's a process called Ninhydrin. Fingerprints can quite successfully be lifted from smooth paper such as this,' Doug explained. 'But you mustn't get your hopes up.'

'Why not?' protested Rick, 'This is good evidence, isn't it?'

'I don't want to dampen your enthusiasm,' Doug continued, 'But there are many obstacles between you presenting this letter to me today and me being able to tell you who sent it. Firstly, the sender may have covered his hands with socks, surgical gloves or something similar. In fact, he probably did. Then there's the fact that you've handled the envelope and the letter. With your agreement I'll get some elimination prints taken from you today, so we can discount your fingerprints, but in touching the document you could have smeared or spoiled the offender's fingerprints. Think of all the other people who'll have handled the envelope; the collector from the post box in Nottingham, the sorting staff, the postman who put it through your door. And even if we do lift a good print or two, and eliminate your prints and others we find, there's a chance that the offender's remaining prints are of no use to us. If he, or she, has never committed an offence before then we'll have nothing on the fingerprint database to match them with. Don't get me wrong, all the tests that we can do will be done, but the chances of success from one piece of evidence such as this are slim.' Doug looked at Rick's despondent face, and tried to placate him with a resigned look of his own, showing that he too wished the chances of success were greater.

'Have you got anywhere with any other lines of enquiry?' Rick asked.

'I'm afraid not,' replied the Chief Inspector. 'Listen, there's a long way to go yet, but I'll fill you in briefly with what we've been looking into. The actual scene itself is the single most important piece of evidence available to an investigation team. Unfortunately this scene, where Ellie was shot, has revealed nothing of any use. Are you OK with this, Richard?' Doug paused to ask if he wanted to hear more.

'Oh, I want to know everything,' was the emphatic reply.

'Right. Ellie had only one wound and we can't find the bullet, despite hours of painstaking fingertip searching. The weapon must have been taken from the scene by the killer as it hasn't been left anywhere nearby. There were no footprints at the scene, either those of your wife or of the killer. This is probably because neither of them stepped off the dry tarmac onto the verge; for the same reason no tyre tread has been left behind. Whenever one piece of clothing touches another there is a transference of fibres, always, albeit microscopic. No fibres other than clothing owned by you and Ellie were found on her clothes, so the killer didn't touch her. No fingerprints apart from yours and Ellie's were found on or in her car. So as far as the scene goes there was no bullet, gun, fibres, footprints, fingerprints, tyre tread or anything left by the murderer to assist us.'

'Didn't anyone hear the shot?' Rick asked.

'The nearest residence, as the crow flies, is a farm about half a mile away. We've spoken to each of those who live there, and they heard nothing. Obviously, you've probably seen it on the local news, we've issued an appeal for witnesses but there hasn't been any response yet. Another thing is the motive; her purse containing twenty-eight pounds and two credit cards was still on the passenger seat of her car, so robbery can be ruled out. No physical evidence, no known motive and no witnesses; I'll be honest with you, Richard, we're struggling.'

Rick was relieved that Paul, one of his neighbours, had called round at the time Ellie was setting off to visit her mum and dad. He had brought a belated wedding present round for them and had stayed to have a beer with him for about an hour. Without Paul's visit, which coincided with the time of Ellie's death, Rick would have been the prime suspect listening to the lack of other evidence. In fact, he recalled providing this alibi to the Chief Inspector on the night of the murder. He hadn't even thought about being a suspect at the time, but clearly the alibi had been thoroughly checked out by the police and found to be foolproof. Thank God, he thought, it was bad enough without being in the frame for the murder as well!

'It seems you know what you're doing then, Doug,' Rick said in a resigned voice.

'I'm not giving up yet, I can assure you of that,' Doug said emphatically, but Rick knew that the prospects of finding the killer were slim, even with the piece of evidence he had so optimistically brought to the police station.

Chapter 4

Rick shunned the world around him. No visits to the gym with Tom, no trip to the shops and no work. The door remained unanswered, despite persistent attempts by well-wishers to cross its threshold and offer words of comfort and advice. The telephone, too, was ignored.

This was his healing time. The hours and days passed, each filled with countless thoughts of why Ellie had had to die and just who could be responsible. What the solitude succeeded in bringing about, however, was the grim realisation that she was gone, that nothing could bring her back and that he could not live the way he had for the last seven days. Slowly he reached the conclusion that he'd either have to end it all by throwing himself under a speeding train, or pick himself up off the floor and live his life. The choice was his and his alone to make.

Ever since his early days at high school, when he was bullied to the point of despair, Rick had never allowed himself to be a victim. He'd attended kick-boxing classes and excelled at it. Within eighteen months the bullies became the ones with bloodied noses and swollen eyes and Rick didn't look back. He faced every obstacle in life with a determination to overcome it, and his resilience had paid off many times over. Rick Sheldon was no pushover. This tragedy, though, had floored him utterly, and it would take him considerably longer to pick himself up. But he fully intended to do so.

A phone call to DCI Fenton confirmed that no further progress had been made in tracking down the killer. He expected this, and took it well.

Rick telephoned the Personnel Manager at work, Mr Davis, who told him that he must not come to work until he was fully ready to return, and he offered him his sincere condolences.

Rick's 'hibernation' had helped him appreciate that Ellie would not have wanted him to give up. She would have encouraged him to make the most of life and to move forward, not to get trapped in the present.

With a newly-felt determination Rick tidied the house, binning at least three dozen beer cans and numerous ready-made-meal boxes. He busied himself cleaning, tidying, vacuuming and washing, mowing the lawn and sweeping the path. He would not be beaten. He visited the supermarket and bought healthy food, spent two hours persecuting his body at the gym and arrived home, flopping into a chair exhausted. All day he had pushed himself, forcing his mind to accept reality and to leave the depression behind. And it seemed to be working. Rick looked around the spotless living room. The windows were open to let fresh air in and sunshine streamed in and onto his face. 'The worst is over,' he said out loud.

Rick languished in a hot bath for half an hour. He changed the blade in his razor and shaved. Looking at his clean-shaven face in the mirror made him feel that he had won. He had faced grave adversity and survived. The makings of a smile appeared, but it was to be short-lived.

A shadow appeared to his right in the mirror. His heart missed a beat as he turned instinctively to see who was behind him. Nobody was there. Who would be there? He had been alone in the house for the best part of a week. He exhaled heavily, as if the air forced from his lungs would blow away the spectre. But as his face rose to mirror level once more he again glimpsed a figure behind him. He turned, nothing there. Frantically, he wiped the condensation from the glass surface and saw, clearly, Ellie's face.

Rick's heartbeat soared and he began to take short, shallow breaths. Hurrying to the edge of the bed he sat and rubbed his eyes. He began looking around the bedroom as if he was playing some life-and-death game of hide-and-seek. The wardrobe hid no impostor, and there was nothing under the bed. Rick looked around him like a man demented, trying to make sense of what he had seen. He tiptoed back into the en suite tentatively, but there were no clues as to the source of the vision. He forced himself to look in the mirror once more, and grimaced as the face of his late wife looked out at him.

As he stared wide-eyed at Ellie, Rick began to experience a strange warm feeling permeate his being. His alarm subsided and gave way to abandonment. As his fear relented he surrendered to the image in the mirror. What was real and what was happening became inconsequential, the two opposites seemed to merge and Rick couldn't have given a damn any more. Ellie's face was not as near now, as if she had moved back from being close; in fact, Rick could see the whole of her now. She stood there smiling warmly at her admiring husband and beckoned him to her. No words were spoken, no words were needed. She urged Rick to join her. Her hands pleaded with him to come closer, but as his face neared the mirror she gently backed off, taking small steps away from him. He could not follow, the glass was hard and unrelenting, and after a few short moments she had become too far away to see. Despite squinting to keep her in sight, Rick could no longer maintain her image, and she was gone.

Chapter 5

A peaceful night's sleep followed the bizarre occurrence of the previous evening, and Rick awoke surprisingly refreshed. He was oddly unaffected by what he had seen, as though his mind had become saturated with the hurt and pain it had been forced to deal with of late and had refused to accept any more work.

He called Tom at about 7.15 am, before his friend set off for work, apologised for having not kept in touch over the last week, and asked if he could join Tom and Josie in the Old Ball tonight. They often went for a drink and a pub meal on Wednesday evenings. As expected, his suggestion was met with enthusiasm.

***

'So, how are you coping?' Tom asked, as Rick sat opposite his friends at a table, clutching a Guinness. 'We've phoned you five or six times this week but you've not been in.'

'Oh, I've been in. In fact, I haven't been out,' Rick replied. 'I needed some thinking time.'

'The whole thing's unbelievable,' added Josie. 'I mean, I've been quiet this week as well, haven't I?' she said looking to Tom for support. 'I've lost a good friend, but you, Rick…'

'Yes,' Tom interrupted. 'It's been difficult for all us.'

'Listen, you two, there's really no need to feel like you're walking on eggshells. I've done more thinking and crying this week than ever in my life. There isn't anything you can say about this that I haven't thought. I've felt ill with pain, I've wanted to kill the bastard who's done it, I've felt guilt not being there for her. Some of the thoughts I've had you wouldn't believe, but I'm out of it at the other end. So if we could talk normally I'd appreciate it, OK?'

'Fine,' Tom concluded, and he gave a relieved glance at Josie, who looked less convinced.

'Well, I've eaten crap all week,' continued Rick. 'So I'm going for the sweet and sour chicken, and it's my shout so what are you two lovebirds having?'

Tom and Josie placed their orders and Rick went off to the bar.

'I'm not happy with the way he's handling this,' Josie said, watching Rick order the meals.

'He seems to be doing pretty damn well to me,' Tom disagreed. 'His wife's been shot dead and only a week or so later he's pulled himself together. I call that strong.'

Josie knew a great deal more about the workings of the mind and about how to deal with people's pain than Tom. During the day she was a legal secretary, but two evenings a week she was a Samaritan. Josie had helped hundreds of lost souls over the years in her capacity as a skilled listener and giver of advice. She knew that people expressed grief in a variety of ways, and she knew that Rick was still well immersed in the grieving process despite his happy-go-lucky disposition. She told Tom that it was not usual, however, to put an ordeal such as this to the back of the mind so soon. Tom dismissed her concern; he was just pleased to see his pal back in the land of the living.

'What have the police come up with so far, Rick?' asked Josie. Tom gave her a disapproving look, but Rick reassured him.

'No, it's fine,' he said. 'They're stumped, to be honest. I won't bore you with the details, but basically there are no witnesses, even from the public appeal, there's little if any clues found at the scene and the motive remains a mystery because her cash and credit cards were untouched in the car. Oh, you won't know about the letter I received, will you?'

'Letter?' Tom enquired.

'Yeah. Three days after… she died… I got a weird letter in a red envelope saying how did I feel, and what goes around comes around.'

'You've got to be joking,' Josie said, a look of disgust on her face.

'No. I took it to the police straight away. I rang them this morning, and they managed to lift two fingerprints from the letter itself, but there's no match against the criminal database so this pervert, who's probably the killer, has never been convicted of an offence. If only he'd stolen something from a shop in his teens, we'd have him. This DCI who's been handling the case was disappointed.'

'What a bloody shame,' Tom said, shaking his head.

Rick glanced towards the bar, his attention averted from his friends by a tall brunette ordering a drink. 'Hey, isn't that Sarah Bowers?' he asked in a low voice.

'That's all we need,' replied Tom.

As the woman turned her face ninety degrees, offering a profile of her features, Tom realised that she was like her, but that it was not Sarah. 'Thank goodness,' he sighed.

'And who might Sarah Bowers be?' Josie piped up.

Tom and Rick looked at each other, and Rick was the first to proffer an explanation. 'Well,' he said hesitantly, 'you never knew about her. When Ellie and I split about two years ago - do you remember when she went to live with her parents for a few months?'

'I do, yes. She was beside herself.'

'In that time, when we were apart, I saw Sarah.'

Under normal circumstances Josie would have given Rick a piece of her mind, but she wondered whether it was really necessary. Ellie wasn't here any more, and what she was hearing was history; a lot had happened since then.

'Did Ellie know?' she asked.

'No. We'd never have got back together. It was no thanks to Sarah, though.'

'What do you mean?' Josie probed.

'Sarah was frantic when I finished with her. I enjoyed being with her, but I was miserable being apart from Ellie. It was Ellie who I loved, and so I had to call it off with Sarah. But she came to the house and told Ellie about our affair, out of sheer spite. I'm not proud of it, Josie, but I lied through my teeth. I told her that

Sarah was making it all up because I wouldn't go out with her and that I would never cheat on her. I felt dreadful doing it, but there'd have been no chance of us getting back together if I'd admitted it and it seemed a small price to pay at the time. Eventually Ellie told me that she believed me, and as you know we went from strength to strength from there. I had to live with the guilt feelings, but it was worth it.'

'You didn't tell me about this,' she said, looking daggers at Tom, who had remained quiet during Rick's confession.

'I made him promise not to, that's why,' Rick said.

'All boys together,' she added sarcastically. 'Still, what's done is done. I don't suppose there's any point in getting mad about it now.'

'Hang on a minute,' Tom said, thoughtfully. 'I remember you telling me that she'd said some pretty nasty things when you finished with her.'

'She did. I wouldn't have thought she had it in her. I remember her throwing a full cup of tea over me and shouting that she'd see me in hell. When she'd calmed down, though, that was worse. It was then that she sounded really spooky, saying she'd get revenge for what I'd done to her. I remember her saying that she'd never let me be happy, that she'd do everything to stop me having a good life, no matter how long it took her and how hard it would be for her. I thought that was weird, at the time, and so I was prepared when she told Ellie about the affair. I had all the lies prearranged. I had to, I'd never have got Ellie back, and I'd learnt my lesson. I'd not cheated on her before, and I was *never* going to do it again. Sarah's ignored me at work ever since, given me dirty looks every time we bump into each other. Thank God she moved departments.'

'You don't think… that she… you know?' Tom suggested clumsily.

'Killed Ellie?' Rick spelled out his thoughts. 'I don't think so. She did her worst by mixing it with Ellie. I mean, I can't blame her for her anger, looking back at it. I dumped her unceremoniously and then branded her a liar as well. What a mess. I really regret it, you know.'

'I'm surprised Ellie didn't tell me about Sarah,' Josie said.

'Well, I persuaded her not to say anything to anyone. At that time the more people that knew the more chance there was of me being found out.'

'She could have written the hate mail,' Josie said.

'I don't know,' Rick sighed. 'If she did, she did. I probably deserve it.'

The plates piled with steaming food arrived and the three tucked into the feast. They all remained muted, deep in thought, for a while, until Tom broke the silence.

'What about Danielle Harper?' he said insensitively.

Josie almost choked on her food. 'Tell me you're joking,' she said rather angrily.

'Whoa, hang on a minute,' Rick replied. 'What I've told you up to now, Josie, is all there is to tell. Danielle works in the same office as me; she started with the bank about six or seven months ago, and she's been a pain in the backside ever since she arrived.'

'Go on then, what's the story behind this one?' Josie said, making no attempt to mask the suspicion in her voice. 'And you,' she continued, glaring at Tom. 'Some partner you are. You're thick as thieves, you and him.'

'Danielle's been making passes at me ever since she set foot through the office door. I was flattered at first, don't get me wrong, most men would have been 'cos she's an attractive girl.'

Josie looked up to the heavens. She was a stunningly beautiful woman, and the price she paid was men leering at her when she went out and constantly making passes at her. It wore her down sometimes. Rick himself, though not in possession of classic features, was a good-looking bloke and so she sympathised with his plight in this respect.

'She began by asking me out. I turned her down, gently. When she asked me again a week later I let her know that I was planning to get married, but it made no difference. She started asking me questions, about work-related matters, while standing behind me and brushing her breasts on the back of my neck. She was a real tease.'

'Why didn't you tell her to get stuffed, you know, be blunt

with her?' Josie asked.

'I did, but she seemed to treat that as a challenge. One time we passed in the corridor and because no-one else was around she reached out and stroked my dick! I'm no prude, but that shocked me. I was mad about it actually. I didn't want to tell Ellie, for obvious reasons, so I went to senior management and complained formally, you know about sexual harassment.'

'Good for you,' Josie smiled.

'They took it really seriously. I thought they'd laugh because it was a man complaining about a woman, but they had her in the office and she was given a good dressing down. They told me to report any further problems; they were really good about it.'

'Did anything else happen after that?'

'No, I think it must have been the embarrassment for her. She didn't give me any more hassle.'

'A woman scorned, eh?' added Tom, to Josie's annoyance.

'So you've two prime suspects, then?' Josie said.

'Hardly,' Rick replied. 'I don't think the police would be impressed with me putting those two forward as murder suspects on the grounds of one being jilted two years before, and the other being turned down for a date.'

The conversation seemed to reach its natural conclusion at that point, and they ate their meals without further conjecture. Various normal topics of conversation were broached over the following hour and a half, and then Rick decided to tell them the news.

'I saw Ellie in the mirror last night, as I was getting shaved,' he said without warning.

Tom's face dropped. He remembered Josie's words of warning earlier in the evening, and kicked himself for believing that everything could suddenly be back to normal.

'Is that right?' Josie answered calmly.

Tom admired her intelligence, coupled with her level-headedness and obvious experience in dealing with the unexpected. He read the motives in her tone; she wanted Rick to explain in his own words what he meant without laughing at him, and without showing either disappointment or disbelief.

'Oh, yes,' Rick continued. 'I could scarcely believe it at first but she was there all right. She didn't speak, she just seemed to want me to go with her. She backed away, and I couldn't follow her.' He swallowed hard, and held back the tears, dropping his head.

'I believe you,' said Josie gently, placing her hand on his.

Rick accepted this statement unconditionally, as though he felt there would be no reason for anyone to disbelieve him. Nothing more was said about the vision, Rick said his goodbyes a short time later and left Tom and Josie finishing their drinks in the Old Ball.

Chapter 6

Sunshine and blue skies added to Rick's cheery demeanour. He occasionally had feelings of guilt at coping so well so soon after losing his wife, but he shrugged these off. Neither did the vision three days before affect his outlook. He had come to the conclusion that it was real, in his mind, and that his subconscious had created it as a way of allowing him to say his final farewell to Ellie.

As he sat on a sun-lounger in the garden, he remembered what Josie had said in the Old Ball. 'So you've two prime suspects, then?' The more he thought about this, the more he felt that it could be true. Josie had not meant it literally, after all there was no real reason to suspect either woman of premeditated murder, but the thought niggled away at him all afternoon. At 5.10 pm he decided to visit Sarah Bowers at her home.

***

Rick felt that it was really important to speak with Sarah in person, but being stood at her door diminished his fervour. So much water had passed under the bridge since they last spoke. He dreaded her response when she answered the door, so much so that he turned and began to move away. The longer he deliberated the more chance there was of him failing to resolve his suspicions, and so he approached the door quickly and knocked hard on it to force his own hand.

A few moments past, but there was no answer. He knocked again, more confident this time as it appeared that she was out. Still there was no reply. Rick breathed a sigh of relief and turned to leave. Behind him stood Sarah, staring at him with a puzzled expression. 'What do *you* want?' she said coldly.

'Er... I... wanted to talk to you,' Rick stammered, feeling stupid.

'Look, I've had a long day, I just want to... oh, come in, then,' she sighed.

Rick followed Sarah sheepishly into the house, feeling like an intruder. She ushered him into the living room and told him to take a seat while she fixed herself a drink. Rick looked around; no signs of newspapers or magazines having recently been cut up. He felt silly thinking this, but then he saw a photograph of him and Sarah in the Dales on a coffee table. It sent a chill down his spine. Why would she still have this on display, almost two years after they'd split up, he thought. Something was not quite right.

Sarah padded into the room minus her high heels, a glass of Martini in her hand.

There was no drink on offer for her visitor.

'Fire away, then,' she said, flopping into a comfy chair.

Rick had acted on impulse coming here. He had no pre-planned spiel, and the question threw him.

'I take it you know about Ellie being killed?' Rick said, not knowing what to say initially.

'Yes,' was the reply.

'Well, what do you think of it?'

'What do I think of it?' She pulled an awkward face. 'What kind of question is that?'

Rick was floundering and he blushed. He knew no other way now, and so he cut to the chase.

'Did you have anything to do with her death?' he asked bluntly.

Sarah looked at him for several moments. At first she looked as though she would explode with anger, but then she laughed aloud.

'*Me?* Why me? What the hell makes you think I could possibly do a thing like that?'

Rick got the impression that he had Sarah on her back foot.

'You tell me,' he said.

'Sorry, Columbo, no. I'm not in the fucking dock here, this is my house and unless you explain yourself sharpish you can get your arse off that chair and get out.'

'OK, OK, I'm sorry.'

'You will be,' she said menacingly.

'Well that's just it, you see. The police have no leads whatsoever, and there isn't even a known motive, so when you make threats like that it gets me thinking. Remember the threats you made when I finished with you?' She winced at the reminder. 'I seem to recall you saying things like you'd get your revenge, you'd do everything you could to stop me having a happy life no matter how long it took and that kind of shit.'

Rick had been looking away from her as he spoke, and as he trained his accusing gaze on her once more he saw tears rolling down her cheeks. She made no attempt to hide them.

'You stupid man,' Sarah sobbed. 'I've loved you ever since we began dating. Have you any idea how it felt when you dumped me like a sack of spuds? I was suicidal, but I didn't have the guts to end it. Realising that I'd lost you was like nothing I'd felt before. I regret telling Ellie about it now, but I was just hitting back. I wanted you to hurt too. And yes I said some awful things, I admit it, but I was distraught. Does that make me a murderer?'

'It gives you a motive,' Rick said, looking at her wet face and wishing he'd never started this conversation.

'Oh, come on. If that amounts to a motive then you must be able to put half a dozen people in the frame.'

Rick looked again at the photograph on the coffee table, and Sarah realised immediately what he was thinking.

'I'm an ordinary girl,' she said, picking the photo up and looking at it herself. 'I've only been out with two lads since we split up, and neither of those relationships got serious, so why not keep a good memory of you and me…is *that* a crime?'

'No, it's not,' he said gently. He got up and put his hand on Sarah's shoulder in an attempt to apologise, but she shrugged it off.

'I think you should go now.'

'Look, I'm really sorry for everything that's happened in the past,' Rick said.

'And I'm sorry about your wife, but be fair,' she replied.

Sarah showed Rick the door, and he left contrite, giving her a warm smile as she closed it behind him.

As the door closed Sarah smiled too, inwardly.

Chapter 7

Lying in bed the following Monday morning, Rick thought how foolish he'd been speaking to Sarah the way he had. It was true he had treated her badly; he had slept with her, told her about his problems with Ellie, spent three months in her company, then gone back to his other lover. To add insult to injury, he had denied their liaisons and denounced her as an obsessive liar. Then, two years later, he had turned up unannounced at her home and virtually accused her of being party to a murder.

It was little wonder that she had shouted and sworn at him. If someone had hurt him in the past and then arrived on his doorstep years later asking him such cutting questions, he would probably have reacted in that way too. Worse.

There was no way Sarah was involved, he thought. She was an up-front character; she said what she thought and wouldn't stab someone in the back. Sarah was very emotional and showed her feelings freely. If she was hurt, you got a mouthful, if she was ecstatic she displayed that equally. To think he could seriously have thought that she was anything to do with Ellie's death was ridiculous, to accuse her of it was outrageous. Rick thought of re-visiting her to apologise properly and to explain how he felt, but he dismissed this for fear of making the situation even worse. Sarah may take it as a re-kindling of feelings he once had for her, or she may become even more angry.

He had made a complete fool of himself, that was obvious. In view of this he decided that to approach Danielle Harper in the same vein would be equally ill-advised. He was not trained to interrogate people, that was glaringly apparent from the interaction with Sarah, and in any event there wasn't a shred of evidence against either woman. Rick vowed to forget his misplaced suspicions and leave the investigation to the police.

His thoughts turned to his job. It was over two weeks since that fateful Saturday night and despite having a sick note for stress that didn't expire for a further two weeks, Rick felt that he was ready to return to the bank. Not only would working take his mind off the million questions he still held inside, but he was an important cog in the wheel at work. He was the manager of the debt recovery department and the thought of Danielle Harper, the team-leader, performing his duties while he was away made him shiver. It wasn't so much the dislike he harboured for her, but the fact that she simply wasn't good at her job. He had met all his team targets in the seven months up to July and was not at all happy that she would continue the trend. Not only would the team suffer, but she would get comfortable in his chair, and he wasn't having that.

Today was the day when he'd get his life back on track. It was soon after Ellie's demise, he knew, but what was the point of sitting at home alone for the next few weeks, or months? That would only serve to make him as depressed as he was that first week. He quickly showered and dressed, fully intent on speaking with Mr Davis again and arranging when he could come back to work. Andrew Davis had been understanding when he telephoned him before, and made him feel valued, so he was the man to see.

With a spring in his step Rick descended the stairs, fastidiously adjusting his tie, and stopped dead in his tracks. The red envelope sat there, as if in pride of place, contrasted against the beige carpet. A single, lifeless object that caused his innards to lurch. To have found a thousand cockroaches in its place would not have engendered a worse reaction.

Rick approached the envelope slowly, as if it had the ability to take the end of his fingers off, and he picked it up with trembling hands. He could not discern whether the typed address on the front was the same as that on the first letter. He breathed a sigh of relief, however, when the postmark showed Newcastle.

The contents swiftly destroyed any premature hopes that Rick had. He again saw the uneven lettering comprised of newspaper and magazine cuttings, and he read the text with a twisted expression on his face.

HOW'S THINGS RICKY BOY? IT HURTS HAVING NO-ONE
DOESN'T IT? NO-ONE WHO CARES FOR YOU ANYWAY.
STILL, THAT'S NEW TO YOU ISN'T IT? NO DOUBT
YOU'RE FULL OF SELF PITY. FEEL THE PAIN, IT WON'T
KILL YOU.

Who had the right to torment him like this, he thought. He
was doing so well controlling his anger and frustration and
loneliness, and then this. It had to be from someone who was
jealous of the fact that he was normal, and had normal
relationships with people, and someone who had no partner
themselves. Sarah fitted the bill. Danielle had been out with two
or three lads from the office since his rejection of her. 'Christ, it
could be anyone, anyone,' he shouted out loud. Red in the face,
Rick tore the letter and the envelope into tiny pieces, some of
which fluttered onto the carpet. Slamming the handful of vitriolic
paper shreds in the kitchen bin, he proceeded to vacuum the
remaining pieces from the carpet where they had fallen. He then
emptied the dust bag into the kitchen bin, and this bin into the
dustbin outside. He knew that his actions would not erase the
memory of the wretched letter, but it gave him some satisfaction.
Washing his hands thoroughly, he promised himself that he
wouldn't let this weirdo get to him, more than superficially,
anyway. Momentarily, Rick regretted destroying the letter
because it was further evidence of someone who maybe involved
in Ellie's murder. 'Further evidence,' he said under his breath
scornfully. 'The police have found sod all.'
As if to continue where he left off before being rudely
interrupted, Rick straightened his tie in the mirror. Externally, at
least, he looked the part. Picking up his leather briefcase he
opened the door, to see a brown parcel on the step. Oddly, Rick
felt no apprehension as he had done upon seeing the red
envelope. It would have been perfectly understandable, expected
even, for him to freeze with fear. He didn't suspect for a moment
that the parcel could be from the sender of the letters, or that it

may even harm him in some way. Instead he took it into the house and sat down to open it.

Rick tore at the paper eagerly like a child on Christmas morning, and inside he found a hard-back book. The title read 'Beyond the Mirror'.

Unlike any book he had seen, there was no picture on the cover to accompany the title, which stood out in white text against a black, featureless background. The back of the book had no words on it. He peered inside the front cover, but found no description of the story-line. Neither did the back cover introduce the author. Rick looked perplexed as he thumbed through the pages and discovered that there was no writing on them. Except for the very first page.

He read out loud. 'Be with me – Help me – I need you – You must come to me'. Reading the words aloud over and over again, as if mesmerized, gave Rick a glowing feeling, one he had felt before when he forced himself to look in the mirror at Ellie. He knew beyond any doubt that this was not the work of the letter-writer. In fact, the letter and its evil intent seemed to lose its influence entirely as he fell into a spellbound fascination with the words before his eyes. He nodded as he read the message again. At that moment the book slipped from his hands and thumped to the floor. Rick jumped. He gathered his thoughts and looked towards the clock on the wall. It was twenty past nine, nearly a whole hour since he had opened the door and found the parcel, yet it was only moments earlier that he had unwrapped it.

He picked the book off the floor. 'Beyond the Mirror' was still the title, but now the front cover depicted a mirror in which there was an image of a young woman. Her appearance was faded such that her features were indiscernible. The inside cover contained a gripping overview of the story, and the rear cover gave the author's background. Rick looked at the front of the book again to see the author's name emblazoned across it, Ruth Stocks. And the pages were full of vibrant prose.

Quickly flicking to the opening page, Rick felt his heart sink as the words from Ellie, his beautiful Ellie, were gone.

Chapter 8

What do you make of that? Rick thought to himself, placing the ordinary-looking hard-back on the mantlepiece. One of three things was happening to him, he concluded. First, he was suffering from some sort of post traumatic stress which manifested itself in these visions or 'occurrences'. Secondly, he was going mad. Or thirdly, everything he was seeing and experiencing was real.

Although Rick had visited church regularly throughout his life, this was the extent of his belief. He believed in God, but not in ghosts or extra-terrestrial life, and certainly not in alien abduction or the suspension of time! Ellie used to love 'Star Trek' and 'Arthur C. Clarke's Mysterious World', but he considered all that to be a waste of time and utter nonsense. So what was happening to him? He felt perfectly sane, but isn't that what all psychopaths and schizophrenics feel? They exist in their own worlds and even sound plausible in their beliefs when justifying why they did this, or saw that.

He had seen Ellie in the mirror, and had read her message to him in the book on the mantlepiece. And that message was the same each time; he had to join her, she wanted him with her. Did this mean he had to die? Why would she want him to die? None of it made any sense, but he saw what he had seen, and no-one was going to convince him otherwise. Maybe there are 'happenings' outside our present realm of understanding, Rick thought. Because we don't understand something doesn't mean that it hasn't happened, surely. He tried to reason with his stubborn down-to-earth self, but found himself confused and agitated. He needed some help.

Josie seemed to understand when he said he'd seen Ellie in the mirror. Tom had reacted in the expected way, not intending to show that he thought Rick was losing his mind, but showing it nevertheless. Whereas Josie, her face assumed a look of interest at his revelation, even comprehension. Maybe she had experienced an unusual happening at some time in her life and was relieved to hear that she was not the only one. She had undergone training into the workings of the mind in her capacity as a Samaritan, so perhaps she recognised something in him which he himself was not aware of. Josie had said she believed him, and he would speak to her about the book rather than Tom.

Forgetting about his intended visit to the office, Rick set off for his friend's house, on the off-chance that Josie was in, but there was no answer to the door. He was so enthused with the morning's events that he decided to go to the solicitor's office where Josie worked and speak to her there. All the while the curious book remained closely at his side.

Rick had visited the practice where Josie worked as a legal secretary only three months before, in connection with the purchase of his house, and so he knew exactly where her office was. Breezing in, he approached her desk unannounced.

'Look at this beauty,' he declared, holding the book out for Josie to see. She jumped, almost falling sideways off her chair.

'Rick. What are you doing here?'

'I've come to show you this book,' he replied, like the cat that got the cream.

Vanessa, another secretary working in the office, looked bewildered.

'So it's a book. Why have you come here when I'm working?'

Rick's face dropped. 'Look at the title,' he continued.

Josie took the book from him and looked at it. She raised her eyebrows on reading the title and seeing the picture depicted on the front cover. She looked up at Rick who gave her a half-smile, as if seeking her approval. Handing him the book back, she stood up and told him to wait for her while she saw her boss.

Feeling awkward Rick looked around the office. He caught Vanessa looking at him out of the corner of her eye and he smiled at her genially. She blushed and continued with her work. He scanned Josie's desk. The documents said so much about people: two wills being drawn up, the clients preparing themselves for the fair distribution of their assets on their demise; conveyancing papers, no doubt there was an excited couple connected with these, eager to move into their new property and the next stage of their lives together, just like he and Ellie only a few short months ago.

'OK,' Josie said as she walked back into the office, 'Mr Reynolds said I can have my lunch-break early today,' and she gathered her personal things. 'See you after, V.'

'Yeah, all right, Josie,' replied her timid colleague.

Rick followed her down the carpeted stairs and they walked into the park directly opposite the offices. As they sat on a bench, Josie opened the conversation.

'Please don't come barging into my office when I'm not expecting you; it's embarrassing.'

'Sorry, I didn't mean to show you up.' Rick felt he deserved the mild reproach. He should have either waited until she had finished work or rung to see if he could meet her at lunch-time.

'What's so important, anyway?' Josie continued in the same irritated tone, 'I admit the book you've bought is a bit spooky in view of what you saw last week, but come on...'

'No,' he interrupted, 'You don't understand. I didn't buy this book, it just appeared on the doorstep this morning wrapped in brown paper.'

'What, appeared before your very eyes?' she chided, still not looking pleased at having her day involuntarily re-arranged for her.

Rick got up to walk away. How could she speak to him like that? She had believed him about Ellie's image in the mirror, and he hadn't even had the chance to explain about the book yet, but she was acting cold and annoyed.

'Hey, sit down. It's my turn to apologise,' she said. As he

turned to look at her she smiled and patted the seat beside her. 'Come on, don't go. I didn't mean to be offhand with you, it's just that…'

'What's the matter?'

'Well, me and Tom. We're going through a bit of a bad patch at the moment.'

'You and Tom? But you're like… couple of the year.'

'Not really. We get along most of the time, and Tom loves me very much but…'

'But what? That sounds pretty good to me.'

'Rick, you know almost as well as me how Tom and I met.'

'What's that got to do with it. You've always got on like a house on fire, haven't you?' Rick was beginning to doubt his faith in their relationship.

'If I tell you this, I don't want you to repeat it to Tom, OK? I know you always tell each other everything, but I don't want to hurt his feelings.'

'I'm not going to like this, am I?'

'Probably not. You promise?'

'Promise.'

'As you know, I came to Leeds from Sheffield about four and a half years ago. I didn't want anything to do with my parents because of how they treated me, so I was alone here. It was awful, living in a bed-sit on my own, looking forward to work because I had no life. I wasn't interested in all the passes the guys made at me, and I got drunk in town one night. As you know, I collapsed in the road on the way home, and Tom found me.'

'I know this, Josie, but you're not telling me why there are problems now.'

'Tom was brilliant,' she continued. 'He took me to his house in a taxi. He could have taken advantage of me easily but he didn't. I really appreciated that. He made breakfast for me in the morning, and then said something along the lines of he'd never be able to get a girl as beautiful as me, and so I could leave anytime. A really nice guy.'

'And? I still don't see the problem,' said Rick.

'I like him. A lot. But I've never loved him. I'd been let down so badly by my family there was no way I was going to let this lovely man down. So I gave him love, or so he thought. I wasn't deliberately misleading him, or playing games with him, and I enjoyed giving him pleasure in his life. He deserved it, I mean, there aren't many men like him. This went on and became... the norm. The trouble is, I can't go on hiding my true feelings, and he's beginning to realise how I feel, no matter what I do.'

Josie looked straight ahead of her as she spoke, as if she felt too guilty to face Tom's best friend with this betrayal.

'It's been over four years, and yes we've had good times, but I'm nearly twenty-eight now and...' she looked at the ground pensively, 'I have to move on.'

Rick sighed deeply. He knew that Josie meant the world to Tom, and he would be devastated if he lost her.

'Another thing,' Josie said. Rick wondered if it could get any worse. 'Tom's getting more and more possessive. He can't bear it when we go out and men look at me. Lately, we either don't go out at all or he insists that I wear clothes that don't, you know, show me off. I feel completely trapped, and it's my fault.'

'Why are you telling me this now?' Rick asked her. He felt a little cheated in that he had come to her for help today, and not only did it seem inappropriate now to talk to her about the book, but Josie's announcement put extra weight on his shoulders as well.

'I don't know, I suppose you had to know sometime, and I always used to talk to Ellie about these things. If I look at it logically, I'm probably telling you now because in a way it gives me the freedom to finish with Tom.'

'How do you work that out?' he said in disbelief.

'Well, you're the only person who I'd have to justify it to, other than Tom,' she replied.

'Yeah. Is it definitely over, then?'

'It's looking that way. I can't live a lie, Rick, and I won't. A lot of people do, you know. They endure decades of a loveless marriage and in the end it's too late to find love, just because everyone thought they were happy and they got used to each other and couldn't find the courage to face the truth.'

'And some people get a person they love snatched away from them,' Rick said bitterly.

Josie felt a pang of selfishness. Here she was offloading her problems onto a man who's wife had been killed two weeks before, and who had sought her out today for help.

'Rick, I'm sorry,' she said. 'You obviously had something important to tell me.'

'Oh, it doesn't matter.' He sounded dejected.

'It does. Never mind my problems,' she said more cheerily, 'They're ones that people have every day. Now what were you looking so smug about earlier, and what is it about this book?' Josie prised the hard-back from Rick's grasp and read the title again.

'I'm not sure this is the right time to discuss it,' Rick said.

'Look, forget other people for a while. Tom and I will sort ourselves out one way or another, it won't be easy but that's life. You're going through a lot at the moment, and if I can help I will. We've been good friends for years now, and if you feel comfortable coming to me to discuss something then, that's fine. Now, what's bothering you?'

'OK then.' Rick took a deep breath as if he was planning to talk for an hour.

'This book was on the doorstep this morning, wrapped in plain brown paper.'

'Hey, the neighbours'll be thinking you're having naughty things delivered,' Josie giggled. Rick did not find it funny.

'I took it into the lounge,' he continued, 'The weird thing was that I wasn't frightened of it.'

'Why would you be?' Josie asked puzzled.

'Oh, sorry,' he said, 'Before that I got another sick letter. Even worse than the last.'

'Another? Why would someone want to torment you, for God's sake?'

'I don't know.'

'Are you taking it to the police?' she asked.

'No. I tore it into small pieces and threw it in the bin.'

'But, the evidence…'

'Look, they got prints from the last one. As I explained, the person who's sending them has no criminal record, so the police haven't a clue who it is. In any case, it felt good tearing it up.'

'Right. So you took the book into the living room,' Josie resumed.

'Yes. I took the packaging off and there it was.'

'The book, yeah.' Josie looked perplexed.

'When I looked at it, all this wasn't here,' Rick explained, and he pointed to the picture on the front cover, the name of the author, the description of the story-line inside. He drew closer to Josie and said, almost menacingly, 'None of the pages had writing on them. But the first page read, "Be with me - Help me – I need you – You must come to me." I read it lots of times. But listen. That was at about half past eight. I got a really warm feeling, like when I saw Ellie in the mirror, and then I dropped the book.'

Josie looked worried, but Rick interpreted the look as one of wonder.

'When I picked the book off the floor, it was as you see it now. With the picture on the front, the author Ruth Stocks, all the pages full and Ellie's message gone. But it was twenty-past nine. Fifty bloody minutes had gone by; I'd just sat down moments earlier with the package.'

Josie instinctively drew on all the knowledge of people she had gained over the years working as a Samaritan, but she was no psychiatrist. And the person relating this tale was no Mr Anonymous at the other end of a telephone line, but a close friend pleading with her in person to make sense of a story that couldn't be true other than in his damaged mind.

Josie looked at Rick's face. He awaited her reply with bated breath. The next thing Josie said would be of profound importance to him, and could well affect their friendship. But what was the best thing to say? Should she shoot his story down in flames in an attempt to force him back into the real world, and then suggest that he seek counselling, or pretend that she believed him wholeheartedly and collude with him in this ridiculous fantasy? Surely, in the long run that would only confuse him and encourage him to dream up further delusions. There was no obvious third option, and she didn't have the luxury of time to make a decision, nor the ability to walk away and pretend that it wasn't her sole responsibility. She had to decide, now.

'Where has Ellie's message gone?' she said, to buy her thinking time.

'In here,' he replied, prodding his right temple.

'How could that have happened, you know, the book changing like that?' Josie posed the question carefully as though she was genuinely intrigued. If she had sounded incredulous it could have tipped Rick over the edge.

'Mm.' Rick thought for a few moments. 'It couldn't happen really, could it?' he asked.

Josie felt tested again. Despite her attempts to avoid Rick's direct approach, he had asked her again in a roundabout way whether she believed his account. 'Things like that don't happen…'

'Oh, no,' Rick interrupted, putting his hands to his face.

'Hang on, I've not finished yet,' she said. 'They don't happen to just anybody.' Rick looked up as if Josie had revealed the secrets of the universe in one short statement. 'You have to be a very special person, someone open to suggestion.' Rick had no idea that Josie was making this up as she went along, but from her perspective it was working. 'Maybe you should visit a clairvoyant,' she suggested.

She had given him further food for thought. A medium was the sort of person who he would have derided and taken pleasure in ridiculing a few weeks ago. All that mumbo-jumbo about 'the other side' and talking to family who had died; but wasn't that what was happening to him even without a psychic? Ellie communicating with him, trying to pass a message to him? Maybe a medium would make it easier to understand what Ellie was trying to tell him.

'You might be right,' Rick said, still contemplating.

'Well, you've nothing to lose,' she continued. 'Except a few quid.'

Thinking that she had weathered the storm without upsetting

him, Josie looked at the confused soul sat beside her to see tears streaming down his face. Rick was a proud man yet he made no attempt to hide his sorrow. Feeling a little awkward she gently put her arm around him and pulled him closer to her. He did not resist her tenderness, but innocently languished in it like a child in need of motherly comfort.

The two remained there for ten minutes or more, in silence. Rick was a man stripped of dignity, and Josie a friend doing what she could for him. He was physically and mentally drained, and he drifted into semi-consciousness leaning on her shoulder.

Suddenly, a shout from behind them!

'Oh, that's just bloody great!' bellowed Tom, his hands on his hips, looking accusingly at the pair on the bench. Rick jumped to his feet, immediately recognising Tom's voice, whereas Josie took a sharp intake of breath, startled by his arrival.

'You conniving bitch,' he snarled. Several couples on adjacent benches looked round at the commotion. 'I've always known you'd go with someone else, but him?'

'This is what I mean, you see?' Josie said to Rick, referring to the earlier conversation.

'So, not only have you been secretly meeting him, but you've been talking about us as well, have you?' Tom sounded really menacing.

'Eh, we've not been meeting anywhere secretly,' Rick said.

'Look you, if you weren't going through so much at the moment I'd…'

'Stop being so bloody stupid,' Rick said emphatically.

Tom looked at him, and then at Josie. 'You're welcome to each other,' he said through gritted teeth, and walked off at a pace.

'It's my fault,' Josie said. 'I should have known he'd probably be coming to the park on a sunny morning like this. He only works at the garage over the road and he always comes to the park at about eleven when it's not raining.'

'But we haven't done anything wrong.'

'I told you, didn't I?' Josie said, shaking her head.

Chapter 9

'Danielle, I'd like a word,' Frank Parsons called across the office floor.

Parsons was Rick's immediate boss and, although he did not have the influence of the managers above him who had reached director status, he nevertheless had plenty of power as regarded the running of this and two other departments. And he liked to throw his weight around.

A forty-three-year-old decidedly unattractive man with a personality to match, Parsons lived with his ageing mother, who suffered from Parkinson's disease in its advanced stages. He couldn't wait for her to die; he wanted her house, her money and his freedom. Having long since given up trying to win girlfriends and cultivate friendships, he had worked with an unbending commitment to achieve his present position at the bank, from which he could command respect through fear rather than earning it. A second rate acknowledgement, but one he was more than satisfied with.

Danielle felt her heart rate increase as she quickened her pace towards Parsons' office. It was not wise to keep him waiting, and she didn't want to jeopardise her current position. She was acting manager of the department in Rick's absence and keen to make a good impression whilst he was away.

'Yes, Mr Parsons,' Danielle said, peering into his office.

'Come in,' he replied, 'and close the door.'

He told her to take a seat, and then he let a few moments pass in order to make her feel uneasy. This was his domain, and Danielle knew she would have to play the game his way, whatever the game was. Having sat with his arms crossed looking at her like a disapproving parent for a short time, Parsons spoke.

'I've been evaluating your work with the team whilst you've been filling in for Mr Sheldon,' he began. This was the moment, Danielle thought, where he was going to either tear a strip off her mercilessly, or praise her to the hilt, and if body-language was anything to go by she was finished. 'And I think you've done a good job up to now.'

Danielle beamed at Frank Parsons.

'But your chance to prove yourself maybe short-lived,' he said, smiling back at her. 'Mr Sheldon's likely to be back at work within the week.'

Her faced dropped. He truly was a bastard, she thought. 'However, there maybe a way,' he continued in a cryptic tone.

Danielle thought that he must be impressed with her work if he was considering finding a way for her to continue in Rick's stead, or possibly be acting manager in another department when Rick returned. This would be preferable, she mused, because not only would she gain the relevant experience for promotion but she wouldn't have to work alongside a man who had not only rejected her advances but reported her to the highest bosses.

'What would you say if I said I could organise for you to continue as you are?'

'I'd say thank you, sir.' She added the 'sir' in an attempt to emphasise his importance, a base form of flattery even by her standards.

'Well, you've done well in the short time that Mr Sheldon's been away, like I say, so it would benefit the firm. And there'd be personal benefit for me, of course?' He looked into her eyes to ascertain whether she understood what he was saying.

Danielle looked at him. He raised his eyebrows, asking the question again without speaking. Her mind raced. She must not get this wrong, she thought.

'What are you saying, exactly?' she asked in a quiet voice.

'What I'm saying is this. When Rick went upstairs, above my head, to report you for sexual harassment they asked my opinion. I told them that you were a good worker and that he was exaggerating the situation. I said that the department would miss an efficient team-leader such as you, and not to treat you harshly. Because he's worked here for a number of years; because he's your manager, and because sexual harassment is a political hot potato for big companies like this, they were all for sacking you.' Danielle was visibly shocked. 'So, I've effectively saved your job. In addition to that, I'm prepared to manipulate it so that you can continue getting managerial experience. Don't ask me how, but it can be done. But, like everything in this world, there's a price to pay, and I don't have the luxury of pretty young women queuing at my door to satisfy my needs.' He paused. 'You do realise that if you make it to manager, after showing your worth, there's a nine thousand a year rise from team-leader, and you're currently how old? Twenty-three?'

Parsons had said it all. If she performed for him he would give her the keys to a lot more money, and a position of authority, maybe even higher than Rick. She looked at him, very careful not to betray her feelings of disgust at the thought of him pounding away at her like some dog let loose. Albeit there were no witnesses to this conversation, the suggestion made was patently disgraceful both from an ethical viewpoint and in the work context, as it would directly affect the fair advancement of others, but due to its sordid nature she decided to let *him* sweat on this one. All the time looking him in the eye, she considered his offer. She was only twenty-three, yet if she put herself through this 'ordeal' she could do really well at the bank in the long term. She could be a manager well before her time.

She looked again at his puny physique, his pale complexion and balding pate, complete with a wispy goatee and yellowing teeth. If she agreed, it was hardly prostitution, more using her position as a young attractive female to further her life prospects. Who knows, she maybe able to hold it over him one day if she played it carefully.

'OK,' she said.

Chapter 10

Despite several phone calls to Tom's mobile and a personal visit, Tom refused to speak to his old friend.

Rick could not believe it. They had been best buddies since they were eleven years of age. Both had been bullied badly at secondary school, but less than two years after Rick's kick-boxing classes began, the bullies found themselves at the receiving end. On one occasion Rick had fought three of them off, preventing Tom from getting a severe hiding, and they had hit it off ever since.

To think that a misunderstanding could end all those years of friendship. People change, though, Rick thought over a bowl of muesli. It was obvious that Tom and Josie's relationship was nearing its end, and it was understandable in a way that Tom would lay the blame elsewhere than at his own or Josie's door. Tom loved her with all his heart, Rick knew that, and so he didn't ultimately want to blame her, and people rarely blame themselves. He'll come round, Rick concluded, as he downed his second cup of tea.

He had arranged an appointment with Andrew Davis, the Personnel Manager, this morning, one he had promised to keep after failing to turn up last time. The vision in the mirror and the message in the book were mysteries he could not solve, either in themselves or in his mind, and he had decided to go back to work and try to forget about them in the hope that eventually the memory of them would fade and he could return to normality, albeit without Ellie.

***

The glass lift conveyed Rick to the top floor of the building. He had only visited the sixth floor on three or four occasions during his five years with the bank, and each time he had smiled to himself at the outward show of opulence the décor presented. Incredibly thick royal blue carpets, pine wood and fine paintings served to remind visitors from the lower floors that this was where the big money was earned, and where the power was wielded. Those impressed by money and material ostentation marvelled seeing the sixth floor for the first time. But not Rick. Not only had he seen it before, but the events of late put such matters into perspective.

After speaking to Mr Davis's secretary, Rick knocked and entered the Personnel Manager's office.

'Come in, Richard,' Andrew Davis said cordially, 'and sit yourself down.'

Rick sat in the Chesterfield, at ease with himself as well as the leather. 'Have you managed without me, then?' he joked.

Mr Davis immediately picked up on the joviality. 'Well, it's been touch and go at times, but we've struggled through,' he said. 'Now, how are things with you?'

'As well as could be expected, really. I want to come to back to work as soon as possible because I'm finding it hard to cope with things at home on my own and if I was at work keeping my mind occupied it would help.'

'That may well be,' Mr Davis said, 'and your enthusiasm is a credit to you, but there are two things I have to consider. Firstly, your state of health; you don't need me to tell you how difficult it is dealing with a tragedy like this, and I have to be sure that your doctor is happy with you returning to work so soon. Secondly, I have to be satisfied that you are capable of doing a good job. The department could suffer if your mind isn't on the job as it should be. I'm sorry if I sound callous, but until these things are sorted out I can't really make a decision. Believe me, I'm thinking of your long term prospects here; it would be a real shame if you came back and then made some costly errors. It could affect you and the bank. Do you see the dilemma I'm faced with?'

'I understand what you're saying,' Rick replied, 'But I've had a conversation with my doctor and he's satisfied that I'm OK. I can get you written confirmation of that if you need it. I can spend the next month at home if that's what you want, but I can honestly say that I don't think it would benefit me. I know it's only three weeks since it happened, but in that time I've done nothing but think, and more thinking won't do me any good.'

'Have you had any counselling?'

'No. It's been suggested to me but I don't want it. I can sort things out myself. Look, if I find that my mind isn't on the job, or I'm having trouble concentrating, I promise I'll accept it and I'll see the doctor again about counselling, but I need the chance to come back to work and to get on with my life.'

Mr Davis rubbed his chin and thought for a moment.

'Would you mind giving me a few minutes, Richard? I'll ask Jayne to make a cup of coffee for you if you'd like to take a seat outside.'

Rick drank the treacle-like percolated coffee more out of courtesy than enjoyment, and about ten minutes later Jayne asked him to step back into the manager's office.

'Right, then. I've decided that you should speak with Frank Parsons. As long as you can produce the doctor's note to the effect that in his opinion you are fit to return to work, and Frank is happy after speaking to you, then you can start back on Monday. How does that sound?'

'Great, thank you.'

'I've asked Frank to see you now, so if you want to go straight down to his office, he should be there.' Mr Davis stood and shook Rick's hand with a firm grip. 'And once again, Richard, I'm very sorry about Ellie.' Rick nodded.

***

All eyes were on Rick as he strolled across the office floor. Most people wondered how he was, and hoped that they would never have to go through what he had. He smiled awkwardly at a few people, and then knocked on Frank Parsons's door.

'Come in,' Parsons shouted.

Rick went in and closed the door behind him. This was not a conversation to be heard by all and sundry. Parsons extended his hand, and Rick shook the limp, sweaty palm.

'So, how are you?' Parsons asked in an indifferent tone.

'Feeling better, you know,' said Rick.

Although Parsons was above Rick in the hierarchy, the recognised gap between them was not nearly as wide as that between Parsons and a team-leader, and so he could not exercise the same degree of control and disdain as he could over Danielle Harper. Rick knew he had to be careful, though, because Parsons was quite capable of causing him considerable problems if he so wished, and the two men had not seen eye to eye on several issues lately.

'You've been through a difficult time, no doubt,' Frank began, pointing out the obvious.

'Yeah. It's been surreal. One minute she was here, and the next gone. No reasons, just gone.' Rick was thinking aloud more than explaining what had happened.

'I'd like to take this opportunity to offer my most sincere condolences,' Parsons said, as if the phrase was rehearsed. It sounded anything but sincere, Rick thought.

'As you know, Mr Davis has been speaking to me, and he's asked me to test the water, so to speak. I understand that you feel ready to come back to work?'

'Yes, I do. I was explaining to him that it wouldn't do me any good festering at home any longer. Also, I want to continue where I left off, I had a few things unfinished.' Rick was 'testing the water' himself, now. He knew that Danielle would be acting manager in his absence, unless in view of her indiscretion she had not been entrusted with the role.

'Well, you maybe surprised to hear that everything's been running like clockwork while you've been off. In fact, Miss Harper has done a really good job.'

Yes, Rick thought, and she would happily have done a good job of making his life a misery if he hadn't reported her to senior management. 'No doubt she has, she's a capable team-leader,' he said, forcing the words out to fit the tenor of the conversation.

'I don't know why you dislike her,' Parsons continued. Under normal circumstances Rick was able to deflect his boss's snide comments and innuendo, but these were not normal circumstances. This was the first time he and Parsons had spoken since the tragedy, yet the insidious worm was already badgering him.

'I thought you'd have been astute enough to realise that, Frank,' he retorted. 'It's not long ago since she was making a laughing stock of me in the office, remember?'

'There's no need to be rude, Mr Sheldon. I've found her to be a likeable person, and she comes across very well with the team. In fact, she excels in the post, more so than as team-leader.'

'Right, I'll take your word for it. Now, about me starting on Monday...'

'It seems to me that you're a bit on edge, still,' Parsons interrupted. 'You have an underlying aggressive tone, you see. Look, it's perfectly understandable in view of what you're going through, but maybe it would be wise to give yourself a little longer. The grieving process often takes its time, you know, and everyone's different.' His condescending tone, together with a glaring absence of honesty, quickly fired Rick's temper.

'Listen, don't you tell me what it's like to grieve. You haven't got a clue. I'm doing my best to get my life together, and I need to come back to work to do that.'

'Just listen to yourself,' Parsons said calmly. 'Raised voice, pointed finger, and that's towards me, so what would you be like towards those on your team, not to mention clients?'

'What's the matter with you, don't you want me back at work? Why are you being so obstructive?'

'Well thank you, Richard. I'm trying to assess whether you're in a position to come back, and you're raising your voice and accusing me of being unhelpful.'

'I'm sorry,' Rick said, 'Mr Davis seems happy with me starting on Monday, so I don't see why you'd have any objection.'

'I don't think you're anywhere near, to be honest. It simply wouldn't be fair to the department, or yourself, to place further burdens on you at present. I'm sorry, but it seems to me that you need at least a further six weeks recuperation. We'll talk further then, OK?'

Rick slammed Parsons's desk with his fist and put his face close to that of his boss. 'You little shit,' he said through gritted teeth. 'You didn't back me up when Danielle Harper was pestering me, you treat me like dirt in front of others in the office, and now this. What is with you, you power-mad little...' With that, Rick cleared the desk of its contents with one sweep of his arm and gave Parsons a hateful look as he banged his office door closed behind him.

Glancing over towards Danielle as he stormed across the office floor, he saw a smirk on her face.

***

'Andrew, would you mind coming to my office for a moment, please? I know you're busy, but it's important.'

'Really, Frank. You come to see me, say in quarter of an hour?'

'No, I need you to see something here, sorry.'

'Very well. Give me five minutes, I'm speaking with someone.'

'Yes, of course, I wouldn't ask if it wasn't serious. Thank you.'

Frank was worried that the person Mr Davis was speaking with was Rick, and that he may have failed to have the first say after the fracas. The confrontation had gone far better than he expected, and he wanted to fully utilise Rick's outburst, the consequences of which would be diluted if Rick had gone to Mr Davis and explained his reaction before he could stir things up further.

'Right, Fr...what on earth has happened here?' Mr Davis said, aghast.

'I thought I'd better let you see first hand. It was Rick, he just went crazy. Has he been up to see you since?'

'No, no. What did you say to him, for God's sake?'

'I was as nice as pie. I offered him my condolences and told him that things in his department were on track, and he became aggressive for no apparent reason.'

'Well, he was fine with me. He wanted to come back to work.'

'He told me that too. I said that Miss Harper had done a good job in his absence and that I was looking forward to having him back.'

'That was a bit insensitive, wasn't it? You know, about Danielle Harper, in view of what happened before?'

'Look, I didn't mean anything by it. I was trying to tell him that targets were on course and he started raising his voice and accusing me of stirring it up with her. I asked him to calm down and the next thing I knew he trashed the office.'

Andrew Davis sighed deeply. 'I like Richard, but this is no good. Hell, the lad's been through a lot but if this is how he reacts to the slightest thing then he can't come back, until he's had a good deal of therapy at least.'

'I agree. I don't mind admitting it, I was bloody scared. I've never seen him like that before.'

'Right, I'll let Mr Kemper know.'

'Do you have to? I don't want to get him into trouble.'

'I know that, but he has to know. We'll have to visit him at home and make sure he sees a counsellor before he steps through the front door again. I've got to consider people's safety here.'

'Are you sure you're not making a crisis out of a drama?'

'Don't question my decisions, Frank, I don't appreciate it.'

'Sorry. Listen, if there's anything I can do to help, just ask. Are you happy for Miss Harper to continue as acting manager for the time being?'

'Yes, yes. If you're satisfied she's doing a good job, she can stay put for now, that's the least of our worries. Now tidy this lot up, it looks like a bomb's hit it in here.'

Andrew Davis left Parsons's office genuinely concerned for Rick, in his estimation one of his best managers. Frank Parsons smiled broadly, another day's social manoeuvring completed. Well, he'd never really liked Rick anyway.

Chapter 11

Josie loved to languish in the bath, only her head visible above the masses of white bubbles sitting on the steaming water. This was her haven from the stresses and strains of the world around her, where she found peace.

Today was different, however. The hot water and foam offered her no hiding place, in fact the bubbles had long since dispersed without her noticing, as the internal wrestling match between her conscience and her true wishes took place. The bout had lasted for many rounds, over a number of days, and she was both physically and mentally drained as it neared its end.

The winner was her desire to be happy. The loser, who came a very close second, was guilt. She didn't want to hurt Tom, but she would have to in order to free herself of a man who was becoming increasingly possessive and stifling, a man who she was fond of but did not love.

If she was truthful with herself she had wanted to finish with Tom before Ellie had died, after that most vivid of dreams where a figure had appeared and told her that her true happiness did not lie in a life with Tom, but elsewhere. That dream had made her realise that the path she was about to take was absolutely necessary if she was to live the life that she deserved to live. She concluded that Tom would have to go.

Josie dried and slipped on her silk dressing gown, ensuring that it covered her properly. She descended the stairs and sat opposite Tom who was reading the paper.

'Tom,' she said gently, easing the tabloid from his grasp, 'I want to talk to you.'

'Here it comes,' he said. 'What I've been expecting for four years.' He did not look at her, but stared out of the window instead with glazed eyes.

'I've always been very fond of you, and I'd be lying if I said we hadn't had some great times together...'

'But...'

'Yes, but,' Josie confirmed as kindly as she could, 'Despite everything, I'm not in love with you. I'm really sorry, I know that must hurt, but I have to tell you. It's only fair.'

'And you *love* Rick do you?' he said sarcastically.

'Look, this is about you and me. When you saw me and Rick the other day I was just comforting him. He was distraught, Tom. You should be offering him more support, you know.'

'Maybe, but it's not easy helping someone who's moved in on your girlfriend.'

'He's not moved in anywhere, it's all in your mind.'

'Is it really? So when did you stop loving me, then?'

'We all define "love" in different ways...'

'Don't give me that counselling claptrap, I want the facts,' Tom said coldly, still looking at the neon lights at the opposite side of the street.

'OK. You helped me when I came to Leeds, and I felt close to you then. You didn't take advantage of me and you were modest and kind. I was attracted to those qualities in you, but...but I didn't fancy you.'

'Oh, fine. So all these years you've been repaying the debt. Looking at it that way, I suppose I've not done badly then, really. A beautiful woman to make love to for four years, a companion who feigns that she cares for me for all that time, and all the local blokes as jealous as hell of me. Yes, it was worth picking you off the street and not giving you one straight away, I must admit.'

'Tom, listen to me. I care for you and I've never treated you like that. I can tell you truthfully that I've enjoyed our times together, including in the bedroom, and in spite of what you might think I would never look at our relationship as repaying a debt. That's bloody nonsense, OK?'

The aggression that Tom had formally displayed as a defence mechanism subsided and gave way to sadness. He looked at Josie, his eyes filled with tears, 'Please, tell me this isn't true.'

'Sorry,' Josie said. She did not need to elaborate or explain any further. As Tom cried as unreservedly as a baby, she took him in her arms and sighed.

Chapter 12

10th August 2001

The journey only took an hour and ten minutes, considerably less than other times in the past when he had made the trip with Ellie sitting beside him. But those times had been at weekends when more people travelled to the coast. Today was a weekday, albeit during the summer holidays, and the rain fell heavily.

Despite the fact that he had made the journey to Filey in record time, it did not seem that way. Ellie's former chattering and laughter had felt irritating at times, but had clearly entertained him because today's excursion with only the radio for company had felt decidedly longer, and lonelier.

Rick parked the car and walked across Reighton Sands, as he had done on so many occasions with Ellie. With the exception of Rome, the wooden bench on the cliff side to the north of the Sands was their favourite place, their special place. They had sat on that bench and discussed everything from Josie's terrible news that she couldn't bear children, to their own work-related problems. Rick had proposed to Ellie on that bench, and made love to her on it that same night.

As Rick sat there he looked over to his left, where Ellie used to sit. There was only a space instead of her. The wind howled and the rain lashed his face, hiding his tears, although he was the only one within a mile of the place on such a ghastly day.

The inclement weather attacked him with unrelenting fury for hours, but Rick did not see the rain nor feel the gale. His inner turmoil far surpassed anything that nature could throw at him as his mind ebbed and flowed with emotions in tune with the sea below.

To have watched him as an invisible observer would have given the impression that he had lost his mind. Smiling one moment, the next crying and the next angry. And that was how it went for almost three hours, but even that failed to purge Rick of his pain. He felt as if he wanted to rip his insides out to rid himself of the anguish that was destroying him. Physically fit in every way, but emotionally crippled. How do you deal with this, he asked himself over and over. But the answers did not come.

Rick looked up to the heavens. The police were no nearer to identifying the killer and the letters proffered no evidence of value. He was sure that Sarah Bowers was not responsible for writing them; it could be Danielle but how would he go about suggesting it, let alone proving it? He had effectively lost his best friend, and now maybe his job as well. Then there was the vision in the mirror and the message in the book.

He sighed because he felt worse than he had that week after her death when he shut out the world to grieve. In fact, he felt now that there was no way he would recover. He had been fooling himself believing that a shake of his head and a spring-clean would give him his life back. He was no nearer to catching the killer, but a damn sight nearer to losing his sanity.

Racked with a sense of utter defeat, Rick walked to the cliff edge, leaving only a few inches of turf between his feet and…freedom?

Chapter 13

10th August 2001

The rocks below almost beckoned Rick as he looked down at them. Was this a coward's way out, he thought, or a quick fix? A simple step forward would do the trick. It would be frightening for four or five seconds, no doubt, but after that the prize would be eternal peace. A single stride into thin air would immediately rid him of the need to worry about bringing the killer to justice, about trying to cope with the loss and all those other material concerns which ate away at him like an unstoppable disease. He inched forward, his toes now protruding over the rough grassy edge of the cliff.

As his baggy jumper flapped in the wind Rick felt an invisible finger caress his neck, just below the ear as Ellie had done so many times during tender moments. He did not jump or reel back, in fact he welcomed the sensation. He knew Ellie was with him, helping him through his torment. She had always been a trusty shoulder to cry on in times of need, particularly when his father died, and she was here with him now. Rick looked out to sea. His tears ran into the corner of his mouth and they tasted salty. Why did things have to end this way, he thought. It was so unfair. Two, no three, lives destroyed for no reason. 'E...L...L...I...E,' Rick shouted at the top of his voice, the wind laughing at him as it threw the outburst back in his face. There was no reply. He shouted again, still no response.

A gust of wind whipped up behind him and threw him off balance. Instinctively, his arms windmilled to prevent him from going over the edge, and somehow he managed to prevent the fall. He sat on the grass, weeping uncontrollably for half an hour, before finally taking the long walk back to the car.

Chapter 14

Josie rapped at Rick's door. He peered around the side of the curtain and sighed as he looked at her worried face. Reluctantly opening the door, he gave his visitor a less than warm welcome and she followed him into the hallway.

'Nice to see you too,' she said.

'Look, I'm not good company at the moment.'

'You haven't been for the last four years,' Josie said, in an attempt to snap Rick out of his self-pity.

'Sit down. Do you want a drink?'

'I'll have a sensible one,' she replied, looking at the spent beer cans which littered the living room.

'Eh. If you've come here to have a go at me then you can sod off.'

'And if that's how you treat your friends, I think I will,' she retorted. Josie knew this was the best way of handling Rick. Submitting to his mood would have done him no favours. She stood up and made for the door.

'Sit down. I didn't mean it. I'm stressed out at the moment, sorry.'

She looked closely at Rick, trying to assess the quantity of alcohol he had consumed. Although he wasn't drunk, the effects were plain to see. 'I've been ringing you since Friday; where have you been hiding?' she asked.

'Oh, I've been here. I didn't want to speak to anyone.'

'I thought you said you'd turned the corner, you know learned to cope with what's happened?'

'I thought I had.'

'Listen to me. I'm not going to lecture you or ramble on

about this, but no-one deals with a tragedy like this in three weeks, OK? Not you, not anyone.'

'Don't I know it? Just when you think you're coming to terms, it hits you again like a bloody train.'

'Yes. And that's normal. You're normal. It shows that you loved Ellie.'

'How long am I gonna feel like this, Jo? It's been nearly a month and...I was going to end it all the other day.'

'What?'

'Yeah. I went to a cliff edge and nearly threw myself off.'

'What stopped you?'

'I don't know. I was ready to do it, then...I just couldn't.'

'Tell me that you won't do that again. Promise me.'

'Why? Who are you, my mother?' Rick injected a scathing tone into his words, but Josie knew how to deal with it.

'That's nice,' she said, looking away from him and feigning upset. 'I came here because I care about you, and you throw it back in my face.'

'I told you I wasn't good company. Just ignore me, I don't know whether I'm coming or going at the moment.'

'Do you want to talk about something else?'

'Why not?'

'Me and Tom, we've split up.'

'How did he take it, as if I need to ask?'

'Not well. I'm glad I did it though. It was awful, for both of us, but better that than me pretending that I love him for the rest of my life and eventually resenting him for it.'

'Has he mentioned me at all?' Rick asked, hoping for some good news.

'I won't lie to you, he said you've betrayed him.'

'How the hell does he work that out?'

'I've told you he's a very jealous and possessive bloke, and at the moment he'll believe what he wants to believe. Let him come round, he won't want to throw your friendship away for long. He's gone to stay with Michael in Birmingham for a week or so, after that I don't know.'

'Where's he going to live? Your house is yours, not his.'

'I don't know. It's not a good idea for us to sleep under the same roof though. It has to be final otherwise there could be misunderstandings.'

'Mm. Aren't you sad, then?'

'Of course I am. You don't spend years with someone and have no scars when it ends. We've grown apart this last year though, and I've not treated him well for the last couple of months, probably because I knew it had to come to an end. Anyway, the hard bit's over now.'

'For you, maybe.'

'That's not fair.'

'Well, he's suffering like me now isn't he? In some ways it's worse for him; I have to come to terms with never being able to touch or talk with Ellie again, but Tom. He's lost you, but you're still around. You're there, but he can't touch. Now that's hard.'

'You're right, I hadn't thought of it like that. But what's the alternative?'

'There isn't one, is there?'

'Not really, Rick, no.'

Josie got up and made her way into the kitchen. 'Coffee?' she called.

'Please.'

He followed her. As he approached the kitchen, he stopped in his tracks. The door was half open and he could see Josie busying herself. As he watched her, he could not help noticing her natural beauty. In no way was he consciously spying on her, but momentarily he was captivated by her elegance.

Her long strawberry-blonde wavy hair moved ever so slightly as she glided across the room. She wore stretch jeans which accentuated her perfect bottom and long legs, and her ample yet firm breasts moved temptingly under the tight white T-shirt she wore, a cropped top which revealed her flawless, tanned midriff. Rick remembered her icy blue eyes and alluring smile. He could not think of any model or film star as beautiful as her. She could have made a fortune, he thought to himself.

Becoming aware of his own thoughts, and the hardness building in his track-suit bottoms, he felt tremendous guilt. He remembered going out as a foursome with Ellie, Josie and Tom on numerous occasions in the past and thinking how gorgeous Josie looked. He hadn't felt the guilt then. Ellie was an attractive woman, but Josie was stunning. He would never have made a play for her, though, because he genuinely loved Ellie and he wouldn't have wanted to hurt her or Tom, so the occasional fantasies were OK then. In his head, and no-where else. But as Ellie was dead now, and Tom was officially out of the equation, Josie was technically available and his physical feelings for her were no longer acceptable in this context. He hurried back into the lounge and waited for his coffee.

'Here, sober up a bit,' Josie said.

'So, we're *both* single all of a sudden,' Rick said.

Josie looked at him and gave him a warm and almost affectionate smile, causing further stirrings in him. 'Life throws you around, doesn't it?'

'You can say that again.'

'Life throws you around, doesn't it?' she repeated, mischievously glancing at him out of the corner of her eye.

'You're nuts, Josie Hinds.'

'It's been said,' she replied. 'Anyway, I thought you were going back to work. Some of us have to earn a living, you know.'

'Don't talk to me about work. Actually I've been thinking, what with the mortgage paid off on Ellie's death, and the insurance moneys due, I could stay off work for a long time to come. Stuff 'em.'

Josie looked perplexed. 'But I thought you were itching to get back?'

'I was, until that prat Parsons put the dampeners on it.'

'What do you mean?'

'I went in and spoke to Andrew Davis, the Personnel Manager. He was fine. OK, he was a bit concerned that I was going back too soon and was worried that my mind might not be on my work, I can understand that. He wanted to see a doctor's note that showed I was coping with the stress, and he was happy. But not Parsons.'

'He's your immediate boss, right?'

'Yeah.'

'Well isn't the Personnel Manager above him?'

'Yes, but he wanted Parsons to speak to me and be satisfied that I'm ready to return as well. When I spoke to him he twisted everything and made me mad.'

'Hang on, what do mean made you mad? What did you do?'

Rick hesitated for a moment. 'Trashed his desk,' he said sheepishly.

'What are you like? Mr Hot Head.'

'He's a malicious twat, though,' he said defensively.

'What could he possibly have said that made you do that?'

'Look, I hate the man. All the office does, he's a slimy little git who likes throwing his weight around. Look at the business with Danielle Harper. Top management backed me up, but Parsons? He managed to get her to remain as team-leader in my department, and kept making the odd comment to me about how I wasn't a man turning her down. He talks to me like a child in front of staff I supervise. He's just a arse.' Rick was raising his voice.

'Calm down,' Josie said, putting her hand on his. 'What did he actually say about you going back to work?'

'He started off by offering his "condolences" like he really meant it. Then he went on to tell me that Danielle was doing my job and that she was every bit as good as me. I tried to ignore his attempts to wind me up, but then he said that in his opinion I was no-where near ready to start work again and to come back in six weeks.'

'Maybe he was right.' Rick looked at Josie with annoyance, but his anger quickly subsided as he saw genuine concern on her face. 'It seems that his reasons were all wrong, but you spending more time getting to grips with your feelings and emotions can only be good,' she said.

'But I've done nothing else for almost a month,' he protested.

'And it takes longer, whether you like it or not. You are a human being, and human beings need time to cope with loss, it can't be rushed just because you don't like it. It's a cliché, I know, but Time is a healer, and you *will* get over this.'

'It just feels like Frank Parsons is laughing at me. The stupid things he's been saying to me about Danielle, and now this. Why does he do it?'

'Well, in a nutshell people have motives for everything they do and say. The motives often have to stay hidden because they're immoral, based say on revenge or jealousy. Obviously, it would be socially unacceptable for Parsons to say "I'm jealous of Rick Sheldon because Danielle fancies him, so I'll stick a spanner in the works for him and make him suffer because she doesn't fancy me" so he dresses it up. He still achieves his objective, but in a way which is acceptable in the environment he's in. In the same way, he lords it over others because he probably lacks respect or recognition elsewhere in his life.'

'That figures. He's a sad man.'

'In what way?'

'He's in his mid-forties, but he lives at home with his mother. I've never known him go out, not even to works functions, and no-one has ever seen or heard of a girlfriend. He's a bit of a weirdo, really.'

'How long has he disliked you in particular?' Josie asked.

'For a long time. But this situation with Danielle seems to have made him worse.'

Rick was getting upset, and Josie decided to let the matter drop for now, although she was beginning to wonder whether Frank Parsons was vengeful enough to concoct a hurtful letter or two.

Chapter 15

Rick visited the gym usually alone, sometimes with Josie; he decorated the kitchen and changed his car for a newer model. Most of his time in the last few days, however, had been spent engrossed in a couple of books he had bought. One concerned paranormal events, the other was a book written by a late clairvoyant.

Rick felt embarrassed choosing these books because in a way he felt as though he was giving in to stuff and nonsense as a way of coping with his grief. Yet, if he believed in himself, he was convinced that the two unusual occurrences had actually happened and this was a practical way of finding out more about a subject which he no longer dismissed out of hand. If the things he'd seen had not happened, he was delusional; if they had happened then he was sane and wanted to know more about what they meant.

Reading the book 'The Other Side' reminded him of Josie's off-the-cuff suggestion that he visit a medium. He had spoken to people at work who'd been for sessions with a medium and had gained a great deal from the experience. At the time he'd laughed at these people's stories, deriding them as outlandish and plain silly, but now he wondered if there was an element of authenticity in the anecdotes. Indeed, the 'witches' as he used to refer to them, had on reflection produced some pretty intuitive insights which he chose to ignore in favour of his out and out cynicism.

The last couple of days' reading had made him more receptive to the unknown as he perused numerous examples of people's encounters with loved ones who had passed away. He was not sure whether he believed all the accounts wholeheartedly, but his former dismissive attitude was giving way to an element of hope that he maybe able, through a clairvoyant, to establish the meaning of the visions.

With this in mind, Rick contacted a local medium whose name had been bandied about at work as synonymous with pure genius. She told him that under normal circumstances he would need to book a reading with her at least eight weeks in advance, but luckily for him she had been notified of a cancellation only ten minutes earlier. If he could be at her address in two hours, she could see him.

Rick's emotions were mixed. He had expected a week or two's acclimatisation to the idea before he went along, but on the other hand there was no time like the present and he had made the decision on making the phone call, so why back out now?

***

Ms Begrum's house was not what he expected. Rick sat in his car opposite, ten minutes or so before the agreed meeting time, and looked over at number 37. He had pictured a large detached with sweeping gardens, maybe due to his preconception that such people would make a fortune as well as telling one. Instead was a modest-looking town house in a row of six, with a four year old car sat on the road outside. Either this medium was not very good at her job, or money was not a priority in her life, he thought.

He began to regret his decision to meet the woman, but before he talked himself into switching the engine back on and driving off he alighted the car and made his way to the door of the house. As he walked down the garden path his stomach turned over. He had not felt such apprehension for a long time, but in the circumstances he concluded that it was only natural. Firstly, seeing such a person would have been inconceivable to him only two months earlier. And secondly, the outcome of this visit would either affirm his life-long assertion that the whole thing was twaddle dressed up to make a quick buck, or would frighten him to death.

Rick knocked on the door. To his surprise, a perfectly

normal- looking woman opened it. In his mind's eye he had anticipated a swarthy middle-aged woman, slightly overweight, with a bandanna covering her thick black hair. At this point, Rick told himself to stop making assumptions and to take it as it comes.

'Mr Sheldon?'

'Yes.'

'Please, come in,' she said reassuringly.

Rick followed Ms Begrum along the hallway and into an attractively decorated room. Pine furniture sat on beach-wood flooring and the walls were painted azure blue with pine coving and dados. The style was minimalist and it appealed to him. He felt much better having entered this room.

'Take a seat. You said your name was Richard?'

'That's right, yes.'

He sat on a leather chair, which seemed to mould itself instantly to his shape, and she sat opposite in an identical one.

'Have you had a reading before, Richard?' she asked. Her voice was soft and relaxed.

'Well, no,' he replied.

'I didn't think so. If you don't mind me saying, you look very uneasy. Let me tell you that anything you don't want to discuss will not be discussed, and you can feel free to ask whatever you like at any time. OK?'

'Thanks, yeah.' He heard the apprehension in his own voice, and felt a little embarrassed.

'Right then, if I could explain how the next forty minutes or so will go, you may feel more relaxed with things. I don't use a crystal ball or cards, all I need as I explained on the phone is an intimate piece of jewellery or an item which has special significance to you. We'll spend the whole time in this room, talking to each other, and there will be no need for me to lay hands on you or go into a trance or anything like that. Now, have you brought an item for me?'

'Will my wedding ring do?'

'They often work very well, yes.' Rick removed his ring and gave it to Ms Begrum.

'The only other thing I would say to you is please don't take anything I say out of context. Basically, there are all sorts of people who come here, with a variety of reasons for coming. All I ask is that you try to keep an open mind.'

'That's fine,' Rick said, not really knowing what she meant.

The medium then turned her attention to the wedding ring. She rubbed it gently between her thumb and finger, gazing at it for over a minute. Rick instinctively knew that this was not the time to ask a question. He left her to ruminate further, and after a short while she looked up and sighed.

'Your life is difficult at the moment, isn't it?' she said. Rick nodded. On the one hand he was amazed that she had reached this conclusion, but on the other he was conscious that he mustn't give her any information that she could use to structure the meeting. He was considerably more open-minded than he had been, but he still felt it necessary to test her authenticity by letting her find her own path. 'Married for such a short time.' Rick's mouth opened slightly as he heard her words. 'I'm told that India was beautiful.'

Rick cleared his throat. 'Well…the Indian Ocean. It was the Maldives.' Ms Begrum nodded and smiled. It was as though she was holding a two-way conversation and did not want to offend either party by paying too much attention to one of them in particular. 'How do you know that?' His query did not sound disbelieving or aggressive, simply intense.

'I'm with her now, Richard. She's a little playful, I have to say, and she won't tell me her name other than it begins with an 'E'.'

'Ellie, her name's Ellie,' Rick volunteered hurriedly.

'Yes. Ellie. She loves you very very much.'

Rick swallowed the lump in his throat. Lost for words, his thoughts were no longer centred upon whether this woman was a fake, but on his wife and his love for her.

'She says not to worry about anything that's happened in the past, before you were married.'

'The affair with Sarah,' Rick said without thinking.

'None of that matters. You love her, and that makes her very happy.'

There followed silence for a moment or two, and then Rick asked, 'Who did it...? I need to know.'

Ms Begrum inhaled sharply. Her face contorted and it took a few seconds for her to compose herself. Rick stared at her aghast. 'She won't give me an answer to that,' the medium said flatly.

'What happened there?' he asked.

'Sometimes the subject breaks the communication suddenly. I've experienced this three or four times in the past, but it's fairly rare. I can't give an explanation, it just happens on occasion.'

'Can't you get her back?' he asked desperately.

'Usually it spells the end of the session, I'm afraid, but I'll try.'

She fell into a reverie for almost five minutes, and then raised her head, smiling. Rick smiled back.

'Ellie says not to be naughty.'

'Why has she been calling me?' Rick enquired.

'She's says if you can't work out the message then it is of no use.'

'What does it all mean?'

'Ellie is shaking her head and she has her finger to her mouth. "Shhh. It's our secret," she is saying.' Rick looked down in despair. 'She has to go now. She says she is sorry she can't help any more, but always remember that she loves you.'

With that, Ms Begrum told Rick that there would be no further contact today.

'Are you upset with what you've heard?' she asked him.

'I don't know. To be honest with you I used to think that this was all a load of rubbish. I mean, how can you contact Ellie...? How can you speak with the dead?'

'"Dead" is not a word I use. I prefer "existing elsewhere". Your spirit, my spirit and Ellie's leaves the body when it fails. I can't tell you where exactly it goes, but I do know that it's usually receptive to contact, particularly the loving and caring elements of the soul.'

'How do you contact the soul, then?'

'Some people are more able to feel its presence than others.

I'm lucky, so I help those who are not to establish a link, and it often makes them feel close to those who have gone.'

Rick explained the vision he had seen in the mirror, and the message he had read in the book. Ms Begrum nodded and smiled as he related what he had experienced, and not once did she interrupt him. 'Do you believe all that?' he asked her.

'Certainly,' she said. 'You've been very lucky. No doubt you were frightened at first, but not many people get the opportunity to see their loved ones after they've gone. Those who tell me that they've had contact often refer to things said in dreams or things that happen in their everyday lives which they interpret as a message, but you have had closer contact.'

'I get the impression that Elllie's trying to tell me something, though,' Rick continued. 'She beckoned me in the mirror that day, and the text in the book. What do you make of it?'

'Oh, sorry to disappoint you. I couldn't possibly hazard a guess, first of all because I genuinely don't know and secondly because if I were wrong you may act on my interpretation and what you do could change your life. No, it wouldn't be fair of me to try and make sense of what she means, *you* must do that. On the other hand, you could simply forget about the messages and thank yourself lucky that you got them. Not many people are as fortunate as you.'

'That doesn't make me feel any better,' he said.

'Look, why don't we see if anyone else is interested in linking with us?'

'OK.'

She closed her eyes, clasping the gold band in her right palm. 'Margaret is coming, and...and...no, the other person, a man, won't show himself. Margaret says he's too tired.'

Rick was in awe. Elaine Margaret Sheldon was his mother, and she had always preferred Margaret. And during the last year of his dad's life, after his mum had died of cancer, he always complained of being tired. Every time he went to see his father he was forever tired. No wonder the girls in the office had some interesting tales to tell after seeing this woman. It was incredible, he thought.

'Margaret is smiling. She says she is proud of you.' Rick's eyes welled and he nodded unconsciously. 'She has a word of warning for you as well. Always think carefully before you make any important decisions because those you make in the next six months will shape your future profoundly. More so than at any other time in your life.'

'What does she mean?' Rick asked seriously.

'She's shaking her head. She says you must remember what she's said.'

'How's Dad?'

'Mum says he's happy.'

'Right.'

'Mum's gone now, Richard. I have Ruth here. She won't say if she's a relative.'

'Ruth? I don't know a Ruth.'

'She says she's an author. She's very evasive, almost as if she doesn't want to be with us.'

Rick's face fell and he felt short of breath. The book, the one with the message in it. The author was Ruth Stocks. He knew no other Ruth. 'What does she want?' he asked in an almost frightened tone.

'She says to listen to Ellie.' There was a pause. 'I sense something different about this person.'

At that point the medium's eyes rolled into the back of her head and she stared at the ceiling. Rick was stunned. He could not take his eyes from the woman. She began making a hideous sound, as if she was gargling with a mouthwash, and her eyes flickered entirely involuntarily.

'Excuse me,' Rick said in a confused tone. 'Excuse me,' he said, this time louder. No reaction. He took hold of the medium's arm, now beginning to panic, and he could feel her entire body shaking. Saliva ran down the left side of her chin and her face began to redden. Rick stood in front of her, observing her physical deterioration before his eyes. Not knowing what to do for the best, he struck her with the flat of his hand hard across the face, and she was knocked sideways off the leather chair. She thumped to the floor, but continued her fit as if possessed.

'S...T...O...P!' Rick bawled at the top of his voice, but the woman thrashed about unabated. He stood back from her with a feeling of utter helplessness and watched, wide-eyed, as she squirmed and writhed on the floor. Blood, mucous and spittle spoiled the otherwise spotless beach flooring.

The spectacle was too much for a man who, until recently, had believed all this to be hocus-pocus. Fear overcame Rick and he was about to run headlong from the house and away from this indescribable horror, when the victim in front of him suddenly lay still. At first he thought she was dead, but then he saw her hand move. Her eyes were closed now, but curiously she began wiping the floor with her dress. He watched her movements transfixed, and before long the wooden floor was clean again, yet her dress remained unstained. She picked herself off the floor and stroked her face with her hands. Moments later her features, like the floor, showed no evidence of body fluids and she sat calmly in the chair. Even her hair had assumed its former neatness. Her eyes opened and she spoke to the terrified man stood near the door. 'You are needed to undo the work of a selfish and ruthless man,' she said in a detached voice.

'What?' Rick said, unable to move from the spot.

Ms Begrum showed none of her previous geniality. The voice was hers, but it was as if the speaker was someone else. 'Listen to your wife. Heed her missive. If you ignore the path she advises you will be responsible.'

Rick turned to leave the room, but found himself rooted to the spot. He could not lift his legs. He looked in sheer panic back at Ms Begrum who said, 'Do not turn from the path, do not ignore the voice of reason.' And with that, she sank into the chair. Rick's head was spinning; he nipped his arm hard in an attempt to wake from this nightmare, but the room was still there. He approached the woman, whose eyes were closed again, and shook her violently. There was no response. He felt for a pulse but could feel none either in her neck or her wrist. No breath came from her mouth.

Rick manhandled the woman to the floor and ripped open her dress. He tore off her bra and began massaging her chest, trying all the while to remember the first aid classes he attended last year. Fifteen compressions, two breaths…fifteen compressions, two breaths…fifteen, two…fifteen, two. He breathed hard and sweated, but still no response. Leaving the limp and prostrate woman on the floor, Rick dialled 999 on his mobile and summoned an ambulance. For what seemed to take an eternity he continued his rudimentary attempts to bring her back from the dead until the paramedics arrived with their equipment. For twenty minutes they worked on her, but to no avail. Eventually they told the police officers, whose attendance they had requested, that there was nothing anyone could do for her.

'Could I have word with you, please?' a weather-beaten looking policeman said to Rick, and he was led into the kitchen. 'Are you a relative?'

Christ Almighty, Rick said to himself, his thoughts turning to the reality of the scene before him. Here he was, a man who had come to have a 'reading' from a clairvoyant, who had supposedly died before his eyes and he had tried to save her. When the ambulance crew had arrived she had been on the floor, clothes ripped off. And she was only about forty years of age. 'Er, no, not really,' he stammered.

'Are you a friend, then?' the officer asked, a suspicious look forming on his face.

'No. Look, I came here as…er, a client.'

'I think you'd better explain,' came the inevitable question.

'She's…I mean the woman in there…she's, was, a medium.'

'Stay here,' the policeman said, and he nodded to his colleague. Rick realised that he was going nowhere whether he wanted to or not. Craning his neck to see where the first officer had gone, he could see him speaking on his mobile phone in the front garden. A few minutes later he returned with two rolls of blue 'POLICE' tape and instructed the younger policeman to begin 'taping off the scene.'

Then came the words that shocked Rick almost as profoundly as the earlier encounter. 'You are under arrest on suspicion of murder. You do not have to say anything, but it may harm your defence if you fail to mention when questioned something which you later rely on in court. What you do say maybe given in evidence.'

The handcuffs clicked shut and Rick was led to the police van outside.

Chapter 16

19th September 2001

Some holiday this turned out to be, Josie thought to herself as she sat opposite Frank Parsons's house for the fourth day in a row. She had given a lot of thought to Rick's description of his boss's hermit-like existence, and how unusual he was. She was acutely aware of how unfair stereotyping could be, but not only did Parsons steer clear of socialising, he also lived with his mother despite being forty-some years of age and he had no partner that anyone knew about, female or male. That was not 'normal'. Furthermore, his behaviour towards Rick had always betrayed an underlying jealousy, which had reared its ugly head quite noticeably following the Danielle Harper affair. Josie concluded simply that Parsons was incredibly envious of Rick. He was jealous of his looks, the fact that women found him attractive, in short he was jealous of Rick's life. And jealousy could be a dangerous emotion.

She knew that it had been some time since Rick had received the last piece of hate mail, but in her view this Parsons character was by far the strongest suspect. It was dreadful for Rick to have to endure the pain of losing his wife, and child to be, she thought, but sometimes life throws these things at you and however awful it is at the time you have to bear the pain and soldier on. But to take advantage of a person's misfortune in order to satisfy some sick jealousy, to cause that person additional and unnecessary pain and to derive pleasure from it, she found abhorrent and it sickened her to her stomach. If Frank Parsons was the one responsible for sending the letters, she would be his undoing.

Josie had no particular plan in mind. She simply sat outside his house, watching. She had taken a week off work, the last week of leave she had in the current year, and she intended spending it gathering any information or fact, no matter how insignificant, that would put meat on the bones of her suspicions. Parked opposite his house and slightly down the street, Josie observed the bungalow, with its perfectly trimmed lawn and matching curtains. She had first taken up her position at 7.30am on the Sunday morning, but neither Frank nor his mother had showed their faces all that day, until she went home at 9.20pm, unless of course they sneaked out and returned in the half hour when she went into the town for a break. There had been no movement whatsoever.

On Monday morning, Frank had appeared at the front door at 8 o'clock sharp and left for work. Josie had gone about her business and returned at about 4pm. Frank had got home at 5.15. He had not emerged for the rest of the evening. The same routine on Tuesday, and today. A creature of habit, she mused. Or maybe a man with nothing better to do with his time than cause pain to others. He did it at work with his overbearing and domineering manner, so why not out of work?

The time was now 9.55 pm on Wednesday, and Josie began to question her original suspicions. She yawned, sick to death of the same old music repeating itself on the radio. Rubbing her eyes, she turned the key in the ignition and looked over her right shoulder before moving off. Turning to look forward she saw, to her surprise, Frank Parsons opening the front door of the bungalow. She turned off her lights and peered towards his driveway. He got into his Mercedes and reversed into the road. At first her heart missed a beat; where was he going at this time of night? As she followed him at a safe distance her initial excitement faded, in fact she laughed at her own impulsive notion: he may simply be going to the off-licence to buy milk for his morning cereal, and here she was acting like a rookie copper following a known drug pusher en route to do a million pound crack cocaine deal.

Ten minutes passed and she found herself on the M62 motorway. Following Parsons was not difficult on this road because there were no junctions and bends that took him out of her sight, and the road was surprisingly quiet at this time of the day. She made sure that a gap of least two hundred yards was maintained, just to allay any suspicion on his part that he was being followed. Josie again quietly chided herself; people were followed for tens of miles on the motorway by the same car, so why should he grow suspicious? No, she would never make a surveillance expert, she thought.

Seven miles sped by, and Josie began to wonder where Parsons was going. This was clearly no longer a trip to the shop. She became aware that the gap between the two cars was widening, so she stepped on the accelerator to close it. Despite her increased speed, however, she failed to reduce the distance between her and the target car. Her speed was now in excess of ninety miles per hour, but the car in front was getting no nearer. She floored the go-faster pedal and reached a touch over a ton but still the gap was widening. The fact was that he drove a sporty Mercedes and she was sat behind the wheel of a 1250cc Fiat. His rear lights were still visible along the sweeping downhill ahead of her, but there was at least half a mile between them now. 'Shit,' she said aloud as she pressed her foot hard against the floor. Her car worked hard and she heard the racing engine trying its best to squeeze out a little extra speed, but to no avail; one hundred and two miles per hour was its ceiling and that was downhill. She realised that there was a long climb ahead over the Pennines, that his car would steam up the incline and that hers would labour at seventy or eighty if she was lucky. Josie slapped the steering wheel as if to punish her nearly-new but modest vehicle. Parsons was out of sight now. She had lost him.

As anticipated, her car struggled up the mountain-side. How the hell was she supposed to keep up to his expensive beast? Two or three miles farther on, however, she thought she recognised its rear in the distance. Spurring her car on like a jockey in the final furlongs she began to gain on the car ahead. A minute or two later she whooped with joy as she strained to see the distinctive number plate, FOP 21, on the Mercedes. But she realised instantly how she had managed to catch up, as the blue lights of the police car behind her beaconed their warning for her to stop.

Parsons had slowed to prevent points on his licence, but in her single-minded determination not to lose him she had defeated her own ambition. It wasn't the sixty-pound fine that would hurt her, but the chance to find out where he was going, and why.

A little eyelid fluttering and a few coy smiles prevented the fine, as the young traffic cop gave her a warning about travelling at ninety miles per hour. She had known male friends pick up tickets on the motorway for going only fractionally over the limit; the face of Justice, based on the face of the offender.

After issuing his warning, and giving her a form requiring the production of her driving documents, the cause of her failed mission sped off in his lemon-striped Jaguar, no doubt in a ridiculous attempt to display his driving skills in front of the pretty lady despite having nowhere in particular to go.

Josie cursed her luck. There was no chance now of picking up Parsons's trail, he would be five or six miles ahead oblivious of the fact that he had shaken off a determined amateur detective.

It was five miles before she reached the next junction where she could turn back towards Leeds. The radio remained silent and the otherwise quiet journey was punctuated only by heavy sighs from the driver. Four bloody days of sitting, watching, waiting, she thought, for what? To be pulled up by some spotty-faced policeman who didn't even have the confidence to prosecute her. What a waste of time. As she turned onto the M621 approaching Leeds, Josie decided despite her tiredness to park outside Parsons's house again. She wanted to know whether he would return home tonight. There was always the possibility that he was going on holiday and was simply en route to Manchester airport, quite innocently. But would he leave his ageing mother alone for a week, or two, and travel abroad alone? Probably not.

Assuming her now familiar parking spot on Tranquillity Crescent, she reclined her seat fractionally to ease her aching neck, continuing the vigil she had held for the last four days. An uneasy realisation was building that she maybe forming an obsession with the motives of a man who she did not even know, and against whom she had no evidence to substantiate her suppositions.

Half an hour passed, no sign of Parsons. On more than one occasion Josie had shaken off the predatory nature of slumber, but eventually had given way to its persuasive seduction in that semi-conscious, resigned way. The body's defence mechanism kicked in. Sleep was required urgently, and so it set about its task in earnest by deploying one of its most powerful of weapons, Shutdown.

Bright lights bluntly prodded Josie's bubble of awareness. Instinctively, she dismissed the intrusion in favour of continuing with her much needed regeneration, but suddenly her waking sentience took control and she jumped through several states of consciousness in an instant, momentarily disorientating her. There he was, parking his Mercedes in the drive. She rubbed her eyes in an attempt to inject a dose of keenness into her thought processes. The time, what time was it? 11.42 pm. Right, she'd started the journey behind his car at about ten o'clock. Then she'd been stopped by the police on the M62. Looking at the document the policeman had given her, that made it 10.20. Then she'd given up the chase, gone five miles to the next junction and turned round, then headed back to Parsons' and parked up again. That must have been about 10.50. She remembered being awake for at least half an hour, so she'd only been asleep for about twenty minutes. He'd been out, along the M62 Westbound towards Manchester, for around an hour and three-quarters. Time to get to Manchester and back? Certainly with the roads as clear as that, the answer was yes. Why, though? she thought. Why would an ordinary guy travel to Manchester and back between ten o'clock and midnight?

Josie explored the possibilities. Maybe a meeting with someone in a work capacity. Unlikely, plus there would have been no time to hold the meeting. A liaison, outside his own town, with a prostitute? More likely in view of his way of life. Yes, a quick fumble in the back of his car or in some seedy flat, or a straight-forward blow job, probably wouldn't take more than five minutes. Or he could be into drugs, more likely buying for his own use than dealing. A whole host of less than honest activities went through her mind, most of which were plausible.

She looked at the house, now in darkness again. He must have gone straight to bed. Whatever he had been up to would probably have been without the knowledge of his mother. Josie knew, from what Rick had told her, that Parsons's mum was both old and unwell, so the likelihood was that he had tucked her up in bed and then gone out to do whatever it was after he had checked that she was asleep.

The previous feeling of frustration washed over Josie again. If only she'd been in a more powerful car following him she'd have seen what he was doing, and that could have shed some light as to whether he would have been capable of sending Rick the disgusting letters. Then she had a thought. One that turned her stomach with apprehension, but excited her with equal measure. What if she actually got into Frank Parsons's house? If she was in there, she could look around, gather evidence. It could prove or disprove her wild theory once and for all. There was no way she could break in, even when he was at work, because the old lady would probably die of fright. So she would have to cajole her way in.

Josie had never backed away from a challenge, no matter how daunting, and having reached the conclusion over the next fifteen minutes that speaking to Parsons himself as well as gaining legitimate access to his house would give her a personal and intimate insight into him, she got out of her car and made for his door there and then. After all, she had the advantage of knowing something about him and his life, whereas he did not know her at all.

Moments after a quiet knock she saw his gaunt face appear at a window to her right, peering around net curtains. His eyebrows raised as he saw her at the door. Then he appeared before her with a dressing gown on and a smile on his face.

'I'm so sorry to bother you at this time of night,' Josie said before he could speak, a worried look on her face. 'My car, it's cut out. It won't start. I'm not from round here, you see.'

Before she could say any more, Parsons ushered her inside and into the lounge. He closed the door behind them with a click. Josie was not particularly worried; she was approximately fifteen years his junior, she trained regularly at the gym, she was as tall as Parsons and probably weighed as much as him. She was not afraid of him overpowering her. 'You can use my phone if you wish,' he said.

'Thank you,' she replied, feigning relief at his offer of assistance.

'Would you like a hot drink, or maybe something stronger?' he suggested.

'Tea would be nice,' she said, smiling at him. He urged her to use the telephone and scuttled off from the room, again closing the door firmly behind him.

This was the perfect opportunity, Josie thought. She picked up the cordless phone from its holder and held it to her ear, whilst scanning the living room. The neat garden belied the interior of the bungalow, which was old-fashioned to say the least. The modern wide-screen TV and surround sound speaker system looked absurdly out of place among thirty or forty year old furniture. A faded yet sturdy dark-wood escritoire stood in the corner of the room, complemented by a coffee table and a display cabinet from the same era. The carpet was patterned beige and cream with brown swirls and an archaic brass standing lamp with a plain white shade adorned the opposite corner of the room from the sixties. Clearly old Mrs Parsons still had the final say as to the important things, whilst allowing her nonconformist son the occasional 'treat'.

With one eye on the closed door, Josie gently opened the bureau. There were two old fountain pens in there, and a host of recent bills and letters which she daren't open for fear of insufficient time to replace them should the living room door open. Nothing looked untoward, however. She sat near to the coffee table, under which there were numerous magazines on the floor. Most of the reading material comprised the usual women's publications, but among these she spied a GQ magazine and a couple of other close-to-the-bone men's issues, though nothing pornographic. She would, no doubt, have found his bedroom of interest when it came to 'girly' magazines and the like. She quickly flicked through one or two of the mags, but saw no evidence of anything improper. Similarly, the DVD and tape collection near to the television gave away no secrets.

As Parsons entered the room with two cups in his hands, Josie pretended to finish a conversation with the RAC. 'Yes, that's right. Excuse me a minute.' She turned to her host. 'Is this Tranquillity Crescent, or Avenue?' she asked him. 'Crescent,' he replied. 'Crescent,' she told the non-existent person, and then paused for a few seconds. 'Thirty minutes? Yes, that's fine.' She pressed the end-call button and replaced the handset. 'They'll be about half an hour,' she told Parsons.

'Don't you worry your little head, my dear, you're OK here until they come. Now, where was it you said you lived?'

She already despised his patronising and demeaning manner, and she had spent only a few minutes in his company. She knew she had to humour him, though, for now. 'I'm from Manchester, I was on my way to visit a friend when I broke down.'

'Visiting a friend at midnight? That's an unusual time to call on someone.'

It's an unusual time to go to Manchester and back, with no time to do anything in between, she thought. 'Yes, I know, but I'll be staying with her for a few days, and it's still not too late to go to a club. I've been working all day.'

He was about to ask how she had found herself in the middle of an estate, but the comment about her having been working intrigued him more. 'Till this time of night? You should be tucked up in bed by now. What do you do?'

Josie was getting in too deep here. She hadn't anticipated a detailed line of questioning as to where she lived and what she did for a living. But to maintain her deceit she had to answer these simple queries. 'I'm a police officer,' she announced, giving the first occupation that came into her head that involved shift working.

'Well, well,' Parsons sneered. 'All the police women I've ever seen look like lesbians. But not you.' He looked her up and down in a way that made her skin crawl. Throughout her adulthood, hundreds of men had leered at her, but usually within what was generally regarded as social protocol. A sideways glance, a lustful glare removed as soon as she spied the man drooling, repeated little glimpses when the onlooker thought she couldn't see. But this creature, he examined her features clinically, lingering on reaching her breasts, in a way which surpassed rude and insensitive. It was positively shocking, so much so that she braced herself expecting him to reach out to touch her at any moment. He was attempting to exert power over her by making her feel weak and undervalued. She knew all about the kind of man who did this, through her counselling, but to have one try it on with her was extremely unnerving. His actions worked, temporarily, because at first she had no idea how to tackle his overt behaviour. She looked at his face in momentary disbelief, and as his gaze rose to her eye level she succeeded in dealing effectively with him.

'Had a good look have you? Thanks for your help with the phone and the tea, but that doesn't give you the right to fuck me, you know.'

Her underlying aggression took Parsons by surprise. He did exactly as she expected, and backed off. To have pandered to his bullying tactics would almost certainly have placed her in greater danger. 'Oh, I'm so sorry,' he said. 'I didn't mean to be rude. You're so beautiful, I wasn't thinking.'

'Yes, well I'd better be off now.'

'Don't go…you're welcome to stay until the breakdown people arrive.' There was a mild pleading in his voice and as he reached to pick up his tea Josie was not surprised to see his dressing gown form a mini tent, housing his excitement. She had the time to form, and remove, a look of disgust before he turned to face her again.

Her mind began to reason things out at lightning speed. She had the upper hand now in this bizarre self-created situation, despite being on his territory and despite his play for dominance. This was a strong position to be in. She held his attention both sexually and psychologically. Maybe she could capitalise.

'So you like playing mind games, do you?' she ventured.

Parsons wasn't altogether sure what she meant, but he was

spellbound by her utterly. 'In what way?'

Josie deliberately threw an impatient look his way, as if she was disappointed by his lack of understanding. 'Oh, come on. You mean to say a man of your age hasn't experimented with the irrational…the inner mind?'

Parsons began to look slightly out of his depth, but he didn't want to appear naïve or inexperienced. She was making him squirm. 'Only once or twice. But I found it a bit weird.'

'Look, we've got a little time before the breakdown man gets here, so I'll tell you something if you agree to tell me the equal.' He was lost, but just as he was about to pull out of the game Josie purposely opened her legs a little and he could not resist the temptation to look. She wore tight, faded jeans, and her shape was displayed to him through the clinging material. He exhaled slightly without realising he had done so, at which point Josie clicked her fingers in front of her face. 'Come on, are you playing?' she coaxed.

'Yeah, OK,' he said. She was now in total control.

'Right, we'll play just one round. I'll tell you the worst thing I've ever done in my life, and then you've got to tell me the worst thing you've done. There are only two rules. One, we *must* tell the absolute truth. And two, what we say must *never* be repeated to another living soul. Do you understand?'

'Yeah.' Parsons's hard-on was virtually bursting through his clothing. He made a poor attempt at hiding the fact that he found this unknown woman, mysterious and domineering, the biggest turn on of his entire life. His non-verbal communication told Josie that she had him eating out of her hand completely, and she continued the macabre game.

'OK then, I'll go first. You agree to the rules, don't you, before I begin?'

'Yes of course,' he said hurriedly, almost seeming to climax in expectation of an utterly depraved story from this sex goddess sitting in his living room at midnight.

'The most horrendous thing I've ever done…I'm trusting you now not to repeat this…is…knock someone over in my car and drive off,' she lied. She looked at him for his immediate reaction.

Parsons looked at her steadfastly in the eye, smiling nervously partly in disbelief and partly realising that what she had told him maybe true. 'And it gave me a thrill,' she continued, giving him a half-smile and stroking her inner thigh provocatively. She hoped beyond hope that her display would be sufficient to get him to confess to the letters.

Parsons responded to her teasing. He gripped his hard-on as though she had given him written permission to do so and he let out a moan. Before he could indulge himself further, Josie interrupted.

'Come on, it's your turn. Confession time.' She elongated the last two words and raised her eyebrows as a way of asking him again. What the hell, he thought, engrossed in the erotic machinations, 'I fucked the young team-leader at work over my desk, by promising her quick promotion, and I used a twelve inch dildo to fuck her again a few minutes after that.' He was in his own world.

Josie was disappointed. Yes, what he had told her was awful, but it wasn't the admission she had worked so hard to elicit. She realised immediately that it was Danielle Harper who he referred to, and that he had purposely put Rick off from returning to work in order to offer such promises in return for sexual favours, but still it fell far short of what she wanted. Maybe she had put herself to these outlandish lengths for nothing, risking her safety and prostituting herself almost in pursuit of information that simply didn't exist. She hid her chagrin, and pretended to find his depravity amusing. Then she changed her mood in an instant, thanked him for the entertainment, and said she would wait in her car for the breakdown company to arrive.

Parsons tried to persuade her to stay, but she was in charge and he knew it. Having been snapped out of the sexual games he even felt embarrassed at what he had told her.

Josie thanked him again for his help, as if a perfectly normal conversation had taken place, and made for the door. He followed her sheepishly.

As she strode along the hallway towards the front door she

caught sight of two small square pieces of paper contrasted against the brown carpet. One had a 'P' on it and the other an 'N' in italics.

Chapter 17

19th September 2001

The inside of the cell door was supposed to be blue, but years of bored inhabitants had scratched away the paint with their inane scribblings. 'John was ere' and 'Scott 1999' was the level of vocabulary on display. But who was Rick to judge those responsible? He was sat on the same hard bench as the artists had sat on, he breathed the same stale air as they had, and he would protest his innocence just as vociferously.

Everything about this place was hard. The door was solid metal. The floors and walls, despite a recent covering of flame-proof paint, were rocklike, and the safety glass in the window was so thick that it hardly made a sound when tapped. The wooden bench he sat on was unyielding under his weight.

In spite of his unexpected incarceration, Rick felt no malice towards the police. The scene in the medium's house had given the officers there no choice but to take him in for questioning. No, it's not their fault, he thought. Life had dealt him so many unfortunate twists lately he was becoming accepting of them. After all, how could anyone fight against fate? With the best will in the world, no-one knows what's around the next corner. You can't decide to accompany your wife to her parents in case she's murdered on the way there; you can't not visit a medium in case she becomes possessed and drops dead before your eyes. These are things over which there is no control, things that cannot be avoided by using common sense or by weighing up the risks beforehand. Things that are destined to happen to you no matter what you do, because you are not in a position to foresee them.

Rick was deep in thought. He concluded that decisions must be made by a higher authority, one which could not be consulted or persuaded, and that the things which were destined to happen would inevitably occur no matter what course of action the subject took. Ellie was due to die on 21st July 2001, Ms Begrum on 19th September. His presence, intervention or ignorance of these events was entirely irrelevant. 'So, just take what comes,' he said under his breath. If that meant going to prison, then that was what was pre-ordained, if it meant being released and then getting run over by a lorry on the way home, that was fine too.

'Are you feeling all right?' the tall gaoler asked, craning his neck to see through the door hatch he had just opened.

'I'm on top of the world,' Rick replied, a sardonic smile on his face. 'What time is it?'

'Five thirty. Would you like something to eat?'

'What's on the menu?'

'Whatever the canteen upstairs rustles up. Are you a vegetarian, or are you allergic to any foods?'

'No.'

'OK, I'll bring it to you in about ten minutes, then. Here's a cup of tea.'

'Thanks. What's happening now? When will my solicitor be here?'

'Well, I spoke to the DI dealing with the case about half an hour ago. The plan is to interview you as soon as your solicitor arrives.'

'Yeah, OK.'

The door-hatch closed firmly shut again, and Rick felt loneliness close in on him: the solitude in the hard room manifested itself in a strange claustrophobia, a feeling which defied definition but was nevertheless real. He would have liked to discuss the pros and cons of the evidence with the man who was bringing his meal, if only to pass the time, but he knew the gaoler was busy with other people because he could here other door-hatches opening and closing and the muffled sound of voices at various distances away down the corridor. The endless cycle of cells filled with prisoners, then empty as the occupants were released, only to be filled again the next day with different wrongdoers, most of whom were either unconcerned with their plight, or loudly rebellious.

Over two hours in the cell had worn Rick down. He wondered why solitude had not been used as a form of punishment in the past, rather than hard labour or flogging, because it certainly seemed effective. His palms began to sweat as he unconsciously rubbed his hands together, willing something to happen.

The door-hatch opened again, and a hot meal was passed through. Fish, chips and mushy peas. At least this would give him something to do for the next ten minutes.

'Thanks,' he said.

'When you've finished push the "call" button next to the toilet flush,' the policeman told him. 'They're ready to interview you in about ten or fifteen minutes, and your solicitor will be here very soon. OK?'

'Yeah, OK,' Rick replied in an almost grateful tone. His slightly lifted spirits soon deflated, however, as the reality of the situation hit him. He was about to be interviewed for *murder*, for God's sake. A wry smile appeared on his face as he ate the crispy chips. He, interviewed for murder. What a joke. It was his wife who had been murdered; had the bastard responsible for that been grilled by detectives or sat alone in a cell? No. Had this Ms Begrum actually been murdered, by anyone? No. Everything was upside-down as if some god, like in the old mythology films, was controlling events from above and having a bloody good laugh at his expense.

The door opened just as he took his last mouthful of fish. 'Finished?'

'Yeah.'

'If you'd like to step this way, your solicitor's waiting in the interview room.'

Rick followed the lanky custodian down the corridor and towards the charge area, then right into Interview Room 2.

A short, stocky, well-attired man with ruddy cheeks and round glasses stood up on his arrival. 'Hello, I'm Mr Williams, you must be Richard Sheldon. Sit down.'

First appearances were often deceptive, Rick knew that, but this man, there to protect his rights and advise him in this couldn't-be-more-serious issue, looked every bit like a figure out of a Charles Dickens novel. He half expected the bloated brief to clasp his paunch and say 'Ho, ho, ho fellow my lad.' Twenty minutes later, however, Rick's opinion of the solicitor had changed entirely. Mr Williams knew exactly what he was talking about, as he extracted all the relevant facts from his client, and asked questions, and probed motives. He gave the impression that he was here not just for the money, but to mount a formidable defence to the allegation levied against Rick. And he believed his version of events, which engendered an air of trust and hope in the accused. At the conclusion of the consultation, Rick felt almost smug. He couldn't see how the police were going to make the crime fit the person, and he felt reasonably relaxed.

Mr Williams also explained to him that, before a post mortem had been carried out on the deceased, the cause of death itself could not be ascertained with sufficient certainty to justify him being charged with an offence. This made Rick feel better too.

A fairly nondescript detective entered the room, with a smart-looking female detective alongside him. She had a curious look of Ellie, not in stature or general appearance, but in her eyes, which were the same greeny-blue and the same shape. Rick was momentarily taken aback by the similarity, but averted his gaze when the officer showed an inkling of disapproval in her expression.

The usual caution and preamble which precedes the main body of questioning was carried out, and this in itself made Rick feel more relaxed. He felt somewhat pleased that both detectives were obliged to give their names as well as he providing his, placing them all on a strangely even footing.

'As your solicitor has probably pointed out to you, Mr Sheldon,' the male officer said, 'Until such time as the results of the post mortem are released we will not be able to say exactly what caused the woman's death, but as that won't be for at least four hours there are some preliminary questions we'd like to put to you.'

Rick nodded his understanding.

Now it was the turn of the female detective, who had introduced herself as Inspector Walsh. The male was a detective constable. 'Can you explain why you were in the deceased's house?'

Rick hated that phrase 'the deceased'. It was so cold and matter of fact, and he had heard it used several times after Ellie's death, with reference to her. 'Yes. I went to see Ms Begrum, sorry I don't know her first name, for a reading.'

'A reading?' DI Walsh asked. Clearly, she was to be the one asking all the questions.

'She was a medium.'

'Right, I see. In my experience, men don't often visit such people alone. Women sometimes do, but even then it's more common for two or three to go together, you know for a bit of fun. I've never heard of a man visiting alone before.'

'I don't see anything wrong with it.'

'Oh, there's no law that says you can't, it just strikes me as unusual, that's all. And unusual is my business, particularly when it comes to the unexplained death of a young woman.'

'I'd like to intervene, there,' said Mr Williams. 'By all means ask pertinent questions, but I would urge you to refrain from eliciting responses from my client based on supposition and innuendo.'

'And I'd urge you to talk as though you hadn't swallowed a dictionary,' the confident DI retorted. 'But point taken,' she said with a slight smile. 'When did you arrange your appointment, Mr Sheldon?'

'Look, call me Rick. It was today, actually. She told me that there was a long wait normally but that she had a cancellation, so I went along a few hours after I'd rung her.'

'Do you know this woman? Have you ever met her before?'

'No.'

'You've never been for a reading with her on a previous occasion?'

'No, I've never been to any clairvoyant before.'

'Why did you go this time?'

'Well, I feel a bit stupid saying so, but I've heard others in the past say how much they've got out of a reading and...' Rick swallowed hard, 'I wanted to contact my wife.'

DI Walsh gave an understanding smile. Although Rick had not wanted to mention his wife's murder it was clear from the woman's face that she knew all about his loss. This was, after all, the same police station in which he had spent hours giving statements and demanding updates in relation to police enquiries. However, she had a job to do, and the questions resumed.

'And did you?'

'No.' Rick was in no mood to reveal what was said and what happened to the medium. In any case, nothing he said would give the police any tangible evidence as to why or how she died. Also, if he told the truth and nothing but the truth, that she had become possessed, they wouldn't believe him. So, keeping it simple was the best policy.

'What happened to her, Rick?'

Same question, just a little more probing. 'She was just beginning to talk and then she fell to the floor. She looked in pain and she clasped her chest...' Not too much detail, he said to himself, and halted his account swiftly.

'What happened then?'

'I couldn't feel a pulse, so I tore off her top clothing and tried chest compressions. Then the ambulance came, but they couldn't help her either.'

'Did she say anything to you before she fell to the floor?'

'No. She just stopped talking.'

'What was she talking about?'

'She was telling me that the reading would last about forty minutes, and that I must be open-minded. That kind of thing.'

'So you've never met her before, and never been to her house previously?'

'No, I've told you.'

'What parts of the house did you visit?'

'Just the downstairs hallway and the lounge. Oh, and the kitchen after the paramedics came.'

'You definitely didn't go upstairs at all?'

'No.'

'Did you visit the bathroom?'

'No.'

'So your fingerprints couldn't be found anywhere in the house other than the living room, the downstairs hallway and the kitchen?'

'No. Why are you asking me that?'

The male detective was about to butt in, but the DI raised her hand to prevent him. 'The reason is simple, Richard. If this turns out to be a murder investigation, which it may or may not do, then we need to know such details. You say you were there when the woman was alive and well; you were also there when she died and at this stage, other than the brief account you've just given us, we have no idea how or why she died. I'm not suggesting you're lying to us, but I've seen people lie convincingly about much less important things. If I took your word for it and released you without ascertaining the cause of death, and you'd been in any way responsible for her death, I'm sure we'd have a problem picking you up for further questioning. Do you see where I'm coming from?'

'Yeah. Look, I'll help you as much as I can. I visited her for a reading, and she collapsed when I got there. That's the story. I didn't go upstairs and I was only there for five minutes before it happened. I've never met her before in my life, but I've heard some of the girls in the office say she's good at what she does, er, did.'

'That's fine. Was your phone call to her made from your home?'

'Yes it was.'

'And was it the last call you made from that phone?'

'Yes.'

'How did you find this particular medium?'

'Like I said, I've heard her name mentioned at work and I used the Yellow Pages. God, I wish she'd not had that cancellation.' Rick raked his hair in frustration.

'Right. I'm going to ask you to go back your cell for the time being. Whilst you're there I'm going to follow up a few things from the information you've given me in this interview, and I'll find out as soon as I can when the post mortem is to take place. After that, I'll be in a better position to let you know what's happening.'

'The post mortem is definitely taking place this evening?' Mr Williams asked.

'It's planned for about 10 o'clock, but as you know things can change. Pathologists can be fickle creatures.'

Rick looked at the clock on the wall. His watch had been taken from him when he was booked in. 6.13pm. The examination was not due to take place for almost four hours, at the earliest.

Chapter 18

20th September 2001

'If you press that buzzer again, I'll mute it, do you understand? The time's half past two, now shut up and go to sleep.'

The earlier shift who had booked him in had long since gone home to their families, and the Custody Sergeant now in charge was a direct descendant of Hitler, Rick thought. The tall, stick-thin gaoler had also been replaced by a police woman who appeared totally uninterested in her job and even less in the needs of the prisoners.

OK, so he kept pressing the 'call' button to ask the time, but his watch had been taken from him and they wouldn't let him have it so what was he supposed to do? He hadn't had a minute's sleep in the eight hours since he was interviewed and repeated requests concerning whether the post mortem had been carried out and other such matters were dismissed out of hand. He hadn't so much as seen the faces of the new staff that had taken over, and the place wasn't nearly as busy as it had been earlier. A drunk wailed and moaned in a cell down the corridor, but if there were other full cells the occupants were sound asleep, most no doubt in their second homes.

There was nothing here to occupy him. He had tried to sleep but couldn't. He had asked for something to read but had been told there was nothing available. He began to feel like a dog in a locked hutch who had been wrongly accused of biting the postman. The caring demeanour of the DI, and the reasonable manner of the previous officers, began to lose their influence. In short, Rick was losing his temper.

Another half an hour or so passed as if it were a day, and Rick pressed the "call" button again. No answer. He pressed it repeatedly, but nothing. The sergeant had clearly muted it at the central console. Now he was being ignored. Anger rose within him like acid bile rising from his stomach.

'LET ME OUT OF HERE,' he bellowed. 'I'VE DONE NOTHING WRONG,' and he beat his fists on the door.

Still no response.

Then a key in the door. Thank God, he thought.

A man-mountain entered the cell. The chevrons on the officer's epaulettes glinted as he passed under the overhead light. This was the new sergeant. Weighing in at twenty-something stones, and at least six foot six, he wasn't even a little overweight. His bulk was solid muscle, honed from endless hours in the gym. The combination of his mass and the enraged expression on his face as he strode into the cell made him very dangerous.

Rick instinctively stood up. Within two or three milliseconds his brain performed the primeval function of assessing the degree of danger before him. The electrical impulses were infinitely quicker than the movements of the man in the cell, as Rick's adrenaline responded to the brain's conclusion that this situation represented grave risk to its health. Internal alarm bells rang and 'fight or flight' was the almost readable message in Rick's eyes. Just one simple choice for the speedy computer to make, fight or flight. But flight was not an option. The sergeant, now reaching out with his spade-like hand to take hold of Rick, blocked the only exit from the small, hard room. Yes, its hardness would be oh so apparent if he hit it with force under the influence of the officer's anger. So, fight it was. Years of kick-boxing stood Rick in good stead, and his movements were practised and fluid. They did not have to be considered. One strong uppercut connected at the most devastating point under the giant's chin, throwing even his head back with force. The full-weight kick to his solar plexus which followed left him gasping for air in the corner of the room, one of his white teeth sitting contrasted against the black floor, and blood flowing from his bottom lip.

Rick automatically adopted a fighter's stance, despite his opponent's incapacity. He did this not out of conceit or a feeling of triumph, but because that was what he had been taught. The fact that there were no other attackers behind him or within reach of him was irrelevant. Right now he was a survivor who would do everything to preserve his safety. It was an impenetrable mindset.

A loud buzzing sound entered his awareness as the panic alarm was activated by the female gaoler via a black strip on the wall. She looked into the cell, aghast that her massive colleague could have been taken out so emphatically, but Rick also saw fear on her face. He was about to re-assure her that he wouldn't harm her when he felt a cold splash on his face, wetting his left cheek. Then came hell.

Rick couldn't breathe, he couldn't see. A thick haze seemed to envelope him and he felt as if a swarm of a thousand bees was attacking his head and his senses. He rubbed his eyes furiously, but it was as though someone had poured liquid fire into them. His lungs were not getting air, and he began to panic as rivulets of mucus flowed from his nose. This was an invisible enemy, one impervious to a thousand years of martial-arts training, and one he could not fight. As he hit the floor, he heard shouts around him.

'Get Paul out of there. He's badly hurt, and the CS won't help him. What the hell were you doing spraying gas into there?'

'What was I supposed to do. Jackie Chan here had floored Paul, what would he have done to me or to you lot?'

Rick squirmed on the floor, his eyes and nose streaming. Spit ran down his chin. He thought he was going to die. He heard complaints from a number of uniformed and plain clothes officers who had arrived to assist after the alarm that they were being affected by the spray. The sergeant's bulky form was dragged out of the cell. Then he himself was manhandled from the hard room as well. In fact he was being carried down the corridor. Another large metal door opened and Rick found himself on a wet concrete floor. 'Bastard,' one officer said, as the door slammed shut.

Rick's breathing became slightly easier, and this allowed him to take stock. He was now outside, in an enclosed yard. There was no roof, but the walls were really high. And it was raining hard. The rain was a blessing. It fell on his face and soothed him. The pain in his eyes, his throat and his nose was still extreme, but subsiding to the point of tolerance, and his breathing was becoming easier by the minute. He lay there, a heap of physical and mental misery, thanking God that he had survived.

***

'Sheldon, the doctor's here to see you,' a gruff voice yelled into the echoey yard. About an hour had passed, and Rick had lain in the rain the whole time. The clean, cool water from the sky had diluted the effects of the CS gas to the point where he felt fairly comfortable, and being soaked to the skin was a small price to pay for such relief.

Rick hauled himself from the floor and trudged into the corridor, dripping. Doctor Simmonds stood at the end of the short passageway, and gestured for Rick to remain where he was. As he stood, making a small pool on the polished floor, he heard the doctor in the charge area. 'I'd like you to get his clothes off him and put him in a hot shower for a few minutes. Then give him a paper suit to wear.'

'Look, doctor,' a voice answered, 'That animal in there…'

'Never mind that,' the doctor interrupted, 'My responsibility is the welfare of the patient. Get him showered and dry, before he gets pneumonia. I'll see him in ten minutes when he's ready.'

Rick was shown to a cubicle by a male officer who did not deign to speak to him or look at him directly. He showered and dried in a matter of minutes, and slipped on the paper suit and polystyrene slippers provided. He was then shown to the doctor's room. 'Do you want someone in with you, doc?'

'I'll be fine.'

'But he's violent.'

'I'll be OK.'

The door closed out the ill-feeling towards him which hung palpably in the air.

'Right, young man,' the middle-aged doctor began. 'I'm here

110

because police policy dictates that a doctor must examine anyone who's been sprayed with CS. I'm not here to judge you, I just need to examine you to make sure the effects of the spray are wearing off as expected.'

'Right.'

The doctor carried out various tests and asked some questions, and was satisfied that Rick's respiratory system was returning to normal.

The patient's emotional condition, however, was deteriorating at a rapid rate. Rick looked at the brown paper suit. He looked around him, considering his plight. Here he was in a police station, soon to answer further questions about the death of a woman he had never met before today. He had hurt a police officer and was public enemy number one, at least in the eyes of all those working at this station. How would this affect his situation with DI Walsh? The police were no nearer to catching his wife's killer, and his employers did not want to know him. Then there was the vision in the mirror, the book, and the communication with Ellie, and Ruth whoever she was, the one who had possessed the medium.

So many things to sort out. Where was he going to begin? Would he ever succeed? He suddenly felt completely overwhelmed by the immensity of the problems that had thrust themselves upon him in the last two months. One after another, after another. The straw that broke the camel's back. Normally a strong and resilient character, Rick felt himself collapse emotionally; his resistance to adversity, formally a solid wall within him, crumbled into dust as he sat before the doctor. Weakness was something which Rick was always careful not to display, but the obstacles before him seemed insurmountable. If this was some sort of test, he had failed. He put his head in his hands and wept like a baby, despite the doctor's presence.

'Mr Sheldon, what's the matter?'

'You wouldn't understand,' he sobbed.

'Try me,' insisted Doctor Simmonds.

'All right then. My wife was murdered two months ago. Since then, I've seen her in my bathroom mirror. She wants me to go with her, whatever that means.' Rick's inhibitions, together with his sense of privacy, had left him. He no longer cared what others thought of him, or how he sounded. Bottling it all up was killing him and he simply couldn't go on the way he had. 'Then there was the book. The book with no story in it, just a message from Ellie on the first page. Then the book became normal when I looked at again. Look, I went to see the clairvoyant, and she became possessed...possessed by Ruth, the author of the book I told you about...'

'Whoa, hang on a minute. You've seen your deceased wife?'

'Yes. It was real, honestly. She was in the mirror. She walked away and beckoned me to follow.'

'Right. What did you say about the clairvoyant?'

'She's why I'm here. I went to see her so that I could talk to Ellie. But Ruth, the author of the book that Ellie used to pass a message to me, she took hold of Ms Begrum and killed her...she bloody killed her.' He sobbed aloud.

There was silence for a minute or two, as Doctor Simmonds wrote down some notes.

'It's Richard, isn't it?'

'Yeah.'

Rick was a broken man. His face was wet with tears and he cried unreservedly as the doctor watched him.

'Richard, I'd like you speak to another doctor, whilst I'm here. Do you agree to that?'

'Whatever. I don't give a toss. What do I care any more? I've tried, so hard. I've tried to put things right, and I've tried to understand what the FUCK'S going on in my life...but...I...just...' He covered his face and cried some more. 'WHAT'S HAPPENING TO ME?' he shouted at full volume, his fists clenched.

The door of the doctor's room burst open and several burly officers piled in thinking that the doctor was Rick's latest victim, but Simmonds raised his hand calmly, said everything was OK, and asked them politely to leave.

He asked Rick to wait in the room while he spoke to the Custody Sergeant, the third sergeant in charge since Rick had been there. Five minutes later he was ushered to a cell in another block, the corridor containing his first cell having being put out of use, and the doctor asked him to wait patiently, and gave him a hot cup of tea.

As the key turned in the lock Rick realised that he had fallen asleep. Mental exhaustion had forced him to shut down. 'To the doctor's room,' the policeman said, flanked by two other officers. He was about to explain that he wasn't going attack anyone, but decided against it. As far as everyone in here was concerned, he had been tried and convicted, and if they had their way five years' hard labour would follow.

He sat opposite Doctor Simmonds, and a plump young woman wearing the most ridiculous thick round glasses. Another man was sat with them as well.

'Hello Richard, I'm Doctor Wade and this is Mr Brown from the Social Services. Do you mind if I ask you a few questions?'

'No,' he replied. Questions were the order of the day. First the detectives, now two doctors and a Social Worker, then the CID again later.

'Have you had any form of counselling since your wife died?'

'No.'

'Have you seen your own doctor at all?'

'No.'

'How has it affected you?'

One he couldn't answer monosyllabically. 'It's been bloody awful. How do you think?'

'You said to Doctor Simmonds earlier that you saw Ellie in a mirror.'

'That's right. I did.'

'Afterwards, maybe two or three days after seeing her, didn't you think that it may have been…your imagination?'

'Yes. But now I'm sure it was real.'

'How can you be sure?'

'Because of the book. No doubt he's told you about that as well.'

'Yes, he has. What was the message in the book?'

'To be with her, just like her gesture in the mirror.'

'OK. Then you said the book became normal again.'

'It did. Almost an hour passed by in an instant and the book fell to the floor. I picked it up and it was a normal novel.'

'Did that seem strange to you…? Did it frighten you?'

'It was weird. It didn't frighten me though, no. I think she's watching over me. I think she wants me to end it all and be with her.'

'I'm sure she doesn't.'

'And how would you know?'

'I don't know, Richard. I'm trying to find out from you. What happened to the medium you visited yesterday?'

'She was good, to start with. She had Ellie there.' He paused, and the psychiatrist watched him intently, purposely not breaking the silence. 'Then Ruth came.'

'Tell me who Ruth is again.'

'She's the author of the book I told you about. Ruth Stocks. She spoke through the medium, and told me to listen to Ellie, and do as she asked. She said not to stray from the path.'

'Did you get cross with Ms Begrum?'

'No. She began acting strangely. She fell to the floor and she was bleeding. Then she stopped moving. I tried to save her, honestly I did.'

'Did you hit her? Did you do anything else to her?'

'No. I tried to get her breathing again.'

'What will you do if you get released from here?'

'I want to be with Ellie now. I've had enough trying to solve problems. Things just get worse every day.'

'Would you mind waiting here with Doctor Simmonds and Mr Brown for a short while?'

Rick shrugged his shoulders.

'I intend to section him, Sergeant Willis.'

The sergeant looked skyward. 'So he gets away with assaulting the other custody officer, does he?'

'It's not really a question of getting away with anything, sergeant. Under the surface he's suffering acute depression that he hasn't had any medication for since his wife was murdered two months ago. He's also displaying the classic features of Post-traumatic Stress Disorder. But most significantly, and in addition to those ailments which in themselves are significant in shaping his actions, he is delusional and exhibits a genuine desire to end his life. I'm sure you don't want a death in custody to deal with.'

'We can have someone sit with him the whole time.'

'And that'll cure his mental problems, will it? No, I want him taking to Ward 40 at St. James Hospital as soon as possible. I'll prepare the papers with Mr Brown now.'

'Before he goes anywhere, I'd like to speak to DI Walsh. He's here in connection with a suspicious death as well you know.'

'That's fine.'

As if summoned, DI Walsh appeared in the custody suite, looking somewhat bleary-eyed. 'What's going on here?' she asked.

'Your Mr Sheldon's knocked Paul Kemp out in the cell. He's in hospital with concussion.'

'Paul Kemp? Bloody hell. What happened there?'

'I don't know, but it looked like he'd gone six rounds with Lennox Lewis.'

'Is Sheldon injured?'

'No. But the good doctor here's sectioned him.'

Doctor Wade intervened. 'He's depressed, Inspector. He's suffering PTSD and he's been having delusions. Also, he wants to take his own life and I believe that his desire is genuine.'

'Well that turns things around somewhat,' she said. 'Anyway, it's for you to sort out sergeant because the result of the post mortem is that she died of a common or garden myocardial infarction. Apparently, heart problems ran in her family. There was nothing in or on the body to suggest foul play, so Sheldon needs releasing without charge, on the Begrum matter anyway. Personally, I'd let the assault go as well under the circumstances. Let's face it, Paul's intimidated many prisoners over the years, maybe this had to happen to him eventually. Goodnight.'

'Bye, ma'am.'

'Oh, can I have a quick word with Richard before I go for some sleep?' she asked the psychiatrist.

'No problem.'

'Hello again,' she said.

'Christ, you're all I need,' came the reply.

'No, it's good news. The post mortem's over, and you're cleared. She died of a heart attack, nothing more. I'm happy with your version of events, and thank you for trying to help her.'

Help her, Rick thought. God knows how he would have done that. 'Thanks,' he said, as if someone had given him a boiled sweet.

How best to end his life was all that filled Rick's thoughts now, as he sat in the back of the police van en route to Ward 40.

Chapter 19

21st September 2001

'Hello, Rick here. Sorry I can't come to...'

'Damn,' cursed Josie. 'Where the hell is he?' She had heard that same answerphone message a dozen times in the last twenty-four hours. And she'd called at his house a couple of times, but he hadn't been in. Even his mobile was switched off, which was unusual.

She tapped her fingers on the windowsill next to the telephone, cupping her chin in her left hand. She was itching to tell Rick the news about Frank Parsons, his pervy boss who she'd virtually pinned down as being responsible for sending the hate mail. Josie was feeling rather self-satisfied; a few days self generated under-cover work and she may have reached a breakthrough. Hell, if she could do it without an iota of training, what on earth were the police playing at? A simple suspicion and a sprinkling of application and...progress. She rang his mobile again, but it was still inactive.

Rick had provided her with a key to his house about a week earlier. It wasn't that he wanted her wandering in and out as if she lived there, but he had planned to take a short break in the South of England and Ellie's cat, Tiger, needed feeding. Josie had agreed to help out but the excursion hadn't taken place and she had forgotten to return the key.

What if he needs my help, she mused. Her thoughts ran away with her as she imagined that he may have reached the end of his tether and done something stupid. Maybe he had hit another low in the recovery process and was isolating himself as he had done that first week. Their friendship had grown since then, though, so he might appreciate her concern if she went into his house uninvited to help him.

It was 11.30 am, so it wasn't an unreasonable hour to check on him.

She set off.

Josie stepped gingerly over the threshold, feeling partly that she was overstepping the mark in so doing, but partly that she owed it to Rick as her close friend to ensure that he was safe and well.

'Rick,' she called. No answer. 'RICK.' Silence. Still no reply to another call as she climbed the stairs. A feeling of apprehension gripped her stomach as she peeped around the door of the bathroom. The worried expression on her face gave away her fears. He could have taken an overdose and be lying dead, or worse comatose or in pain, his insides never to recover from the effect of the pills. Or, in a state of utter hopelessness, he may have decided to do away with himself by other means; immersing a hair drier in a full bath of water, or hanging himself from the loft hatch. Was she ready for this, really? And was it her responsibility?

Her heart beat every bit as fast as when she pushed hard on the rowing machine at the gym. Josie visited each room in turn. Having ascertained that Rick was not upstairs, she repeated the chore downstairs. The whole house inspected, she stood mentally drained in the entrance hallway, beads of sweat forming on her brow.

A couple of brown envelopes lay on the carpet, and a red one hung from the inside of the letter box. Josie picked them up, she put the official looking ones on the half table near to the door, but examined the red one closer. She saw immediately that the postmark was Salford. Manchester, the way Parsons had headed two nights before on his unusual errand.

Discarding any thoughts of whether or not she should open the letter, Josie walked into the kitchen and, using a sharp knife, carefully sliced away the top of the envelope. Pinching only the slightest edge of the single sheet within, she withdrew it and placed it virtually untouched on the carpet. She read with horror the evil message, comprised of uneven cut-out letters.

HOW'S TRICKS RICKS? COPING YET?

APPARENTLY NOT.
ELLIE'S DEAD. THERE'S NO GOING BACK, SO GET HOLD
OF YOURSELF.
ELLIE'S DEAD – DO YOU UNDERSTAND.
SHE'S DEAD, DEAD, DEAD.

Open-mouthed, Josie covered her face with her hands and let out a sigh. How could he, she thought. Because he's jealous of Rick he goes to these lengths to persecute him. She looked at the offending sheet before her again. Some letters italic, others not. All cut out of magazines. Many different sized letters. No handwriting. And on the front of the envelope, typescript.

Her hands trembling Josie ran into the kitchen again, this time returning with a plastic lunchbox, in which she placed the envelope and the letter, using two forks to handle them. She mustn't destroy any of his fingerprints. The police must have the best evidence available to nail this sociopath.

Chapter 20

21ˢᵗ September 2001

'MURDER. Are you bloody mad?' Frank Parsons said with utter horror, the volume of his response tapering off towards the end as he realised that beyond his office door curious ears maybe listening.

'That's what I said. You did understand the caution, Mr Parsons?' DS Moore asked calmly.

'Sod the *caution.* Whose murder?'

'I can't discuss that here in your office. Now will you please come with us to the station?'

'I'm going nowhere 'til you tell me what the hell you're talking about. Who do you think you are coming in here? I'm a very important...'

'Look, we can do this the easy way, or the hard way. You can walk out of here with us as if we're businessmen or we can handcuff you in front of everyone in the office. It's your call.'

'You arrogant...'

'Cuff him, John,' DS Moore instructed his colleague.

'No. I'll walk out,' Parsons said.

All eyes were trained on Frank as he strolled across the office floor, flanked by the detectives. Despite his feigned nonchalance, he was sure one or two of them must have heard his short outburst and spread the word within seconds. 'Nothing to worry yourselves about,' he said, looking around at all the faces. 'Now get on with your work.'

In truth, none of the faces displayed the slightest worry, except for Danielle's. If he were never to return the biggest party would be thrown, celebrating the downfall of the office ogre. But Danielle did not want to see him go. He was her passport to management, plus he had had his filthy hands, and more, all over her, and she grimaced to think that her harlotry might go unrewarded.

***

'It's a simple enough question. Where were you on the evening of 21st July this year? It was a Saturday.'

'I just don't know. It's two months ago.'

'Well, let me see if I can help you,' DCI Fenton said, sounding genuine. 'Do you often go out on Saturday nights?'

Frank listened to the whirring of the dual-deck tape machine. The interview was being recorded, of course. Everything he said, complete with nuances in his voice, sighs, everything, was under scrutiny. He was being examined. The walls were coated with sound-proof tiles to prevent echo, or the intrusion of unwanted sounds from adjacent rooms. The DCI interrogated him, the DS who arrested him looked on, probably ready to pounce at the first sign of a discrepancy or irregularity in his account. Even his solicitor awaited his answer, her pen poised to write down any reply of significance. He felt trapped by claustrophobia generated by the pressure of questioning, and the small room.

'Well? Do you?'

'Er, not usually, no.'

'OK, so you normally stay in on Saturdays.'

'That's right, yes,' he replied with a half-smile on his face. The incongruous expression displayed a hatred for authority, but also an element of humiliation. The detective was asking questions which required him to reveal private things about himself, and he didn't like it.

'Any reason for that?'

The DCI had years of experience dealing with odd-balls, and knew instinctively when a raw nerve was touched.

'Should there be?' Parsons answered a question with a question.

'There's really no reason to get annoyed, Mr Parsons. I simply need to know whether you were in or out on that evening.'

'All right then, in.'

'How can you be sure you were in?'

'For God's sake, I was in. I know I was in, because I very rarely go out,' he said, reddening somewhat. DS Moore scribbled a few notes down.

'Was anyone in with you?'

'Yes. My mother.' Yes, my mother was, he thought to himself. She'll vouch for me.

'I don't wish to upset you, but isn't it true that your mother suffers from the late stages of Parkinson's disease?'

'So?'

'It just weakens any alibi you may present, that's all. Was anyone else there with you during the evening?'

'Look, I was in that night, and I was in with my mother. I can't help you any more. Can you tell me why I was locked up for nearly four hours before this interview? Come on, I want a few answers now.'

The DCI looked at his sergeant, and they nodded in agreement.

'Fair enough, I don't see a problem in bringing forward a little what I was intending to cover later in the interview. Obviously, in serious cases such as this, we have to carry out various enquiries. Basically, although we have to have "reasonable suspicion" to believe that you may have committed the offence in question before we can arrest you for it, we must have substantially more evidence if we are going to keep you in for lengthy questioning, or charge you with that offence. All the enquiries that we carry out are to fact build. We won't charge you with any offence until we have sufficient facts to base a charge upon. So, before we did this interview, we spoke to your mother, and we searched your house.'

Frank let out a long sigh.

'Why did you send nasty letters to Richard Sheldon?'

Frank's eyes widened and his mouth opened slightly in response, positive indicators of his guilt. He looked at Fenton, but there was no way the detective was going to let him off this hook by asking another question and giving his adversary time to formulate a credible answer. He allowed silence to intimidate the suspect, while fixing a stony gaze on him.

'What are you accusing me of now?'

The question did not need repeating, so it wasn't.

'I... I... did no such thing,' Parsons stammered, embarrassed by how unconvincing his reply sounded.

'We have a good set of fingerprints from your latest letter, and your first one as well. Just to prove to me that you're not lying, would you agree to give us your fingerprints so that we can compare them with those we've lifted from the letters? It will prove your innocence if you're not responsible.'

'You don't have to agree to do that,' Parsons's solicitor intervened. 'Am I correct in believing that my client has no previous convictions, Chief Inspector?'

'That's right, yes.'

'So you have no record of his fingerprints on a database?'

'No, we don't.'

'I advise you to decline the offer, then,' the brief said to Parsons.

'I decline the offer,' he said, smiling.

'No problem. You don't have to give your consent, that's true. But I can obtain the superintendent's authority to take your prints by force if I believe that it will prove or disprove your involvement in a serious offence.'

Frank's face dropped.

'Ask your solicitor.'

He turned to her, and she nodded.

'Then do it,' he said confidently.

'OK,' Fenton replied. 'This interview is suspended in order to obtain the...'

'All right, you win. YOU WIN,' he shouted. 'I sent him the bloody letters.'

Parsons waived aside his solicitor's intervention.

'Why did you do that?' The DCI's calm tone remained.

'Because he's a spoilt little shite, that's why.'

'I think you'd better elaborate.'

'It took me years to get where I am now at the bank, and I've worked my fingers to the bone to achieve that. But blue-eyed boy comes along, straight in at team leader, then manager within two years after that. Christ, he'll be knocking on my door next, the jumped-up... I'll tell you straight, I hate him.'

'How many letters have you sent him altogether?'

'Three.'

'Just to verify it was you, can you tell me where you posted them?'

'I've admitted it, haven't I? I posted the first in Nottingham, the next in Newcastle and the one the other day near to Manchester. I thought by spreading them round a bit, I'd avoid suspicion. Plus, I knew my fingerprints had never been taken. How did you link the letters to me?'

'Well, your old typewriter is the same model as the one used to type the addresses on the envelopes, all of which were the same make, and all red. Now we have your admission, and your prints if necessary. Plus information from a little birdie, who will remain nameless.'

'OK, OK. But it doesn't mean I'm a murderer.'

'So, we've established that you hate Richard Sheldon with a vengeance, so much so that you'd send him hate-mail designed to...make him hurt, shall we say...and the messages you sent relate to the murder of his wife. How did you kill her, Frank?'

'I've told you everything. I didn't kill anyone.'

'Did you know her?'

'No.'

'Here I am, investigating the murder of Eleanor Sheldon.' He sat back, as if to begin a long story. 'For weeks and weeks, there's no motive. She has no obvious enemies. Then you come along with the oldest motive in the book. Revenge, hatred, whatever you want to call it. You've admitted hating the dead woman's husband. The letters are despicable, and they show the depth of your hatred and jealousy for a man who is simply doing well for himself. Until his wife is killed, that is.'

Parsons' lips tightened as he came to the realisation that he was trapped.

'And lo and behold, you live with your ageing mother.'

'Didn't she tell you that I was in with her on that night?'

'Mr Parsons, your poor mum didn't know what day it was when we spoke to her a few hours ago. Don't worry, we gave her a believable tale as to why we were there, but I'm afraid you can't rely on her for an alibi. You're a man, full of hate and jealousy, who sends a murdered woman's husband taunting hate-mail, and no-one to give you an alibi as to your whereabouts on the night of the murder. As I said, how did you kill her?'

'And I said I didn't.'

'You'll have to do better than that.'

Parsons put his head in his hands and sobbed.

'My client is clearly upset at the moment; I'd like to request a break in the proceedings for...'

The suspect stopped her in her tracks. 'Hang on, just let me think a minute. Yes. John Bridges, a neighbour of mine, he came across on a Saturday evening in late July. Shit, I can't remember whether it was the 21st, or the one after. What time was the murder?'

'Never mind that, you continue,' Fenton said.

'It must have been about eight thirty because I'd just put my mother to bed, she goes between eight and half past. He came to ask me if I'd seen anything funny at his house earlier; he'd been out to the coast with his family and when they got back they'd been burgled. I went over to his house for a few minutes, but I hadn't seen any burglars.'

'So this John Bridges can vouch for you being at home at half past eight in the evening on the date his family were burgled?'

'Definitely. God, I hope it was the same night.'

'How well do you know John Bridges?'

'Hardly at all. I lent him my lawn mower last summer when his broke down. Apart from that, and that Saturday night, I don't think I've ever spoken to him.'

'OK. We'll take a break at that point. I'll be checking out your story, and the times and dates.'

'Yes, yes,' Frank said gratefully.

***

'Can you come to the charge desk, Mr Parsons,' DS Moore said, opening the creaky cell door.

Tamed by his period of solitude, and desperately worried, Parsons was a sorry figure as he approached the Custody Sergeant, his former petulance and aggression having subsided.

'Your version of events has been thoroughly investigated, Mr Parsons,' the Custody Officer explained. 'And the conclusion is that you could not have been at the scene of the murder at the time it occurred.'

Parsons looked up to the heavens and breathed an audible sigh of relief.

'However, the DCI wants to bail you to come back to this police station in four weeks time. He has other enquiries to pursue in relation to this matter, so you are obliged to surrender to custody at the set time and date. Do you understand?'

'Whatever. I mean, yes, no problems.' He was free.

'Now I'd like you to listen to this officer, please.'

DS Moore read from a prepared charge sheet, first cautioning Parsons. 'You are charged with three offences under Section 1, sub-section 1 (a) of the Malicious Communications Act 1988, for the sending of three letters to Richard Sheldon which contained grossly offensive messages intended to cause distress or anxiety to the said person. Have you any reply?'

'Sorry.' He wasn't sorry, he was simply relieved to have the burden of the other matter taken from him.

'What could I get at court for that?' he asked.

'Up to six months imprisonment or up to a level five fine,' the sergeant informed him. 'Having admitted the offence, and it being your first time, you would be eligible for an adult caution, but due to the circumstances the DCI wants you to go to court for it.' He smiled at Parsons. 'Now get his photograph, fingerprints and DNA taken,' he added. 'Oh, and Mr Parsons, we *don't* need your consent to take them now, because you've been charged with an offence.'

Chapter 21

22nd September 2001

Rick awoke with a start.

He was a patient now. The staff at Ward 40 were pleasant and helped where they could, but he was a patient nevertheless. A psychiatric patient. The nurses and doctors did not look at him, or speak to him, as they would a 'normal' person. He could see scrutiny and suspicion in their eyes as they communicated with him. Why? Because he had displayed violence, because he was depressed beyond the level experienced by most people, and because essentially they saw him as unstable, unpredictable, a loose canon.

And the other 'patients'. There was Molly, a woman in her fifties. She sat all day long in the so-called recreation room, facing the wall in the big leather chair and clapping to the music. Joe, he spent the day walking up and down the long corridor. He said he was a guard patrolling, to prevent a Nazi invasion. And then there was Mary. Little Mary, only in her early twenties, her face scarred with sores and her arms like pin-cushions, betraying years of heroin use. She cried most of the time, in mourning for the twin boys who had been taken from her by Social Services.

These people were all in their own worlds, suffering their personal torments alone. Emotional or nervous breakdown, as people referred to it, didn't even begin to describe the hell these people were enduring every day. No doubt sleep was a blessed relief to them, unless the spectres haunted them there too.

Rick sighed. What could this place really do for him? He knew there was no wonder drug able to make him forget the past and look to the future with optimism. He knew that, despite the concerted efforts of doctors, counsellors and advisers, his feelings of loss and confusion with the messages Ellie had sent him, would remain.

A knock at his bedroom door.

'Richard, here's your breakfast.'

Rick jumped out of bed, dressed only in his boxer-shorts, and opened the door. He had asked if he could eat alone in his room, because the sight of Mary, Joe and the others at the dining table almost drove him mad.

'Thanks, John,' he said, and sat on the bed with his cereal and boiled egg.

Only 8.40 in the morning. How would he fill his day? He had scarcely taken two mouthfuls of cornflakes when he noticed a wet patch on the blue plaster wall opposite his bed. The moisture seemed to be spreading before his eyes. Yes, it was. A minute earlier it had been the size of small saucer, but it had grown to a dustbin lid size. At first Rick thought there must be a water leak, but the wet patch had maintained its current size now for a few minutes. Also, water always runs downhill, yet the wall above the dampness was dry.

He was about to get up and feel the wall, when he thought he saw bubbling from a point near to the centre of the wetness. As he watched, the surface of the wall surrounding the moisture grew a translucent mould, as though an invisible person had coated it with clear glue. The sticky material increased in thickness before his eyes and before long the wall played host to a gooey, clear mass, about eighteen inches in diameter, which protruded at least an inch and a half from the vertical surface.

As Rick stared at the phenomenon, he recognised instantly the same warm feeling he had experienced when he opened the brown parcel containing the book. He felt no fear, only intrigue at what was facing him.

Time seemed to stand still. Nothing mattered in the whole world except what he was looking at here, now.

The entity on the wall remained the same size. Then he thought he saw a tinge of red within it. Within seconds, the jelly-like substance changed to a vibrant flame red. Some of it began to break away from the mass. The defecting red portion eventually freed itself from the whole and hung, inexplicably, in the air above its creator. Still Rick felt no fear, only wonder. The material on the wall returned to its former clear appearance, and nothing seemed to happen for a moment or two. Dissatisfied with the lack of colour, Rick imagined a deep blue, and the jelly quickly transformed into an azure blue more beautiful than any summer sky he had ever seen. And again, a part of it tore itself away and nestled next to the larger red portion in mid-air.

Rick began to experience a feeling of control. As soon as the clear, nondescript colour returned, he pictured a blazing sun and moments later the entity was almost too brilliant to watch, as a yellow section shrugged off its larger relative to achieve independence. Then a verdant green, followed by exquisite shades of indigo and orange.

The numerous colours began to merge, and Rick's attention was drawn away from the wall. Red joined with blue, which in turn amalgamated with two other colours. Then the others combined. The strange thing was, red and blue did not form purple. Yellow joining with other darker colours failed to lighten them. Although the colours came together, each retained its individuality, a paradox which Rick did not question as he gazed in awe.

Then, before his brain had time to assimilate what was happening, the physical colours were upon him. They encased his head as he sat on the bed. His sense of touch told him nothing. There was neither pain nor pleasure, and he felt nothing tangible as he gripped his crown. He could no longer see the colours, as they were out of his line of sight. Despite his senses giving him no information, Rick became aware of increased brain activity. It was as if a machine had been switched on in his head after being idle.

A faint sound entered his consciousness and he felt a desire, a longing to hear it more clearly. He strained to hear the sound, which gradually seemed to come closer. A whisper. 'You're so near now, my love. So near. Take that final step. Take the last step. You are so strong. You can do it. Please... let me see you.'

Then the sound faded, like an echo losing its resonance. Try as he might to hear more, the voice was no longer within earshot.

It was just like Ellie's image fading beyond his sight in the mirror, her voice fading beyond his ability to hear.

Then came an unpleasant sensation. Rick felt as if his head was bursting. The inside of his skull felt overcrowded, and the population wanted out. It couldn't hold the contents any longer. Then, excruciating pain. He tore at his hair and screamed out in agony.

The colours danced once more together near to the point of their origin, and Rick felt the pain leave him. His brain slowed, and he watched the colours quickly separate and join the clear entity still clinging to the wall. They appeared to be in a rush, now. As the last colour merged, the gluey substance lessened, until only the wet patch remained. The reversal was complete as this, in turn, shrank and dried in an instant leaving no clue as to its ever being there at all.

The bedroom door flew open, and John rushed in. 'Richard, are you OK?'

He nodded, still trying to make sense of it all.

The cornflakes were soggy in the milk and the boiled egg was as cold as a stone.

Rick looked at the clock on the bedside table.

11.25 am!

Chapter 22

Despite hours of futile attempts in search of further communiqué with Ellie, Rick was left disappointed and downhearted. No more colours, only his face in the mirror, and only ordinary novels in the makeshift library.

But did he really need her messages clarifying? They were unambiguous… she wanted him with her, and she had gone to great lengths to tell him so. A person had died, for Christ's sake, to emphasise the importance of the missive. And there was no let up. Every time he convinced himself that she could not possibly want him to die, she repeated the request, each time more forcibly than the last.

His experiences far surpassed the strangest tales he had read in books of the paranormal. And *he* had been a sceptic.

Lying on his bed Rick surrendered himself to the inevitable.

But this was not the place to do the deed. He wanted a sweet reunion with Ellie, and this mad-house did not feature in the plans.

Calmly walking into the staff room Rick smiled at the charge nurse and asked her for his property. He needed his credit cards and a little money, nothing more.

'And where do you think you're going?' she said.

'Please, I just need my things.' He looked around and saw a small bank of lockers, one had his surname near the top of the door, scrawled on a post-it. He reached out to open it, but it was locked.

'Hey, what do you think you're doing?' the nurse protested.

He had no time for explanations or apologies. He pushed her gently off balance and into a soft chair behind her, then punched the little locker door with sufficient force to smash the lock and send it banging open and closed, open and closed. He removed a brown envelope from within and smiled again at the young nurse, now looking on in horror.

The place had been fairly quiet at the time, so the unexpected crash from the staff room sent two male nurses charging down the corridor. One saw Richard heading for the way out. 'Get back in here now,' he shouted authoritatively.

'Sue me,' replied Rick, and walked from the ward, down the steps and into daylight behind the main body of the hospital.

* * *

'A single room, please, just for tonight. The name's Walters.'

'Thank you sir. Will you be requiring a morning paper?'

'I don't think so,' Rick said. He had £156 in his wallet, which enabled him to avoid using his credit card and so give a false name. He knew that, having being sectioned, the police would have been notified of his absence from the psychiatric ward and would be looking for him. So using a false name would delay his capture easily long enough for him to do what had to be done, and would prevent him from having to look over his shoulder all evening.

To allay any suspicion he had also paid for the room, and an evening meal, in advance. Despite wearing the same clothes for the third day running, since the time of his visit to the unfortunate medium, he had kept himself showered and clean. The clothes he wore were smart-casual; a blue shirt, black trousers and black brogues, and a waist-length leather jacket, so he didn't look out of place in the four star hotel he had checked into.

The meal was delightful and Rick chose Ellie's favourite red wine to accompany the Beef Wellington. As he ate alone he sensed her presence, and her approval of his decision to join her that night. He smiled to himself whilst eating, steeped deep in memories of the good times they had shared. The laughs, the fun and the tougher times intermingled and gave him that warm feeling again. He knew she was with him, there whilst he ate and drank to her memory, their shared times. True, he couldn't see,

132

hear or touch her, but her love, her aura surrounded him and he felt closer to her now than he had even on their wedding day. This was spiritual closeness, a bond of souls that uplifted him to the highest level, surpassing any physical pleasure.

Having finished the meal Rick retired to his room, a well decorated bedroom with an en suite. As he sank into a hot, deep bath he had the sobering thought that the waiter downstairs was the last person he would ever see alive. 'Do not disturb' hung on the door handle in the corridor, and he felt at peace with the world. No longer did he have to concern himself with the aftermath of the atrocity in the United States on September 11th; no longer did he have to worry about Frank Parsons and work; no longer was re-acclimatisation to life after Ellie's death at the forefront of his mind. All that concerned him now was the meeting he would soon have with his soul-mate. He could almost feel Ellie's anticipation ahead of their rendezvous.

Rick wanted to be at his best when he met her. He had eaten, and now he was sprucing himself up, as if in preparation for a hot new date. He shaved, cleaned his teeth with the complimentary toothbrush, and splashed on the after-shave. Ensuring that his hair was neatly brushed back, he walked over to the window and looked out. A little after ten o'clock, he could see from his lofty position the city centre bustling with life. It was Saturday night. Laser lights pierced the night sky, and the multi-coloured neon lights adorning night clubs and bars made a pretty picture. But those days were over for him.

Suddenly, he thought of Josie. He hadn't seen her for a few days and she was probably worried. She was the only true friend he had in the world. No mum and dad, no brothers and sisters, and no *real* friends. Plenty of acquaintances, but none who really cared about him, except Josie. She would miss him, and this was his only regret. He didn't want her to feel as though she hadn't done enough to help him, so he decided to write her a short note on the paper from the bureau:

Josie,
Thank you for being such a fantastic friend!

You listened to my moans and groans, you even looked like you believed me when I told you about Ellie's antics with the mirror and the book.

It is important that you know how I feel when writing this letter. I do not feel that you have let me down. I truly believe that you have helped me, in more ways than you can imagine.

My decision to leave is based on things which you probably wouldn't understand, things that have happened to me over the months which give me no choice.

I have always believed in God, and I am sure you and I will meet again.

Thanks again, for everything.
Rick.

He placed the note prominently on the bed, and next to it another one for the finder requesting that the note be given to Josie, and giving her name and address.

All life's business having being attended to with the message to his friend, Rick left his room and made for the roof.

Ignoring the 'DO NOT ENTER – DANGER' sign at the top of the short, metal staircase, Rick opened the unlocked door. Closing it behind him, he stepped out onto the roof of the hotel.

What had been a light breeze a few hours earlier had, with time and altitude, whipped up into a squally gust. Seven floors above the ground gave the zephyr free reign. Rick's hair became a mop instantly, and the lapels on his jacket flapped wildly, as if warning him of the dangers. As he stood, bracing himself against the elements, they decided to give him a little more to consider. Rain, seemingly from no-where, suddenly lashed his face and drenched him within moments.

But the tumult failed to prevail. Its force was insignificant compared with its victim's resolution, his drive and intent to finish what he had started.

Rick peered over the precipice. Heights had never troubled him, but he took a step back from the edge of the hotel roof as the wind whistled about him. Only a foot high rail came between him and death.

Below was a fairly busy street. Attracting attention to himself was the last thing he wanted to do; neither did he wish to cause people distress by dying before their eyes. No, that wouldn't be fair. Leaning against the wind, he walked to the other side of the roof. A large enclosed yard was now below him. Although the person who found him would be upset at least it wouldn't involve a lot of people.

He stood a few feet from the edge. It must be when *he* decided, not the wind.

Two minutes passed, three.

In spite of being determined, his inner self-preservation mechanism was arguing with him, not in words, but in fear. Fear of pain, fear of death, fear of having got it all wrong. What if his experiences were delusions? Ones which he would overcome in time if he gave himself a chance. What if he didn't die instantly on the concrete below? What if Ellie wasn't there, after all?

'No. No,' he said between gritted teeth, fighting his human instincts to live longer.

Then... he had done it!

He had stepped over the edge.

The adrenaline rush was such that things really did slow, sufficiently for him to think. The feeling of *nothing* below his feet was extraordinary. The wind whistled passed his ears now, and his stomach lurched as though he were on free-fall on the biggest white-knuckle ride in the world. He was on free-fall. He saw windows, lots of them, fly passed as he fell at a tremendous rate, and his heart beat in his chest as though it would burst through ribs and skin.

Although this was precisely what he had intended, the fact that there was no turning back suddenly hit him like a hammer between the eyes. He *was* about to die. In the next second. His longing to be with Ellie now played second fiddle to the greatest fear he had ever experienced. Fear was what filled every last nook and cranny of his consciousness, and every physical sinew of his being. There was no room for any other emotion.

This was Fear's domain.

Terror and abject surrender enshrouded Rick, as his muscles tightened to the point of spasm in their futile attempt to protect his body. No mercy would be afforded them from seven floors. His mouth opened and took in litres of air within a tenth of a second, and he closed his eyes awaiting the impact. Please be final, he prayed. Please be quick.

A soft sensation gently engulfed him. No bang, splinter or thud. Instead a serene and muted yielding.

But how was he able to think these thoughts? Perhaps it was the brain's swan song moments before oblivion, a paradoxical afterthought.

Yet moments were passing. He felt them tick, tock, tick. Was he dead? He opened his eyes gradually, apprehensive as to what would be there.

Ellie was before him.

Only her head and her bare shoulders were visible, the remainder strangely faded out. Her lovely face was near to his, but was at least three or four times its normal size. The same went for her smile.

Rick looked down and saw that he was whole, his feet dangling mere inches from the ground.

'Ellie,' he said softly. She smiled lovingly at him. 'Am I…dead?' She slowly shook her head. This was not the response he expected.

'How… how?' he stammered.

'That is not what is intended,' she said. Her voice was unusual; she seemed to sing her reply to him, not in that the pitch of the sound was higher or the words elongated, but there was a resounding quality in the sounds.

'Then I'm alive?'

'Yes.'

'How? Why?'

Her smile broadened. 'I was allowed to intervene,' she said slowly. 'Please, lose your fear.'

'OK,' Rick replied, tears filling his eyes as he became entranced by her manifestation. 'Have you been calling me?'

'Oh yes. I have. But I need to speak to you. It will be hard for you to understand, but listen.' Rick nodded. 'At the moment before a violent death, where a person realises that he is about to die, fear is so intense that it opens the mind to the influence of the next phase.' She spoke slowly and emphatically. 'In most cases, those who have the ability to act upon this window between the worlds choose not to do so, but I chose to act.'

'Who killed you?'

Ellie shook her head. 'There are some things that I have no knowledge of, and others that I am not permitted to tell. I cannot simply tell you that…the consequences would affect things. You must see…' Both her voice and her image began to fade.

'See who?' Rick said, reaching out to her.

'You must see Ruth. Ruth Stocks. She has the powers of a go-between.'

'What, the author of that book?'

'Yes.'

'Why couldn't you tell me this in the book, or in the colours?'

'They are very transient, and messages through them are limited. Using this window I can at least tell you in person the right path to take. To get you to this window, you had to attempt to kill yourself by violent means to achieve the necessary degree of fear, which is found nowhere else. That is why I asked you to join me.'

'Where is this Ruth Stocks?'

'I do not know. But you must speak with her.'

'Why?'

'She wishes to right a wrong.'

'In relation to your murder?'

'I believe that is a small part of it, yes.'

'How do you know about her?'

'I cannot tell you the answer to that either. I simply know, that is good enough.'

'What will she tell me?'

'She knows a great deal. She will be able to spend time explaining things to you that I cannot for even this window, so difficult to find, is only for the moment.'

'I love you,' Rick said, pensively.

'Then do as I ask. You will be given a great opportunity. Grasp it.'

With that Ellie faded.

'Wait, there's more I want to ask,' he pleaded.

'Ruth... see Ruth... see...' She became translucent, then indistinct, then at one with the rainfall.

Rick slumped to the ground. Soddened, aching, but palpably alive.

Chapter 23

'Come in, quickly.'

Rick ushered Josie into his room, looking furtively along the corridor to ensure that no prying eyes saw his late visitor.

'Thanks for coming. I know it's half two in the morning, but I needed you.'

Josie smiled. 'Where've you been for the last three days? I've been calling you.'

'Did the reception staff downstairs see you?'

'No. I did as you asked. I didn't have to wait long before she wandered off from the desk, and I quickly got in the lift while she was away.'

'Good, good,' Rick said, sounding short of breath.

'Listen, mister, I should be the one asking the questions. Now what's going on?'

'Sit down,' he said.

'That bad?'

'Worse. Well, some of it.'

'What are doing in a hotel anyway?'

'I'm on the run.'

'What?'

'From the police.'

'Why, what have you done? You're frightening me now, Rick.'

'No, it wasn't my fault.'

How many times had she heard that phrase over the years as a Samaritan? It was the common plea made by the paedophile who felt guilt for his heinous activities with innocents, the cry of the wife who had just killed her violent husband as a reaction to years of cruel beatings; in short, a universal excuse to escape culpability of every kind.

'Answer my question.' She suddenly looked deadly serious. 'What have you done?'

'I ran from the psychy ward at St. James'.'

Josie looked into his eyes. He was on a high, as if he had taken Ecstasy or Speed. She forced herself to remain calm.

'Have you taken any drugs, or have the hospital given you any drugs?'

'No.'

'Right, start at the beginning, and just tell me why you were there.'

'I went to see that Ms Begrum...'

'The medium?'

'Yeah. How do you know her?'

'I went there a couple of years ago. She's fairly well renowned.'

'Well, now she's dead!'

'Shit. You killed her?'

'Thanks very much. You think I'm a killer?'

'Well, how did she die?'

'She died giving me a reading. She became possessed.'

'Possessed?' Josie sounded incredulous.

'Yes. She stopped breathing. I tried to give her mouth to mouth but it didn't work. The paramedics couldn't help her either. I ended up getting arrested.'

'Well...what were you doing in St. James'?'

'I hit this police sergeant. He was coming for me so I floored him...'

'Oh, God... sorry, carry on.'

'Then I got sprayed with that CS gas stuff, and a doctor came to see me. I broke down and told him what really happened to the medium. I also told him about Ellie in the mirror, and the book.'

'Oh no,' she said.

'Anyway, the results of the post mortem came back, and it showed that Ms Begrum had died from a heart attack. But I know different.'

Josie shook her head, choosing to ignore the last comment. 'So they sectioned you...you know, sent to the psychiatric ward because of what you'd said about Ellie?'

'I think so, yeah.'

'And you've left there without permission?'

'I wasn't staying in that nut-house.'

'Let me get this straight, then. You're "on the run", as you put it, because you left the hospital. And the police are satisfied that the medium's death has nothing to do with you?'

'That's right.'

'What about the assault on the sergeant?'

'I think they've decided to drop that.'

'In view of your mental condition?'

'There's nothing wrong with me.'

'No. As they see it.'

'Yeah.'

'So, you're not wanted by the police for any offences, just the hospital thing?'

'Yes, but I'm not going back there.'

She breathed a sigh of relief.

'Josie, I met Ellie again in the hospital. She came to me in colours. And that's not all. She told me again that I should join her. So I did.'

Josie's face dropped. 'What do you mean you did?'

'I did it. It took some doing, I can tell you. Listen,' he said, edging closer to her like a child about to tell his best friend a secret. 'I went to the roof of this hotel, and jumped off.'

She curled her lip and backed off from Rick. This was too much even for her to take. She had done everything to help her friend since his wife died, but this was the final straw. How could she collude with this level of fantasy and still help him?

Unperturbed by her withdrawal, Rick continued his incredible tale to its conclusion.

During its telling, Josie felt a great sadness. Over the months, the friendship they had had prior to Ellie's demise had changed and flourished, in her eyes at least. Her feelings for Rick had blossomed as she took it upon herself to be his emotional

141

crutch. He needed her, and she felt good. She had always liked Rick, even when Tom and Ellie were on the scene, but circumstances had led to this very different situation, one in which, with time, she could win his love.

She looked on as he recanted the impossible. As he recalled each ridiculous fact she saw her hopes fade away. For one, Rick was still very much in love with Ellie, despite her death, and he was hanging onto memories and fabricating reality to assuage his sorrow. And second, how could she love a man who was literally driving himself mad? He was on an unstoppable ride; the destination, Insanity.

For the first time during this roller-coaster two months, *she* broke down. Not only would Rick never be hers, but he was heading for a life of quenchless madness. Both cut her to the quick. As Rick showed her the note he had written to her earlier, she burst into a flood of tears, letting the dam of her emotions empty.

Not knowing what else to do Rick took her in his arms and comforted her. She nestled into his chest like a cat languishing in its owner's lap, thinking that this was as near as she would ever come to a true embrace with this man, a man soon to be completely unreachable.

No, she thought, I'm not letting go just yet. She hauled herself from his grasp, and began to question his latest apparition.

'Rick, you know I've always been honest with you?'

'Yes.'

'Well, what you've just told me, do you realise how hard it is for me to believe that those things really happened?'

'You don't think I'd lie to you, do you?'

'No. I don't. And let me make that absolutely clear to you. I don't think you've ever lied to me.'

'Good. It's true, you know, all of it.'

'Yes. But I know a little about the workings of the mind. So you could say I know some things about you that even you don't.'

Rick listened to her. He valued her opinions and respected her knowledge. He would not have entertained a contrary view from anyone else, but Josie was different.

'When a person faces something dreadful, something really horrendous in his life, certain things begin to happen in his brain. This person is you, at the moment.' She squeezed out every bit of knowledge, experience and persuasiveness in her armoury. 'It doesn't mean that you are weak, it means that you are *human*. What your brain is doing is selecting certain things that it likes, things that make it happy, things that will let it, let you, cope with life more easily. You want Ellie, so your brain throws up images of her, in various forms, and persuades you that they are real, that she is actually there. She is there, in your mind. You've conjured her up. Such is the power of your mind.'

'How do you explain me sitting here now in this hotel dressing-gown, and my clothes wet through in there?'

'You will rationalise every event... explain how it couldn't have been any other way than how you saw it. Your mind tries to tell you two things; first, that what you experienced was real, because that satisfies your need, and second, that you are not mad. Maybe you got wet by simply walking outside.'

'No. What happened to me *was* real. I know it.'

'You are not mad. Rick, look at me. You... are... not... mad. You don't have to convince me, I know you're as sane as me. Now understand what I'm saying. What's happening to you is normal, but you must break this cycle that you're in. You have to tell your mind to stop the games, now. I believe you can do this; you *can* live a normal life without Ellie. I know it hurts you to hear that, but she is gone, and she wouldn't want you to torture yourself. Think of her, now. How she was, how she loved you.'

Rick held back the tears.

'Let them come. Cry, there's only me here, no-one else. Would she honestly have wanted you to kill yourself? Answer me.'

'No, but that was how she opened the window between the...'

'No. No,' she said emphatically. 'That's rationalising it. That's giving yourself a reason. Would Ellie have wanted you to commit suicide?'

'No.'

143

'Would she persecute you, by…haunting you like this?'

'No.'

'Did she love you, Rick?'

'You know she did.'

'Did she?'

'Yes. YES.'

'Then accept that. Accept that she loved you, and realise that she isn't here now. Not in the mirror, in the book, in the colours or in the yard at the back of this hotel. Once you do, you'll break the cycle and you will be able to live your life, just like she'd want you to. Don't let her down by driving yourself crazy and allowing your mind to rule your life. I want you to recover. You're my best friend.'

She smiled lovingly at Rick, and he responded in kind.

'It all seemed so bloody real,' he said, 'In fact…'

'Shhh. Things will improve.'

Everything that had happened, everything that Josie had said, swirled around in Rick's mind. Her explanations were more feasible than his sense of reality. Ellie's image, her voice, the suicide attempt all seemed infinitely more vivid than any dream, but had they actually happened? Could they have happened?

They talked for over two hours. Josie was steadfast. She would not give him an inch now, explaining away his beliefs time and time again, until he slowly came round to her way of thinking. By 5am, Rick nodded his head in agreement with her, and she felt mentally exhausted.

'How do you feel,' she asked.

'Still confused. But what you say has to go, doesn't it?'

'If you want a life, yes. You know I'm right, don't you?'

'Mmm.'

'And you have to go back to the ward.'

'I know.'

'Give it a month or so, and for heaven's sake take the counselling seriously. If you stick to what I've told you tonight and do what the doctors advise you'll walk out of there whole. I promise you. And listen, I'll take Tiger to my house and look after your place while you're there. OK?'

'Yes, boss.'

'Never mind that, you just get yourself sorted.'

He embraced her again and this time she felt gratitude, even affection, in him. She held him and was so tempted to kiss his lips, but she didn't want to spoil things. He had a lot to cope with at the moment and any advances now may push him away.

'Hey, I've got some *good* news for you,' she said, her face lighting up.

'Oh, yeah.'

'No more disgusting letters from "the crank".'

'Why?'

'Because I've found out who was sending them to you.'

'Who?'

'Only that weasel Frank Parsons.'

'PARSONS,' Rick said in a loud voice. 'How did you find out?'

'Women's intuition,' she said with a smirk, and touched her nose with her forefinger.

'No, come on. How?'

'After you'd described him to me and said what he was like it was obvious to me that he was jealous as hell of you. So I sat outside his house for days and watched him. Eventually he took off near to midnight and headed for Manchester, but I lost him on the M62. So I paid him a personal visit when he got back about an hour and a half later.'

'This is a joke, right?'

'No way. I pretended my car had broken down and while the recovery people were supposed to be on their way I played a sick little game with him.'

Rick was dumbfounded. He looked at her intrigued.

'The lecherous old git couldn't take his eyes off me, so I... played up to him a bit, shall we say.' Rick chuckled, both at Josie's ingenuity and at Parsons's gullibility. 'I said we had to admit to the worse things we'd ever done in our lives. Obviously, I was trying to get him to admit to writing the letters, but do you know what he said?'

'No, go on.'

'That he'd fucked one of the girls from the office over his desk, then given her the best part of a twelve inch dildo afterwards.'

They both laughed aloud, Rick falling back onto the bed.

'So that's why the little shit doesn't want me back at work. I bet it's Danielle. But that doesn't explain the letters.'

'When I left I saw two individual letters, one in italics, cut out from some magazine, on his hall carpet.'

'Go on then, what happened next?'

'I found another letter from him at your place post-marked Salford, so I went to the police and told them. I tried to ring you but you were too busy playing silly buggers. They arrested him and he was charged with whatever offence it is.'

'You're a bloody hero, sorry heroine,' he corrected himself. 'Hey, *he* could be the murderer, Josie.' Suddenly he looked very solemn.

'No. The police rang me after he was released; he has a cast iron alibi as to where he was when…when it happened.'

'Oh well. Shit, I just can't believe it. Parsons. And you, detective Hinds.'

'I'm not just a pretty face, you know.'

'And you're certainly that,' Rick replied, looking deep into her eyes. Temptation came knocking again, but again she resisted its call.

'Come on, get your stuff. I'll go back to the hospital with you.'

'Now?'

'Well you don't want to be Leeds' most wanted man forever, do you? In any case, the sooner you concentrate on getting better, the sooner you can treat me to a slap-up meal. The effort I've put in for you.'

'Will you visit me, you know at the ward?'

'Will every day do?'

He felt almost normal again. With Josie, and a degree of effort, he may just get through this.

Chapter 24

31ˢᵗ October 2001

The period of Rick's forced residency in Ward 40 came to end, but he stayed a little while longer as a voluntary patient.

Doctor Heptonstall had been invaluable. He had discussed every aspect of Rick's life since the tragedy, and had expanded greatly on Josie's somewhat rudimentary explanations of the visions. She had kept her promise, and they had chatted daily, mainly about what Doctor Heptonstall had taught him. She was interested both in the psychology and in his enlightenment.

Rick began to find a renewed happiness, a feeling which had totally deserted him of late. There had been no more unusual occurrences to cloud his recovery, and the day he found out that Parsons had served a fourteen day prison sentence, and been demoted to assistant manager at a small branch of the bank (a substantially less prestigious position) and that he had no further prospects of advancement, he felt vindicated. Parsons hadn't been sacked, but in some ways this punishment was worse. He deserved the humiliation.

It had taken a while coming, but he had a sudden thought. Life *was* worth living.

And Ellie was gone.

He had phoned Mr Davis, the Personnel Manager, a few days ago, and it was he who had informed him of Parsons's downfall. He told Rick that Josie had rung him and filled him in as to Frank's jealous antics, and that upon verifying her information he had taken immediate action. He wanted to see Rick in person with a view to discussing his return to work, and to commend him on his recovery.

At last, he thought, things are coming together.

Having said farewell to Doctor Heptonstall for the last time,

Rick made his way through the rush-hour traffic. He had intended to take Josie out tonight to celebrate his last visit to the hospital, but he felt tired. Ending his treatment felt like a milestone, and he really just wanted to relax at home; a hot bath, maybe a film, and bed. She would understand.

His eyelids were heavy as he watched the ten o'clock news, sprawled across the sofa. He was just about to turn off the television when he saw a news report:

Up to thirty people in a small village deep in the heart of Chile have contracted an unexplained brain disorder. The illness, which has been called the 'evil madness' locally, causes its victims to stammer and lose co-ordination of movement within days, followed by the person foaming at the mouth and literally losing his mind during the next seven to fourteen days. Two people have died so far, one within nine days of displaying the first symptoms.

Many inhabitants of nearby villages and towns have fled northwards with their families as speculation grows that the disorder is contagious.

There are no reported cases outside the village, but scientists and doctors have declared the area closed. No-one is to enter or leave until more information is available as to the nature of the disease.

If the illness were to prove contagious, it would be the only disease connected with the brain ever to spread from person to person.

We will keep you fully updated of any developments.

And finally, the six year old girl whose bravery in helping her...

Rick turned off the TV and had the best night's sleep he had had for weeks.

Chapter 25

12th November 2001

Things were different in the office.

There was a good atmosphere in the place since the departure of Parsons.

It was clear to Rick that senior management had excelled themselves, contrary to the every-day derision they received from all and sundry. Parsons's career had died a death, quite rightly so, and Mr Davis had moved Danielle Harper out of the department in time for his return. He felt like the Prodigal Son sitting at his desk, Mr Davis having made every effort to ensure that there would be no problems for him. He had even come down from the sixth floor personally and ordered a temporary respite to the hubbub while he said 'a few words'. Rick had been formally welcomed back and presented with an appropriately worded card, signed by everyone, and a solid silver fountain pen to assist him in the Acting General Manager's role, until the appointment of a permanent replacement for Parsons.

Rick had never been one for playing along with the office ethic that had grown in popularity over the last five years or so, whereby 'equality' and 'fairness' were pushed down people's throats, and where a general air of niceness and family was encouraged. He gave praise to people when they deserved it, not gratuitously for the sake of adhering to a contrived code. But his welcome was not in furtherance of 'the new way'. It was genuine, and heartfelt. Those who had worked alongside him prior to the tragedy really were pleased to see him back at work. Their faces expressed unalloyed sympathy for what he had been through, mixed with their relief that he was back on track and looking well.

Having emerged from the abyss, he felt at home here.

Rick felt a little strange driving home, because every time he had made the journey in the past Ellie had either been there with his tea made, or he had prepared the meal awaiting her arrival from work. The house would be empty when he got home.

But Rick realised that these feelings of sadness would linger for months, even years, to come. He knew that such feelings were normal and so didn't feel the deep hurt and resentment he had formerly experienced. In short, he was dealing with the loss.

Taking his coat off in the hallway, Rick almost jumped out of his skin as a familiar face appeared from the lounge.

'Phew, Josie. You scared the life out of me.'

'I hope you don't mind, but I thought you might want a bit of company tonight, your first day back at work and all that?'

'No…great,' he said, kicking off his shoes.

'I took the liberty of getting one of those Chinese meals for two from Tesco's. Sweet and sour chicken,' she said, raising her eyebrows.

'That'll do nicely,' he replied. 'I'm famished.'

The dining kitchen was beautifully laid out. Sodium lights from the street were shut out by the blinds, the dimmer switch had been used to great effect so that the table, adorned with flowers and wine, was just visible.

'Would sir care to take a seat?' Josie said playfully. 'And sorry, takeaway's off the menu.' Rick frowned.

As he neared the table, he saw what must have been a 16 ounce steak steaming lusciously on a plate. Alongside it were roast potatoes, peas and carrots cut into petal shapes. Fried mushrooms and onions swam in a gravy boat filled to the brim.

'Well. What can I say?'

'Say nothing, just enjoy,' Josie said, pulling his chair back from the table as would an attentive waiter in a good class restaurant.

Josie had the same as Rick on her plate, halved.

The food was consumed in its entirety, together with two bottles of wine, and five thirty turned into nine o'clock before either of them realised it. Rick suddenly became aware that the time had passed without him giving Ellie a second thought. He ushered away the guilty feeling by reminding himself that she would want him to be happy, and that he must dispel such feelings if he was to move on. After all, nearly four months had passed since she was killed, and he hadn't so much as looked at another woman in that time, with the exception of a momentary glance at Josie in the kitchen. There had been no self-gratification, in fact no sexual arousal of any description, so there was no need to beat himself up by enjoying Josie's company so much. She had become more than a friend to him over the months; without her God only knows where he would be now. And here she was, looking more beautiful than ever, thinking of him after his first day at work. No, there was no need to feel guilt or shame about this at all, he concluded.

'I don't know about you, chef, but I'm getting a numb bum sat on this chair. How about retiring to the lounge?'

'Retiring? You've only just gone back to work,' she said. Both burst out laughing, partly at the poor joke, partly due to the effects of the wine.

They sat close on the settee, each aware of the other's proximity. The TV prevented any awkwardness as it demanded a large chunk of their attention. A quiz show had them shouting out answers, trying to beat one another to be the first to get ten correct.

After a short while, however, Rick could not resist a sideways glance at his guest. She wore a short blue leather skirt, and a lighter blue blouse. The central heating had been blasting out for two hours at least, and the house was warm, so Josie had no shoes on, and bare legs. One more open button on her blouse than would be acceptable in a work environment showed enough cleavage to cause stirrings in Rick. He stole a look at her legs, all of which were on view except for the five or six inches below her hips. They were closed, knees together, and how he wanted to part them and show his gratitude to her for all the help she had given him.

He instinctively sat back further on the sofa to hide his growing pleasure, and Josie turned to him and smiled, as though she was able to read his every thought. Her blue eyes plumbed the depths of his, fishing for something special that may, due to coyness, be hiding beneath the surface. A thrill shot through him like electricity, and without consideration or permission he leaned towards her and kissed her lips. She greeted his advance with a warm, wet tongue which instantly and with vigour danced around his own. Her mouth was sweet and inviting, as was she.

Opening his eyes just a little, Rick saw hers closed; he saw the passion in her expression, and realised that the depth of his physical longing for her was shared. He thought how stunningly attractive she was, and could scarcely believe that he had her, here. But she had personal qualities, too. A sense of humour, understanding, intelligence, empathy and affection, more than any Miss World or glamour model in his eyes. He stroked her right thigh, fully expecting to meet resistance, but instead she opened her legs invitingly and exhaled with the pleasure of anticipation.

Her inner thigh was softer than anything he had ever touched, and raking the smooth skin lightly with his fingertips persuaded her to open her legs wider, whilst throwing her arms around his neck to kiss him deeper. His phallus emulated a Coldstream Guard, stood steadfastly to attention. She released her right hand from around his neck and found his throbbing member eager to greet her through thick trousers. Expertly, she downed his zip and her hand adeptly found its way into his underwear to meet its prize. Still kissing wildly, Rick let out a groan of satisfaction at Josie's enthusiasm.

It was a long time since he had had sex, and he didn't want to spoil it, so he gently eased himself from her grasp, removed his mouth from hers, and smiled at her in a triumphant manner. Josie smiled back...both knew that this was just the beginning.

Rick stood up and, urging her silently to remain just where she was, he took off his shirt, trousers and socks. 'These just get in the way,' he said.

'Oh, absolutely,' Josie agreed, unabashedly fixing her gaze on the tent that formed in the front of Rick's boxer shorts. He lingered for a moment and then knelt before her. Slowly, he edged her little skirt around her waist, and forced her long legs apart to the maximum, revealing black lace panties. They were so brief that part of her womanhood teasingly peeped around the sides. He used one finger to stroke her, through her knickers, making small circles on the wet lace, and producing gasps of delight.

Then he edged closer and with one, swift movement he tore the lace apart. 'I'll buy you some more,' he said in a tone suggesting that protest was futile.

'Make love to me Rick,' Josie said, unable to hold back her elation, but he wanted to do more for her first.

Kissing the inside of her soft thighs slowly, and in no hurry, made Josie puff and blow, craving more intimate contact. She took hold of his head and guided it towards her crotch, but he pushed her away and continued as before. A minute or two passed before he plunged his tongue into her hot, expectant cavern, as she groaned aloud. Using the very tip of his tongue now, he came up and caressed her clitoris with wet, snaking movements until her legs closed vice-like around his ears and she shouted out in ecstasy.

The moment past, Josie unbuttoned her blouse and unceremoniously removed her black bra. Rick saw her perfectly formed breasts, pert despite being a good size, with erect nipples coaxing him to play. Still with boxer shorts on, he straddled her and his tongue again went to work, this time on her hard and pointed nipples. Unexpectedly, Josie pushed Rick off her and he tumbled to the floor. Before he knew it, she had his underwear off and was sitting on top of him up to the hilt. He couldn't remember a time in his life when he had been more sexually excited, and his raging, solid cock bore testimony to that fact as Josie rhythmically undulated and writhed on top of him, shamelessly moving to get every last millimetre of him inside her. She leaned down to him, throwing her golden hair across his face whilst she thrust her pelvis strongly back and forth, her breasts bouncing uncontrollably.

Well before Rick wanted he felt the volcano erupting and, powerless to prevent the flow, he came in strong frenzied waves.

Josie felt his lava fire into her and she moved ever quicker, coming a second time, this time silently but no less enjoyably.

She laid on his stomach, he still inside her. 'Sorry,' Rick said.

'Sorry? What *are* you talking about?'

'Well, I hardly stayed the course, did I?'

'Listen, if that's one of your poor performances, I don't know if I dare come near you on a good day.'

'Thanks,' Rick said, unconvinced.

'No. Thank you. That was fantastic.'

'Do you know how I feel?' Rick asked.

'Go on.'

'If I smoked, I'd light one up now.'

'Good in bed, but not too hot on the compliments front, hey?'

'No. Listen. I feel...decadent. You were brilliant.'

Josie stopped short of saying that she loved him. She didn't want to frighten him off. 'What about we have another glass of wine, then you can phone me a taxi.'

'Sod the taxi, you can stay here.'

'I hope your intentions are honourable, Mr Sheldon.'

'Are they hell, Miss Hinds,' he replied.

Chapter 26

6th January 2002

The weeks passed like days. Work was no longer the chore it had been with Frank Parsons as his boss, and Josie moving in with him just before Christmas had turned an otherwise horrendous year on its head.

Rick had never been one to make rash or hurried decisions about the important things in life, but his feelings for Josie were strong, and hers for him. He had no family, and she had long since consigned her parents and her brother, Mark, to oblivion. In spite of always trying to please her mum and dad, Mark had stolen the limelight and she was always second best. The final straw came when Mark graduated from university, and her father didn't want her on the photograph of the family with Mark in his cap and gown. She was twenty-three then, and she vowed never to speak to any of them again. Moving cities to find a new life away from them, she would punish their betrayal, and turn her back on former attempts to be a daughter they could be proud of.

Each had the other, and it suited them both. Most right-thinking folk would consider it rather unusual, or unorthodox, for Rick to set up home with the best friend of his murdered wife only five months after the event, but why not? She had been steadfast in her support for him through the hard times, she was bright and affectionate, beautiful...and available. If he didn't seize his chance to love her, she would be snapped up in no time, like a wrongly-priced diamond. He had once owned a book of 'wise proverbs' and the one which came to mind now was *'poor is the man whose pleasures are dependent on the permission of others'*. So sod what 'they' think, those who judge him behind his back and say otherwise to his face; he would do what *he* thought was right, and that was committing himself to Josie. It made him, and her, happy, so that was that.

But the dreams would not go away.

Night after night, he would see Ellie. It was always the same. Her words were always the same. *'Take your chance, why do you ignore me? Take your chance, why do you ignore me?'* Every time, the same. And every time he woke short of breath and sweating. Since the new year the dreams had taken a turn for the worse, in that he had developed an awareness whilst asleep of when the dream would come, but could not avoid its arrival. A book on subconscious thought he had purchased called it 'lucid dreaming', where an element of realisation that one is asleep is present, even to the point where the dream can be consciously controlled. But this... nightmare... forced itself upon him. He felt it coming, but was powerless to stave it off, utterly unable to shut it out. Josie comforted him time and time again, but eventually she began to worry and suggested he seek counselling again to help him.

Today was Sunday, a lovely blue day. The air was breezeless and crisp. A light frost covered the ground. Rick had left Josie fast asleep under the covers and set off for the park nearby for a walk. He needed desperately to clear his head after the dreams had haunted him twice in the night.

Golden Acre Park was quiet, almost deserted at 8.20 in the morning. A man walking a ridiculously ungainly Great Dane was the only person spoiling the tranquillity. The lake was like glass in its stillness, mirroring the cotton wool clouds above. The evergreens, motionless, silently begged not to be disturbed by the forthcoming children kicking footballs, swinging sticks and shouting their zest for life. Save for the birds chirping to one another, all was calm and serene. Rick wondered if the park slept during the quiet hours, and whether his intrusion encroached upon its slumber like a dream did, often interrupting the perfect solitude of a human being. The nothingness and luxury of deep sleep ruined by surreal images.

The newly-laid gravel rustled under Rick's feet as he meandered along the pathway by the water. But the serenity of the surroundings and the beauty of it all was not enough to stop his mind racing this morning. The dreams were taking their toll and dragging him down beneath the surface of reason, a place he was determined not to visit again. Despite reminding himself that the dreams were all part of his psyche coming to terms with recent events in his life, he felt inextricably drawn to the doldrums. It was all well and good enjoying his job, enjoying Josie and having no money worries or health concerns, but what use were all these things if he was going to live a life plagued by the past? How long would it be before he finally shook off its grip on him? Would he ever?

A splintering and crunching sound suddenly filled his ears. Instinctively, he looked in the direction of the sound, upward, and in so doing tripped over a tree-root and fell heavily onto his left side. Above him, a massive branch from the oak tree under which he had walked was now silently falling through the air to the ground below, to the very spot where he lay, aghast.

He rolled quickly to his left, 360 degrees, and looked above him again. But the girth of the branch, its sheer size and the speed at which it fell meant that his efforts, though swift, were insufficient to move him out of its path in time. Rolling again he endeavoured to escape the falling tons of wood, but as he moved he felt an unstoppable force pin him resolutely to the ground.

His face was pushed into the dirt to the point where there was no daylight. Neither was there any air. It was as if his body had been struck by a million ton hammer. The shock of the impact had removed his senses entirely. He couldn't feel any part of his body. There was nothing to see or hear, and taste and smell didn't even enter the equation. Even pain had not had fair warning that it was required. He felt like a human fly, swatted.

Try as he might, Rick could not breathe. Not only were his mouth and nostrils filled with clay, but his chest was crushed beyond the ability to even begin to expand and take in air. And the cruellest blow of all was that his consciousness was intact, making him aware of all these terrible facts.

Rick felt a numb abandonment, a relinquishing of life. He drifted into a dream-state he had never experienced before. There was no unpleasantness, no pain. Then he heard Ellie's words again, *'Take your chance, why do you ignore me? This is the last time I am permitted to help you Rick, you must listen to me. Your death could mean the death of many, and my help is now spent. You will have no more dreams...there is no more of me left to give, no more of me to give. Ruth is the key...Ruth is the gateway. Take your chance... take your chance... take it... take it...'* Her words faded. Rick tried to breathe in but could not. As his panic grew, the immense weight became less and less still, until he felt himself rolling to his right. He gasped for air and filled his lungs. Still rolling over he thought he saw the colossal branch rising from the ground. He felt as if his movements were being controlled by a force other than his own, beyond his understanding. He moved backwards now, as if in reverse of reality, and suddenly, things were as they were moments before the accident. He stopped, for no other reason than to look across the lake, and as he did so he heard a loud splitting sound. Before his eyes, the branch of the great oak separated from its trunk and crashed to the ground ten or twelve feet from his present position.

Rick sat on the wet grass, and cried.

Chapter 27

7th January 2002

Yesterday had been really difficult. Not telling Josie about the incident in the park had been almost as harrowing as undergoing the trauma itself. Rick did not want to upset her by revealing what had happened, but at the same time he felt as though he was letting her down in some way. She had made him promise to discuss any future 'happenings' with her, rather than bottle up the feelings that followed them, and he had agreed.

Pretending that everything was fine had been a mammoth task. It wasn't easy coping with the fact that you've just cheated certain death a second time within six months due to the intervention of your dead wife. Josie thought that the dreams were to blame for his being out of sorts, and Rick wasn't about to tell her otherwise, not yet anyway. His life with Josie was brilliant and he didn't want to jeopardise that. And whilst he was sane, he wouldn't.

He would simply have to cope with this latest situation, and any future ones, on his own because losing Josie would finish him, for good. There would be no getting over losing two special people in the same twelve months. So his mind was set.

Josie set off for work at the usual time, about half an hour before him, and as she drove down the street Rick picked up the phone and told his boss that he had a migraine, and that he would no doubt be back the next day after a good rest.

He simply needed time and space to think, on his own.

One of the most worrying things since yesterday was the fact that last night he had slept soundly, with no sign of the usual nightmare. Ellie had told him that there would be no more dreams, and for the first time in over two weeks he had not seen her face or heard her voice whilst asleep.

There was an uncanny change in the air, one which perturbed him deeply. He had fully understood all the psychological reasons put to him by Josie and Doctor Heptonstall in their attempts to explain the visions, and the interpretations were logical. But the tree branch hit him. That was fact. Did Fact not outrank Logic? Logic told him that if he had been hit by a five-ton tree branch he wouldn't have walked away, yet he felt it hit him. That was a fact. Because he walked away didn't mean it hadn't happened just because logic dictates. It did happen, full stop.

Rick mused over reality and his place in it all morning. Furthermore, he felt absolutely compos mentis. He no longer doubted his sanity as he had done in the past, because thanks to his extensive counselling he was able to reason with himself. Mentally stronger, he was now able to face up to the unusual. But he was trying to find an answer, and maybe there simply wasn't one. It wasn't a question of finding how to work out a complex quadrilateral equation, this was abstract. There were no books or teachers to provide the answers. Or were there?

Laughing at himself for even bothering to look, Rick picked up the telephone directory.

Christ, she was there, as large as life! Stocks, Ruth... hypnotherapist!

He stared at the tiny letters, half hoping that he had misread the entry, but he had not. He looked away, and then back again. Stocks, Ruth... hypnotherapist. The telephone number was 0987 654321.

'NO, NO,' he shouted and banged the directory shut, throwing it to the other side of the room. After composing himself, he went to pick it up, to find that it was open at the very page he had seen her name. His eyes homed in on her details once more, and the implausible number remained. Rick slammed it shut again and put it back where it belonged, giving it occasional glances of disapproval as if it was a naughty child.

He sat silently for over an hour. Then he opened it again. Stocks, R; Stocks, RS; Stocks, RT; Stocks, Richard V; Stocks,

SA. It had gone!

Rick rubbed his eyes and looked closer, but the entry had vanished.

'WHO THE HELL ARE YOU, RUTH STOCKS?' he bellowed, as though the volume of his voice would conjure up an answer.

'OK, you win, you bloody win,' he said angrily, picking up the telephone. 'Nought, nine, eight, seven, six, five, four... ridiculous number... three...' His finger faltered. 'Two...' Rick looked at the phone as though it was about to explode, and he stopped in his tracks. What if it rings? Not that it will dialling this nonsense number. 'Sod it, one.'

A pause. No sound. No ring tone, engaged tone, computerised voice, nothing. 'Ha,' he uttered, as if he had won a mental battle with an unknown opponent. Then... brr, brr... brr, brr... But how could that number be correct?

Click. 'Rick... I have been waiting so long for you...' The woman's voice sounded similar to Ellie's when she saved him from suicide.

He cleared his throat. 'Who... who... are you?'

'Ruth is good enough for now. When can you visit me?'

'What? Visit you? Who the... who *are* you?'

'I need to see you. I will explain whatever you wish then.'

'Well, *where* are you then?'

'Wherever you want me to be... name the place.'

'What do you mean name the place? Where are you?'

'Listen to my words. I give no hidden meanings. Where do you want me to be?'

'All right then, here. Here, in my fucking living room,' he said scathingly.

'In your fucking living room,' she repeated with no intonation in her voice at all. 'Please, allow me a minute or two. And Rick, I would ask you to accept what you see with no fear. I will not harm you in any way. Do you understand?'

Her calmness frightened him.

Rick replaced the handset and sat on the settee waiting for... for what, he had no idea. One thing was certain, this was no dream or imagining. He had just had that telephone conversation and he was awake and fully aware. In fact, he was apprehensive almost to the point of being sick.

Two minutes went by, three minutes, four. Ten past twelve became quarter past. Thank God, he thought, nothing's happening. Then he saw a shimmering in the air above the rug. The otherwise invisible air displayed movement, like eddies and currents in water. Ever so gradually, the movement of the air became more frenzied and eventually a mini typhoon whirled three or four inches above the carpet, but made no sound. Rick watched awestruck as the silent tornado grew in size and slowed in speed. In time it began to die away, and as it did so a figure became visible from within the vortex.

The wind disappeared, leaving a woman stood in its place. She was like no woman he had ever seen. Tall was an understatement; her head almost touched the ceiling, making her virtually eight feet in height. She was of proportionate build, and so nothing short of a giant. Her white hair flowed down her back beyond her bottom, and her face was extraordinarily long, with sharp features. As she opened her eyes, Rick saw that her pupils were cat-like and her irises a piecing yellow.

The few minutes he had had to prepare himself for her arrival proved sadly insufficient, as he shuffled along the sofa away from the spectre in his midst. The visitor raised her right hand, and Rick felt the fear within him melt away in an instant. He no longer felt threatened by the creature.

She slowly sat cross-legged on the Persian rug, which brought her head level with his as he remained rooted to the spot on the settee. Then she smiled. A warmth emanated from her being, and Rick could hardly bear to look at her teeth, they were so white and bright. As her smile faded, the warmth went with it, but the fear stayed away.

The woman, approximately twenty years of age in appearance, wore a skin-tight black outfit, like a cat-suit, which accentuated every curve and crease of her perfectly shaped body, but Rick felt no sexual desire for her. He saw her as a living being, and nothing more. For all he knew she could be God, or

Satan.

He looked at her, but couldn't speak.

She looked at him.

The woman glanced at the window through which sunlight streamed, making the room bright. As she looked towards the window a cloud passed in front of the sun, darkening the room somewhat. The vertical blinds at the window then turned and closed of their own volition, creating a more appropriate level of light for the meeting.

'That is better,' she said.

Rick nodded, his brain still acclimatising itself to everything that was happening.

'Rick, my name is Tal. I am really pleased to meet you.'

Silence.

'I understand that you are having trouble believing what is happening. Do not let that worry you. There are two things I cannot do here. One is to harm you, and the other is to force you to do something you choose not to do.'

'Who are you?'

'I am Tal.'

'I thought you were Ruth Stocks.'

'I could not use my real name here.'

'And where is "here" to you...Tal?'

'A place which once existed, and whose existence is again of great importance.'

'Look...I have a million questions I could ask you...'

'I am here as a potential go-between. You may ask me any and every question you wish. I have fashioned a cessation, a pause in time. You could speak to me here for ten of your years if you wish; the world outside this room would wait for you and resume when we part. Neither will you become tired, hungry or thirsty, or feel the need to exercise any bodily functions. And the answers I give will brand themselves onto your memory engrammes... you will *never* forget an answer or an explanation I provide you with. There is no need for you to concern yourself with the world outside of your head, it is taken care of. You may wish to use one minute or one hundred years to find the answers

163

you need to carry out the task in hand. The choices are yours.'

'Right, then. Why are you here?'

'I am here because I have been called. There has been an occurrence which requires my intervention.'

'Does it have anything to do with Ellie's death?'

'Yes.'

'Who killed her?'

'I do not know the answer to that question.'

'Why?'

'Because the rules of existence dictate.'

Rick covered his face with his hands, rubbed his eyes and exhaled loudly. The mysterious woman sat patiently observing him.

'Let me get a few things straight, otherwise I won't know where the hell I am,' he said. 'Am I dreaming?'

'No, you are awake.'

'How do I *know* that, though?'

'Your concern is of no significance. Dreaming is the reality of the subconscious, the waking hours are the reality of the conscious, both combine to make the whole.'

'Try this one then. Where are you from?'

'Where is not important in itself, when is more appropriate.'

'When then?'

'I am a human being, like you. I am female. We are the same, you and me, separated only by time and the changes that time has brought upon us. I live with other human beings, as you do, but approximately seventeen thousand years ahead of this time.'

'You're…from…the future?'

'Yes, Rick.'

He struggled to take it in.

'I know it cannot be easy for you. But you must believe what I tell you.'

'Easy? It's crazy.'

'You have had more to contend with than most people in your time. Think as I know you have thought recently. Because you do not understand something does not mean that it has not happened, or that it is not possible. The knowledge you have is relative to the time you are in.'

'I can live with that, yeah.'

'Two hundred years before this point, a man looking into the sky would have considered himself insane if he had seen an aeroplane fly passed. A woman would have been imprisoned if she insisted that she saw a horseless carriage travelling along the road. You question your sanity when you see me here, saying that I am from your future.'

'But you're so different to me. So big, your eyes and face. And time travel... well...'

'It is true that our physical form has changed at a more rapid rate over the millennia. As for our scientific growth...not more than in the past. Look at your technology now and compare it with only one hundred years ago. Your ability to measure the size of the universe, to communicate by mobile telephone, to transmit live pictures world-wide via satellite. Total nonsense to your great grandfather. I am almost one hundred and seventy times as far in your future as you are to a person one hundred years ago. Are you surprised that transportation through time is now possible, or that I look different from you?'

'When you put it like that.'

'You are also hindered by the fact that you have never read or heard of an experience such as this.'

'That's true enough.'

'That is because there has never been one.'

'What do you mean?' Rick said.

'This is the first and last time that a communication between your time and mine has, or will, take place.'

'Can I start with some simple questions?'

'Certainly.'

'Why do you talk so correctly, every word precise and no abbreviations or slang?'

'Because I have no spoken language of my own. I have spent a great deal of time learning how to speak effectively in order to be able to communicate with you. Do you have any problem understanding me?'

'No, not at all. Sorry.'

'That is good.'

'Why have you contacted me, then?'

'Before I explain, which I will do in detail, I would ask that you accept my words as truthful and spoken with knowledge and good intention. Some facts you will obviously find difficult to believe, or comprehend, but I will expand on any point if you so wish.'

'OK,' Rick said, feeling calmer, even relaxed. He thought he heard a noise outside and looked briefly through a gap in the blinds. A crow was still against the sky and a car motionless in the roadway, its driver displaying a grin which made him look mad as it remained frozen on his face.'

Tal sensed his thought. 'We are in a time within time,' she said. 'There can be no interaction between the two without my say-so. Ignore what worries you, and concentrate on me, Rick Sheldon.'

Rick resumed his former line of thinking. 'Why are you here?'

'Have you heard of a timeline?'

'I've never really been one for reading science fiction and all that, but I think I know what you mean. A series of events over a period of time.'

'Good. The timeline that you occupy is the one in which I live also. It is the one in which all human beings have lived. It began with single-cell life in the oceans and continued through your time into mine. Beyond that is irrelevant to me and outside my scope of influence. The timeline has remained pure from the beginning up to my present. But now there has been a disruption.'

'A disruption?'

'Yes. An alteration of an event which fundamentally changes the line. For you, that is.'

'You've lost me. How can something that has already happened be changed?'

'It can, once, and at any chosen point in the line. It could have been an occurrence in Egypt ten thousand years before your present, or the change of an incident ten thousand years after you go to the next phase…sorry, after you die.'

'The next phase? What happens when I die, Tal?'

'I almost made a mistake. I am not permitted to discuss that.'

'What stops you?'

'The tenets. If they are breached, there would be calamity.'

'Why?'

'The tenets are… compare them with the laws of physics that you know. Gravity, if you drop an apple, it will fall to the ground. Centrifugal force. The sun rising and setting. Such things are law, the rules that we must abide by, that we must live with. Rules which have no compromise and form a certain outcome. In the same way, the tenets. If I avail you of certain information before your time it *will* influence time to come, just as gravity *will* cause the apple to strike the ground. There are many tenets, and I have an obligation to abide by them and keep things in tact. A timeline can be altered once, and once only. It is fragile in its composition and further disruptions would tear it apart.'

Rick's mind was working at a pace. He could almost feel the cogs turning at full pelt. It was not painful or uncomfortable, but required a degree of concentration that he had never experienced.

'A disruption in the timeline. Why has that happened?' he asked.

'A man named Rusak has caused the disruption. Many have hankered over the years to achieve what he has done, but he is the first to carry it out successfully.'

'Why would he want to cause this…disruption?'

'To be the first to do it. It is, no doubt, a significant scientific achievement. But the choice of the change he has fabricated will have momentous consequences for the development of our species, particularly during the next hundred years from this point in time.'

'What's gonna happen?'

'If the change goes unchallenged, ninety eight per cent of the world's human population will die by 2096.'

Rick looked at her in disbelief. 'What?'

'That is the way it will be.'

'Won't that affect you, in your time then?'

167

'No. Cyclical shifts would prevent that occurring.'

'Cyclical what?'

'Rick, please do not be offended if I liken this situation to you attempting to explain the workings of a computer chip to a Neanderthal Man. It is simply not possible...the gap between you and me is too wide. My purpose here is to explain this situation to you according to your level of understanding. You can walk away from me at any time you wish, I have no hold over you. Or you can choose to listen to me and accept certain things as fact which you are not yet capable of understanding. You have the ultimate choice. Walking out of this room will break the cessation and you can forget our meeting ever happened. I cannot contact you, the tenets dictate that. Conversely, you can choose to stay and accept me for what I am. I can only ask, I cannot command.'

'So if I walk out, there won't be any more dreams, visions or weird things happen to me again?'

'I give you my promise. They were the Petitioners, employed solely to persuade you to contact me. Their role is fulfilled.'

Rick felt a great sadness wash over him. In some ways he had been uplifted by Ellie's visits, they had made him feel that her death had not been final but had afforded him the opportunity to say a few words before she left him for ever. But they were aberrations, nothing more than ghosts put in place to serve a purpose.

Tal smiled. 'You are a kind-hearted man,' she said. 'Ellie was with you, Rick. In the mirror, at the hotel, in your dreams. It was her. She is very brave, but now her involvement is at an end.'

'Does her... soul, sprit, whatever you want to call it, still exist? Does she watch over me?'

'Sorry. I am not permitted to speak of that.'

'If she's tried so hard to get us to meet, then I won't walk away. I choose to stay.'

'Thank you.'

'What do I have to do?'

'You have to restore the timeline to its former pattern. I said before that it can withstand only one change, that change includes a restoration. If you succeed, it cannot be tampered with again, if you fail it will continue from today bound to the new pattern.'

'Where most of humanity dies?'

'Correct.'

'But why would anyone want to cause such mass death?'

'To see how the human race copes with it, how it pulls through and regenerates. The hard times, the setbacks and so on. To Rusak that is intriguing. Plus, due to the rules, such a change can have no effect upon his life or anyone in his time.'

'Vivisectionist,' Rick scowled.

'In a sense, yes. I am the appointed guardian of the timeline. My predecessors have watched over it for centuries, ever since technology made it possible to do what Rusak has now done. Scientists have edged ever closer to achieving a disruption, but this man has beaten them all to it, and his choices are unpalatable. I am here to achieve, through you as the rules dictate, a satisfactory restoration. Then my job is done and the timeline can rest, never to be interrupted again.'

'Why can't you just go back in time a bit further and do the job yourself...? You've got the knowledge.'

'That is not how it works. A person from your time was "persuaded" to carry out the act that formed the disruption, and it *must* be a person from your time who initiates the restoration.'

'And that person's me, right?'

'If you accept the challenge.'

'Who's the person who was "persuaded" as you put it?'

'I do not know.'

'This disruption... was it Ellie's death?'

'Yes. The timeline did not include the death of Eleanor Sheldon on 21st July 2001. This will be hard for you, but you need to listen carefully. She was due to give birth to a daughter.' Rick's face fell, the weight of disappointment hitting him hard. He would have had a beautiful little girl to love and raise, but this bastard Rusak had decided otherwise. 'Your daughter, Rebecca she was called, became an eminent scientist of her time. This is part of *my* history, Rick, before the disruption. She was instrumental in finding a way to kill an invasive new bacteria which attacked the human brain. Within weeks it ate away chunks of brain tissue, leaving the victim mad and soon after dead, then it became airborne and into the head of its next prey. Basically, without two major findings attributable solely to your daughter's genius, the bacteria wreaked havoc and went on to virtually wipe out mankind before it was checked. You see, I have knowledge of both timelines. One untouched, and the other changed. I know the outcome of each. The altered world became a hell on earth for years. Rusak knows the outcome of each scenario as I do, but he wants to watch how the problems were solved, how people suffered and how they interacted during the hundred years' struggle with the deadliest bacteria in history. He could not do that without changing history, without ensuring that your daughter never lived.'

Rick felt a chill travel the full length of his spine as he remembered the news report about the Chilean village whose inhabitants were dying of an unexplained brain disease. There had been no follow-up reports and nothing more had been thought of the situation. A mystery one-off illness that killed a handful of people then died away itself. Not so. That was clearly only the beginning. It was also the material link between what he knew as reality and what he faced today. The two *were* connected. Tal was no figment of his imagination, there was a definite association between her words of warning and what had happened in Chile.

'But how can *I* prevent Ellie's death?'

'I can place you before the event. You must then prevent its occurrence.'

'Oh, this is madness! Now you're telling me that you can send me back in time?'

'That is exactly what I am saying. You must prevent Ellie from being killed at that time on that day. If you succeed in that task, you will restore the original pattern and the line will continue as it should have done, and will never be altered again. If you fail, the new pattern will prevail.'

'But I don't even know who killed her.'

'That is the only information you do not possess. You know where and how she was killed, and the approximate time. That gives you all the information you need, at least to attempt the restoration.'

'So if I persuade her not to go out that evening, will that do it?'

'Unfortunately it will not be so simple. You will not have the power to prevent her being at the very spot she was murdered. The disruption event occupies mere seconds in the timeline of the person whose life is affected, so even if you tied her to the floor with chains it would not prevent her from being at the place she met her altered fate. It is that very moment, when the change took place that you can influence. No other.'

'What you're saying is I have to be there to stop the killer shooting her.'

'That is what you must do.'

'If I can find out who the murderer is though, could I stop them from going to kill her?'

'No. You can only influence the moment when the event change took place. You cannot alter any other moment in time that affects another.'

'So I have to kill the killer at the time Ellie was murdered?'

'You do not have to kill, though that would suffice.'

'But what would happen if I went to prison? Would that change things in the timeline?'

'Your significance in the timeline came to an end after fertilising Eleanor. After that point, nothing you did played a part in the line.'

'Thanks,' Rick said. 'Why didn't this Rusak just kill me off earlier then?'

'He could have done. He chose to eliminate Ellie instead. He can only make one change. He could have chosen to have your father removed, or Ellie's great grand-mother; the result would have been the same, but as it is he made this choice. And you are the best equipped person to appoint as Restorer.'

'Why me?'

'You are strong, in body and mind. Not many people would

have coped mentally with my appearance, let alone with what I had to ask. Deva Begrum could not tolerate my presence in her thoughts.'

'The medium. You killed her?'

'It was not my intention. It saddened and surprised me. I sensed that she was stronger, but I was wrong.'

'If I succeed, will I find myself here in the living room, now, but with Ellie and... Rebecca... here?'

'No. Whether you succeed or fail, you will continue in the timeline from the point of the event change onwards.'

'Hang on,' Rick said cagily, his hand out in front of him. 'You mean to tell me that if I can't stop her being shot I'll have all this to go through again... this last six months?'

'That is unavoidable, and a risk only you can decide whether to take. If you do decide to take up the challenge you will take back with you all the information I give you, none of which you will forget. And think of the rewards if you prevail. Your wife back with you, your daughter, and the safety of billions from pain and death.'

'Don't remind me,' he said.

Tal smiled broadly, recognising his sense of humour. As she did so, a warmth filled him, as if he stood before an open fire. A feeling of absolute contentment pervaded him and, despite the emotional turmoil, he experienced an all-embracing relaxation. For a short while nothing mattered and he basked in the sensation, never wanting to leave that moment in time. He looked towards Tal and saw her expression, one of hope and happiness intermingled. As his gaze lingered on her face, her smile slowly gave way to a serious aspect, and he felt the pleasure subside.

'What was that?' he asked.

'How we communicate.'

'It felt lovely.'

'I wish I could show you more of how we developed, but I cannot,' she said. 'It is forbidden. Now, have you decided, or do you need time to consider?'

'What happens if I fail?'

'If you fail, you fail. You can only try.'

'What about Josie? If I don't manage to turn things around will she still be there for me?' It was a selfish thought, but after everything he had been through Rick simply could not face loneliness again.

'There are no guarantees Rick. If Ellie dies a second time you would have to cope with that again, but this time with the knowledge of how things will be for the world, with the knowledge that you had failed and that I would be powerless to help. There would be no visions in the mirror, no messages in books or escaping death, just you alone. It is not a pleasant prospect, but could you live with yourself having *not* tried to help your family and your fellow man?'

Rick thought for a few moments. 'Tell me about going back,' he said resolutely.

'Very well. I will apprise you of the relevant laws. What I tell you is solid fact, and not to be taken lightly. If you try to act outside the laws, to the slightest degree on even one occasion, you will fail. You must adhere to the laws absolutely, do you understand?'

'Yeah.'

'First, as I have already said, you have one chance only to avert her death. Time loops do not apply and the chance will never present itself again.

'Second, you cannot discuss me, anything I have told you or anything connected with what you are doing, your intentions, anything to a living soul once you have gone back. If you do, you will instantly fail because the awareness you bestow on another will at some point along the line affect its course.

'I can give you no help in any form once you have made the journey. In fact, I will never be able to communicate with you again in any way once you return to the time before the event.

'And finally, reciprocation. Up to the point at which the event was changed, Ellie's shooting, you take on a pseudo form. When you jumped from the hotel roof and Ellie appeared, saving you from death, she took on what we refer to as a "pseudo form"…there but not there. Up to the event, you are effectively a figment, a visitor to that period of time, though no-one with whom you interact will realise this. To them, you are as real as anyone else. But the important element of your pseudo form is this. The intensity of the fear of death which opened the window for Ellie to be able to intervene and save you, works conversely during your pseudo form. In short, this means that if you experience that level of fear again whilst in pseudo form it will work oppositely, or in reciprocation, to the way it did before. Where it saved you, it will cause your death. The "favour" will be returned in reciprocation.'

'I don't know whether I can do this,' he sighed. 'There's so much to take in. I'm just an ordinary bloke, not Bruce bloody Willis.'

'Again, this rule is very difficult for you to comprehend. Do not try to understand the workings of it, simply know that if you allow your mind to undergo that degree of fear again, whilst in pseudo form before the event change, you will die.'

'Well why should I have that much fright again? I'm not going to be jumping from any more buildings, am I?'

'If I send you back Rusak will know that his disruption has been challenged. He will become aware that you are in pseudo form and will know that you are attempting to reverse his work. The tenets do not allow him to intervene in person, so he may well use reciprocation to attempt to remove you from the equation. He is quite able to fill you with fear sufficient to bring reciprocation into play, so you will have to be strong to fend off the fear if he uses that tactic. I will not be there to help you, but neither will he be there in person, so my warning plus your strength will have to be enough if you are to succeed.'

'What will he do?'

'I do not know. He may do nothing. As long as you are aware that he may use fear to invoke reciprocation.'

'Right. So, let me cover the basics again. You send me back to a time before Ellie was shot. I have to be there at the point when she was killed, and to prevent her death at that moment in time. I only have control over my movements and no-one else's up to that point, and I can't discuss what I am doing with anybody. I will be a visitor to that time and take on a pseudo form, though nobody will realise. If I allow myself to feel the same level of fear that I experienced when I was near to death, that will kill me and I will fail. I will assume full human form and continue as a normal person after the event time whether I succeed in restoring the timeline or not, and I will have to live with the result.' Rick was surprised that he had remembered all the important points with such clarity. 'How exactly am I going to be able to stop the killer from shooting her?'

'That is for you to work out at the time, I do not know the answer.'

'Is there anything else I need to know?'

'What I have told you is sufficient for you to restore the timeline. The rest is for you to work out and endure. You have the ability and the courage but your will is yours and not for me to question.'

Rick looked through the gap in the blinds again. The crow was still there, and the grinning motorist had not moved an inch. It remained quarter past twelve. They awaited his decision, oblivious of being trapped in time whilst he considered the most difficult task ever to face a person. Far greater than climbing Everest or trekking to the North Pole. He could appreciate those challenges, but this was beyond his sphere of understanding. He was being asked to comprehend the incomprehensible, do the impossible, brave invisible storms, *change history.*

'Do I have to decide now?' he asked.

'No. I will be here for you whenever you wish. I will wait here until you give me your final answer.'

'Here in the lounge?' he asked, surprised.

Tal laughed quietly. 'Yes, it took me a few moments to establish your location at first, but now I know where you are, when is easy. I will stay here, but I will not be with you, I will be in my time. You may decide to dismiss the idea entirely, and I cannot influence your decision, but I would ask that you inform me either way. When you wish to speak to me again, stand at the point at which I now sit and concentrate your every thought on me. Blot out every other notion in your mind and think of me. Your meditation will travel through aeons to me, as long as you occupy the same place.'

'But it won't be the same place, will it? The Earth won't be in the same place as it is now.'

'Rick, such matters are easily dealt with. Do not concern yourself with things which to me are trivialities.'

As Rick looked at her she became a little hazy. He rubbed his eyes, thinking that tiredness was creeping in, but Tal's form was changing. She was losing her acuity, her solidity, as he watched. It was as if Rick had developed myopia in the space of fifteen seconds; the blurring of her image made him feel dizzy and off balance. Her black suit merged with her white hair and her skin colour to make a grey cloud, shapeless and indistinct. The misty mass then turned and swirled in the air, finally evaporating into nothingness.

Rick felt a jolt, as if he had been shaken or shoved by someone, and he realised that time had resumed its course. The second hand on the clock moved passed the six, a noisy car roared down the street and a crow rasped a caw as it flew overhead. The sudden sunlight hurt his eyes as it flowed in through the window, the blinds now wide open as they had been before Tal had arrived. Everything was as it had been before her appearance, and it resumed just as she had promised.

THE RELOCATION

Chapter 28

26th January 2002

Life with Josie remained on an even keel since Rick's meeting with Tal. Good company, great sex and friendship. Pangs of guilt and self-reproach tapped at the door of his mind from time to time, but he dismissed them as destructive.

Despite being happy in himself, he could not shake off what the mysterious woman from the future had told him. Try as he might his thoughts turned to her when he woke in the night, when he drove along in the car, every time his mind drifted from the specific. He did not feel coerced, he simply couldn't elude the enormity of reality. As promised, there were no more harrowing dreams and no inexplicable happenings. The last three weeks or so had been tranquil, like a pond on a still day, except for the thought that he was letting so many people down by his inaction.

Rick knew that he could live this life, now rich and happy again, until his dying day if he wished. He knew, he could feel, that he had the dignity of choice. If he decided against taking up the challenge, which after all was the easiest option because it required nothing else than to continue enjoying his life, he simply *knew* that he would never be approached or pursued by Tal. He trusted her implicitly. Yet she was there for him if he decided otherwise. When he was a boy his parents often made him do a certain thing, or stopped him from doing something else, and he remembered kicking back against the deprivation of free will. He hated being told no. This situation was the antithesis. The choice was definitely his and his alone, and this freedom played with his emotions. He was effectively choosing to decline the challenge simply by allowing the days and weeks to pass and by living his life like the next man. But 'the next man' had no option; he had to go from day to day. What blessed ignorance, Rick thought, and wished he was as lucky.

He had contemplated discussing the entire last six months of his life with Josie, from the time he saw Ellie in the mirror to the present day, but he dismissed this as foolhardy. It would upset her and set their relationship back, plus it wasn't fair to expect her or anyone else to believe what faced him. Without having experienced what he had been through first hand, would anybody really give credence to his story? Of course not, and if they did they would be gullible fools. Only he had seen and heard Ellie, faced death head-on and met with a person from a time to come. Only he could work out what to do.

The decision would be so easy if it weren't for Josie. If he was faced with loneliness and had nothing to live for the choice would be simple; but Josie was beautiful and fun and a great life was there for the taking if he wanted it. And the other option involved risk, a hell of a risk. He may die trying to save Ellie, for one. Then there was failure, having to go through her loss again, knowing that the future of mankind was bleak, and with no guarantees that Josie would be there for him.

The problem facing Rick now was one of conscience. He did not have to worry about his sanity, whether he had seen what he had seen and all that, because he believed in himself. He was as sane as anyone, despite the last six months, and this made him a strong and resilient individual. No, the problem wasn't one of recognising what was reality and what was fantasy, but how to justify to his Jiminy Cricket the final decision. After weeks of internal wrangling he reached the conclusion that Jiminy simply would not accept the status quo. Continuing on this path with Josie and turning his back on his wife, his daughter and humanity was just not good enough, and his conscience would not let him live with that.

He waved Josie off as she drove down the street, en route to join a work-mate for a visit to the cinema.

Taking up his place on the Persian rug Rick closed his eyes and thought hard of Tal.

***

In spite of thinking as hard as he could, she failed to appear.

Thoughts of what she had told him, of the terrible consequences of the disruption, and other more mundane matters infiltrated his mind. He tried hard to blot out all interruptions and concentrate solely on Tal, but the task was difficult. He had never meditated before and his lack of ability manifested itself in failure to invoke her.

The harder he tried, the further he seemed to be from his goal. A full hour passed and still he had been unsuccessful; he lay on the rug exhausted.

Rick drifted into half-sleep. The image of Tal's yellow eyes appeared before him and he snapped awake as if from a nightmare. He felt his body shiver, then shudder. Rick moved from the rug and saw a familiar movement in the air. Within minutes Tal appeared as the vortex which had transported her through time disappeared.

The flawless female, larger than life and dressed this time all in red, stood majestically as she looked down at him sat on the carpet. Rick felt humbled both by her beauty and her grandeur. Tal smiled warmly at Rick and the feeling completed enveloped him, with double the intensity it had on the last occasion. He sat in unadulterated ecstasy, a sensation which far surpassed the strength of emotion on sexual climax. This was an inner feeling, not physical but mentally impassioned and thrilling to the extreme. He was in absolute bliss and given the option he would have remained in its influence forever to the exclusion of everything. Rick felt wrapped tightly in love and it seemed a long time before it left him. He let the feeling go grudgingly, and as its effects finally drifted from him he felt awake and alert, ready for anything.

'Tal... you make me feel so...'

'I know. You truly have a great deal of love in you, Rick Sheldon, more than I attributed to men of your time. Now... I trust you have reached a decision?'

'Yes. Life with Josie is good, but it should never have been. My place is with Ellie and Rebecca and I'll do everything to stop Rusak.'

'I admire your courage, but the risks of failure are great. Rusak is a very resourceful scientist and I cannot see him letting your challenge go unchecked. He may use reciprocation as I said before, but in view of the fact that your mind is not quite as resilient as I had expected, suggestion and imagery are weapons he may utilise also.'

'What do you mean about my mind not being as strong as you expected?'

'Your calling, it was very weak. I anticipated a strong link between us when you summoned me, but the power of your mind sent the most frail of messages, almost too indistinct to discern.'

'I tried for an hour to contact you,' Rick protested.

'Then I have reservations about your ability to fight the battles ahead. The problem with estimation, which I cannot avoid when assessing the capabilities of people from different times, is its scientific inaccuracy. It maybe that what I request of you is beyond your power. You have spirit, but I fear it may not be enough.' Tal looked serious, and let out a sigh. Rick felt abject depression wash over him. His body seemed to drop significantly in temperature in a matter of moments and he experienced a feeling of disillusionment as he had never done before, even deeper in its intensity than when he heard of Ellie's death or when he stood in the rain on the hotel roof. Depression gripped him to the point where, if he had had a loaded gun in his hand, he would have used it there and then to extinguish the growing pain within him. Tears of anguish filled his eyes as a feeling of isolation grew. And then, a slow reversal of emotions until normality returned.

'My apologies,' Tal said. 'I must not let my feelings show to you.'

'Just tell me this,' Rick said in a shaky voice, 'If I go back will this Rusak character be able to make me feel fear as easily as you fill me with pleasure and other feelings?'

'No. If that were the case you would not last a single minute. The distance in time between you dilutes the effects of his power over you. However, he will still be able to play havoc with your senses in an attempt to generate the necessary level of fear. You will need to be on your guard at all times, for the moment reciprocation is invoked your life will end and the disruption will stand.'

'What about when I'm asleep? I can't control my thoughts then.'

'I am permitted to assist you in that respect. My promise to you is that you will not dream for a single second when asleep prior to the event change. After that, as I said before, your pseudo form will be gone and you will continue a whole person. Of course, Rusak will not be able to reach you after the event change moment in time, and neither would he have any reason to.

'So no dreams to contend with?'

'You will find you have enough to contend with during the waking hours.'

'Don't you think I can do it, then?'

'I am less optimistic than previously, but the task is not impossible.'

'Well, that fills me with hope,' he said sarcastically.

'The choice is still yours to make. I will not deceive you by giving you false hope... what I have said to you is the truth. The rewards are great, but so is the likelihood of failure.'

'Then I choose *not* to go,' Rick said emphatically. He was testing Tal, her promises and her power over him.

Her face remained without expression and she paused. Then she turned and looked him straight in the eye. 'Then I thank you for listening to my entreaty. I will leave you now, Rick Sheldon.'

Rick knew that she had devastating power over him. She could swat him from existence without laying a hand on him, simply using the power of her mind. Instead, she didn't even allow her disappointment to show; she respected his final decision and thanked him. That was enough for Rick to know that everything she had said to him during both meetings was true. When the chips were down, she accepted his decision as she said she would. Tal did not force his hand, she didn't even attempt to persuade him, and that engendered a tremendous level of trust in him, sufficient for him to take up the challenge, not only for Ellie, Rebecca and all those who would suffer, but for *her*. She was a true ambassador, and he would do it for her.

'You've stuck to your promise that you wouldn't force me to do this, so my final decision is to do it. I'll go back, and what's more, I'll succeed.'

'Then I wish you good fortune and strength,' Tal said.

'Is there anything else I need to know before I go?'

'I have told you all the important and relevant facts. Going into greater detail would not benefit you.'

'Oh, one thing I did want to ask. When I go back, what happens here? Will I be missing?'

'Time and the events since the disruption will never have been! Not only will it cease at this point, but everything that has happened since Ellie's death will be extinguished entirely from the timeline. Two lines cannot run alongside one another. This is how Rusak will know of the challenge. The timeline will resume from the point at which you join it and its course from there forwards will be determined by your success or failure. The last six months will be cut from the line and eradicated in its entirety. This is why only one disruption and restoration can occur, because the timeline can be severed only once.'

'So where exactly will I arrive, and when?'

'That cannot be guaranteed, though it will not be in excess of three months before the disruption, nor nearer to it than three days. The place you arrive depends upon the point in time you arrive. So, if your destination is 16th July 2001, for example, you will be where you were on that date at the time you arrive.'

'Will I have to live out exactly what happened before?'

'No, otherwise you would be powerless to change the disruption event. Your destiny will be yours from the moment you arrive. Time will resume at that point, and Rusak will see the shift and see that you are the one who has instigated it.'

'What will the… journey… be like?'

'I do not know, but you will survive it and remain in tact I can assure you of that.'

'Let's do it,' Rick said, and felt every bit as though he were at the top of a roller-coaster ride awaiting the gut-wrenching drop.

'Use your mind, Rick Sheldon; the power of your mind is the key. Your mind… your mind… your m… your… y…' Tal's form once more became indistinct as it had done when she left him before, but he realised that it was he leaving her this time.

Tal shrank in size as he maintained his gaze on her; the red shock of colour which greeted him five or ten minutes before became blurred and small. The ride did not resemble a drop, rather a spin. He was turning at a phenomenal rate. He saw Tal's red suit ten times a second, a hundred times, a thousand. It became a red line before his eyes, yet he felt no panic. He sensed that she was supervising his journey, metaphorically holding his hand while he travelled into oblivion. The red line whittled to pencil thinness as a high-pitched whistle entered his senses. The sound climbed the octaves until it was indistinguishable.

Rick felt his body rotate at an impossible rate such that his sight was effectively useless. At this speed nothing was visible, everything was simply a white moving smear. His hearing too was of no use.

Then he felt his arms rise above his body and his feet lift from the solid floor. His limbs seemed to extend above and below him beyond their capability, and he felt pain shoot through him as if he were on a rack, its operator having become demented with sadism. In spite of his attempts to fight off the pain the spinning intensified further and his arms, legs and torso stretched ludicrously whilst being flung at a million rpm.

Rick cried out in agony as his body parts tore and wrenched themselves from their homes in sockets and ball-joints. His eyes broke through the vitreous humour that had held them steady all his life and extended beyond his cheeks, whilst his ears were ripped from the side of his head.

His heart beat at what felt like thousands of times a second and his head was close to exploding as every muscle, sinew and tendon was rent and ruptured. 'Use your mind...the power of your mind is the key,' rang in his consciousness amid the pain and panic. In spite of physical chaos Rick steadied his thought processes. He told himself two things. One, that he did not understand *what* exactly was happening, and two, that Tal had promised he would survive the journey. He clung onto the latter and as he did so he discerned an almost tangible sensation fill his mind. The trust he afforded his mentor seemed to be repaid by a calming air which grew in strength as the moments flew by. Rick felt a confidence envelop his being and as its influence took over his body resumed its former wholeness. He felt strong and in control, like David of old with a Goliath to take care of.

The spinning slowed and with the exit of the vortex came a breath of fresh air, literally. Rick sucked in the rich-tasting oxygen and his lungs filled with the gas, just as his mind had filled with hope and strength. But the journey was not quite over. Still unable to make out colours and shapes, Rick began to feel as though his body was being squeezed into a space far too confined for it to fit. It was as if he was a child's cloth doll which the youngster was determined to cram into an already full toy-box.

Then, freedom.

He breathed the air, his legs walked and his arms swung at his sides. He was whole. People were talking all around him, children were crying and music was playing. Lastly, his vision returned, clear and crisp.

Rick strolled along the supermarket aisle.

'Come on darling,' a frustrated voice said from behind him, 'The tea's there, where it's always been. Wake up, dopey.'

Eyes wide with a growing realisation that the inconceivable trip through time had actually happened, Rick turned slowly to face the woman speaking to him.

'In dreamland again, I see,' she said, a loving smile on her face.

'Ellie. Ellie, it's you.'

'Well, who did you expect, Julia Roberts? Rick, are you feeling all right?' A concerned look replaced her smile.

'Yes,' he said, pulling himself together. 'The tea, right.'

Having placed the tea in the trolley Rick said that he needed the bathroom and he shot off in that direction whilst Ellie, slightly bemused by his odd behaviour, continued the weekly shop.

Rick picked up a Daily Mirror and his eyes searched frantically at the top of the front page.

Saturday, 5th May 2001.

Chapter 29

'Eh, give me a hand.'

'Sorry sweetheart,' Rick replied.

'I know you don't feel too well today but I shouldn't have to remind you that I'm eighteen weeks pregnant, and I shouldn't be lifting these heavy bags.'

Rick brought the shopping in from the car and set about putting it away in robotic fashion, his mind still coming to terms with what had happened.

'Have you thought any more about names recently?' he asked.

'I have actually,' Ellie said, half grimacing. 'Look, I know you're not hot on traditional names, but you chose all the decorations for the nursery and I'd like to have the final say on names.'

'So we're talking Edna or Herbert then.'

Ellie laughed out loud. 'Nothing so modern,' she joked. 'No, seriously, I thought Joe or Mark for a boy, I can't decide between the two. But Rebecca definitely for a girl. What do you say?'

Rick gulped hard and looked at his wife-to-be as if he had seen a ghost.

'Don't be so bloody dramatic,' Ellie snapped. 'You'd think I'd come up with some stupid name. Well I'll tell you this, if you think you're gonna give our child a name like Kyle or Kylie you can sodding well think again.'

'Hey, calm down. Rebecca's nice, I like it.'

'OK. What about the lads' names?'

'It won't come to that,' he replied, not thinking.

'Oh yeah... fortune teller.'

'Just a feeling,' Rick said dispassionately. 'Listen, I'm off for a lie down for half an hour. I've got a splitting headache.'

'OK, I'll make us a nice meal.'

Rick lay on the bed, but found no solace in the ceiling. The decision had been made and there was no turning back. He felt dreadfully lonely in spite of Ellie and his future daughter downstairs. Tal was no longer at hand to offer any further advice and Josie, in a matter of moments, was once again Tom's unhappy live-in lover. He knew that she liked him which made it worse.

He felt like an intruder in his own home. For the last six months he had battled to come to terms with Ellie's death, with the incontrovertible fact that she was gone, forever. But that was not the case. He had struggled with losing a child, one he had marvelled over on finding out that Ellie was pregnant, but now the child lived again. Against all the odds he had moved on and found love a second time, with Josie. That was off. His life had been turned upside down and it had taken hospital treatment to cure him and now, by his own choosing, its direction had been reversed again. This time there was no help to seek, however; he was on his own.

'Wake up, sleepy head,' Ellie said, stroking his face gently. 'Your half an hour's turned into nearly two.'

'Oh, right, sorry love,' Rick said, only half awake. He had slept the sleep of the dead. Then he remembered Tal's promise. It was true, he hadn't dreamt during the last two hours, which was unusual for him. Not a single thought or image had entered his mind. Two hours had passed without recollection, as if a dark cloak had enshrouded him, protecting him from unwanted intervention.

It had.

Chapter 30

7th May 2001

The pub interior had bare dark wood floor-boards, decrepit chairs and stools stood before tables with graffiti scratched into the wood, and a perpetual blue cloud masked drug deals and God knows what else.

The Peacock and Sparrow was the agreed meeting place, and the pre-arranged time was 10.15pm.

The vendor would be recognisable by his long side-burns and a small looped pink brooch positioned over the left breast on a red woollen jumper. His sister had died of breast cancer seven months before.

The buyer entered the smoky pub and coughed as the nicotine filled air tickled the back of the throat. The buyer's eyes scanned those present, those who could be seen through the blue fog. Eventually, the vendor was spotted and approached. He leaned nonchalantly against the bar, purposely ignoring the arrival of the buyer by taking another drink from his pint.

The buyer stood inches from him and looked him straight in the eye.

'ID?' the vendor said, his words drowned by the heavy metal track on the juke box.

'Russian,' came the reply.

On hearing the correct password the vendor gulped the remainder of his beer and gestured with a flick of his head towards the door. The buyer followed the man into the unlit car-park at the rear of the premises and then into a narrow, muddy pathway which led from the pub grounds.

The vendor lit the way with a torch powered by almost spent batteries, a deliberate tactic to avoid detection or unwanted attention.

The vendor stopped after thirty or forty strides and began to examine a brick wall to his right. After a few moments he began scratching and picking at a brick until it gave way and he removed it from the middle of the wall. The man reached into the wall, up to his elbow, and eventually pulled out a small bundle.

The dimmed light from the torch made the faces of the conspirators look eerie as the man slowly unwrapped the dirty cloth. Both players fixed their gaze on the lump within the material.

'What are you planning on doing with this?' he asked.

'You don't need to know,' came the curt reply.

'Hey, just interested that's all.'

'Yeah well I'm paying you for the gun, not for your interest.'

'Touchy.'

The vendor carefully wiped the small black hand-gun with the cloth, ensuring that none of his fingerprints remained.

'This little beauty's all yours now. I've cleaned each bullet in the magazine and it's not registered to anyone, so over to you, after payment of course.'

'Here,' the buyer said, handing the seller a small wad of notes.

'Two hundred and eighty... three hundred. Nice doing business with you.'

The buyer did not answer, but followed the seller back into the car-park and out onto the main road, the gun clasped tightly inside the buyer's coat.

Chapter 31

9ᵗʰ May 2001

'Come on, lover boy,' Danielle Harper whispered in Rick's ear, the one not occupied by the telephone.

'Excuse me a moment,' Rick said politely, pressing the secret button on the base unit. 'What are you playing at,' he scolded. 'I'm on the phone to an area manager here, now for God's sake leave it, will you.' He gave Danielle a disapproving look and resumed his telephone conversation. She strode across the office, not discouraged in the least.

When Rick came off the phone he felt really weird. He remembered the conversation he had had the first time round with John Simmonds, the area branch manager, and he also remembered telling Danielle off for her behaviour. Things were repeating themselves; it was uncanny. And yet he knew, in reality, that events were not actually repeating, this was the first time they had happened in the eyes of every living creature on earth except for himself. Danielle had not whispered her sweet nothings in his ear before, only in his memory had that occurred. He was the impostor here, no-one else.

Things would pan out just as they had in his memory unless he changed events as he went along. Rick began to think more deeply about this. If he remembered something happening, before it happened this time round, could he actually change it as he had remembered it? So, for example, if he had recalled Danielle whispering to him whilst he was on the phone, could he avoid it happening again? He decided to try out his theory. After racking his brains, Rick remembered that whilst he was sat at his desk in the afternoon on the same day as Danielle had interrupted his phone call, Frank Parsons had dropped his briefcase on the office floor and the contents had spilled everywhere, much to the stifled

191

hilarity of those who witnessed it. Furthermore, he remembered that this had happened at 2pm precisely because his watch had stopped and he had phoned the Speaking Clock to get the right time when the accident occurred.

When the time arrived, Rick looked at his watch. It had stopped. Instead of phoning the Speaking Clock, which he had a strange compunction to do, he met Parsons half way across the office. As they grew closer Rick saw his boss's briefcase slip from his grasp and as it did so Rick reached out and caught it just before it fell to the floor.

'Thanks, Rick. Bloody hell, lightning reactions.' Parsons frowned, bewildered by the incident.

It worked. He could change things if he wished. He didn't have to sit about for months waiting for that fateful moment in time where he had to stop the unknown killer from putting a bullet through Ellie's head. He remembered, word for word, Tal's warning that there was nothing he could do to prevent Ellie or the killer from being at the place she died at the time in question, but in view of the way he could divert something inconsequential from occurring maybe his scope of influence was more potent than he realised. Tal had also said that he must use his mind to succeed in his quest; well he would do just that. If he could stop Parsons's briefcase from spilling all over the floor, maybe he could directly affect other more material events and so avert the disruption event without the need for violence.

As Rick sat down at a table with his lunch, deep in contemplation, Sarah Bowers exhaled angrily and left the table he had chosen without realising she was sat there, taking her meal with her.

Chapter 32

12th May 2001

For reasons known only to herself Ellie had developed an obsession for swimming in the last couple of months. She had been told by her doctor that it was the most all-round exercise and that it was the least invasive on the body. She saw it as great exercise whilst she was pregnant and completely safe, and not a week passed without her making three or four visits to the pool.

'If you don't want to come with me, that's fine. I'm the one carrying this baby, remember, and I'm doing my best to eat healthily and keep fit. You just sit around and do your own thing, Mr Selfish.'

'OK, OK, point taken, I'll come.'

'Not if you don't want to,' Ellie pouted.

'I do, but you've been twice this week already. I only went with you on Thursday night: this is the weekend, I like to chill out a bit.'

'Lay about like a couch potato, you mean.'

'I've said I'll come, haven't I?'

The fact was that Rick knew their baby would be fine, as long as he did the job he set out to do, and her welfare needn't involve numerous trips to the leisure centre to swim up and down a pool. In fact, he'd never liked swimming. Plus he needed all his mental and physical energy to get through this next few months, to formulate a plan or at least some strategy to find out who the killer was and to stop them in their tracks. Time on his own was what he really needed, but what with Ellie and his job requiring the majority of his time it was difficult to find quiet moments.

'Don't you fancy me any more?' Ellie asked as they drove along.

'What do you mean?'

'You haven't so much as looked at me this week. Is it the bump?'

'No, I've got a lot on my mind at the moment. Work things, you know.'

'You haven't mentioned problems at work for ages.' Her face suddenly became angry. 'It's not that bitch Sarah Bowers is it? If she gets her claws into you again I swear I'll...'

'Don't start jumping to daft conclusions,' Rick reassured her. 'I hardly ever see her, and if I do all I get is an evil look, so there's no problem there.'

'Yeah, well I've seen her twice in as many weeks driving down Main Street. Has she moved round here or what?'

Rick could hardly hide his concern. He had visited Sarah after Ellie's death and she lived at least ten miles from their home, so what the hell was she doing round here? 'You probably thought it was her,' he said weakly.

'I'd recognise her anywhere,' Ellie interrupted. 'When a woman's confronted in her own home by a ...predator like her claiming to have had an affair with her fella 'cos she can't stand rejection, you don't forget what she looks like.'

'Will you calm down,' demanded Rick, realising that he had to take control of this situation before he revealed something he shouldn't. 'She could have been visiting relatives, shopping with a friend, anything. You've got to put it behind you and stop being so suspicious. Now listen, I've not been feeling too well this week,' he fibbed, 'But I didn't want to worry you, you've got enough to deal with. That's all it is, OK, nothing more sinister.'

'Sorry love. This pregnancy's playing havoc with my emotions, just ignore me.' She leaned over and kissed him on the cheek. 'And thanks for coming with me.'

'Let's just enjoy the swim and relax, eh?'

'Good idea.'

Up and down. Up and down. Rick was bored.

On reaching the deep end for the umpteenth time, Rick dived beneath the surface. With his goggles on he could see almost a full breadth under the water. He swam down six or eight feet and looked above him. Ellie swam along the surface of the water, her former flat tummy protruding a little, the sanctuary for his genius daughter-to-be. Ellie's legs kicked frog-like as she swam the breast stroke, her arms pulling hard through the blue water as she breathed deeply, the extra weight she had put on placing an additional strain on her beating heart.

Rick smiled. As he stroked the pool floor with his belly he felt an unusual tug on his right foot. As he turned to see what was happening, his foot was sucked into what looked like a vent on the floor. The grill which should have covered the outlet was sat a couple of feet from it. In spite of pulling his leg upwards his foot remained trapped in the outlet and he could not free it, in fact his leg up to mid calf was now in the hold of the under-water vent. Rick summoned all his strength and gave a hefty pull, but still he was held in a vice-like grip. He pulled at his leg with both hands but there wasn't so much as an inch of movement. He looked around under the water in a panic, but no-one had seen his plight. Surely one of the pool attendants sat up on those high chairs would see him floundering under the water and come quickly to his aid. But nobody had seen him. Looking upwards in a vain hope that Ellie would notice his disappearance and raise the alarm, all he saw were other swimmers pursuing their relentless strokes, and children far away in the shallow end splashing and fooling around. Ellie was actually on her way back down the pool away from his present position. By the time she realised what had happened it would be too late. Instinctively he shouted for assistance, but the suffocating water drowned his cries, as it would drown him in the next minute. Further frantic pulls of his leg proved fruitless as he inhaled deeply and took in a lung full of chlorine-filled water. His coughs too were muffled beyond recognition. Someone must have seen him by now. But what if they had? There was no time left. There was no air and he needed it now, not in two or three minutes when one of the attendants eventually dragged him to the surface.

Terror dominated his thought processes. He writhed and squirmed whilst trying to hold his breath longer than was possible. He had already been under the water in excess of a minute and a half. He coughed again, unable to prevent his body from expelling the unwanted water it had taken in, and immediately after his respiratory system forced another inhalation which he was powerless to prevent.

In short, he was dying.

The profound and deep inner feeling which pervaded his being when he travelled that short journey from the hotel roof to the ground below began to take hold a second time. He could feel the sensation rising in him like acid bile from his stomach. He recognised it.

It was true, Rick's body was virtually past the point of recovery, and he knew it. That was what triggered the intense panic, the aura which presented itself to the consciousness moments before death. Despite his apparent hopelessness, Rick's brain was still working independent of the rest of his functions. 'Use your mind' rang in his awareness, not actually a physical sound but a reminder from a friend. In less than the time it takes a computer to work out a simple equation, Rick's brain remembered in minute detail Tal's explanation of the rule of reciprocation, and how Rusak would use it to defeat him by generating the level of fear required to kill him.

A battle raged in his cogitation. Fear contested strongly for supremacy, but Reason was winning the day. Rick knew from what Tal had taught him that if fear took over he was a dead man, whereas if he used the power of his mind to recognise a ruse, a fabricated circumstance in which he was placed to fashion his death, he could overcome the fear and avoid it.

In the space of milliseconds Rick concluded that despite his two minutes or so below the surface, this could be a trap set by Rusak. He was in what had been described to him as a pseudo form, and whilst in this state he was vulnerable to the scheming of the professor from the future. It was also possible that the whole incident was entirely unconnected with Rusak and a bizarre but not unheard of accident was taking place. He also knew that this had not happened the first time around, so why now?

Rick's glimmer of hope and his questioning of the Reaper, so close to claiming him as his own, gave him a strange and incongruous sense of confidence. Who had ever been faced with certain death and asked questions of it, or had the impunity to challenge its finality? Rick did, and in so doing the fear was lifted from him like a ton weight hauled from his back. He stared at his leg, still caught in the underwater vent, but it no longer worried him. He inhaled and his lungs filled with air even though it was not possible. His mind had achieved the impossible, just as Tal had intimated it could.

Rick laughed hysterically, expelling water and taking in air. He taunted death and Rusak's attempt to finish him off. The suction released his leg as quickly as it had taken it and as he looked down at the open vent the circular grill which had laid to one side of it moved slowly of its own volition along the floor of the pool, eventually nestling into its place. Calmly, Rick broke the surface of the water, not even out of breath.

Ellie waved to him as she swam towards the deep end and the two pool attendants continued their petty conversation about last night's television unaware that a miracle had taken place before their eyes.

The experience drained Rick and he had to ask Ellie to drive home he was so exhausted.

Blessed sleep came over him quickly that night. Sleep and Tal's teachings were his only *real* friends. Ellie, Josie, Tom and all the other people he knew were ghosts to him. He could not ask their opinions or seek their help in any way. Their future depended entirely on him, a fragile and semi-real barrier between biological calamity and normality.

Take just one day at a time, Rick assured himself as he fell into Sleep's protective arms.

Chapter 32

'Excuse me, do you mind if I join you?'

'I can't stop you coming in here, can I?' Sarah sighed. She was sat in a quiet room, one designed for contemplation and relaxation. Not many people took advantage of the facility, preferring instead the bustling canteen or the television room to catch up on the soaps.

'If you wish I'll go,' Rick said.

'Look, do whatever you want,' Sarah said impatiently, giving him a hard stare.

'What I really want is to talk to you for a few minutes, if you can spare the time.'

Sarah's magazine slapped the desk hard. 'I don't believe you. First you cheat on your long-standing girlfriend, then you go steady with me for over three months. You know, I really thought there was a future for us. But Rick wanted to change again, and what Rick wants he gets, so back to the first and dump the second. As if that wasn't enough, you didn't even have the balls to admit it to Ellie and you denied our time together as if I was some kind of obsessed schoolgirl, so sad that I had to invent a relationship. Have you any idea how that made me feel?'

'I don't blame you for having a go at me. I was a total jerk, I know that.'

'And leopards don't change their spots.'

'I don't know about that.'

'Oh, so you've told Ellie all about me now have you?'

'No.'

Sarah laughed mockingly. 'Why aren't I surprised?'

'I just wanted to say I'm sorry for everything that's happened, and that my own selfishness stopped me from admitting what I'd done.'

'What you'd done? That's flattering. I take it you're referring to a sexual relationship with me for over three months. I take it you mean sweet nothings and a fantastic Christmas, the best I've ever had?' Her eyes began to well with tears. 'I loved you, you bastard!'

'Sarah.' Rick felt dreadful. 'I truly am sorry. I enjoyed the time we had together, honestly I did. But Ellie was the one I really wanted, and if I'd told her about us I may not have got her back. I *know* that means nothing to you, but it's two years ago now and we're getting married and having a baby, so it's pointless telling her now.'

'That makes me feel a whole lot better… not.'

'What I wanted to say to you was this. What I did was wrong. I hurt you so that things would be easier for me, and looking back now I really regret that, I genuinely do. It probably means nothing to you coming from me, but you are a lovely person and you deserve to be treated better than how I treated you. Having said that, there's no turning back time (he thought how wrong that was for him) and what's done is done. Life goes on, but I don't want us to be enemies. Believe it or not it upsets me when you give me hateful looks in the corridor. I certainly don't hate you and I hope, deep down, you don't really hate me.'

'I hate what you did to me.'

'I hate myself for what I did.'

She looked at him without bitterness etched on her face for the first time in years. 'So, when's your baby due?'

'October.'

'Boy or girl?'

'We didn't want to know.'

'Right, well I'll be off.' She made for the door.

'I hope my apology means something to you. It can't wipe out what I did, but I wanted you to know that I'm not a monster and…well…I hope everything works out well for you.'

'Yeah. Thanks.'

The door closed and she was gone.

Rick's strategy was to identify those people who may have a

motive or incentive, however tentative, to harm Ellie or himself, and to try and remove that motive. Albeit two years ago, Sarah Bowers had been devastated when he drew their relationship to a close, and when he denied the affair had taken place at all she had threatened to do whatever it would take to prevent him from being happy. What better way to achieve that than by removing the object of his happiness, a new wife and child?

Of course it was all speculation and guesswork. All he could do was look at the facts as they presented themselves and assess whether an individual had a motive or not. Sarah did, so he had to taken action to reduce the incentive. In any event he had killed two birds with one stone because he had always felt guilty about the way he had treated Sarah, and it felt good to atone for his wrongdoing. Everything else aside, an apology was the least she deserved.

***

'Danielle, can I have a word please.' Rick said, ushering her into Frank Parsons's office. 'Please, sit down.'

'Hey, Mr P would hang you out to dry if he knew you were using his office,' she said cheekily, anticipating Rick seducing her there and then.

'Well he's off today, and this is the perfect place for a private chat,' he replied.

Danielle's eyes lit up, and she crossed her legs slowly, temptingly, revealing her inner thighs.

'Listen, what you're doing is just no good you know.'

'Oh, I thought I was a good worker,' she said, smiling broadly.

Rick had planned how to approach her. 'Danielle, you're driving me crazy.'

'Why is that, Mr Sheldon?'

'Look, I won't beat about the bush. You're bloody gorgeous, and I'd love to have you right now here over Frank's desk.'

She feigned a shocked look. 'What's stopping you then?'

'Everything, unfortunately. I've been thinking about you a

lot recently, and I can tell you the things that have been going through my head have been… shall we say… not work related. But…' Rick held his hand in front of him as if to stop himself in his tracks. 'I have to hold myself back.'

'That's a shame… why not let yourself go instead?'

'Because I couldn't live with myself if I did. I need you to listen to me very carefully, I know you'll understand because you're a intelligent woman. I'm getting married in a couple of month's time, but more than that Ellie's pregnant and our baby's due in October. I haven't told anyone this, but the doctor's think that our baby girl is going to be brain-damaged,' he lied. He hated telling such a story, but he had to be very careful not to turn Danielle into a woman scorned by rejecting her. 'They're not a hundred per cent sure, but the chances are that she'll have seriously impaired brain function, and Ellie won't consider an abortion. In any case it's almost past the time when a termination is allowed by law. Ellie wants this baby whether it's normal or not, and I can foresee some really tough times ahead. You're a beautiful woman, but if I make love with you I can see me wanting so much more and to leave Ellie with a handicapped child… I'm not that much of a bastard. So, you see, it's not you, Danielle, I just can't…' Rick dabbed his eyes with a handkerchief.

The theatrics worked. Danielle's face changed from lustful to attentive to empathetic.

'Rick, that's terrible. I'm sorry.'

'No, no,' he continued. 'I didn't want you thinking I was being pig-headed, or that I thought you were unattractive. It's just that I've got so much going on in my life at the moment.'

'It's me who should be apologising. I knew that you were getting married, but my motto has always been that if he's not hitched he's available. I didn't know she was pregnant or that… you know.'

'Look, it makes me feel good that someone as nice as you fancies me. We blokes aren't that different from you, you know. But at the end of the day, you coming on to me is killing me… I've not explained myself very well, but do you know what I'm saying?'

'Don't apologise. My antics are gonna stop right here, and if there's any way I can help...?'

'There is one thing. I really would appreciate it if you'd keep all this to yourself. I've purposely not told anyone because sympathy's the last thing I need right now.'

'Consider it done.'

'OK, well that's all for now. Oh, keep up the good work in the office. A good team-leader is just what I need for the next few months, and don't hesitate to tell me if you think I've slipped up or my mind isn't on my work.'

'Right.' She made for the door.

'And Danielle.' She looked back at him. 'No hard feelings?'

'None whatsoever,' she replied, and smiled.

Sitting in Frank Parsons's office, Rick smiled too. This time senior management would hear nothing of her sexual harassment. She would not undergo the embarrassment of being told by those who had the power to sack her to desist, nor of having to move departments as a punishment. Today had not been wasted, in fact building bridges with Sarah and Danielle could even have averted the events of July 21st. And he was fairly confident that Parsons himself was not the murderer. He knew how twisted and weird his boss was, and how he secretly despised him, from the revelation that he had sent the hate-mail letters to him after Ellie's death. But he also knew that Parsons's actions had led to him being arrested and interrogated regarding Ellie's murder, and that he had an alibi which the police had checked out. Yes, Rick felt decidedly happier today that things were working out, or at least that he was doing all he could to prevent Rusak's evil plans.

Rick rolled Parsons's swivel chair back from the desk. As he was about to get up a silvery speck caught his eye near to the desk leg. He looked closer and saw a small piece of metal protruding from under the leg of the table. Lifting the heavy desk a few inches, Rick could see that a key had been placed under it. He edged the key from its hiding place with the toe of his shoe and then put the desk down. On the right side of Parsons's desk there were three drawers, the top two of which were unlocked. Rifling through, whilst making sure that nothing remained out of place, Rick searched around for anything unusual. Papers, various stationery and books were all they housed. Intrigued, Rick opened the third drawer with the key. Again, all he saw was fairly unimportant stuff, but just as he was about to close the drawer and replace the key he spied what appeared to be a marked out square in the wood on the floor of the drawer. Using a letter opener he inserted the sharp end into one of the corners of the square and was surprised to see it sink a quarter of an inch or so into the wood. Gently prising upward the square gave way to a little compartment in which he could see a dark coloured cloth. Rick picked up the cloth, unravelled it and stared open-mouthed at a small black hand-gun.

'But… but, it's not Parsons,' he said under his breath. 'He had an alibi. What's he doing with this?'

Rick pocketed the weapon and put everything else back where it belonged in the drawer. He locked it and replaced the key under the leg of the desk. Looking as nonchalant as possible he strode across the office, told Danielle that he had to leave an hour early today and left the building.

***

Ellie had slept like a log for the last three or four weeks and so creeping out of the bedroom unnoticed was not difficult at three-fifteen in the morning.

As the drive was on an incline Rick was able to freewheel the car a short distance before firing it up, furthering his chances of leaving the house without being detected.

He had to get rid of Parsons' gun before it was found, and the dead of night afforded him the best chance of doing this. He would drive to the River Aire near to Swillington and throw the weapon into the water. He had contemplated travelling a considerable distance, maybe to the Midlands, to dispose of the gun, but what benefit would that have? The chances of it being found were remote to say the least and even it was discovered by some twist of circumstance and its origin investigated by the police, as long as his fingerprints weren't on it, it couldn't be connected with him. It would be a miracle if it was traced to Parsons, let alone himself.

Rick was sure he was doing the right thing. It may have taken Parsons a great deal of time and effort to obtain the weapon, and its loss could dissuade him from procuring another. It opened up new worries for him, however. Frank was supposed to have had an alibi, but what if that alibi was not checked out properly, or what if it wasn't as water-tight as he had made out? Examples of mistakes and poor investigation by the police formed the subject of books and television documentaries, so it was not beyond the imagination to suspect that Parsons may have wriggled out of a tight spot and escaped unscathed through a combination of luck and shoddy work by the police. It certainly wouldn't be the first time such a thing had happened. And why else would this sad recluse, full of jealousy and hatred for him, possess a gun? Getting rid of the gun was a good move because he may not be able to get a replacement easily. In fact, he could be plotting Ellie's murder for 21st July now and he may not even open the draw to get the weapon out until the day in question. Then he would be stuck.

Venturing out at night was new to Rick. He was used to queuing in the morning or the evening traffic whilst listening to the news or a tune on the radio. He felt strangely alone as he drove slowly along Wakefield Road, not a car, bus or lorry anywhere in sight. The radio was off and his mind was whirring, sifting through all the people he knew, any of whom could have shot his wife. He considered what the odds were of the killer being a maniac unknown to him, Ellie or their circle of acquaintances. A random and anonymous lunatic who took pleasure in taking the life of young women he had never met before. It was possible, but he decided that it was unlikely.

As he mused, he vaguely became aware of lights behind him. The lights were not sufficient to break his reverie, but they did so as the vehicle quickly drew close to his own. Twin blue lights flashed behind him.

'Shit... oh God no,' he said aloud as he realised it was a police car requiring him to stop. How the hell did they know he had a gun? 'Calm down, just bloody calm down,' Rick said. His mind was racing, as was his pulse, but he managed to persuade himself that it was impossible for this police officer to know he had a gun on him, and that it was probably just a routine check.

'Hello, sir,' the officer said.

'Have I done something wrong?' Rick replied guiltily.

'Apart from your rear left light being out, no. I thought you were a motorbike from a distance.'

'Oh, sorry about that,' Rick said, still facing forward and not looking the officer in the eye. The fact was that Rick was not a born liar, he had to work at it, and the officer was trained to spot a liar from ten paces, so he smelt that something was not quite right.

'Have you been drinking?' he asked in a matter of fact tone, and beckoned over the young police woman who was still sitting in the police car.

'No,' Rick replied.

Then he remembered that he'd had a couple of glasses of wine at about 11.30-ish. 'Er, yes, I had a glass of red wine a few hours ago.' At that point, Rick looked at the officer, and visibly flinched. The sergeant asking the questions was a huge man, and he recognised him instantly. Sergeant Paul Kemp, the recipient of a perfectly delivered uppercut and kick to the solar plexus in the cell, smiled at him with a full set of even teeth. Rick's reaction, one of alarm, caused the police woman to snigger. It was not the first time she had seen a petulant or aggressive man take a step back upon seeing the man-mountain and reconsider his actions. But it wasn't Kemp's size that shocked Rick, simply his presence. It took no time for his brain to realise that in this timeline the two had never met, but the sight of him took him by surprise nevertheless.

'Then if you'd step into my car my friend here will give you a breath test.'

Rick began to worry. Should he try to discard the gun while the officers weren't looking? If they saw it he was a gonner. But if he failed this wretched breath test he would be arrested and he knew from experience that he would undergo a thorough search at the police station. There was no time to consider the options. He made sure that the gun did not fall out of his coat pocket as he trudged to the police car under the watchful eye of the sergeant.

The police woman began the procedure as the sergeant checked out Rick's car on the Police National Computer.

'Right, I'd like you to blow into this tube long and hard enough to produce a beep. There's no need for you to touch the device. When the sample has been provided it will give a reading after about thirty seconds. The green light means you are under the limit, the orange light is warn and if it goes to red you will be arrested on suspicion of being over the limit. Do you understand?'

'Yes,' Rick said sheepishly.

This could ruin everything, he thought. One too many glasses of wine would result in them finding the gun and could prevent him from stopping Ellie's death. How could he have been so stupid?

He blew into the device.

The police woman removed the tube and waited, watching for the result. Sergeant Kemp also watched the hand-held machine transfer Rick's breath into a life or death reading. Rick stared intently at the black box. Green. Still green. About fifteen seconds had elapsed. Still green. Amber! Still amber. Still amber. B e e p.

Rick let out a sigh of relief and sunk into the back seat of the car.

'Oh dear,' said Sergeant Kemp. 'It looks like you're coming with us.'

Rick felt as though his world had closed in around his ears as he looked at the serious expression on the officer's face. He knew nothing of such procedures, but he knew that his quest had come to an end. When he was searched back at the police station they would throw the book at him. He looked a beaten man.

'Just kidding,' laughed Kemp. 'I do that with all first-timers who blow a warn.' He laughed further, until his colleague interrupted.

'This amber light means that I should give you a warning

about the alcohol level in your system. It shows that if you had drunk any more you would almost certainly be over the limit. So, please be careful in the future.'

'I hear you,' Rick said, and he smiled at the sergeant, making a conscious decision not to challenge his stupid behaviour. The last thing he wanted here was confrontation, he simply wanted them to go and leave him alone.

'Take care, and don't drink and drive,' Kemp said as Rick climbed back into his own car. The police car sped off and Rick rested his head on the restraint as he looked up to the heavens.

The river was deep below the bridge as it coursed around a tight bend. Rick looked at the black water, a perfect place to dispose of a thing that could kill someone. Its insides would become wet and unworkable, emasculating it as an instrument of death. There was no-one around and, for no pre-meditated reason, Rick pulled the trigger, half wondering whether or not the weapon was loaded. The gun let off a sound crack and the bullet penetrated the water with a muffled whistle.

The whole point of him venturing out at this hour, and almost falling foul of the law, was to put this gun beyond use. Rick looked at the matt black, cold metal. The power of the thing made him shiver.

He placed it back into his pocket. 'If the worst comes to the worst, I'll be needing you,' he said reluctantly, and wondered if this very gun was the one used to end his wife's life.

Chapter 33

19th May 2001

'Look at that white skirt, Josie, it's gorgeous. Not that I come anywhere near fitting into it.'

'You're nothing like as big as a lot of women who are twenty weeks pregnant, you know. In fact, if you didn't know,' Josie said looking at Ellie's tummy.'

'Yeah, yeah. That size ten'll come nowhere near me. But I really like it. Sod it, I'll get the fourteen, I can't stand all these frumpy maternity dresses. Oh sorry, love.'

'Don't apologise,' Josie said. 'I came to terms with infertility years ago, I've told you before. Don't ask me to come baby clothes shopping with you though, all right?'

'I'm a thoughtless cow sometimes.'

'Look, because I can't have kids doesn't mean I begrudge you getting all excited about yours. You go ahead and revel in being big and fat, having mood swings three times a day and puking up when you least expect it, it's fine by me,' she joked.

Ellie laughed out loud. 'It'd be great if you didn't lose your figure. Look at you, Miss bloody World, you make me sick. All the guys look at you when we're out.'

'Yeah, and half of them you wouldn't touch with a barge pole,' Josie said.

The two shopped for an hour before Ellie said that she was getting a little tired, so they found a quaint tudor-style café and sat down with a cup of coffee.

'Any improvement between you and Tom?' Ellie asked.

Josie sighed. 'I don't know what to do for the best really. I just…don't *fancy* him any more. It's not that he's pig ugly or anything or useless in the bedroom, I just can't seem to muster the enthusiasm these days. What's worse is that he's beginning to notice.'

'That bad?'

'Well, men can tell when you don't, you know, enjoy it like you once did. I've started faking it because I feel guilty. It's not his fault, it's mine, but I haven't got the bottle to tell him 'cos he's so damn decent.'

'Oh dear,' Ellie said, a sympathetic look on her face. She could see her friend was unhappy but didn't know what to suggest.

'I feel like breaking free, but he wouldn't understand. How do you tell someone you've lived with for ages that you want to finish the relationship but you can't really put your finger on why?'

'I wish I knew how to help. All I can say is you have to do what *you* think's right. Josie, if your feelings for Tom have gone, then you have to deal with it one way or another, you can't carry on ignoring it. You need to spice up the relationship and see how that goes, or he has to go.'

'You're so together, aren't you?' Josie said almost enviously. 'You seem to be able to see a problem and see a way to tackle it, whereas I get myself deeper in it and it gets worse.'

'Do you love Tom or is it a bad patch you're going through?'

'I don't love him, and the more I tell myself I should because of all he's done for me in the past the more I resent him. It's tearing me apart.'

'And every month that goes by it'll be more difficult for him when you tell him it's over, because you will, eventually.'

'You're right. And it doesn't help when you really like another bloke.'

'Oh yeah, you're a dark horse. Who is he, anyone I know?'

Josie hesitated.

'Ah ha,' Ellie's eyes lit up with interest. 'I *do* know him. Come on, spit it out, who is he?'

'Well…'

Ellie dropped her almost empty cup onto its saucer with a bang, but she made no attempt to pick it up. Josie looked at her friend and saw that Ellie's gaze was over her left shoulder, towards the door. She turned to see what had suddenly captivated Ellie's attention in such an all-consuming way, but all she saw was a scruffily dressed woman. No-one that would interest Ellie.

'It can't be,' Ellie said under her breath, her stare fixed firmly on the face of the woman who had entered the café.

'Anna,' she said in a slightly raised voice. The woman looked shocked at the outburst and instinctively turned her head towards where Ellie was sat. No sooner had she set eyes on her sister, than she turned on her heel and made for the door.

'Don't go, please don't go,' Ellie called after her, but she was out of the door and gone.

Ellie moved like lightning despite her condition. She was up and out of the café in a flash leaving Josie sat alone with only the bewildered stares of the other patrons to keep her company, and Ellie's shopping.

'Anna,' she said, pulling at the woman's dirty denim jacket to slow her progress along the street. The woman turned and their eyes met. The sisters looked at one another. The differences they had had in the past were of no consequence at this precise moment. The chemistry between them brought tears to their eyes, before Ellie finally broke the silence.

'It's good to see you,' she said, stumbling over her words.

Anna nodded in agreement, still shocked at coming face to face with her younger sister. She looked at Ellie, numbed by the unforeseen circumstance, and left her to make the next move.

'Please, come back to the café with me and let's sit for a while.'

'All right, but I'm not staying long,' Anna said nervously.

'Fine.'

The two walked back to the café in silence, neither knowing what to say or how to deal with the unexpected rendezvous.

'Josie, this is my sister, Anna.'

'Pleased to meet you,' Josie said politely. Anna curled her lip at Josie, looking her up and down disdainfully.

Josie sensed the animosity immediately and made an instant decision. 'I'll leave you to it, love. Give me a call,' she said, picking up her shopping.

'Yeah, see you soon,' Ellie replied, not even looking at her friend.

'I... don't know what to say,' Ellie confessed. 'It must be... thirteen years since I've seen you.'

'You could get me a hot drink,' Anna said curtly.

'Yeah, sure.'

She ordered a tea which was brought to the table almost straight away.

'Thanks,' Anna said, without sounding in the least appreciative, and she gulped at the tea as if it was the first she had tasted in days.

Ellie watched her sister as she drank. Her face and hands were bony, yet the last time she had seen her she was curvy, if not full in figure. Anna had dark rings under her eyes and Ellie stifled a gasp as she saw deep horizontal red lines across Anna's left wrist. Her hair was unkempt and her clothes less than clean.

'What's wrong? Don't you like what you see?' Anna said.

'No... no, it's not that.'

'Then what?'

Ellie felt awkward. 'What happened to you?'

'Oh, sorry,' Anna replied sarcastically. 'Don't I meet with your approval?'

'Look, I know it's been a long time but you've changed so much. I hardly recognised you.'

'Changed for the worse, you mean?'

Ellie was a down-to-earth character and tiptoeing around people was not one of her strong points, but she suppressed her urge to put Anna in her place for her rudeness because she didn't want to drive her away.

'Listen, I'm not judging you, I just can't believe how you've changed.'

'Well that's life sis. In your life you probably have a steady, well-paid job, a six foot gorgeous man and a detached house. You probably go to the gym and drink decaf' coffee. Not forgetting a well-earned fortnight abroad at least once a year. Am I right?'

Ellie had to admit she broadly fitted into the category of

lifestyle described.

'And what's so wrong with that?' she said, her hands held open.

Anna laughed. 'Nothing, nothing at all. But if I tell you about my way of living I'm sure you won't approve, so why should I approve of your neat little life?'

'Why are you being so defensive?' Ellie asked.

'Don't fucking analyse me, Eleanor.'

'Hey, now that's out of order. I'm only concerned for you because you're my own flesh and blood.'

'That's true enough. If I weren't your sister you wouldn't have given me a second look, would you? In fact you'd have turned your nose up at the way I look and had a laugh with your snotty friend as soon as I was out of earshot.'

'All right then, tell me about you. Where do you work?'

'Can't you tell? On the street.'

Ellie looked shocked. Her reaction was not due to naivety but due to the fact that her own sister who she once played with in the garden, who she once laughed with and once loved dearly had admitted to prostitution.

'Why do you do that?' Ellie asked.

"Cos I've no exams to get *me* a job. I've no-one to put in a word for me and I've no big brown eyes to help me. But you don't need those things to earn honest money, babe.' She took a packet of cigarettes out of her top pocket and threw one into her mouth. She lit it with a cheap lighter and sucked on the fag as though it offered her life blood. 'The oldest profession in history. There's never a shortage of businessmen in Mercedes who want a stranger to suck them off or want to fuck you up the arse. And it pays well. I can still make a ton fifty any night of the week.'

Ellie looked at Anna blankly. There was no disgust on her face, no disbelief, simple numbness.

'And that money comes in very handy,' continued Anna, blowing second-hand smoke into her sister's face. Ellie didn't flinch, she wasn't going to be intimidated. 'Look.' Anna pulled the sleeves of her denim jack up to the elbows, unconcerned that others sat close by were beginning to pay attention to her. Track marks from years of injecting heroin scarred her otherwise flawless skin.

'Smack,' she said. 'Once you're on it it's got you, for life. There's no turning back. So you give your ass to the suit or you snatch old ladies' handbags to get the money. Both sometimes. Hey,' she said with a smile, 'What do you think of your big sister now?' and the smile disappeared as quickly as it had come.

The mix of emotions running through Ellie's system confused her. She felt hatred towards those who had so willingly shown Anna the way to go when she was young and desperate. She felt deep sadness that her once innocent and happy sister had ruined any chance of a meaningful life, and she felt helplessness. It was beyond her ability to help Anna; nothing she could say or do could even begin to reverse the path that Anna had chosen to follow.

As Ellie looked into her sister's eyes, tears streamed down her face. Silent tears was all she could offer in reply to the revelations just made. Anna stared back at her, and Ellie thought she detected a fleeting look of warmth, love and regret in her eyes, but if it was there Anna extinguished it as she would have done her cigarette. It wouldn't do in her world to allow sentiment a place. That could destroy her, so the protective stone-heartedness instinctively returned.

'Don't patronise me. And I don't need your sympathy either. You have your life and I have mine; so they're different, why does that cause you such a problem?'

Ellie had heard enough. She had been bombarded with coldness, aggression and hard facts. Her sister was lost to her, so why should she take it lying down?

'You selfish bitch,' she said quietly, trying not to be heard by others. 'You left home at eighteen. Mum and Dad were devastated, and I was studying for my exams. You didn't even tell us where you'd gone, or why. You may as well have been dead, in fact none of us knew otherwise until you sent a bloody Christmas card. And that was your only communication, Christmas cards each year. Getting your card each year ruined every Christmas for Mum, do you know that? Then you go on the game and start taking drugs. Listen, don't come here blaming me or anyone else, *you* made those choices, not me.'

'And how do you think it was for me living with little miss perfect? You couldn't do anything wrong. You were so pretty. You were so bright. It made me sick. Well, I got out before I did something I would have regretted. I hate you and them; you're the reason I'm like this.'

'Oh, no. Don't you pin your hang-ups on me, Anna. You are what you make of yourself.'

'And you're successful, of course.'

'I think I am, yes.'

'Well I think you're a stuck up, self-centred bitch.'

'Self-centred? I'm not the one who abandoned my family and left them to stew. Look, I've got better things to do than talk to you. I've got a baby on the way and you're upsetting me.'

Anna's face dropped. 'A baby. It doesn't surprise me, you get everything in life and I get nothing.'

'Oh grow up, will you.'

Anna looked like thunder. She stood up, leant menacingly over the table and thrust her face inches from Ellies. 'Look forward to disappointment girl, because it's sure to come your way sometime. How will you deal with it, I wonder? You never know, I might be there to see how. Then we'll see the *real* you.'

With that she stormed out of the café, slamming the door behind her.

This time, Ellie was in no rush to follow.

Chapter 34

19th May 2001

'What's the matter, love, are you all right?'

'No, I'm not,' Ellie said, her eyes red with crying. 'You'll never believe who I've been talking to.'

'You've been out with Josie, haven't you?'

'Yeah. We were sitting in this coffee house when Anna walked in as large as life. Can you believe it?'

'What, Anna, your sister?'

'Got it in one.'

'But… I thought she'd left home never to be seen again?' Rick had never met Anna Greening but Ellie had mentioned her on occasion.

'We all did, but she was here in Leeds today. And she's…' Ellie put her hands to her face and sobbed.

'Hey, come on.' Rick put his arms around her and sat her gently on the settee. 'Take your time, and if you want to cry, you cry.'

She did. Rick let her get the grief out of her system without disturbing her, save for the occasional hug and words of encouragement. Eventually Ellie dried up.

'Now, what were you saying?' Rick said softly.

'Oh God Rick, she's a bloody prostitute and a heroin addict. Can you believe that, my sister on the street. And heaven knows how long she'll live, injecting that muck into her veins.'

'I know she's your sister, but every prostitute is someone's sister or daughter. And most of them are hooked on drugs. I know that's no consolation to you, but I'm a little surprised that you're so upset, I mean you haven't seen or heard from her for what, ten years?'

'Thirteen, actually. We all suspected that she may have got

herself into trouble and because of that not wanted to make contact with the family, but *knowing* that she has, and seeing her so aggressive and hateful of me and mum and dad... it's just awful. She's a twisted wreck, you should have seen her. Pale, thin and scabby. And it's screwed with her mind; everyone but her is to blame and she loathes me for making something of myself.'

'Are you going to tell John and Mary?'

'You're kidding, aren't you? It would finish Mum off if I told her what I've told you.'

'I'm sorry, love,' Rick said, realising that there was nothing he could say to placate her at this time. She would have to come to terms with it herself, sort her own grief out.

'She even threatened me,' Ellie said.

'What do you mean?' Rick's ears pricked up.

'She actually snarled at me like a dog out of control. It was after I told her I was pregnant. She said I was due a "disappointment" and she hoped she was there to see it. Then she stormed off. I just don't deserve this, Rick.'

'Idle threats made in the heat of the moment, don't worry yourself about that,' Rick said, hugging her again.

It was as if the odds were stacked against him, weighted firmly against his efforts to prevent those around him from wanting to hurt him or Ellie badly. He had done his best to quell the anger in Sarah Bowers, but he was by no means sure that she did not harbour a grudge against him and his future happiness. He regretted having had an affair with her, as many people do after the event, but his actions, entirely irreversible, may have been the catalyst that sparked an inner hatred sufficient to cause the death of an innocent person and her baby, along with humankind. No-one in history could have foreseen such devastating consequences from an elicit liaison.

Then there was Danielle. Rick was certain that he had done enough to prevent her wrath. In this timeline he had not reported her to senior management and he had successfully avoided her advances without upsetting her. In fact he had done nothing but compliment her.

Up until last week Frank Parsons was no longer on his list of suspects, but then the gun, and now Ellie's long-lost sister had turned up, a hateful and possibly vengeful druggie.

'How the hell can all these things be happening when they didn't happen before?' he said aloud in the bath. He found the answer without a great deal of difficulty. It was him. Because he was saying things differently, because he was going to different places at different times and because he had an entirely different agenda it was affecting the movements of those around him which in turn was presenting them with different situations. He could not remember precisely, but on the original 19th May he could have gone shopping with Ellie, they would have visited different shops and she wouldn't have bumped into her crazy sister. Did that mean that her sister could not possibly be the killer, he thought. In the first timeline she did not meet with Anna, Anna would not have rowed with her and discovered that she was pregnant. No threats would have been made and so there would have been no obvious motive. That reasoning was flawed, he concluded. Anna was in Leeds to start with. Why? From what Ellie had told him she already had a deep-seated hatred towards her sister and her parents before their unexpected meeting. And who was to say that Rusak had not conveniently planted her there to do the killing? After all, Tal told him that the other timeline had ceased to exist completely. Anna could be the murderess in this timeline.

'Shit,' he said, slapping the bath water with his fist. How was he supposed to work out who the killer was when things changed around him faster than he could follow, and when he had no understanding of time and its nuances? He was just an ordinary man expected to deal with events set up by someone with an evil yet clever mind, someone with superior knowledge from a time beyond his imagining. But there was no turning back. This was the choice he had made and his efforts, though seemingly trivial, would simply have to do. His despondency would only serve to work against him.

217

Chapter 35

It had been ten days since the incident at the swimming pool, and Rick was becoming increasingly apprehensive. Looking on the bright side, maybe Rusak was not able to fabricate life threatening situations very often, ones that were able to frighten Rick to death, literally. Tal had said that his influence was limited due to the amount of time which separated the professor and himself. On the other hand, if such scenarios were presented to him frequently he would become used to them, or how to deal with them, and Rusak's chances of disposing of him would be diminished. In any event the prospect of dealing with the next one, whenever that was going to be, filled him with dread. And the anticipation had his nerves constantly on edge.

Having reached the premise that what he did and said had a direct influence on events around him and on other people, Rick decided to visit the travel agent. He remembered all too clearly what Tal had told him about his inability to prevent the killer and Ellie being at the very spot she died in the first timeline. She told him that this was something he had no influence over. But since his attempts to find the likely murderer were becoming slimmer by the week he decided, in spite of the information given to him, to extend the honeymoon by a week. This would place Ellie in the Maldives with him on the date of the murder. It was all he could do. He had racked his brains trying to find another solution, but there didn't seem to be one. If he was destined to fail then so be it, but he would try everything and anything to foil Rusak's plans, however slim the chances. Rick was simply not prepared to wait for the inevitable to happen. He was too stubborn for that.

The first obstacle he expected to be put before him when he walked into the travel agent was being told that it was not possible to extend his current holiday by a week. So if necessary he would lose the deposit on that holiday and book an entirely different one. But there was no problem. The additional nine hundred and twenty pounds was a small price to pay if it worked. He wrote a cheque there and then.

***

'So, are you all set for the big day, then?' Tom asked astride an exercise bike next to the one Rick was on.

To Rick the big day was 21st July, not his wedding day on the 6th. 'As ready as you can be, I suppose,' he said without conviction.

'Cold feet?'

'No, it's just that I've so much on at work at the moment.'

'Don't give me that bullshit,' Tom smiled. 'I know you, you're getting windy about being wed.'

'Why would I? It's not as if we haven't lived together, I mean she's washed my dirty underwear and I've interrupted her on the loo. We've had disagreements and reached compromises, so a piece of paper saying that we're married won't make any difference to our lives, will it?'

'Not technically, no. But there's no turning back after the fateful day, though. No going off each other and deciding to call it a draw, or having a fling with a bit on the side, not without major grief anyway.'

'You're such an optimist, aren't you? And listen here, pal, I've only ever cheated on Ellie with one woman, and that was when we were separated, so don't make out I'm some sort of Casanova.'

'Ooo...touchy. I take it Ellie still doesn't know about Sarah then?'

'No, she doesn't, so don't go blowing it.'

'You got out of the wrong side of the bed today. What's bugging you?'

'Nothing, really.' Rick longed to tell Tom everything that had happened, but he knew that would be disastrous. If only he could talk to his friend, or someone, and get a second opinion on how to tackle the problem. But he couldn't. 'What about you and Josie, how's things?'

'No better, mate. I don't know what's wrong with her these days. I've not changed a bit since we met but she doesn't seem happy any more.'

'Have you asked her why?'

'A few times, but she skirts around the issue. We still have great sex two or three times a week, no man could lose interest in that body, and she still enjoys it, but other times she seems distracted, you know miles away like something's bothering her.'

'Well, what is it?' Rick asked.

'She just says she's tired or menstrual, that's all I get out of her.'

'Maybe it's just a bit of a bad patch,' Rick suggested. He knew that Josie wanted to finish with Tom, but there were no grounds on which to base that assumption as far as telling Tom was concerned, so he changed the subject. 'You seem to be losing a bit of weight.'

'Yeah, I've lost seven or eight pounds in the last couple of weeks. I think it's worry about me and Josie.'

'Listen, I'll buy you a pint after we've finished here. I might even stretch to a pack of nuts if you work hard.'

'You're on.'

Time passed quickly when Rick was with Tom. He remembered how close they had been for so many years and how Tom's suspicions had torn their friendship apart after Ellie's death. At the time Rick had thought his friend was possessive and plain stupid, but it wasn't long before Tom's suspicions were justified. He looked at his friend stood at the bar and wondered what this life had in store for him. If Rick had his way Ellie would survive this nightmare and they would enjoy a long and happy marriage. He wondered if Tom would patch things up with Josie, and hoped that he would.

* * *

Rick parked his car in the drive and was just about to lock it when he saw Laura, the next door neighbour's three-year-old, toddle along their drive towards the road. He instinctively looked towards the road and was horrified to see a bus travelling in the direction of his house. Rick looked again at the situation unfolding before him. Laura was only three or four metres from the road and she was running headlong. The bus was twenty or thirty metres away and travelling at about thirty miles per hour, its driver looking not straight ahead but to his right. He had not seen the impending danger.

'LAURA!' Rick shouted at the top of his voice. The little girl heard her name and turned to see who had called, but continued running forwards, a carefree smile on her unsuspecting face.

Rick bounded towards the girl who by now was in the roadway. The bus driver had seen the hazard and slammed on his brakes, but it was too late, he was sure to hit her. Rick leapt into the road and pushed the toddler forwards. She fell onto the tarmac on the opposite carriageway out of the bus's path, and Rick lurched forward himself in an attempt to avoid being hit. He strode a full step and had time to think that he had done just enough to save them both when...THUD.

Rick's head reeled as he lay on the ground. He saw the girl scooped up by a passer-by and knew that she was safe. He also saw the look of horror on the bus driver's face. His head swam. He couldn't see clearly, nor could he hear with clarity the shouts of those around. Everything was blurred and indistinct. His thoughts were clear, but his senses were letting him down. He felt intense pain on the right side of his head, a headache times fifty. He put his hand to the throbbing temple and when he withdrew it his palm was covered with blood. He tried to get up but his head caused him such agony when he moved that he surrendered to it without question and lay still on the ground.

His blurry vision became more vague with each passing minute, until the small crowd that had gathered seemed to him a grey mass of colour and their voices intermingled into a low drone. Rick knew that his injury was serious and as his consciousness grew in ambiguity he became afraid. The

221

transition from awareness to unconsciousness lying in bed whilst awaiting sleep was a pleasant experience, but it was a frightening one if forced upon a person. After all, it could be that person's last ever waking thought. Despite his physical state Rick was able to reason. He realised that he may die, there and then, on the road outside his house. Head injuries were often killers, as opposed to broken limbs which often mended with time.

Nausea suddenly hit him. He felt himself retch several times, and had a vague awareness of some warm material in his throat and in his mouth. He thought he heard a woman shout 'Jesus' and at that point he knew things must be pretty bad. He was struggling to hold onto consciousness now in spite of his best efforts and he felt fear grip him, not for the first time recently. It was almost becoming his most regular visitor.

Yet he still had the presence of mind to recognise Fear as his executioner. He focused every remaining ounce of his strength into fighting off this most persistent of emotions. He even managed to ask himself whether this was another of Rusak's fabrications, but this time his endeavours failed to reverse the process and Fear began to take a real hold of him. He recognised its touch all too well, but this time he was too weak to stave off its power. He knew that at any moment its influence would be such that it would kill him, and that his quest to save Ellie and mankind would fail; but his body was weak and his mind was giving way.

If only the…

He slipped into oblivion.

Chapter 36

23rd May 2001

'Mr and Mrs Greening? Come in, he's in the far bed on the left. You've just missed your daughter, she's been here all night and had no sleep whatsoever. I advised her to go home and call later today.'

'How is he, nurse?' Mary Greening asked.

'Not good I'm afraid. He's in a coma. Don't worry about all the tubes and drips, they're just to feed him and tell us about his breathing and other things, OK?'

'Thanks.'

'Could I ask you to slip these polystyrene shoes on while you're here? It cuts down on germs from outside.'

'Of course,' John Greening said.

Rick's mother and father-in-law to be walked slowly through the Intensive Care Department, aghast at the horrendous-looking injuries that some of the patients had. Some were conscious and in obvious pain, others lay asleep.

The nurse's warning about tubes and drips did nothing to lessen the Greenings' shock at seeing Rick, whom they thought the world of, tied up in medical technology. They knew that he was in good hands and would not question for one minute the need for all the regalia and the expertise of the hospital staff dealing with him, but nevertheless it reduced Rick to a level of dependency that they never thought he would require. In their eyes Rick was a strong young man, in mind and body, someone who in their somewhat old-fashioned way of thinking would look after and protect their daughter from the unpleasant and undesirable things in the world. Yet here he was, as helpless and reliant as a new-born baby.

'Look at him, John,' Mary said quietly. 'Do you think he'll

pull through?'

'I'm sure he will,' John reassured her. 'He's a fighter, this one. If there's so much as a glimmer of hope he'll cling to it and come out at the other end. Believe me.'

The fact was that John had by no means convinced himself. He had seen a documentary on coma victims. Some snapped out of the coma in a day or two, others took months. And some had to have their life-support machines turned off with the consent of their families; that was too awful to think about, particularly for Ellie and her unborn child. He sighed to himself, not wanting to share his pessimism with Mary.

The Greenings sat with Rick for over an hour. John felt duty-bound to be at his side, although at times he wondered why they had made the effort. Apart from the rise and fall of the patient's chest, assisted by a machine, there was no sign of life there at all. Rick's head remained in exactly the same position the whole time. Not so much as a finger moved throughout their stay and his eyes did not flicker. It was if he were dead. Maybe he was, John thought. The only evidence of life came from the machines. A constant blip, blip, blip from one and a flashing heart symbol on another. Others displayed readings that he did not understand. Yet he was there, enshrouded in a forced sleep, baffling even the doctors and professors as to whether he would wake from the slumber. No-one knew, nor would they even offer an educated guess.

'Come on, love,' John said to his wife, 'He probably knows we've been.'

'Yeah, you're right,' she said, with a smile. 'They say that even in the deepest of comas a person can sometimes hear the voices of those around and recognise them. You've heard of these pop stars visiting young children in a coma and singing to them. It's worked, you know, sometimes.'

'Listen, Mary, we did the right thing coming here, but the person we need to help most is Ellie. She must be devastated; she's the one who'll be hit worst by all this.'

'We'll go and see her later when she's had some sleep.'

Chapter 37

23rd May 2001

'Hi, love, it's only us,' Josie said as Ellie opened the door.

Without saying a word Ellie left the door half open for her friend and Tom to enter and she walked back into the house, as if in a daze.

'A drink?' she said, motivated only by etiquette and manners.

'I'll do that,' Tom volunteered, and he scuttled off to the kitchen.

Josie put her arm around Ellie, whose eyes had already begun welling-up for the umpteenth time that day. 'I can't believe it,' she said. 'Your mum rang me this morning and told me the news. How is he?'

'God knows. He's in a coma. The doctors say he's got hardly any injuries, just a few cuts and bruises, but his head suffered a bad knock. They've done a CAT Scan and things look OK, nothing's physically damaged, but he just… won't wake up,' and she began crying.

'He will soon though, right?'

'No-one knows. I sat with him all bloody night and he didn't move an inch. Why did this have to happen to Rick?'

'What exactly happened anyway?'

'Oh, the little girl next door ran into the road or something and silly bugger ran after her into the path of a bus. The girl's fine, but he was hit. It was terrible, Josie. I saw a crowd gathering outside the house and when I went out to see what was going on, he was lying there in the road, blood all over the place. What am I gonna do?'

'First, you're going to calm down and stop imagining the worst. The doctors have said he's not badly injured in himself, haven't they? Well it's just a matter of waiting for him to come round.'

'But they *don't* come round sometimes, do they? You must have seen stories on the news of families agreeing to turn off the life-support machines after months of hoping that their son or daughter would wake up. I just couldn't cope with that... I couldn't.'

'And it probably won't come to that. Listen to me, you've got to be optimistic, for Rick's sake.'

'I know. But it's one thing saying it and another doing it. We're supposed to be getting married in six weeks.'

'Here we are, girls,' Tom said, trying to lighten the mood a little. He handed the coffee around.

'I'd like you two to visit him, if that's OK,' Ellie announced. 'They say that friendly voices can help.'

'Of course we will,' Josie agreed. 'You try and keep us away. Have you had any sleep at all?' she asked.

'Do I look that bad? I've a little, a couple of hours maybe.'

'Why don't you let us take you to the hospital, whenever you're ready, and we'll come with you?'

'Would you? I'd appreciate that.'

'You go get a bath and put some war-paint on and we'll all go, eh?'

'Thanks, Josie, and you, Tom.'

'No problem,' Tom said.

Half an hour passed. An hour. An hour and twenty minutes.

Deeply asleep in the bath, Ellie's mind conjured up fantasies of her and Rick swimming in a beautiful lagoon, no-one else to disturb their tranquillity other than their raven-haired daughter, who dived into the water from a rocky ledge and splashed them both. 'Me Beccy, you Tarzan and Jane,' the teenager laughed.

'Ellie, is everything OK in there?' Josie enquired.

The voice was just loud enough to penetrate her awareness, and when the request was repeated a second time Ellie jumped from her utopia with a start.

'Er, fine. I'll be with you in ten minutes.'

'Right, we'll be downstairs.'

Ellie sank back into the cool water and wept some more.

***

Rick's position had changed from when Ellie was last at his bedside, but when she asked the nurse about it, it transpired that Rick had not moved of his own volition. A nurse had given him a bed-bath.

The three most important people in Rick's life sat around his bed, looking at his vacant, unresponsive face. None knew what to say nor how to express their feelings. Ellie occasionally leant forward and whispered things in his ear, but her utterings went unanswered. Tom agreed to talk to Rick about the gym and other laddish things, which he did despite feeling foolish, but again his words fell on deaf ears.

After about an hour Ellie and Tom went to get a bite to eat from the cafeteria on the ground floor, but Josie said she wasn't hungry. Instead she stayed with Rick.

Josie moved close to Rick and used the back of her right forefinger to stroke his stubbly cheek. He was usually clean-shaven and fresh looking, but his enforced hospitalisation had left him scruffy and unkempt. She stroked his cheek over and over.

'Come on, Rick,' she said very softly. 'Please wake up. We all need you. Ellie, the baby, Tom. I need you, Rick. Can you hear me? You can't leave us like this. Do you know how many hearts you'll break if you don't wake up and be with us again? So many. Listen to me. You have to wake up. We all love you so much. I love you.'

The blip, blip, blip quickened in pace momentarily and the heart symbol flashed more rapidly than it had of late. Josie heard the difference on the machine and thought she saw Rick's eyelids flutter, ever so faintly.

'Nurse,' she called. 'Nurse, over here quickly.'

The nurse hurried over. Josie explained about the blips and the eye movement, but after Nurse Brown had checked everything out she told Josie that it was probably just wishful thinking. His condition had not worsened, but neither had it changed for the better.

Josie looked at Rick, and tears rolled down her cheeks.

Chapter 38

26th May 2001

Ellie held an almost continuous vigil over her fiancée's bed, but she began to tire as the days wore on. All the support she received from her mum and dad, from Tom, but particularly from Josie helped her through the ordeal but it was visibly sapping her strength.

The demands from the life within her vied for her attention. When she wanted to stay with Rick she had to visit the toilet because of the strain on her bladder. When she thought only of Rick she felt guilty for ignoring the baby by not eating as well as she should, and by not exercising as she had been up to this week.

And he never moved. Not once.

In spite of the effort she was making being with him day after day, in spite of talking to him all the time in an attempt to awaken his senses, of touching him and playing him music, he *never* showed an iota of recognition or awareness.

'Oh, just die then,' she said aloud in exasperation.

She felt in limbo. The waiting was killing her. Ellie simply wanted Rick to wake up. But if he wasn't going to do so, then she wanted him to die. She prayed for an end to the waiting so that she could get on with her life one way or the other. If she had to cope with his untimely death, then so be it, but for God's sake she had to know whether he was destined to live or die.

Rick felt trapped, completely and utterly trapped.

Trapped by the darkness.

Trapped by an all-embracing paralysis.

He could see… nothing.

He could hear… nothing.

Neither could he feel. For all he knew he could be on a concrete floor or floating in the air.

Without the sense of touch there was no taste. He moved his tongue, or at least he thought he did, but there was no taste. There was no mouth.

He sniffed the air, or at least he thought he did, but no sensation, palatable or otherwise, came to his notice.

Without the senses, how could he possibly realise that he was...alive? Obviously the two were unconnected. He knew he could think, yet all the things he connected with sentience were missing.

Where was he?

He tried to move to gain a sense of reality and balance, but he couldn't. The realisation that he existed but that existence was devoid of sensation frightened him.

Was he dead? Had his spirit left his body behind like a snake leaves its dead skin on the desert sand? This was what he had believed since childhood, that when he died his soul lived on but his body rotted away, no longer of any use. But if this was death, it was a disappointment.

He longed to move, ached to see, but instead he was trussed up in an invisible strait-jacket. He tried to shout but no sound was formed.

The feeling of claustrophobia grew as he came to the conclusion that he was entirely at the mercy of whoever or whatever had created this state of affairs. He could not breathe, so how could he continue to exist?

Rick experienced an unusual pressure build up around him. It was as if he was in a giant hand which was gradually exerting more and more crush pressure on him, but slowly so that he was able to feel its effects. An invisible sadist was at work. The pressure grew and grew in measured stages until he felt he would burst. He pleaded with his unknown captor, but the pressure increased unabated.

Despite his predicament Rick recognised the arrival of his old foe, Fear, but instead of it working against him this time he used his knowledge of it to calm himself. If Fear had not previously made an appearance he may have fallen foul of this latest ruse, but now he knew that Rusak was probably behind this he had a defined enemy. Whereas moments earlier he was at a loss to understand what was happening to him, now he had an idea.

He concentrated on being totally relaxed. As he imagined himself laid on a soft, warm bed on a winter's day, the wind howling outside and the rain lashing the window while he laughed at its attempts to ruffle his comfort, Fear departed, beaten by Reason and what Tal called the power of the mind.

He no longer felt in the grip of the invisible hand. As the moments passed the darkness began to give way to light and he heard muffled voices around him. His tongue felt like dry sandpaper in his mouth and the smell of sweat filled his nostrils. He felt an aching which grew into pain as he tried to move. His muscles were seized. Then he suddenly gulped in a mouthful of air. He heard shouts from nearby, women's voices. With a little effort Rick opened his eyes and saw that he was in hospital. As quickly as his senses had returned, so did his memory. He remembered vividly the accident with Laura and the bus.

'Is Laura OK?' were his first words.

'Oh Rick, you're awake,' Ellie exclaimed, and broad smiles adorned Josie's and Tom's faces.

'Please, step away for a few moments,' a nurse said in a matter-of-fact tone of voice, and Rick was subjected to a series of tests over the next five or ten minutes. His body ached from top to toe, but he knew he was alive.

'How bad am I?' he asked the nurse.

'You've been very lucky, Mr Sheldon,' she replied. 'A few days more in here and a couple of weeks of physiotherapy and you should be as right as rain.'

'I love you,' Ellie said loudly.

Chapter 39

28th May 2001

'I must say you're making excellent progress,' the physiotherapist said encouragingly as Rick walked unsteadily along the ward floor, entirely unaided now by crutches or a helping hand.

'I've had a good teacher,' he smiled at Lynn.

'Another day or two and you can go back to the gym, but give it a few weeks before you go hell for leather.' Rick looked at her as if her advice was far too cautious. 'If you don't you'll seriously pull something and you'll have to come back here. Do you hear me?' she said authoritatively, yet in a friendly tone.

'Yes, miss,' Rick joked.

He was due to go home today and he couldn't wait. The consultant wanted to see him first and then he could go, probably around lunch time. He had been in hospital for five days, of which he only remembered two, but being cooped up in a ward was already driving him mad. The rough bed sheets, the endless repetition of having his blood pressure and temperature taken and making small-talk with strangers was getting him down. He longed to plunge into the softness of his own bed and to sleep for ten hours uninterrupted by the hubbub of the ward. But most of all, he wanted to hug Ellie and tell her how much he loved her without a smile from the person in the next bed.

'Mr Sheldon. Mr Sheldon,' Mr Faulks the consultant said, shaking Rick's shoulder gently. He had fallen asleep. 'How are you feeling?'

'Oh, yes, I feel great, doc," Rick answered. 'I can go home today, can't I?'

'I don't see any reason why not. I've spoken to the nurse and the physio and they're happy with your progress. Your charts are satisfactory. You do have someone at home with you?'

'Yes, my fiancée.'

'And she's taking you home, is she?'

'Yes.'

'Then you're discharged.'

'Thank you,' Rick said. 'I hope *not* to see you again,' he joked.

'Likewise,' Mr Faulks replied, without the same degree of humour.

***

Rick cringed as the car turned into the drive. There had been no rain since the accident and the remnants of the collision were still visible in the roadway. A dark red patch could still be seen on the surface of the tarmac where his head had struck it, and various yellow chalk-marks remained from where the police had marked out the point of impact and other material positions of vehicles in their investigation of the accident.

'I'm lucky to be here, aren't I?' he said to Ellie as they got out of the car.

'Too right you are. And I'm lucky to have you here. But do me a favour, think again before you do your Superman act, will you, you frightened us all to death.'

'Well I'm OK, and so is that little rascal next door.'

'Rick.' A shout came from Laura's mum, Jane, next door. She scurried across the shared driveway. 'Thank you so much for everything you've done. And I'm really sorry for what you've had to go through.'

'Mmm. He could easily have died, you know,' Ellie piped up. 'You ought to look after your daughter better.'

'I know,' Jane replied, a tear in her eye. 'I only took my eyes off her for a second and she was gone, out of the door. Dominic screamed in the lounge 'cos he'd trapped his finger in the fireguard and I rushed through to see him. I forgot that I'd left the back door open. I'm so sorry.'

'Accidents happen, don't worry. I survived and so did Laura.'

Rick thought how difficult it must be being at home with

two toddlers; each would constantly vie for attention and like Jane said it was virtually impossible to watch them every waking second and never make a mistake. Mistakes happened, that was a fact of life. Fate decided the consequences of those mistakes. One two year old could wander the streets for an hour unscathed, whereas another could be run over and killed within ten seconds, just as Laura would have been.

'I promise it won't happen again,' she said, producing a bottle of wine from behind her back. 'I know it's not much but I'd like you to have it, just to say thanks, and sorry.'

'Well I appreciate it. Oh, just one other thing,' Rick said.

'Yeah.'

'I expect an invitation to Laura's next birthday party. I love lemon jelly.'

'You're on,' Jane smiled, relieved that the whole business was over.

'Thanks, Jane,' Ellie relented, seeing that her neighbour had genuinely been distraught after the accident.

'You do realise, Miss Greening, that your cooking is the main reason I'm marrying you?' Rick teased as he savoured the lamb and spinach masala Ellie had prepared.

'I knew that all along, Mr Sheldon. Anyway, don't forget it's Mrs Sheldon in less than six weeks.'

It was a bright, sunny day. Ellie had closed the curtains, strategically placed a few scented candles around the room for best effect and set the table beautifully. She had the perfume on that Rick loved her to wear and a low-cut top which, together with the push-up bra, gave her a cleavage that Rick found it difficult not to pay attention to. She had changed her hair as well, and Rick had commented favourably on the new style as soon as he had seen her. In place of the bob she had worn for as long as he could remember her hair was now straight and layered, some of it venturing onto her face in a way he found very sexy. In fact she looked absolutely radiant as her dark brown hair fell across her dusky complexion.

Ellie saw the admiration in Rick's glances and looked into

his eyes long and hard with her deep, brown orbs. He had never been able to discern the iris from the pupil. As they stared lovingly at one another each felt a deep, fervent and intense love, one straight from Cupid's arrow. Rick remembered the good times with Josie, but couldn't recall such a refined, pure feeling of love as he had for Ellie. He had had some great times with Josie, but this was truly special and it brought to the forefront of his mind why he had chosen her above all. It was simple, he really loved her. He had had relationships with more physically attractive women, Josie topping the lot, but it was this feeling, this *bonding*, which reminded him why Ellie was and would always be the love of his life.

He had known Ellie now for five or six years, yet electric shot through him as he reached out and gently stroked her soft face. She pushed her cheek against the back of his hand, like a cat, and closed her eyes. Rick leaned over to her and kissed her warm lips, which parted upon feeling his. Their tongues slowly swirled around each others, wet and sweet with anticipation. Rick slid his hand under Ellie's top and gradually moved it upwards, eventually finding her left breast as she inhaled with pleasure. He pushed her breast upwards and kissed it in a wholesome way which communicated his intentions to his lover.

Ellie stood and took Rick's hand, their meals only half eaten. She led him upstairs and into the bathroom, where she turned on the hot tap and poured a sweet-smelling herbal essence into the flow of water. She sat on the toilet lid and positioned Rick in front of her.

'I nearly lost you,' she said, looking up at him.

'I know,' he replied.

'Don't ever leave me Rick, I don't know what I'd do without you around.'

'You can't get rid of me that easily,' he said. 'Anyway, while ever you're here, why would I want anyone else?'

She unbuttoned his fly and loosened his leather belt. 'You wouldn't,' she replied provocatively. 'Now take off your T-shirt.' Rick obliged. Ellie paused for a moment and took her time admiring his stomach muscles. Rick's tummy was completely flat and adorned with several solid plates of muscle. She stroked his abdomen with the tips of her fingers, ever such a slight touch, which sent tingles of delight through Rick's senses. Then her roving fingers headed south and she prised open the top button of his jeans, easing the rough material over his bottom until the denim fell to the floor. Rick instinctively stepped out of the jeans and picked them up, discarding them in a pile together with his T-shirt.

His manhood stood proud and ready inside the constraints of his tight boxer shorts, but he waited, at his lover's whim. Ellie let out a barely audible sigh as her forefinger alone caressed the length of his member, which twitched at her touch, eager to oblige.

The room was becoming really warm as the steam from the bath swirled in the air. The steam particles were picked out in remarkable fashion by the stream of sunlight that flooded through the closed window. Ellie cupped Rick's buttocks in her hands and drew him closer to her, his hardness now pressing against her face. She nibbled him through the boxers and he groaned as the rising feelings pervaded his body. He raked her hair with his fingers and pulled her face closer still to him. He wanted her so badly it hurt.

Ellie stood and they began a kiss which Rick rated as the best he had ever had. She turned off the taps and felt the water.

'Nice and hot,' she said.

After removing his socks unceremoniously she took her time relieving him of his underwear. He basked in the attention as Ellie fondled his balls and his bottom with fervour, and when she slowly pulled down his boxers he was wet with expectancy. Just as the mouth waters when expecting delicious food, so he was lubricated by love juices as a foretaste of sex with the one he loved.

'Excuse me, madam,' he said stood there stark naked, 'It hasn't escaped my attention that you are still fully clothed.'

'Not for long,' she replied, and began unbuttoning her top, all the while looking Rick in the eyes with a cheeky smile on her face. Rick watched her as if it was about to be the first time he had seen her nude. She pulled the top over her shoulders to reveal a lacy white bra which was a perfect contrast to her tanned skin. Then she flung open her wrap-around skirt and it found itself in the growing pile of clothes in the corner of the room. She too had sported a flat tummy until about two months ago when her child had had a growth spurt and created a bump there. The bump had grown a little since then but was not large by most people's standards at five months pregnant. Rick licked his lips as she opened the front-fastening bra, leaving the straps over her shoulders as her pert breasts invited his gaze.

He could wait no longer and he pulled Ellie to him kissing her deeply and passionately this time. The soul-mate kiss of ten minutes earlier gave way to a hot and sex-driven one; each party bit the others lips just short of drawing blood, each plunged their tongue deep into the other's mouth as if in search of greater pleasure which was there for the taking.

Ellie shrugged off the remaining material from her shoulders and Rick reached down and without a by-your-leave ripped off her panties leaving the torn lace on the carpet. There was no objection raised as Ellie stepped into the steaming water, pulling Rick after her. Their mouths seemed locked inextricably together as they entered the hot, bubbly water. Rick placed Ellie's right leg over the edge of the bath and pushed her other leg up onto the wall as he thrust himself deep into her. At first he couldn't feel her soft wet skin because of the water, but after a moment he felt her inner muscles grip him as she pushed her pelvis towards him, eager to capture every inch of him inside her. Rick realised just how aroused Ellie had been when, after only a few seconds, she cried out in ecstasy and gripped his shoulders tightly as she came in the warm water. Mere seconds later she dug her nails into the skin of his back as she orgasmed a second time, this time even more intensely.

Rick was incredibly turned-on but she pushed him away from her and told him to lie on his back. He lay spread-eagled in the water as Ellie leaned over him and took his aching cock into her mouth. She teased him with alternate sucks and swirls of her tongue driving him to a seventh heaven as he came in long, strong bursts. The short yet euphoric love-making left them totally spent. Ellie sat up in front of Rick among the bubbles which hadn't even had time to dissipate.

'I love you,' she said.

'And I love you,' he replied.

'I can't wait for our honeymoon,' Ellie said.

'Oh, yeah, I can't believe I forgot to tell you.'

'Tell me what?'

'I've changed things slightly, I hope you don't mind. What with the accident and everything it slipped my mind.'

'Changed things, without asking me first? Rick, what are talking about, I've been looking forward to the Maldives for months?'

'Well, it's cost quite a bit more, but I've booked us an extra week.'

Ellie frowned. 'How much extra?'

'Just over nine hundred pounds.'

'Bloody hell! This honeymoon's costing an arm and a leg as it is; why have you decided to do that and more to the point why didn't I get a say?'

'I thought you'd be pleased. I know it's more money but I hope this is the only honeymoon I ever have, and I want it to be *extra* special for us.'

'But it's already special.'

'Listen, if you want to change it back to a fortnight then we'll do it, but just think… *three* weeks.'

Ellie was a forthright individual and didn't like to be dictated to, but she thought about it for a few moments. Then she stayed silent and let Rick stew for a few minutes.

'It sounds great,' she concluded, and she turned round and gave Rick a big hug. 'But listen, buster, when we're married neither of us makes big decisions without the other's say-so, OK?'

'Sounds good to me.'

Rick breathed a quiet sigh of relief.

He and Ellie sat in the warm water, his arms around her, for almost half an hour without speaking a word. They simply enjoyed being with one another, being together as a couple. Such was their understanding of each other that constant chatter and 'filling in the quiet gaps' were not necessary.

Despite the serenity, Rick's heart was still heavy. He looked at the back of Ellie's head and put his face to her wet hair. He wondered how long he would have the privilege of being with her and whether he would see little Rebecca, progressing so well in the comfort of the womb, be born and grow into a wonderful young woman like her mother.

Chapter 40

31ˢᵗ May 2001

A patrol car crept along the leafy suburb by the park.

Sixty or seventy years ago the large Victorian and Edwardian houses, set back from the road, would have been *the* place to live in Leeds. Now they were inhabited by only a handful of respectable families who, when looking at the interiors and the park opposite on considering whether to buy, saw unlimited potential due to their sheer size. The truth was that the majority of the once proud dwellings had been bought by wealthy landlords and butchered, cut up into many small and basic flats, most of which were now run-down and occupied by prostitutes, poor students and undesirables. Their gardens, which would once have been the envy of inner-city dwellers, were now reduced to an untidy mess after decades of neglect. Where trimmed hedges and lawns once showed pride, now used syringes and burnt out shells of cars showed an ever-increasing apathy and indifference.

Incongruously, the streets were lined with beautiful trees which, in the face of reality, gave the district a pleasant look. The park boasted sweeping verdant lawns. In fact, Nature was doing her best to maintain the area's original beauty, but she was being short-changed at every turn by greed, hate and vice. The creators of the suburb would turn in their graves if they could see what havoc their successors had wreaked.

Amber neon lit the mostly deserted streets. Three-ten on a Thursday morning meant that most people were dead to the world. A few were legitimately out and about; late-night take-away owners on their way home, market workers up with the lark for their usual early start, Sergeant Kemp supposedly keeping the peace. Others not in their beds were on the streets, skulking and lurking, up to no good. Night burglars watchful of an opportunity or clandestine drug-dealers using the darkness as a cover for their evil. The occasional new BMW or Mercedes sidled along, ridiculously out of place, its driver on the lookout for his usual bit-on-the-side while his wife slept at home, or perhaps a new slim-line, heroin-filled waif would present herself tonight to fulfil his more depraved fantasies.

So much more was going on than the empty streets revealed.

'A new face?' Sergeant Kemp said to the woman standing on the corner as he drew his car to a halt. She was fairly attractive in the face, deep brown eyes and long dark hair. It was a balmy night and she wore a long, flimsy three-quarter length coat opened at the front, revealing to prospective 'clients' her bare midriff and tight black cut-off jeans.

She had enough experience to know that it was a mistake to antagonise the police. She could be arrested for loitering for the purpose of prostitution and one wrong word could land her in a cell again, for the umpteenth time, which she wanted to avoid at all costs.

'Yeah.'

'Who's your pimp?' Kemp asked, unfolding himself from the driver's seat as he alighted the police car.

'I work for myself,' she replied, taking a final puff of her cigarette and throwing it down onto the grass verge.

'Oh, yeah. They all do. It's funny, really. So, name?' he said, getting a pen and notepad from his pocket.'

'You're not locking me up, are you?'

'Name,' he said, with a slightly raised voice.

'Anna.'

'And the rest.'

'Greening. Anna Greening.'

'Date of birth.'

'December the 8th, sixty-nine.'

'Address.'

'I live with a mate.'

'Address,' he repeated impatiently.

'13, Millers Lane. Just over there.'

'Thank you. That wasn't too difficult was it?'

Anna looked up to the heavens as Kemp ran her details through the Police National Computer. A few minutes of silence past, during which she smoked another cigarette.

'Your last address, which city was it in?'

'Manchester.'

'OK. You're not wanted.' He looked her up and down and, feigning an American accent, said sarcastically, 'Have a nice day now.'

'Wanker,' Anna said aloud as Kemp's police car drove off.

Half an hour passed and she was about to head off home when she saw a red Saab turn into the street. First, the occupant spoke to Janie who was standing fifty yards or so down the road, then he headed her way. As he approached he slowed, viewing what was on offer. The nearside window glided down as he looked at her.

'Do you do blow-jobs?' the middle-aged man asked.

'Bread and butter,' she replied.

'How much?'

She quickly glanced at the car and the look of the man.

'Fifteen,' she said.

'Ten,' he answered.

'Fifteen,' Anna repeated.

'Fifteen it is.'

She climbed into his car and sank into the cream leather.

'Where shall we go?' the man asked.

'Drive up that street,' Anna pointed. 'There are some garages and no-one can see us behind there.'

Having parked behind the garages the man, fairly distinguished-looking with grey encroaching onto an otherwise full head of brown hair, turned off the engine and locked the doors.

'Take off your coat,' he said politely. Anna obliged.

'How much for full sex?' he asked.

'Look, I'm not being funny mister, but what do you actually want?'

'Let's start with you stripping for me, then giving me a blow-job. After that, I want to give it to you from behind.'

'Whoa. One thing at once.'

'Why?'

Anna looked at the man as if he was speaking Chinese. 'Well, usually it takes a while between one thing and another, you know what I'm saying?'

'How about we go to a flat that I own near to here. It's between tenants. We can spend what time we like there?'

'Hey, this a bit freaky. I don't normally…'

'Shh. Do you want to or not?'

'Well, fifteen quid's out then.'

'I'll pay you fifty pounds.'

'For how long?'

'Say an hour?'

'There's no-one else at this flat of yours, is there?'

'No.'

'All right then.'

The Saab moved almost silently through the streets, its automatic gearbox whirring quietly along the straights. Anna was somewhat apprehensive about the arrangement, but she had to face facts. Her line of work was dangerous, per se. Any punter could turn weird at any time of any day, wherever they were. She could find herself screwing the next Jack the Ripper, as could any of the girls, without so much as an inkling as to his intentions. So a middle-aged man taking her to a flat in a nice car was hardly reason for serious suspicion. The fact that most of them preferred a pathetic fumble behind the garages didn't make this man more, or less, menacing. And fifty quid in less than an hour was a little more than she earned with four or five punters on a Friday or Saturday night.

After about five minutes the car drew up outside a new-looking complex of flats in the Roundhay area, and she was led into the complex. Moments later the man opened the door of flat 16 and Anna walked into the most plush accommodation she had ever set eyes upon. Her feet sank into the thick, salmon coloured carpet and the kitchen - to her it was out of this world. She looked around in awe at the expensive, modern décor and wished she had done something more constructive with her life, something that would have given her more of a chance to live like this, or at least not to live the way she did.

'Do you like it?' the man asked.

'There's not a lot to dislike, is there?' she said, still perusing the place.

'Please, make yourself comfortable,' he said, gesturing for her to sit on the sumptuous leather settee.

'Would you like a drink?'

Anna snapped herself from her reverie by asking herself what the hell she was doing here. A beautiful apartment, a rich middle-aged fairly good-looking man who could probably get any woman he wanted, yet he chose to bring her to the flat at three in the morning. Why?

'A drink? This feels like "Pretty Woman". What's going on?'

'Look, do you want a drink or not, it's simple?'

'Martini then. Please.'

'I'm Joe. That's all you need to know, but we can hardly talk and make love when we don't even know each other's names. And you are?'

'Anna.'

'OK, Anna. I've been looking forward to this little striptease. When you're ready.' Joe sat back in a chair.

'I'd like the money first, if you don't mind.'

'Business acumen as well, eh?' and he counted out five crisp ten pound notes from his wallet and handed them to her. Anna stuffed them into her tiny handbag and placed it on a table. Then she began her striptease. Until four years ago she had worked as a lap-dancer in a Manchester 'gentleman's' club as well as a lady of the night and so she knew the moves and what men liked. That was until the owner of the club had sacked her after finding her injecting in the toilets. She told her that she had become too thin anyway and gave her the push that night. Her show seemed to delight Joe and he clapped when she had finished.

Much to her surprise Joe then began to strip provocatively himself. He did not have the finesse or the slinky moves that she had, but she found herself strangely turned on by him. He was about fifty years of age, but he had kept himself in trim condition and regular sun-beds had given him an all-over tan, albeit entirely false. As she sat on her haunches on the rug Joe removed all his clothes and slipped on what she recognised as a ribbed condom. She could not fail to notice that he was extremely well-endowed.

He approached her and spent the best part of five minutes gently stroking her body all over except her erogenous areas. She found herself taking little gasps of delight at his touch as she anticipated more intimate contact. A thought entered her head that she was not supposed to be enjoying this. With other clients she laid back and thought of other things while they had their way with her. She had never had an iota of pleasure from sex with punters before, but this man seemed different.

Gradually, he progressed to licking her nipples in a way which made her squirm, while he made tiny circular movements with his middle finger as he fondled her clitoris. She longed to have him inside her and she did not have to wait for her wish. Without warning he roughly flipped her over so that she was laying face-down on the soft rug. He pulled her legs apart and raised her tummy from the floor with his hand. Then he plunged his enormous manhood into her, not by degrees but with one huge lunge which made Anna cry out. His rhythmic thrusts ventured deep into her, deeper than she had ever been penetrated, and within minutes she let out cries of absolute ecstasy as she came twice within the space of seconds. As Joe reached climax he held himself up to the hilt inside her and Anna thought she would burst, both physically and with pleasure. Then he was gone, off to the bathroom.

As she lay on the white rug, Anna felt carnally satisfied. With the exception of her first boyfriend many years ago, no man had ever given her an orgasm. In private she had used sex aids to satisfy her needs, but Joe had made her remember what the difference was between self-gratification and real sex with another person. She could not believe that she had had this experience, completely out of the blue. But it had excited her, immensely.

As Joe returned from the bathroom she had got half dressed.

'Going so soon?' he asked gently.

'Well, where is there to go from here?'

'Fifty's a lot to pay for fifteen minutes. Stay and chat for a while; finish your drink.'

'OK,' she replied, and finished dressing.

'Tell me a bit about yourself,' Joe said as she sat in the chair opposite his.

'Me? Oh, I don't think you'd be interested in my failed life.'

'What is failure? Everybody has a different view of failure and success?'

'Living in a shitty little flat, working as a prostitute, no money, no family to speak of. Is that enough?'

'What would you want out of life?'

She sighed. 'Some money would be nice.'

'So you wouldn't have to work for your next fix, you mean?'

Anna looked shocked.

Joe pointed to her forearms, where track marks scarred her skin.

'Yes, that's right,' she snapped. 'A fucking smack head as well. Who are you to judge anyway, Mr High and Mighty?'

Joe raised his hand as a gesture of surrender. 'I'm not judging you or anyone else for that matter. So you take heroin, big deal. It's not as if you're the only one.'

'Yeah, and because of that I have to... do what I do.'

'So you've no family at all, then?'

'How do you suppose they'd react if they knew what I did?'

'I don't know. But like you say, judging people doesn't help.'

'I haven't seen my parents for thirteen years and I don't want to either. I've a sister, Ellie. I bumped into her by mistake recently and you should have seen her. Pretty, getting married, good job, pregnant. She turned her nose up at me. Fucking bitch, she's got everything, I've got nothing and she sticks her nose up at me. She was always their favourite. Ellie this, Ellie that. I could kill her.'

'You don't mean that.'

'Don't I? I think I do.' Anna's eyes shone with hatred for her younger sister.

'You'd actually kill your sister?'

'She's no sister of mine. She never helped me when we were younger. She couldn't care less if I live or die. Why should a bitch like that have so much in life, and me, who just wanted some love, have nothing?'

'All things are possible,' Joe remarked.

'What?'

He took a large swig of wine from his glass. 'Like I say, anything can be worked out, one way or another.'

'I was just talking about my sister.'

'Exactly. If you want her gone, it can be arranged.'

'Are you for real?'

'Why haven't you done it already?'

'Since I met her I've wanted to, but I don't know how.'

'Well, first you need a weapon, one that's untraceable, then you need to organise when and where.'

'And you can do that, can you?'

'I can do the first part. I can provide you with a small pistol which can't be traced back to anyone.'

Anna thought for a moment. 'Look, let's get this straight. I've only just met you and you'd get me a hot gun?'

'Everything has to be paid for, Anna, one way or another.'

'Meaning?'

'I'd want you to do some work for me in return.'

'Work? What work?'

'Work that would get you the gun and mean that you don't have to walk the streets on a night.'

'I'm listening.'

'I have seven of these flats, some in Leeds and some in Sheffield. I need someone I can trust to live in them all, when I say. You might be here one day and in Sheffield the next. Joe's not my real name and the Saab is on false number plates. No-one knows where I live or who I am. I 'acquire' large amounts of drugs which I have to distribute quickly and efficiently. I need someone, someone completely anonymous, to help me do that. Someone who wants a better lifestyle, someone who will appreciate the opportunity. That person will *keep their mouth shut*, tell no-one what they do, and reap the benefits. Somewhere decent to live, free heroin for personal use, and a life off the street. Let's call getting you the gun a goodwill gesture, shall we? What do you say?'

'I'm never going to get a better offer. I'll take it.'

'Listen carefully. If you let me down once, just once, I'll kill you. Don't take it personally, it's a matter of my own survival. If you do as I say, you stand to earn a good crust and you won't have to fuck dickheads every day to live.'

'I said I'll take it,' Anna said without hesitation.

Chapter 41

'RICHARD,' Parsons bawled from his office.

Rick knew what this was about. Heads turned as Rick walked over to the tyrant's layer. Parsons had been away to Mexico, holidaying on his own, for the past three weeks and it hadn't taken him long to find the missing item from his bottom drawer. It was only nine thirty.

He decided that attack was the best form of defence, a course of action no-one else would have dreamt of taking with the tin-pot general manager.

Rick closed Parsons's office door behind him. 'I really would appreciate it if you didn't put me down in front of my staff by shouting at me. In fact, I won't stand for it.'

'I beg your pardon,' Frank retorted, challenging him further.

'I'm the manager of this department and for me to do *my* job well I have to have the respect of those who work for me. How can I earn that respect when you put me down like that?'

'Never mind all that…'

'No. I'm sorry, it's just not good enough. I've been in hospital in a bloody coma while you've been sunning yourself on holiday, so don't come back here laying the law down the minute you walk in.'

'Oh, I didn't know about that. What happened?'

'I was involved in an accident. I got run over by a bus.'

'I'm sorry, Rick,' he relented. 'Let's start this morning again shall we?'

'Good idea. Now what did you want me for? I'm really busy today.' He smirked inwardly.

'Are you fully fit now, after the accident?' Parsons tried to atone for his unreasonable behaviour, but Rick wasn't about to let him off the hook.

'Thank you, yes. They were impressed upstairs that I came back to work so soon, particularly with you being on holiday, so if you'd lay off for a while.'

'I've said I'm sorry, now let that be an end to it.' His contrite approach didn't last long as he sensed Rick making a meal out the situation.

'The reason I called you over was to ask whether you've been using my office whilst I've been away.'

'No. Why would I?'

'I don't know.'

'Well, I haven't. I always use my usual desk.'

'Have you seen anyone in my office?'

'No. But I haven't been keeping a look-out either. What's wrong?'

'Something...very personal has gone missing.'

'Really? What?'

He knew that his boss couldn't tell the truth.

'What it is has no bearing on the fact that it was in a locked drawer. That drawer has been opened, my things have been taken out and the drawer carefully put back as it was, together with the key which I hid.'

Rick feigned a confused look. 'Why would anyone go to such lengths? What's been taken, something valuable?'

'Valuable to me, yes. As you probably know my mother is all but senile, so I keep important papers in that locked drawer rather than at home where she might lose or damage them,' he lied.

'Well thank goodness it's nothing that can't be replaced,' Rick said.

'That's not the point,' Parsons said in a raised voice. 'Someone's been sneaking around amongst my private things, and I won't tolerate it.'

'I can understand why you're cross, don't get me wrong, but all you can do is get replacement documents and make sure the office is locked when you aren't around.

'I want you to find out who's responsible, Rick. Ask around, keep your ear to the ground. Any useful information, let me know.'

'No.' Rick flatly refused. For one, he knew that no-one other than him was responsible. Secondly, let the worm squirm, he thought. He could hardly initiate a full investigation involving the police because, by his own admission, nothing of monetary value had been stolen, and he couldn't reveal to them what had, in truth, been taken. Besides, this moron had sent him three disgusting letters after Ellie's death in the other time-line, so why should he humour him by pretending to help him out when he was hiding a weapon? Sod you, he thought.

'What!' Parsons was stunned by his underling's lack of co-operation.

'You heard me. Listen, you might be my boss but that doesn't make me your skivvy. I haven't been in your drawers and I haven't got the slightest clue who has. You won't even tell me honestly what's been stolen, so you do the Sherlock Holmes bit. Important papers, indeed.'

Frank Parsons was an explosive character even when unprovoked, and Rick could almost see his face turn redder by the second. He was the human version of an old steam-engine boiler as it grew hotter and hotter prior to letting off steam.

'GET OUT! GET OUT,' he roared.

Rick calmly stood up, opened the door and walked into the main office. He deliberately left the door open behind him as a mark of disrespect. As he made his way over to his desk everyone looked on. They had heard Parsons's rantings before but this was monumental, something to talk about for weeks to come.

As Rick sat down amid silence from twenty-odd staff, Parsons emerged from the inner office. The boiler still needed to expel more steam.

'If I find anyone in my office, anyone,' he shouted, pointing his finger wildly at no-one in particular, 'their feet won't touch. And when I find out *who's been in my drawers* there'll be hell to pay. HELL.' And with that he disappeared back into his den, slamming the door with sufficient force as to crack the frame on the left side.

'I can't imagine anyone wanting to go in *his* drawers,' Rick said to Danielle, producing laughter from those within earshot, as Parsons looked through the venetian blinds into the main office like a caged animal longing to eat the onlookers.

Rick grinned, yet he knew that today he had made an enemy.

Chapter 41

Danielle kept stealing glances at Rick. Each time he felt her eyes on him and looked up she quickly averted her gaze. He didn't know whether she was doing it on purpose and playing a game with him or whether her interest in him had, through no fault of his own, been re-kindled. He hoped to God she was simply messing about. He felt as if he was at school again in the classroom where teenagers experimenting with their newly found sexuality fluttered their eyelashes, or flexed their muscles, at the opposite sex, inviting exciting new feelings while the teacher droned on about algebra or Chamberlain's naivety.

But this was no classroom. Neither was it time for games. This was an alternate reality, one in which Rick had been given a second chance to avert two disasters; the death of his wife and child to be, and considerable human suffering. There was no place for flirtatious fooling around or elicit liaisons where the only gratification was a quick fumble with a different body. That was tacky and trivial in this context and Rick wouldn't give it a second thought.

He threw himself into his work to help him ignore Danielle's advances and to pass the time. He was no nearer to identifying the killer than he had been a month ago when he arrived in the supermarket, and he had no idea how to find out. All he could do was live from one day to the next, surviving each day that passed until the time came for him to influence the event that changed history. If in the interim he could eliminate those who appeared to have a motive then all well and good, but the task was tiring him mentally.

Danielle clicked her thumb and middle finger together, bringing Rick back into the real world.

'Earth to Rick,' she joked, smiling at him.

'Sorry, I was miles away,' he replied, shuffling his papers.

He really wasn't in the mood for idle chat this lunchtime and so decided to go to the quiet room. He hoped that Sarah wasn't there and he breathed a sigh of relief when the room was empty. Plonking himself down into the comfy chair he let his head rest on the high back. He felt emotionally drained today. After a few quiet moments the door opened and Danielle stepped into the room.

'Are you feeling OK?' she asked.

Rick opened his heavy lids. 'Hi there. Yeah, I'm fine, just a little tired.'

'I thought you might be a bit upset, you know about Parsons this morning.'

'Parsons? Oh, he's the least of my worries.' Rick cringed as soon as he said the words because it gave Danielle the perfect opportunity to quiz him further.

'What is it then, home life? I'm...not prying, it's just that you've not been yourself today and I thought I maybe able to help.'

'No-one can help, Danny, no-one at all.'

'Oh come on, I know you've a lot to worry about but thing's can't be *that* bad.'

'They are, believe me,' he said, not looking at her at all.

'Sometimes it helps to forget about life's problems, just for a short time, and live a little.'

'You're probably right,' Rick said dismissively.

'I am,' she replied, putting her hand on his knee.

Rick opened his eyes again and saw her release a further button on an already revealing blouse.

'No. Don't do that,' he said.

Danielle checked that there was nobody outside the door and she stood above him whilst undoing yet another button. She knelt before him, leaning forwards. This revealed her breasts in their entirety as she wore no bra. Her soft white skin caused Rick to stir, but only for a moment.

'No,' he said firmly.

'Sorry, I was only trying to cheer you up.'

'Danny, I thought we'd discussed this. Like I said before, I find you really attractive but it's just not right. Is it?'

'You need a boost in your life. Everything's against you at the moment. I'm sure a roll in the hay will perk you up a little. After all it doesn't have to go any further, our little secret.' With that she kissed him on the lips hard and rubbed her breasts on his chest. He could feel her erect nipples through her flimsy blouse and his shirt.

Rick pushed her away. 'I said no. What is it about that you don't understand?'

'Fine. It's fine.' Danielle hurriedly fastened her blouse and stroked her hair into place. 'No means no. I can live with that. What exactly is it that your pregnant, sickly wife can give you that I can't, answer me that?'

'Just go away will you,' Rick said as calmly as he could.

'Maybe I should ask her,' she continued. 'Maybe I should ask what a pregnant woman does to keep her man happy. Being out of shape, frumpy and worried about what she's gonna give birth to must be a turn on for you, eh. More than a fit young woman willing to give you anything in bed. You sick fuck,' Danielle said, storming out of the room and slamming the door behind her.

Chapter 42

6ᵗʰ June 2001

Ellie felt fed up. She had left work early today saying that she was nauseous and a little dizzy. In truth she was neither, but her hormones raced and she just couldn't face customers complaining about the bar-codes giving the wrong prices at the tills. Being the deputy manager at the supermarket meant doing all the tough tasks that the manager farmed off in addition to her own jobs. She was good at her job, only narrowly being beaten to a manager's post recently at a larger store by a much more experienced candidate. Under normal circumstances Ellie liked her work, she considered it a career, but today they could all whistle because she was intent on having a little time to herself, time which technically she wasn't entitled to, making it all the more enjoyable.

Having tucked into a fatty cheese and bacon roll and two cups of tea, she headed for the shops in Garforth. It was a warm, sunny day and she loved to window-shop. The town had plenty of shops, mostly contained in one small area, and she fancied an hour's stroll in the sunshine.

The future looks brilliant, she thought to herself as she perused a brochure on the Maldives. The travel agent's was fairly quiet, most people having booked their getaways in the colder months, cheering themselves up with a sunny break to look forward to amid the winds and frosts of the Winter months. A woman that looked similar to herself sat at one of the desks with a beautiful little girl kicking her legs on the next chair, clearly bored with shopping in general. Ellie was convinced that she and Rick would have a girl, and it wouldn't be long before she was sat in the same seat booking a holiday with her daughter sat beside her.

Everywhere she looked, mums had children in tow. It was something that she had never really noticed before. As she sat on a bench and looked around her she saw children everywhere. Most were under the age of five as it was just after two o'clock and the older ones were in school, yet there were so many of them. Most of the mothers looked harassed by their offspring, some even showed signs that they wished the children weren't there slowing them down or cramping their style. Conversely, babies cried in push-chairs, two, and three-year-olds pulled against their parents arms and others looked bored at being dragged out to the shops. In short, the relationships between the two age groups looked less than harmonious. It won't be like that for me, she said under her breath.

Then someone caught her eye, someone whom she would recognise anywhere. Sarah Bowers walked nonchalantly passed her and into the chemists. Ellie's face reddened instantly. This was the third time she had seen this woman in Garforth recently, despite the fact that she lived at the other side of Leeds. This was the woman, the girl, who had lied to her face about having an affair with Rick. Because she couldn't have him she thought she'd spoil it for Rick and herself. A nasty piece of work, Ellie thought. And why was she here, miles away from where she lived and worked? Ellie's imagination began to work overtime. Sarah could be some kind of stalker, looking for a chance meeting with the man she was still infatuated with. Maybe she intended to taunt them by turning up, a bad penny that just wouldn't go away, in the hope that she would come between them and split them up. She had tried it before. There she was, as cool as you like, strolling along as though butter wouldn't melt in her vitriolic little mouth.

Ellie thought of ignoring her, but her fiery temper was much too strong for that. If something needed confronting it would be confronted, no matter how difficult. She stood up and stared at the door of the chemists, her heart beating faster and her breathing becoming deeper. Adrenaline pumped through her body, exaggerating her emotional state even further. The wait seemed like an eternity, but eventually Sarah emerged from the shop slinging her handbag over her shoulder.

Ellie approached her, still unnoticed.

'Something your own chemist doesn't stock, is it?' she said rudely.

Sarah jumped, not expecting anyone to speak to her.

'Oh, it's you.'

'Yes, it's me.'

The women stopped and faced one another.

'Well?' Ellie asked, as if she wanted an answer to everything.

'Well what?' Sarah said, a disdainful look on her face.

'What are you doing round here?'

'Sorry? When was it I became answerable to you? I must have missed that one'

'Don't get funny with me.'

'Look, what do you want? I'm in a rush.'

'I want to know why you keep coming round here. I saw you in Garforth not so long ago as well. You don't live here and you don't work here.'

'My, my. You really *are* insecure, aren't you? I thought you trusted your boyfriend, my mistake, your fiancée.'

'I do. It's you I don't trust.'

'And why's that, then?'

'You made a play for him once, you were turned down and you got nasty. So, I'll ask you again, what are doing here?'

'You're so naïve, for your age. Listen, you know nothing. But I'll not act like you, I'll give you a straight answer. My parents have split up recently and my mum's bought a little semi out here. I'm visiting her fairly regularly at the moment because she's an emotional wreck, a bit like yourself. That's why I'm round here. Satisfied?'

'Not really, no. You're a liar, that's been proven, so what's to say you won't lie again?'

'Look, I've no time for you or your precious boyfriend, so just leave me alone.'

'Yeah, well, you just leave us alone and get your own fella.'

Sarah began to get angry. 'Open your eyes, Eleanor. Look

around you... things may not be as they seem.'

'You stirring whore,' Ellie shouted, and slapped Sarah across the face with the palm of her hand.

Sarah clenched her fists. As she did so she saw terror on Ellie's face as she put her hands to her tummy to protect her baby. Sarah knew immediately that it would be wrong to trade blows with a pregnant woman. She hated Ellie's stupidity and felt as though she wanted to teach her a lesson for embarrassing her in the street, but she wasn't about to be held responsible if anything happened to the baby. Instead, she turned on her heal and stormed away before the situation got totally out of hand.

Ellie watched Sarah stride away, partly pleased with herself for standing up to the brazen woman, but equally as humiliated at the scene she had created and the potential danger she had placed her unborn child in.

Chapter 43

The black ball rocketed into the middle pocket with a resounding bang, as Rick lifted his cue in triumph.

'Excuse me,' the manager said, 'I think it's probably best if you make that your last game, lads.'

'Whatever,' Rick said, the worse for a few pints too many.

Neither he nor Tom drank a great deal, so the seventh pint of lager really took its toll, on both of them.

They sat down heavily on the cushioned seats at the snooker club, away from the tables, the manager keeping a watchful eye on them.

'I'm for the bloody high-jump,' Rick said to Tom, slurring his words, and taking another gulp of lager.

'Ha, ha, ha,' Tom laughed. 'Why?'

'Ellie's getting suspicious about Sarah.'

'Sarah? But I thought all that was finished with. I thought you'd convinced her nothing happened?'

'I had.' Rick looked pensive. Every time he remembered deceiving Ellie he felt a little ashamed. 'But she saw Sarah on Main Street a couple of days ago and it's sparked it off again.'

'But nothing's changed, has it?'

'No. Yes. Sarah virtually told her that what she believed was wrong, and *you* know Ellie. She smacked her one.'

'You've got a feisty one there, mate. I've always said that.'

'Yeah, yeah. I love her though,' he said, the genuineness of the statement patently obvious as he spoke incoherently from the heart. Rick was one of those people who, in drink, became nostalgic and emotional.

'What you gonna do?'

'Nothing I can do. Just hope that it blows over.'

'You're a pillock, do you know that?'

'What?'

'You heard. Why don't you just tell Ellie what happened? It's two years ago now. It was when you and her were separated anyway, so she'll understand.'

'But I've lied, Tom. I've lied through my bloody teeth.' One or two customers looked his way disapprovingly.

'Keep your voice down, you prat, you'll get us kicked out.'

'OK, OK. But you're my pal. If I can't talk to you about it, who can I talk to?'

'Let it simmer down itself,' Tom suggested.

'I can't lose her, not now,' Rick said, emptying his glass.

'Take it easy, will you. Your not gonna lose her, but you've got to keep your head.'

'Keep my head? You don't know the half of it.'

'I don't know whether I want to,' Tom said, and he walked towards the bar.

Rick looked around him. The alcohol produced a hazy glare as he surveyed the room. Sober people played snooker, and tennis on the games machine. They had no idea what their futures held, but he did. The chances were that most of their children were going to die. Not many would survive the modern-day plague that was soon about to rip through humanity. In just a few decades the Reaper was going to be in full employ; the hospitals would be full to bursting with people who, for many years to come, would be untreatable as the world's professors of medicine gathered in vain, clueless as to how to combat the new disease. It would make A.I.D.S. look like measles. Yet they played their snooker, oblivious. Their fate rested with him. A drunk man, blindly heading towards an unknown conflict on a given date. When 21st July arrives, he thought, history will be re-written by a maniac from the future, permitted by those around him to wreak havoc on his own kind for the purposes of entertainment.

'I've got you a black coffee,' Tom said, sitting down beside Rick. 'Me as well. I think we've drunk enough.'

Rick sighed. 'Why not drink ourselves to death?'

'Eh, now pack that in right now. You're getting married in a month, and you'll be a dad later this year, so stop talking crap and cheer up for God's sake.'

'God? I grew up thinking that God protected us. I mean, we've got free will and all that, so you don't expect Him to intervene in wars created by mankind, but you think He'd stop us from getting hurt by…you know, outside influences.'

'What the hell are you talking about? Have you been drinking something different to me?'

'No. It's true, I'm afraid.'

'You've never been madly religious, so what's all this about?'

'I mustn't lose Ellie,' he said, gripping Tom's arm hard.

'Calm down. Why would you lose her?'

'I mustn't lose her. I *have* to be with her, you see.'

'I know, you love her.'

'I have to be with her, at that point in time. If I'm not there, she's going to die.'

'What? What do you mean?'

'She'll be shot. Shot dead, Tom.' Rick put two fingers to his forehead.

'Are you mad?' Tom protested.

'No. I wish I was. Yeah, it's true. At about eight…'

As Rick spoke the words he seemed to slow down. Tom became motionless, the perplexed look on his face seeming to set as Rick looked on. He looked around him as the place became absolutely silent. The music ceased, the games machines were silenced and the players stopped playing, some stood watching the tables and others half way through playing their shots. Everyone around him looked like dummies.

'Tom. TOM,' Rick shouted at his friend, but he may as well have spoken to a dead man. He touched Tom's face. It felt normal, yet Tom stared at him, frozen. Rick's drunken condition left him instantly as the shock of the situation overrode the feeling of inebriation. Then he laughed out loud.

'You. It's you isn't it,' he said in a raised voice. 'Rusak, or whatever your name is. Your trying to frighten me again, aren't you? Well I've beaten your attempts before. YOU'RE A FAILURE. Now let's get back to reality. LEAVE ME ALONE.'

There was no change. All was silent, all was still.

Rick began to think on his feet, only slightly affected now by the alcohol. Use your mind, he repeated to himself several times, but nothing around him altered for better or for worse. He walked towards the bar, behind which several mannequins stood. As he neared the bar, he felt an unusual tug at his clothing. And again, the skin on his face was pulled yet no-one except him was moving here. He concentrated deeply, telling himself that this was a trick, another falsehood designed to implant sufficient fear in him to kill him. He must avoid the effect of the rule of reciprocation. It had saved his life once, and it would kill him if he let it.

In spite of his best efforts, the tugging continued until he could not move. He stood, entirely controlled by whatever force was busy at work, unable to move forwards, backwards, any way. His body was at the mercy of the force. Suddenly, his head was snapped back and he looked involuntarily at the ceiling. Try as he might, Rick could not even move his eyeballs; they were fixed. Next, he felt the tugging at his head. It was as though an invisible plunger had been placed over his head and was being pulled upwards. He used every ounce of his mental strength to fight off what he believed to be the work of Rusak, but he may as well have tried to push a piece of cotton through a brick wall.

His head seemed to be stretching, elongating towards the ceiling of the snooker room. Likewise, his body was being pulled out of shape, as if on an ancient rack. The ceiling drew closer to him and he was in great pain, yet he could not shout out. Again he tried to dismiss the event, longing to be sat with his friend once more discussing…discussing what? Realisation hit him like a steam-train. Rick remembered what he had been saying to Tom before all this happened. In his stupor, he had begun to discuss Ellie's fate; he even remembered telling Tom that she would be shot and mentioning a time. Then he remembered Tal's warning that if he spoke the truth to anyone he would fail in his quest and all would be lost because it would adversely affect the timeline.

'NOOOOOOOOO,' Rick bellowed silently. How could he have been so stupid. He knew the rules. A few drinks and everything was lost; Ellie, his child, his life.

Rick's grief superseded physical pain as he slipped into insensibility.

Chapter 44

Anna had dressed for the occasion. She had become accustomed as to what attire was appropriate for her newly acquired occupation.

Joe, or so he called himself, had bought her a new wardrobe, mainly consisting of 'normal' clothes; jeans, T-shirts, jumpers, wrap-around skirts and so on. He had had to ensure that Anna appeared the single, professional young woman, not a young woman engaged in the oldest ever profession. Her short skirts, crop-tops and tight cut-off lycra leggings had been assigned to the bin and replaced by the other clothes so as to give the residents of the other flats the impression that Anna, or Claire as she was re-named, was a hard-working, run-of-the-mill girl who, through effort and application, had afforded the luxury flat on her income alone.

She answered the door with a smile.

'Can I help you?' she asked the smartly dressed man who stood at the threshold.

'Winston Churchill,' he announced, keeping his voice quiet.

'Do come in,' she replied.

The great man's name was this week's password, and the pinstripe-suited man followed Anna into the lounge.

'I take it you have cash?' she asked.

'Of course,' he said.

'That will be eighty-two thousand then, please.'

'I want to see the gear first.'

'No problem,' Anna said. 'Wait here.'

She walked into the kitchen, closing the door behind her. Opening the cupboard under the sink she removed a bucket containing cleaning stuffs and lifted out the base of the unit.

Reaching to her right she pulled out two sugar-sized bags that were out of sight. Then she put everything carefully back and strolled into the living room where the man waited.

'There we are,' she said, handing the heroin to him.

He opened the two bags and examined the contents without physically removing the smack.

'Alone are you, Claire?' he asked, smiling.

'Yes,' Anna replied looking entirely unperturbed.

'I could take this without paying,' he continued, his face now displaying a more serious expression.

'You're right,' Anna admitted. 'But Joe wouldn't be very pleased with that now would he? Robin Warrener isn't it? 42 Stabler Street West. If I'm not mistaken you have a wife and three kids to support; am I right?'

'So?'

'Joe told me only the other day that someone broke an agreement with him once, before I worked for him. That man's daughter was killed in a road accident just two days later, a terrible tragedy. He ended up paying the money he owed to Joe anyway so his daughter died for nothing.' She smiled broadly at Mr Warrener, and held her hand out for the cash.

Warrener stuffed a wad of notes into her hand.

'A, a,' she said like a teacher. 'Count it for me, please.'

The money counted, Warrener left with the gear in a supermarket bag, his attempt at one-upmanship having backfired to the point of humiliation.

'Hope to see you again soon,' she said as he opened the flat door, eager to leave.

Anna placed the money into another supermarket bag and put it where the drugs had formally been secreted. She flopped onto the settee and gave a sigh of contentment as she flicked the DVD on with the remote.

Moments later there was a knock at the door. The spy-hole revealed that it was Joe.

Anna looked worried. He knew the times of the exchanges, that was his business. She had done four exchanges this week, one in Leeds and three here in Sheffield, and he had always arrived exactly half an hour afterwards to collect the money. That was the agreement.

'Is everything all right?' she asked as he barged rudely into the flat.

'It will be if there's eighty-two grand under the sink, yeah.'

'Course there is, Warrener's just left.'

Joe retrieved the money and counted it.

'Don't you trust me?' Anna asked.

'No. I wouldn't trust Jesus Christ with this sort of money.'

Anna looked offended.

'I'll be following clients in as soon as they've left from time to time, just to check,' he said menacingly.

'Hey...'

'Don't "hey" me miss. This is *my* money, and it's big chunks we're talking so I'll check when and where I see fit, understand?'

'Loud and clear,' she said. 'I thought Warrener was gonna get funny, you know. He said he could take the gear without paying if he wanted. I think he was just testing me out.'

'Did he now? Right, that's the last time I deal with him.'

'Oh, I don't think...'

'No, you don't. *I* do the thinking, you hand over the gear with a smile. Subject closed. Oh, by the way.' Joe added, his mood changing in an instant, 'I've a present for you.'

He pulled a small pistol from the right pocket of his leather jacket.

'Never mention where this came from to a living soul. If you do, I'll deny it. It can't be traced back to anyone, so enjoy. Be careful, though, you're doing a good job so far and I wouldn't want to lose you to Her Majesty's pleasure, if you get my drift.'

Anna held the piece in her hand, trembling slightly. It was heavier than she expected.

'Be careful,' Joe said, 'The magazine's full. Pull the trigger and... boom. Put it somewhere safe until you need it. To be honest, I'd rather you had it should a dickhead like Warrener really put pressure on you in the future.'

'Thanks,' she said.

'Be ready for nine fifteen in the morning. I'll be taking you to a different flat in Leeds for two jobs the day after.'

'OK.' And Joe was gone.

Smack coursed through Anna's veins as she smiled, triumphantly looking at her new acquisition lying dormant on the coffee table.

'My beauty,' she said, as her awareness took on its usual obscurity.

Chapter 45

8ᵗʰ June 2001

The pain subsided.

Rick felt warm, almost cosseted in this environment, like a foetus.

Whispers, indistinguishable in content, fluttered around him. Thoughts, feelings and emotions touched his perception only vaguely, an almost-comprehensible background gibber.

Unable to see beyond the mist which enshrouded him, Rick tried to speak, but no sound came from his mouth.

As his awareness grew, he realised that he was awake. He *knew* that he could think.

'Hello.' He had formed the word and uttered it, yet he did not hear the sound.

'Hello,' he said again, attempting to make himself heard. No sound. Shouting was no more effective.

'Am I dead?' he asked in silence, looking around him at nothing.

The reply was a feeling. He heard nothing, yet he knew instinctively that the answer to his question was no.

'Then where am I?' he said, moving his lips in vain.

Again the answer came as an inner comprehension not requiring physical speech. Rick relaxed, knowing that his questions would be answered shortly. He had to wait until the conditions were suitable. But 'the communication' was enough to convince him that he had come to no harm. He knew that he was not dead, and this sufficed for the time being. Floating in tranquillity he remembered the story related to him many years ago by a teenage school friend. Peter Maidstone he was called. He had been fishing with his elder brother. Peter was ten at the time and had not learned to swim. He had stood up on the bank of the reservoir after having been sat for over two hours and his legs had given way under him due to a lack of blood circulation. Peter had fallen into the water. Unfortunately for him, the banking at that point did not gradually give way to depth, it sank there and then into over twenty feet of cold water, and Peter struggled to stay afloat. He thrashed about in the deep, freezing water, fully clothed. Peter described the sheer panic as he tried desperately to reach the surface. He recalled taking water into his lungs and coughing it out, only to breathe in more.

Then Peter portrayed how, after what seemed an eternity of fighting to survive, he relinquished the battle and gave way. He had reached a point where he knew he had lost the fight to live, and he went on to describe the feelings which followed. The body's will to live caused the mind to be completely panic-stricken, but only moments later, when the mind reached the point where it knew there was no way out of the predicament, it abandoned panic and hysteria, shrugged off the need to protect the physical and replaced chaos with calmness. He depicted an experience which caused his little audience to be envious. A floating feeling, complete abandonment of concern and worry; there was absolutely nothing to care about except enjoyment of that moment. Nothing to be afraid of. A sensation of being wholly at one with the earth and with everyone upon it. Contentment.

The next thing Peter knew he was retching his guts up on the grass, his brother yelling at him and beating the water out of his lungs. He actually pushed his brother away, annoyed that he had rent him from where he felt he belonged.

Rick could relate to Peter's experience. He remembered the episode in the swimming pool, engineered by Rusak, and his present situation resembled his friend's feelings of calmness after giving up the will to live.

But this was slightly different. The pleasant feelings of floating and comfort were similar, yet he still had serious concerns as to where he was, whether he had failed in his aim to stop Ellie's killer and other such things.

This was why he knew he wasn't dead. Peter had been

seconds away from dying, but Rick wasn't. There was a difference.

Sheldon. Sheldon. Sheldon.

The name, his name, was not being spoken. Yet he was aware of it.

This was it. This was where he found out what all this was about. He felt his body gently rising, until he was in a standing position off the floor.

Slowly, a number of figures came into view through the mist, which cleared by degrees, leaving Rick apprehensive as to what would soon be revealed.

The silhouettes gradually became more distinct and it wasn't long before Rick could make out Tal's features. She smiled at him. He looked around and saw a further three people stood with Tal. She was the only woman present, the men towering over her by at least three feet, making them eleven or twelve feet tall. He himself was elevated so that his eyes were at the same level as the tallest of the males. These people were his successors, the world's future. He was their history.

As the scene was set before him, Rick began to experience a hot sensation at the front of his head, which quickly spread across his cranium. The heat became more intense until he began to worry.

'What's happening?' he said, with growing concern. But just like before he heard no sound despite saying the words.

At first, no-one answered his question and the pain grew exponentially to the point where he put his hands to his head and grimaced in agony. Amid the excruciating pain Rick became ever so slightly aware of thoughts passing between the four people before him. Words were not what he recognised, but the meanings of thoughts and ideas travelling between them. He discerned that Tal was telling the others that he simply wasn't developed enough, and that she would interpret for him. He could not tell what they thought, but seconds later the pain in his head faded and suddenly he could hear. It was if his ears had been blocked and syringed thoroughly in the space of a second.

Now he heard the people shuffling about, but detected no

thoughts passing between them.

'I was not expecting a further meeting with you, Rick,' Tal said.

'Have I failed?' he replied.

'That has not been decided at this juncture.'

'What do you mean?'

'A group of…time analysts…that is the best way I can describe them, is looking at the effects of your disclosure of information to your friend Tom. Their findings will determine your future.'

'Where am I?' he asked.

'In the same place as you were, but in my time.'

'Why?'

'Because I won the battle to remove you to this time while the review was being conducted.'

'Won the battle?'

'Yes. Rusak fought hard for two months to persuade the Council that you should remain and tell your friend the whole truth. If he had succeeded in his aim then you would have died as I explained to you and the disruption would have stood. As it is, I persuaded the Council to remove you and to assess the damage you had caused. If they dictate that you have influenced the timeline more than insignificantly, then your death will ensue. If they find that you have not done any appreciable harm you will be permitted the transgression and returned to continue where you left off.'

'When will we know?'

'In a few moments.'

'I'm sorry,' Rick said. 'I've let you down.'

'You have let down only yourself and those occupying your time.'

'But I *knew* I couldn't tell anyone about all this. I just…got drunk.'

'Poisoning yourself with alcohol actually allowed me to convince the Council that your actions were not considered. The involuntary element surrounding the disclosure was enough, together with other factors, to persuade them to conduct a review rather than dismiss you.'

'I just got fed up with getting nowhere trying to find out who the bloody killer was. The more closely I look, the more people seem to have a motive. We're just ordinary people, for God's sake.'

'The only moment of any significance is the event change. All others are meaningless.'

As Tal said this she frowned and faced the men.

'I can tell you no more,' she said. 'The others here will not permit it.'

'Who are they?'

'Rafen and Ula, Judges of Fairplay. And...Rusak.'

Rick looked shocked at her revelation that the scientist himself was among them, the architect of this whole affair. He looked at the three men, not knowing which of them the evil one was. Only one looked straight into his eyes, the tallest of them. His gaze sent a chill down Rick's spine, but the telepathic link between these people and himself had been severed a few moments earlier at Tal's behest, and with the consent of the Judges. He had no influence over Rick right now despite being two strides from him and having the malice to annihilate him from existence with one malevolent thought. Rick smiled at Rusak disrespectfully, but received no acknowledgement from his adversary.

As he watched Rusak, the giant turned to the others.

'The result is about to be delivered,' Tal said to Rick.

He swallowed hard. He wondered what death was like, because it was a reality for him if the wrong verdict came through. The 'Next Phase' Tal had called it when they first met, was a phrase he preferred to 'Death'. One suggested some form of continuance, the other an ending.

Tal, Rusak and the two Judges of Fairplay closed their eyes simultaneously. What seemed only half a second later and they opened them. Rusak turned on his heel and slammed the enormous door behind him, leaving the other three in the room with him.

'Your disclosure did no harm,' Tal informed him with a

smile.

Rick looked at her. 'Thank you,' he said.

'There is no need to thank me,' she replied. 'I am acting only within my remit as Guardian.'

'Right, well thanks anyway,' he reiterated.

'I would be unable to persuade the Council to repeat this,' Tal warned.

'Underst…'

Half way through uttering his agreement with his mentor, Rick found himself on the same roller-coaster as he had ridden on his journey back in time to the supermarket. This time he let the journey go unchallenged by fear and apprehension. He let it wash over him and before long he was sat beside Tom, about to expand on his foolish revelation.

'She'll be shot. Shot dead, Tom.' Rick put two fingers to his forehead.

'Are you mad?' Tom protested.

Rick stopped himself in his tracks.

'Er… yes, I think I am sometimes,' he said feebly.

Tom looked into his eyes, as if he had seen something scary there. 'What are you talking about?'

'Look, I'm gonna call it a night pal, OK?'

'No. I want to know what you meant. Ellie getting shot?'

'Look, forget it. It was a dream I had, it's giving me the creeps, that's all.'

'Right,' he said, curling his lip in disbelief.

'Can we get off now?'

'Yeah, whatever.'

Rick felt the inebriation a second time that night, and was determined not to let it be his downfall.

'You were bloody lucky tonight, mate,' Rick said as they left the snooker hall.

'Why?' Tom asked.

'Well, that blue you potted in the second game…'

Chapter 46

Sleep gave no silent solace to its host tonight.

Rick's mind raced despite being tired and awash with alcohol. He felt like a rat in a laboratory, being tested and pushed beyond his limits by a single-minded scientist, intent on seeing the results of his misguided research whatever the cost. To him the end justified the means regardless of the pain and suffering caused to the subject. The ultimate act of playing God, where the one in control pursued his goal in the face of cries of anguish and pleas to stop. A bully.

A bully. He was being bullied. That was the top and bottom of it. The oppressor this time wasn't a bigger boy as he remembered all too often from his childhood, but a man called Rusak from his future. Essentially, though, the ingredients were the same. Being made to hand over money to the sour-faced older boy was akin to being forced to do things he didn't want to do now. Being punched in the face was every bit the same as being drowned in the swimming pool. Only the degree of the hurt was worse, not the intent of the persecutor.

Anger filled Rick's heart at the thought of being a victim again. The first time around he had done something about it, and he would do the same again. Sitting downstairs at two twenty in the morning, Ellie fast asleep in bed, he slammed his fist onto the breakfast bar in frustration, his coffee lapping over the sides of the cup in response.

'What do I have to do?' he said. He looked up at the ceiling and asked the question again, as if a guardian angel was there to provide the answer. No answer came.

Tal had told him to use his mind. He had concentrated on her and focussed his thoughts successfully in warding off Rusak's attempts to instil fear into him. But maybe his mind was capable of more.

As he drained the second cup of black coffee he remembered what Tal had said only hours before, that the only significant moment in time was the point of Ellie's death. She said that nothing else counted. Could it be that his frantic search for the killer's identity was simply irrelevant? He already knew that there was nothing he could do to prevent the killer from being at the place the deed was done at the allotted time. And, despite his attempt to prolong the honeymoon and stop Ellie from being there, he knew deep down that that strategy was unlikely to work. Tal had also told him that he was powerless to affect the lives of others, except at the time of the event change. So what about little Laura whose life he had saved, almost at the expense of his own? Rick smiled as he realised that Laura had come to no harm on that time and date the first time he lived that life.

He rubbed his face with his hands, feeling out of his depth entirely. Yet the solution must be there. He wouldn't have been sent back to do this if there was no chance of success. As he pondered the way forward, Rick heard a rustling sound in the living room.

'Ellie? Is that you,' he asked as he made his way into the lounge.

Everything was quiet. Rick flicked on the light and saw that a magazine had fallen from its place on the arm of a chair onto the floor. It had landed half open. 'I'm going crazy,' he said as he picked up the publication, one Ellie had had delivered for as long as he could remember. Just as he was about to replace it, he noticed the title of an article on the page at which the magazine had fallen open.

OUR FUTURE POTENTIAL.

He read on.

Doctors and scientists predict that in the future our brains will work much harder for us.

Many believe that a large proportion of our brain remains unused, leaving incredible potential for the future. Using only part of the brain's capacity, humankind has walked on the moon, transplanted hearts and become the most successful ever species on the planet.

In recent years mediums and healers have touched the surface of what is possible with their ability to see into people's lives and predict where a person is going, or by flying in the face of conventional medicine by healing arthritics while doctors look on...

Having read the article twice through Rick sat at the breakfast bar once more. He was a human being, just like Tal, Rusak and the Judges of Fairplay. But they had almost seventeen thousand years more experience than he had. Their brains had developed over this period of time such that they communicated without the need for speech. They passed feelings and emotions to one another through the power of thought alone. And they had begun to master time travel. How the hell could he compete with them?

'But I don't have to compete with *them*,' he said suddenly, conducting a one-way conversation. 'I have to stop the killer from pulling the trigger on 21st July. And the killer, whoever it is, is at *my* level, here in the twenty-first century.'

He recalled Tal's many words of advice, all of which he remembered with consummate ease. She said that using his mind was the key, but that she could not help him to use it, that he had to do it himself.

Clearly Tal was not permitted, or wasn't able, to enhance his abilities to that of hers. So could he do it himself? It was worth a try. Sweating over trying to find who the killer was, was getting him nowhere and even if he did identify the murderer he couldn't *do* anything about it until the time of the disruption anyway, so really his energies had been wasted. Perhaps his time would have been better spent learning how to train his mind to work harder for him. It had worked in staving off Rusak, assisted by the division of time between them, so could it work to benefit him in other ways?

The task was worth immediate attention.

Rick searched in a drawer and found a thimble, which he placed before him on the kitchen table. He closed his eyes and concentrated on the item. He had no idea *how* to concentrate, he just did it. Thinking only of the thimble, and blocking out any other thoughts, he imagined it moving two or three inches to the edge of the table and falling off. He kept his eyes tightly closed and for over two minutes placed images there of the thimble moving and falling, moving and falling, moving and falling. Eventually he opened his eyes. The thimble hadn't moved at all. Unperturbed, he repeated the experiment, but with no success.

Trying a third time, Rick looked intently at the object whilst he imagined it moving slowly along the smooth surface. His concentration became so intense that at one point he thought he was sitting where the thimble sat, and was sure just momentarily that he saw himself looking at himself. This frightened him a little, but he continued undaunted. He would do whatever it took to give him the edge. If he could find anything out which gave him even the minutest advantage over the killer then it was worth it.

For forty five minutes he tried to move the thimble. For forty five minutes he failed. It sat there on the same spot as if to taunt him. Rick was exhausted and, despite his newly found optimism, was becoming disillusioned.

The thimble was tossed back into the drawer and Rick picked up a pack of cards. He shuffled it thoroughly and removed a card from the pack, face down. The card was placed on the table in front of him, and the pack to one side. Again he trained all his attention towards one thing, the card. Was it a king, a jack or a five? These were the images that bounced into his head as he stared at the blue diamond pattern on the rear. King, jack or five; king, jack or five; king or five; king or five; king or… five. Five.

Carefully, the card was turned over. 'Yes,' he said aloud as the five of hearts sat face up on the table before him.

Now he was excited. The pack was re-shuffled and he placed another card face down in front of him. Two, four or five;

two, four or five; two, four or five; four or five; four or five; four or five. Four. The queen of spades sat there, as if laughing at him.

Rick repeated the experiment a further six times, failing on each occasion to predict the number or the picture.

Calmly putting the cards away, he went to bed.

Chapter 47

'Come in,' Mr Davis called.

Danielle Harper walked into the carpeted office on the sixth floor.

'Please, sit down,' he said with a smile. 'What can I do for you?'

'I'm really sorry to disturb you, sir.'

'Mr Davis will do just fine. Now, what's so important that you felt Mr Parsons couldn't deal with it?'

'It's... er... something that I feel only senior management can deal with, properly that is.'

'Go on,' he said reassuringly.

'Well, it's not easy, so I'll come right out with it. Rick Sheldon's been touching me up and it's really getting to me,' she said, feigning unease by making it look like she didn't know where to put her hands.

Andrew Davis was a sagacious man. Fifty-one years of age, he had worked in several kinds of business and met all types of people. Naivety was not one his weaknesses. He leant back in his leather chair and looked at Danielle long and hard before making comment.

'What you're saying is a very serious allegation.'

'I know. That's why I thought I'd see you rather than Mr Parsons.'

Danielle looked at Mr Davis with an unbending resolution. She knew that if she couldn't maintain eye contact with him he probably wouldn't believe her. Yet she averted her gaze after a short while so as not to appear disrespectful.

'How many times?' Andrew said dispassionately, not wanting to side with her or the alleged offender at this stage.

'Three altogether.'

'When was the last time?'

'Friday last week. I've been thinking about whether to say anything all weekend and... well, I shouldn't have to put up with it, should I?'

Danielle tried to take her boss out of the driving seat and place herself in it with a little mild confrontation. But Andrew had more about him than that.

'Have you told anyone else about this?'

'No.'

'Mmm. Have you told Mr Sheldon to stop it?'

'I have, yes. On Friday he just wouldn't listen at all. I got quite frightened.'

'Where were you?'

'In the quiet room; it was lunchtime.'

'And what happened?'

'Oh, do I have to...'

'What happened, Miss Harper?'

'I'd been in the quiet room for five or ten minutes reading. I had a bad headache that day and I couldn't face the canteen or the TV room. He came in and sat beside me. I shuffled along the settee away from him. I saw him look towards the door and then he sat right next to me saying something about how I wanted him really. Then...then he thrust his hand right up my skirt and, you know, touched me.' She concluded the fabrication with a tremble of her lower lip and turned her face from Mr Davis.

'What did you do?'

'I told him that he'd regret it and I walked out.'

'OK,' Andrew said, 'What do you want to happen now?'

Danielle was too smart for his little trap. If she demanded his head on a plate, Davis would smell a rat. He'd suspect that they'd had differences within the work environment and that this was her way of getting back at him.

'I... I just want it to stop. I don't want the police involving or anything like that, I just want to be able to get on with my work without the hassle. It's not a lot to ask is it, Mr Davis?'

He couldn't disagree with her.

'Right, what I'd like to do is speak to Mr Sheldon in your presence. It won't be easy for you, but I'd like to get to the bottom of the matter right now. How do you feel about that?'

She raised her eyebrows in surprise. That required confrontation big style, but she'd gone this far and it was her word against his, so nothing could be proved. Even if she only succeeded in tarnishing his reputation it was a start.

'OK then,' she said sheepishly.

***

Rick frowned as he took a seat in Mr Davis' office, the confusion on his face plain to see as he glanced over at Danielle sitting on the other chair.

'Richard, I'd like you to be open and honest with me. Have you and Miss Harper been seeing each other?'

Danielle almost intervened but was cut short by Mr Davis's raised hand.

'No. Has she told you otherwise?'

'Please, if you'd do me the courtesy of answering a few questions first. The truth is all I'm after. Have you had problems with Miss Harper, from a work point of view?'

'No. She's a good team leader.'

'Right. Have you socialised together at all?'

'Never,' Rick said emphatically. He began to realise where this was leading.

Davis cut to the chase. 'Have you asked her out and been refused?'

'No. I have no interest in her in that way. Did you know I'm getting married in four weeks?'

'I understand so, yes. Mr Sheldon, have you ever given Miss Harper any unwanted attention?'

Danielle looked at the floor.

'Oh, I see now. Well the position is this, Mr Davis. She's been wanting me to take her out, no, to hell with it. She's wanted me to bed her for weeks now. Yes, it's true. I've turned her down on numerous occasions. I'm not proud of it but I've even lied to her by telling her that there's something wrong with Ellie's baby in the womb and that it simply wouldn't be right for me to go behind Ellie's back now due to her emotional state.' Danielle looked over at Rick in astonishment. 'Yes,' he said. 'That's how hard I've tried to get her *off my back*. Even then she came into the quiet room the other day and tried to seduce me. So what's her twisted little tale, then?'

'What you have to appreciate is this,' Andrew said in a conciliatory voice. 'Miss Harper has come to me and said that you've molested her. You've told me the exact opposite. One of you is lying to my face, but in the absence of further evidence I will never know who's telling the truth. Have either of you spoken to anyone else about this, or are there any witnesses to any alleged assaults?'

Both knew that there was nothing other than their individual accounts. One the truth, the other machination.

Rick looked over at Danielle, and she stared back defiantly.

He gazed deep into her eyes. As he looked at her she blinked, but slowly. The blink slowed to the point where it appeared as though she was faking a faint. Her eyelids closed sluggishly and with purpose. Rick turned to see Mr Davis, who was in the process of putting his ink pen on the desk. His hand moved at a snail's pace and his face was fixed. Looking out of the window, he saw a small bird edge across his view. And then it stopped. Danielle's eyes remained closed. Both she and Davis were entirely motionless, yet Rick maintained real time during the 'pause'.

It was almost as if Rick knew what he had to do next. He approached Danielle and knelt before her. Closing his own eyes, he applied every thought to the task in hand. 'Tell the truth,' he whispered. 'Tell the truth. Tell the truth, Danielle. You simply have to tell the truth. You cannot avoid it; you cannot resist telling the truth.'

Rick sat back in his chair, the world around him suspended in time at his behest. He looked over at Danielle as he had been doing and breathed slowly out. Sound entered his world again and as he observed Danielle her blink continued its movement.

Her eyes opened, slowly at first and then at speed. She frowned at Rick, almost an acknowledgement that he had entered her mind.

'Well?' asked Mr Davis.

'I'm sorry,' Danielle blurted out, looking in a state of utter confusion. 'I made it all up.'

'I *beg* your pardon?' Davis said.

'I was jealous, that's all. I shouldn't have done it; it was wrong, I'm sorry.'

'Get out, Miss Harper, and go home. I want to see you in my office tomorrow morning at nine thirty sharp.'

'Yes, Mr Davis.' And she scuttled out looking bewildered at what she had just done.

'Well, Richard, I've seen some shenanigans in my time, but that takes the biscuit. Accept my apologies for putting you through this.'

'You weren't to know who was telling the truth. I'm just glad she came to her senses, albeit a bit late. I mean, I could have been out of a job at the very least.'

'She won't work here any more, that's for sure. The woman's completely unstable.'

'Can I get back to work now?'

'Don't let me stop you. And thanks for taking it so well.'

'No problem,' Rick said on his way out.

Chapter 48

11th June 2001

Keeping his mind on his work was proving difficult after the morning's events. Danielle's lies were surprising, but they took a poor second place when compared with what Rick had done.

Hours of trying to employ his mind more proactively had failed miserably. And then it happened, seemingly of its own accord.

So what was the common denominator? He had parried Rusak's attempts to put fear into him, and he had dealt with an extreme situation today. He remembered feeling intense anger building within him as Mr Davis revealed Danielle's allegations, and he recalled his feelings having reached fever pitch as he looked into her eyes just before time stopped. Similarly, fear had him in its grip at the bottom of the swimming pool before he controlled the situation and breathed freely underwater. Intense feelings; anger, fear. They triggered a rush of adrenaline in his body and this, in turn, seemed to have sharpened his mind and made it more receptive to its inner abilities, more in tune with its future potential.

Yet similar adrenaline-pumping occurrences had faced him at other times in his life. No futuristic abilities had emerged on those occasions. And neither had he read about or heard of anyone else displaying them. Could it be he had the gift of an enhanced mind whilst in pseudo form only? That was all he needed; his pseudo form would continue until the event on 21st July. After that, there would be no use for the gift, whether he succeeded or failed.

He sat alone in the quiet room pondering, when Sarah Bowers walked in.

'Oh good, I hoped I'd find you in here,' she said.

Rick closed his eyes. He knew what was coming, a damn good telling-off for Ellie's behaviour.

'I don't know whether your dear fiancée's told you, but I had the misfortune of bumping into her last week.'

'Yes, I know. I'm sorry.'

'You seem to think that "sorry" solves everything. Well it bloody well doesn't. She humiliated me in front of other people, and if she wasn't pregnant I'd have given her a good hiding. Do you hear me?'

'She was out of order. If it makes you feel any better she was embarrassed about the whole thing herself.'

'No, it doesn't make me feel better. I've got over *you,* but I'll be damned if you think I'm gonna be branded a liar for the rest of my life as well. I want you to tell her the truth, today.'

'But… I thought we'd been through this. It could jeopardise everything for me.'

'Tough. I'm sick of thinking about other people; I'm putting myself first from now on. And that means you telling her that we had a relationship. I want her off my back, and I want an apology.'

'You don't know what you're asking,' Rick said despondently.

'I know exactly what I'm asking. Look at it from my point of view, will you? I don't really want to cause a rift between the two of you, but why the hell should I be looking over my shoulder when I'm out shopping in case your possessive girlfriend decides to have another go at me and make me sound like some sort of weirdo? I'm not having it, Rick, I want you to tell her and that's that.'

'Look, I've had a hell of a day, I don't need this.'

'My heart bleeds for you.'

'I've been hauled up in front of Mr Davis this morning because Danielle Harper said I'd been groping her…can you believe it?'

'Well, have you?'

'No, I haven't. When he spoke to the two of us together she broke down and admitted that she'd made the whole thing up.'

'What have you done to upset her? She obviously hates you.'

'Nothing. I told her I wasn't interested in her when she kept coming onto me.'

'Look, it's all very interesting but nothing to do with me. As I was saying, I want you to tell Ellie about us.'

'What if I refuse?' Rick replied.

'You'll regret it,' she said assertively. 'For starters, I'll turn up at your wedding and tell your guests what happened. I may even speak to Danielle and convince her that you *are* a bastard. I'm sure that if *I'd* seen you pestering her, her story could easily be resurrected. She clearly detests you, and I'm sure that a little help from an unconnected person would cause you untold problems.'

'You wouldn't.'

'Try me,' Sarah said with a smile.

Rick buried his head in his hands.

'You've got until Wednesday,' she said, and closed the door quietly behind her as she left.

Chapter 49

Several opportunities for Rick to tell Ellie had arisen the night before, but he had shied away from them all. He was scared of the consequences. He didn't want to lose Ellie, but in addition to that if the worst happened and they finished up not getting married because he told her the truth about Sarah he would also lose the opportunity to be with her on 21st July. Everything could be lost, absolutely everything.

The alternative was a possible collaboration between Sarah and Danielle which, if followed through to its conclusion, could have equally devastating results. He imagined facing Andrew Davis again, this time after Danielle had told him that her original story was the true account but that she had been hurt and confused and scared. And Sarah's corroboration would be there, another lie but potent in its effect; the word of the victim and a witness against that of the suspect alone.

If the two women maintained their stories convincingly he would lose his job. He might even face prosecution. It would be infinitely more difficult to face Ellie with that situation. Even if he escaped without sanction, which would be unlikely, his wife would always have a degree of suspicion that he was a pervert. He simply couldn't cope with that; he would rather face her wrath having told her a lie in the past, a lie designed not only to alleviate him of owning up to an awkward set of circumstances, but to save their relationship. That was justifiable, at least in part.

Ellie had left for work and Rick ruminated over his toast. Should he call Sarah's bluff? The chances were that Sarah's verbal attack on him yesterday was borne out of sheer anger at being slapped across the face by Ellie the previous week. Her anger may die down. Also, she didn't know Danielle from Adam.

Would she really go out of her way to approach a total stranger with such a scheming and evil plan just to bring him down? And she probably wouldn't have time in any case. According to what Mr Davis said yesterday Danielle was facing the sack this morning, and it would be very difficult for Sarah to track her down if she wasn't coming to the office any more. On the other hand Sarah was similar to Ellie in temperament; each could be explosive in their reaction to things. He liked women with spirit and confidence, but such people often pursued matters to their conclusion with determination and vigour.

'Sod it,' he said. 'It's about time I faced up to the past and buried it, once and for all.' Since he originally told Ellie that there had been nothing between him and Sarah Bowers, lies had led to more lies and if he wasn't careful the whole thing would blow up in his face. No, it wouldn't be easy, but telling the truth now was the only way forward.

***

'Hi, darling,' Ellie called as Rick kicked off his shoes in the hallway, his stomach churning at the task he had to perform. Trudging into the kitchen, he saw his fiancée tending to a delicious-smelling stir-fry. 'I took a few hours off today,' she continued. 'And I've sorted out the flowers. It was so easy with Withers. I can't believe we've had so much hassle; they knew exactly what we wanted from what I described. And you know what that means, don't you?'

'What?'

'Everything's done now. We just have to turn up on the day. No more arranging this and pricing that. Mind you, I don't know what we'd have done without my mum.'

She threw her arms around his neck and kissed him passionately, stroking the inside of his lips with her tongue.

'Come on, you,' he said, gently pushing her from him.

'What's the matter?' Ellie said, looking confused at his reaction to her warmth.

'Nothing. I'm starving, let's eat.'

She didn't take his brush-off to heart, but continued preparing the meal while he put his feet up in the living room. Rick decided that they would eat and clear up before he dropped the bombshell.

'So, what kind of a day have you had?' she asked.

'Same as ever. Same people in the office, same kind of people on the phone. You know.'

'Cheer up,' she said, sounding a little disappointed at his malaise. 'Three weeks and three days and we'll be Mr and Mrs Sheldon, married and looking forward to jetting off to Indian Islands the next day. I'm really glad now you booked that extra week. I just can't wait.' She tucked heartily into her sweet and sour chicken.

Rick stole a glance at her as she ate. She looked so happy, so excited about their future together, almost like a child on Christmas morning. He wished he could love her without fear, worry and uncertainty as to the future intruding upon his love. His deep feelings for Ellie were being inhibited and tainted by his knowledge of things to come. He remembered the undamaged emotions from before; how they filled him with elation and how he shared her vitality and lightness of spirit. Two souls, with butterflies in their stomachs, looking ahead at the good times to come.

Things had remained the same for Ellie, but not for him. She knew nothing of her former existence and its untimely end, the death of their child or the impending suffering facing mankind. This was his burden to bear, and his alone.

Despite her high spirits Rick could no longer hold the tension inside himself and, in the absence of any easy way to break the news to her, he told her outright.

'I *did* have a relationship with Sarah Bowers.'

Ellie choked slightly and dropped her fork onto her plate. She purposely put her food down and turned to face him.

'What?'

It was done. He had told her. Hours of plucking up the courage and he had done it. But he knew that the hard part was to follow.

'When you went to your mum's. I started dating her.'

Tears welled in Ellie's eyes as she looked at him. Like a picture, they told a thousand words.

'Why?'

'At the time, I thought we were finished for good. A few weeks went by and…'

'No, no, NO,' she shouted. 'Not why did you go out with her. Why have you lied to ME?'

What could he say? He felt dreadful not only because of the lies and how they had affected people, but by dragging Ellie from her well-deserved happiness into despair and uncertainty in an instant.

'I lied for two reasons. I was a bloody coward, and it was easier making her look stupid than explaining why I'd started up with someone else only weeks after we'd separated. And secondly, I would have done anything to get you back. Telling you about Sarah would have jeopardised that.'

Burying her head in her hands, Ellie exhaled loudly, awash with emotion.

Rick's head began to hurt. A headache spanning from the front to the back of his skull grew in intensity in the moments that followed. As he looked at Ellie, he became acutely aware of her thoughts. Not the words, but the feelings. Passion, vehemence, hate, confusion, disappointment… betrayal. Each was strong in its own right, and each knocked at the door of his mind demanding to be let in and given an audience. The whirlwind raging in Ellie's mind now raged in his also. Rick began to experience the emotions himself, to feel them as if they were his own. And he knew that it was his responsibility to quell the tempest.

Although she was sat six feet from him, Ellie unwittingly battered and beat him with her jumbled and random deliberations to the point where he felt nauseous and almost out of control. The power of her thoughts was immense. Rick closed his eyes and, without having to consider how to achieve his goal, began to think how much he loved her. He excluded all other emotions, all other considerations. I love you… I love you… I love you with all my heart and soul, he said to himself over and over again. By degrees, the turmoil subsided. The rushing winds of her anger and hate died down as he poured love into the eye of the storm. Rick continued thinking how much he loved her until there was no hate left.

He opened his eyes and looked once more at Ellie sat on the chair opposite him. She dropped her hands. 'I love you too,' she said unprompted, wiping her wet cheeks. 'But you hurt me.'

'I know. All I can say is I give you my word I will not hurt you again.'

Ellie got up and threw her arms around him, hugging him as if she would never see his face again after today. He felt her love for him permeate his being and he let the overflow of feelings out, crying unashamedly onto her shoulder.

Chapter 50

'Oh God, sorry,' Josie exclaimed, taken aback by Rick's unexpected exit from the bathroom.

Rick quickly covered himself with his towel.

'My fault,' he replied. 'Force of habit, sorry.'

Josie watched him saunter into his bedroom, wishing secretly that he had had no towel to hide his modesty.

In his own place Rick frequently wandered around naked, it gave him a feeling of freedom. Your home is your castle, and all that. But he wasn't in his castle, he was in Tom's and Josie's. Ellie had insisted there was no way he was sleeping with her or staying in the same house the night before the big day. She wanted everything just so, and that didn't include waking up beside the groom-to-be today. She had ensured that he had not seen the wedding dress, and in any case the house was due to be bustling with parents, hairdressers and beauticians. You name it, they would be there traipsing in and out, and she didn't want Rick grumbling about the place being taken over by women.

Sitting on the edge of the bed, Rick looked at his grey suit hanging on the wardrobe door, together with the whiter-than-white starched shirt, the dickie-bow and the patent leather shoes. There they were, motionless, beckoning him to move along, to progress along the timeline until that fateful moment of truth, now a mere fifteen days ahead. They seemed to mock him, as if daring him not to wear them.

'Oh, yes,' he said. 'I must put you on, again.'

Little things repeated themselves, constant reminders that he had been there once before. Reminders that he was different from everyone else around him. Rick knew that Josie would reach the top of the stairs to see him coming out of the bathroom without a stitch on, it had happened before. It was funny first time, so why should he change it? He recalled sitting on the edge of the bed looking at his wedding suit and thinking what a big step it was, and wondering how things would turn out in the future. This time his thoughts were different. He knew the immediate future intimately. The question now was, how could he change it?

One thing was for sure. He had to don that suit and turn up at the church, whether he felt like it or not. He had no choice but to go through the motions of it all a second time. It was expected of him. The *real* wedding day had been a fantastic one, full of happiness and the usual apprehension. That now felt like a rehearsal for today. Most people's practice run consisted of visiting the church in scruffs, running through the essentials with the priest and getting a general feel for the surroundings. Where to stand, what to do at various points of the service, and so on. He knew all that in detail. And the hardest thing would be to feign excitement, pretend that it was all magical and a once-in-a-lifetime experience. His show would have to be convincing, too.

In some ways, this part of his task was every bit as difficult to perform as it would be on the evening of the 21st. He knew that the moment of the event change was *the* moment where he simply had to make a difference; he had to change the already changed course of events. That would be the time for truth. But having to go through the wedding day a second time, that was draining. Shaking hands again with the guests as they entered the church; the hour-long service; the children running amok at the reception as they waited for the tables to be prepared; the photographs, they seemed to take an age so this time it would be tedium. But to allow these feelings to show would be to ruin Ellie's day, and everyone else's.

Rick wished he had a fast-forward control. Much as he had enjoyed the original wedding day, in real time eight months ago to him, he really didn't relish a repeat of it. The honeymoon, too, had been the best holiday of his life, but it felt like a chore he had to endure before dealing with the unavoidable and ominous episode to follow. It would not disadvantage his ability to deal with it if it faced him in five minutes' time. He was clueless as to the identity of the person responsible for Ellie's death and what was to face him was, frankly, beyond his imagination. So bring it on, he said to himself. The wedding and the honeymoon seemed like encumbrances. He grew tired of waiting for the 21st and wanted it dealt with, whatever the outcome.

'Come on,' Tom said impatiently as he entered Rick's room. 'It's after ten already. What's the matter, you getting cold feet?'

'No, mate, no. Just thinking things over, you know.'

'Well don't think for too long. It's the bride who's supposed to be late, not you.'

'Yeah, you're right. I'll be downstairs in ten minutes.'

Rick dressed, catching the starched collar of his shirt on that minute shaving cut on his neck. It smarted every bit as much as it had before.

***

Tears welled in Rick's eyes as Ellie looked up at him through her thin veil. He felt her love for him deep in his being, a sensation he would never have experienced prior to his recent growing awareness of peoples' emotions and feelings. As each week passed his perceptibility seemed to extend beyond last week's limits. And he wasn't even trying. As the days and weeks progressed towards the 21st, his mind grew in maturity. He could sense what a person thought of him as he stood at the bar in a pub'; he was able to focus on an individual's thought processes and glean whether that person had any strong feelings towards him, good or bad. The newly found craft didn't worry or frighten him, it was simply there. It had gradually formed part of his general sensibilities, and it gave him an edge, an insight into people. They guessed as to others' intentions and feelings, he *knew*.

Ellie's love permeated his every sinew. It filled him with a warmth and an inner glow which was indescribable in its power. His soul reciprocated without the need to be asked and Ellie took a short and silent intake of breath as she felt Rick's adoration bounce back invisibly into her. The couple could have been the only two in the church, in the world, it wouldn't have mattered. Each realised beyond any doubt that their love for one another was pure and strong. For a moment, only they counted.

'I said you can kiss the bride,' Father Reynolds repeated, a smile on his face indicating an understanding of the love between them.

As Rick kissed her lips he heard her mind working.

'I love you more than I can say,' she whispered almost silently as their lips parted. His smile was all the reply she needed.

Rick turned and looked into the congregation. His general perception was one of happiness. The aura was light and cheery as those at the ceremony inwardly wished them well, and as some of them remembered with nostalgia their own wedding days.

But the atmosphere was tainted, polluted by ill-feeling.

Rick's spirits were dashed by a palpable mood of jealousy and ill-will scattered among the good. It was drowned out by the force of the genuine well-wishers' thoughts and emotions, and yet still discernible despite its minority. Like a bad apple in a bunch, a virus in an otherwise perfect computer programme, the malevolence made itself known to him. Rick was unable to pinpoint its origin among the group of people, there were too many of them. Try as he might he could not find where it lurked, hidden by a smile and a feigned look of happiness for the couple.

But it was there.

***

Contrary to his previous misgivings about the wedding day, Rick was enjoying himself. The deeper love he was able to immerse himself in really lifted his spirits and gave him a renewed optimism as the day progressed. But Fear still skulked around. He was aware of its presence in and among the elation. He sensed it moving clandestinely around, like a tiger among the rushes. Rusak was with him, as well as Ellie, and he had to remain on his guard.

There were so many people around that Rick had not been

successful in singling out the jealousy and resentment among the guests. The group's combined emotions clouded any accurate judgement and he had binned the task as unachievable.

Laughing a second time at John Francis, a clerk from his department, falling head over heels on the dance floor, Rick made his way instinctively to the female toilets. He didn't have to be told this time that there had been a flood in the men's room and that the ladies was being used temporarily while the problem was solved. It was better than the reverse situation where women would be gingerly entering the mens, hoping that no-one was stood at the urinals. In the womens, the cubicles were there to prevent any embarrassment.

He sauntered in, used a cubicle and, as there was nobody else there, examined his face in the mirror.

He thought what Tom had said a few weeks earlier about never being able to look at the top of your own head, and it made him laugh. You never see your own face either, except in reverse, he thought. As he removed a small piece of fluff from his right eyebrow he saw that his face was becoming thinner and paler as he watched. Quickly, Rick put his hands to his face. It felt normal. Yet the image in the mirror indicated otherwise. He felt as if he was stood in a hall of mirrors where reflections were purposely distorted by cleverly shaped glass. He looked behind him towards the door of the bathroom, but everything seemed OK.

As Rick turned to look in the mirror again, he found that he was looking out from it! Blinking several times changed nothing. He looked into the women's toilets, as though he had previously been looking into a one-way mirror and was now standing at the opposite side. Almost wrenching his neck in the process, Rick quickly turned to look behind him to see the empty room there.

The confusion caused him slight nausea. The bathroom was behind him. It was also in front of him. Which was reality? He looked into a mirror yet saw through it like an ordinary pane of glass whereas it had been a mirror only seconds earlier. Rick tried to get up but couldn't move. He attempted to look behind him again, but his head was fixed in a forward-facing position.

The sensation of claustrophobia brought panic on at a pace.

The door swung open and two women entered the room.

'I'll tell you something, Fran,' one said to the other, succumbing to the wine, 'I wouldn't mind taking Ellie's place tonight, if you know what I mean.' She cackled coarsely.

'That one track mind of yours will get you into trouble one of these days. I'm just glad there's no *man* in here. The last thing we want while we're putting the war paint back on, is having to listen to a bloke pissing right into the centre of the water. It turns me right off does that.'

'I know what you mean. There again, there's not a lot about Jack that actually turns me *on* these days. He's not the man I married nine years ago. He's losing his hair, and gaining a beer-belly.'

'I bet he still wants it every bloody night though, eh?'

Rick looked at the women. Fran and Jayne, from Ellie's work. Jayne put her face up close to the mirror, seemingly inches from his own, and applied further coats of lip-gloss. Rick tried moving away but couldn't.

After a few minutes the women left the bathroom as giddy as they had come in. Rick looked around. He could move his eyeballs, nothing more. He became strangely drawn to the white grouting between the terracotta floor tiles, which appeared to move. As he watched, involuntarily, the straight strips of material rose above the tiles and hung limp-like in the air above the floor. There were about fifty or sixty of them in all. As the moments passed, the material moved gradually towards where he was. The individual strips rhythmically merged to form a white, shapeless mass which neared his face as he looked on. He shifted his gaze to the door of the room, willing someone to walk in and disturb whatever it was, diverting the evil from its course.

Predictably, no-one came to his rescue. The white mass then began to mould itself, as though an invisible master craftsman was a work. After a minute or two Rick swallowed hard as he recognised the macabre face floating in front of him. Rusak.

The face had the same look across it as when he last saw it. The anger and the outrage he formally saw when the Judges of

Fairplay announced that he was to be given another chance after almost telling Tom about the whole affair was there in front of him now. And it looked all the more ominous on a head twice the size of his own.

'You're... breaking the rules,' Rick said. 'Tal said you weren't allowed to visit me in person.' He swallowed again.

'You puny, dull animal,' Rusak replied. His mouth hadn't moved, it simply remained down-turned. Rick knew what he had said without Rusak having to speak the words.

One of Rick's life-long mottoes had been that attack was the best form of defence, particularly where the odds were against you, and he flew into that mode almost instinctively.

'You're no better than me, or madmen in my time. You simply exist in a time ahead of me. Bullying is the same in any century.'

The face took on an even sterner look, if that was possible.

'If you do not cease in your attempts to stop my experiment, I will crush your mind so that you are incapable of ever having another thought.'

'You are not permitted to be here,' Rick replied defiantly.

'And you do not understand. I am not here. I am in your mind only. Because you are infinitely weaker than me I can enter your feeble thought processes, though we are aeons apart. *You* are allowing me in, and you haven't the strength to lock me out. As the time nears, my strength will grow and yours will not grow at the same pace. I will crush you into a million pieces if you defy me further.'

'And my life will be over if I don't. I have nothing to lose.'

'You will have Josephine Hinds, and a fruitful long life. You can be happy, but not with this woman Eleanor.'

'She's the only woman I want, don't you understand? Anyway, life won't be worth living the way you want it.'

'That will not affect you in your lifetime.'

'No, but my children and their kids'll have no life will they?'

'Then die,' Rusak said in Rick's head.

The face changed shape by degrees until it resembled a hypodermic needle, its point razor sharp. The shape neared the glass in front of him and then penetrated its surface. The skin of the glass surface broke as if it was water and the needle moved gradually towards a point between Rick's eyes. He tried with all his might to move from the advancing weapon but didn't succeed in moving so much as an inch. Sweat rolled down his left cheek and he became cross-eyed as his widening eyes followed the needle's path.

Remembering previous attempts Rusak had made to place him in grave fear, Rick closed his eyes and opened his mind.

'This is not real,' he repeated over and over again, as he felt the tip of the needle enter the upper layers of his skin.

Throwing himself into a deep and instant meditation, Rick trained his every thought towards banishing the effect of the needle, which he knew in his heart of hearts was an apparition. He also knew, though, that the apparition could easily be his downfall if he succumbed to its power, its fear.

After a few moments he could not feel the needle at his head and it seemed that he had succeeded, but then he felt a sharp and excruciating pain between his eyes. The tip of the imaginary needle had travelled beyond the outer skin's surface and was making its way through deeper layers, severing nerve endings and blood vessels along the way. Rick cried out in pain, but he wasn't about to give in to Rusak's latest ruse. Again, he concentrated hard, harder than ever until it felt like his eyes would burst and his chest would collapse under the pressure. Opening his eyes he saw the needle, still moving slowly forwards, still penetrating his head. Unstoppable, it would soon breach his skull and pierce his brain.

Rick's eyes watered so that he observed the hypodermic's movement unclearly. The pain intensified to the point where he almost passed out. Only his hopeless but stubborn will to beat what was so fundamentally wrong and evil kept him from slipping into oblivion, into death. A red rivulet ran jaggedly across the vitreous humour and tears in his right eye as if to prove to him that this was not fiction, but fact. He was bleeding. The needle *was* there, and it would kill him.

No degree of effort was sufficient to halt the weapon in its path. Rick realised the appalling truth of the situation, that he simply wasn't strong enough to stop Rusak. He had fended him off before, but that was weeks ago. And Rusak had taken pleasure in pointing out to him that as the days and weeks past Rick's ability to fight him off would weaken significantly.

His mind whirred and Rick began to consider the options. If he pursued his goal and continued to defy the professor he would almost certainly die, right here and now. That would mean Rusak would ultimately get his way, *and* he would die to boot. He had done his best, but he feared death as do all living beings and his inner, instinctive self-preservation was busy persuading him that death was not the way to go. Yet if he buckled under the bully's fist he may as well be dead, because he would never forgive himself as the years ahead without Ellie and Rebecca passed.

Being at the point of giving up stirred an intense anger in Rick. An anger he had never felt before. Without consciously intending to, he diverted his attention from the fatal assault to a passionate and intense hatred of the assailant. The feelings surpassed detestation, they were sheer revulsion and repugnance. Formed from a mixture of impending failure, and the horror of the effect of that failure, Rick experienced the feelings such that his heart was rent. It was in contrast to the love he was capable of, that the death throes of a decent man such as he should be enshrouded in the darkest of emotions. If Rusak had been stood before him now, he would have physically ripped his head from his shoulders despite his size.

All Rick's thoughts were hate. Hate at what Rusak intended to do to his own predecessors, hate at what he was doing to him now, hate at what he stood for. The feelings, strong and black, seemed to knot in his chest. They became more apparent than the pain in his head until, without warning, they shot invisibly from within him. One second he felt as if the rage would destroy him, the next he experienced a serenity which he fought to understand. The antithesis enveloped him like the strong and comforting arms of a parent when a child is frightened. He felt at ease, unconcerned about the professor and the needle. Nothing mattered any more other than to bask in the welcome new state of mind.

As he relaxed, Rick's mind presented him with an image of Rusak. At first he saw the man stood, with his serious and angry face, as he had seen him before, as he had presented himself in the mirror. As he watched, Rusak's face took on a surprised and worried expression. Then he appeared slightly afraid, shortly after which he fell to the ground in a heap, his face twitching and moving beyond his control. The scene was almost comical. After a moment or two, the professor stood up and brushed himself down, looking somewhat embarrassed although no-one else was around.

'You are a dead man,' Rick heard in his thoughts.

The mirror seemed to throw out ripples from its centre. As the ripples reached the outer edges of the glass, Rick became aware that he was looking at his face once more in a normal mirror. He could move again. Looking behind him, he saw the ladies bathroom in its glorious normality. His head was unscathed.

A broad smile spread across Rick's face as he realised that he had beaten Rusak yet again. But the smile soon faded. His adversary's strength was growing by the day, and today he almost lost the battle for survival.

Chapter 51

8th July 2001

Ellie marvelled at the beautiful hotel room as the couple crashed in with their luggage, tired after a long night flight.

'Look at the bathroom,' she said, giddy and excited despite her fatigue.

'You get what you pay for, that's for sure,' Rick replied, having spent a great deal of time in the accommodation already.

'Yeah, but... this is gonna be a brilliant holiday.' She threw her arms around him and hugged him as if there was no tomorrow. Rick squeezed her tight. He loved everything about Ellie. Her child-like enthusiasm, her zest for life, her quick temper, everything. And he would do anything to keep her with him.

They made love, gently and slowly now as the pregnancy progressed. Both he and Ellie had enjoyed frenetic, animal-passion love-making frequently in the past, but the growing baby had dissuaded them from their former antics and it had been for the good. Tender, quiet and leisurely sex had proved to be even more rewarding than the former. The absence of muscle-wrenching, energetic and frenzied lust had brought a more intimate and close union between them, where they had time to look into each other's eyes and to feel the sensations rise within them by degrees. The build up to an orgasm proved to be almost as enjoyable as the event itself, as each recognised how close the other was to climax by the growing expressions of pleasure on their faces. It made them realise how skilled at controlling the other's feelings they actually were. It was like discovering sex all over again.

Ellie fell asleep first. It was five-twenty in the morning as Rick gently ran his fingers through her hair, carefully so as not to wake her from her overdue slumber. It was some time before he drifted to sleep, always a short sleep to him in the absence of dreams. The sleep of the dead.

On waking Rick became aware of a cold, wet sensation on his face. He jerked from his sleep, but didn't move. He wanted to assess the extent of the threat. He had been thinking incessantly about how and when Rusak would next strike, but in truth he had no idea whatsoever. He had become resigned to the fact that he would simply have to combat whatever form the next attack took as and when it arrived, and he had begun praying to God as of late to help him in the struggles to come. Religion had helped Rick. Years of going to church as a boy every week without fail had engrained a belief in him that God would help in times of true crisis. Not necessarily when he lost a girlfriend or failed to get a job he wanted, but when real calamity struck he believed deep down that God would come to his aid. He hoped beyond hope that this was the case and that he could trust that God's help would be at hand.

All was quiet around him. He felt slightly suffocated, but he could still breathe. It was so important to keep calm because he knew that Rusak could not physically assault him. The needle in the hotel bathroom two days ago didn't actually pierce his skin, but the sensation surrounding its apparent tangibility caused him pain. Pain sufficient to end his life if he found it too much to bear. So he would stay calm. He gingerly put his hand to his face, unable to completely banish the fear of what he would see. His fingers touched a soft material, which he slowly removed.

'BOO,' Ellie shouted into his face, and she laughed playfully.

'Don't do that again, do you hear me?' Rick snapped aggressively.

'Hey, calm down, tiger,' she giggled.

As he exhaled with relief Rick realised that he mustn't allow normal everyday activities to affect him. If he did so, then Fear would certainly begin to win the day and eventually be his downfall.

'You're in for it now,' he shouted in a silly deep voice and chased Ellie towards the bathroom. She slammed the door shut and locked it before he could grasp the handle.

'Give me twenty minutes to get a bath,' she called. 'Then we'll hit the beach.'

The sea looked welcoming from the fifth-floor balcony as Rick sat with a cup of decaffeinated coffee in his padded pine chair. If only he could hold this day in time, he thought. Live a whole lifetime in a day with the one he loved. Not real, of course, but it would piss Rusak right off. He laughed.

***

'I can't believe we're here,' Ellie said as she turned towards Rick, the towel beneath her preventing the sand from burning her skin.

'I know. It's paradise isn't it?' Rick replied.

'Not a breath of wind, hot sunshine in a blue sky and just us on this beach. Fantastic.' She resumed her former pose.

They had found a secluded little beach in a sparsely populated area, and were taking full advantage of being the only people in their world, just for a short time.

Rick laid under the sun's rays, clad only in skimpy sports trunks and Factor Three lotion. He was swarthy and enjoyed the searing sun darkening his skin. Ellie, on the other hand, though having thick dark hair, had a lighter complexion and was easily burnt. She had learned the lesson four years ago on a visit to Northern Italy where half the holiday had been spent in a cold shower to stop the needles constantly pricking her shoulders and back after over-exposure. She was smothered in sun-block. That way she could enjoy the heat, happy in the knowledge that she wouldn't burn.

Jet-skis whirred passed them, well out to sea, and the more adventurous could be seen straining to hang on as they tried water-skiing for the first time. There was activity all around them, but far enough away to afford them the privacy they wanted. Rick loved water sports, but Ellie was reluctant to exert herself because of the baby. She had said that he could go off and do whatever he wanted, but he was happy to stay at her side, knowing that he could partake on future holidays. In any case, relaxing on a secluded beach with the one he loved made him happy.

'How are you feeling?' he asked her tenderly.

Ellie didn't answer.

'Ellie, are you ready for off?'

No reply.

She was fast asleep.

Rick let his head fall onto the towel under him and he stared into the azure sky, feeling at one with the world. Without warning, a malevolence crept into his head. At first it was the faintest of feelings, but as the minutes past it grew. Swallowing hard, Rick prepared himself for another onslaught, one which he was increasingly afraid of facing.

He stood up and looked around. In the distance he spotted three figures heading towards where he and Ellie were. On the face of it nothing appeared sinister; three figures walking along a beach. But as they neared his position Rick sensed a definite ill-will. Placing his right palm on his forehead to shield the sun, he peered towards the trio which he could now make out as three men, one well over six feet tall and heavily built. They looked European. As they drew closer Rick could read their intent. They were about to rob him and Ellie.

A Gucci watch, bought as a birthday present for him by his wife, adorned his wrist. Ellie had a gold rope-chain around her neck as she slept. Then there were the keys to the BMW they had hired, visible on the road from where they stood.

All hope that the threesome were out for nothing more than a kick about on the empty beach faded as they walked within a hundred yards of Rick's position. He could feel their hearts beat faster as they approached, in anticipation of a fight. He felt the adrenaline course through their veins, as well as through his own, as their serious faces came into view. But Ellie was his main concern. She laid on the towel, oblivious to the impending danger. And, despite her condition, there was no way she would relinquish her jewellery and her pride to three meat-heads, no matter what the consequences. That was the kind of person she was. Principle came before practical, always.

Several things shot through Rick's mind. He would happily swallow his pride and just give the thugs the watch, the chain and the car keys, doing his best to persuade Ellie that it had to be this way to safeguard the baby. Unless they were evil through and through it would ensure Ellie's safety. On the other hand he could fight them. If none had *any* martial arts training at all he could probably take them, if he hit the big one first, hard. But what if one or more of them could fight? He could be beaten, leaving his wife vulnerable to their will. A good compromise might be to offer the watch and the keys as Ellie slept, and only fight if they wanted more, or simply spoiled for a fight in any event.

They were fifty yards away, now forty. Even without his intuition, Rick would by now have begun to worry about the men's intent. Their faces were set and they headed directly for the couple. Still there was no-one else on the beach.

Thirty yards and closing.

Rick walked at a pace towards the three men, who instinctively slowed as he approached them. His main aim was to put distance between them and his wife, who was still asleep.

'Can I help you chaps?' Rick said confidently.

The three men stood still. The ball was in their court now.

'I'd like to fuck the little lady, for starters,' the big one said, licking his lips whilst staring Rick straight in the eye. He folded his arms, as if to allow Rick time to consider his ridiculous proposal.

The evil that had entered Rick's mind a few moments earlier when the trio had first set foot on the far reaches of the little cove was an accurate warning. He was guilty of minimising the feelings that he knew were present, in the hope that he was exaggerating things in his mind, and now he regretted having not reacted more swiftly to the warning. It had been wasted.

'Now you listen to me,' Rick said assertively, ensuring he was out of the big man's reach, 'She's pregnant.'

'SO… WHAT?' came the reply. 'She doesn't look it. And *I* want to fuck her. You ask the lads here. What I want, I get.' The other two laughed, taunting Rick.

Memories flooded into his head. Boys bigger than him at secondary school. Raised voices. Pockets rifled for loose change as he was pinned against hard walls. Being spat at and laughed at. Being punched in the stomach until he couldn't breathe. Being told that he was weak and puny. Just the same as now. Just the same as the way he was being treated right now. The same way as Rusak treated him.

Anger grew within him again. This time it manifested itself within the space of half a second. He was saturated in it, unable to take a breath as it engulfed his chest entirely. He looked up at the big man and coughed, choking as his windpipe became blocked with the tangible vitriol of anger and hatred towards the group before him.

'You'll have to do better than that, weasel,' the big man laughed.

As the leader of the pack threw a hefty punch towards Rick, one which would certainly have floored him outright should he have failed to avoid it, the physical anger left his body and his mind as quickly as it had arrived, and he felt the calmness of spirit he had before when he had fought off Rusak through the mirror.

The bully's fist neared Rick's face, but he didn't flinch. There was no fear in him, just a tranquil, quiet aura. The fist stopped short of his face by an inch or so, much to the surprise of its owner.

'What the fuck…?' the big man said as he threw another mighty blow at Rick, which again failed to meet its target despite the proximity of the two men.

One of the other two kicked out at Rick, but his blow similarly failed to strike its target. Rick fixed his gaze on the big man and, looking him right in the eye, moved his head sharply to his left. The bulky figure moved as if hit by an invisible truck, and landed clumsily on top of the man to his right. Keeping his gaze fixed on the leader, Rick nodded his head gently. The big man's head slammed on the sand, then rose from the ground as if engaged in some weird exercise. Again it hit the sand and rose from it. The bully's eyes were wide with fear as he was made to conduct this ludicrous act of looking up and resting his head, looking up and resting his head. His partners in crime ran off as fast as their legs would carry them, not turning back once, in their quest to escape the inexplicable.

After a few moments, Rick concentrated his gaze to its maximum. The eighteen-stone giant involuntarily stood before him, unable to move a muscle or utter a word. Rick lifted his head slightly and the man's feet left the sand beneath them. He looked down at Rick, having failed to avert his eyes from that of his controller, and remained there, hanging in mid air.

'Take your evil ways away from me and my wife,' Rick said quietly.

The man was unable to reply, but Rick felt fear and confusion fill him utterly. Temptation tickled Rick's thought processes, but he did not succumb to its suggestion. To torment or torture this wretch would be to abuse his newly found abilities and would render he, himself, a bully.

'Go,' Rick said dispassionately.

The man dropped to the ground in a heap, and despite his size he was up and gone in an instant, not once turning back as he ran headlong across the hot sand.

'Use your mind,' Rick said softly to himself, recalling Tal's words of advice. 'I'm beginning to understand.'

Chapter 52

11th July 2001

Sunlight streamed into the room as if there were no curtains covering the double glass doors leading the balcony.

Ellie slept like a baby. It seemed to Rick that she had slept more since they arrived in the Maldives than at any time during her pregnancy. Still, it didn't bother him. It was just the peace and quiet she needed for her own and Rebecca's well-being. And he couldn't argue with that.

Nine thirty was late for Rick to wake, but here it was nothing special for Ellie. He showered, dressed and poured himself a coffee, not surprised that his activities failed to penetrate her sleep.

As he sat quietly looking out to sea, Rick felt an inner confidence. It was refreshing. The past couple of months since his journey through time had been filled with trepidation and frustration. But now he was more accepting of the whole situation, in spite of the 21st July looming ever closer. He had resigned himself to the fact that he wouldn't discover the killer's identity until the day itself, that he wouldn't know how to deal with the big day until it came and that to worry constantly about it was of no help at all. Also, being able to *see* what was happening in the minds and hearts of those around him was a great advantage. And the growing power within him to channel his emotions towards achieving his goals was of great importance. More to the point, being able to control the actions of others through the power of his mind could be the difference between success and failure.

Today felt exhilarating.

As the sun peeped out from behind a cloud, its intensity caught him unawares and snapped him from his reverie.

His thoughts turned to Frank Parsons. How, when a man's wife had been murdered, could he revel in the ensuing misery? How could anyone get a perverted sense of satisfaction out of his sadness, and then add to the despair by sending horrible letters as if they were from the killer? Why? Because he didn't like him. Didn't like him; he must hate him with a vengeance. A man with a gun secreted in a locked drawer in his private office who hates him with a passion. Surely that hatred, coupled with a jealousy thick and green, would be a concoction sufficiently potent to form a murderous intent. There was no doubt about it. Parsons was the number one suspect.

Sipping his coffee, Rick thought for a while about his boss. The man had an alibi, fully checked out by the police when he was arrested. But was the alibi water-tight? Criminals walked free from the courts every day due to shoddy investigation, short cuts and technicalities. Everyone knew that they were as guilty as sin, but in defiance of that knowledge the 'system' allowed them to escape with smirks on their faces.

An understandable antagonism rose in Rick's heart towards Parsons, and he felt a familiar, though relatively diluted, tightening of his chest. Parsons could actually be the one who changed the course of history; the insignificant little tin-god sat at his desk barking his orders to people on a daily basis. Mr Nobody, yet Mr Momentous. Then, the feeling which followed. The feeling he loved so much.

Peace, happiness and equanimity. Abandonment of care overtook him as he became once more at one with himself and the world.

Chapter 53

'Mother, I've told you a thousand times. The key is on the mantelpiece. It's really not difficult.'

'I know. I just keep forgetting. When you get to my age, Frank, little things escape you. You'll find out one day.'

'I'd kill myself before I got into your state,' he said under his breath. 'Why don't you just do me a favour,' and with that he grabbed his car keys and made for the door.

'Frank... FRANK,' Mrs Parsons yelled in a desperate tone.

'What? I'll be late for work.'

'Where's my key?'

Frank sighed heavily and ignored his mother. He could tell her three or four times in the space of five minutes and she still wouldn't remember. Sometimes he thought she did it to make him feel guilty for leaving her in the house alone. But he would not feel guilty, not at any price. Feeling guilty had ruined his life already. Old Mrs Parsons had laid it on thick twenty years ago when her husband died. She had treated Frank's girlfriend with disdain, never welcoming her into her home, and she had persuaded Frank not to leave her by moving into a place of his own with Diane. She blackmailed him emotionally with fake breakdowns and make-believe ailments. Anything to keep him with her. Diane had been Frank's only real partner, but as the months turned into years she grew weary of the unbreakable grip his mother had over him and they separated. It was something he would never forgive his mother for. Since then he had put on weight, lost his hair and turned bitter, opting to stay in as a protest against the world of 'normal' people leading 'normal' lives. He lost touch with the real world, outside a working environment, and felt that it was too big a step to start again with relationships. Too much like hard work. So his energies were spent wielding what limited authority he had at the bank, a pastime which earned him both dislike and derision.

His mother owed him. An only child, Frank would take the money from the sale of her house and her belongings without even thinking of her. He would move far, far away from where he had spent the whole of his forty three years and start afresh. It would be difficult at first, but he would do it. Throw away the old was his motto, and forget about it was his little addendum.

He opened the driver's door of his Mercedes and closed it firmly behind him, sinking into the leather upholstery. 'How much bloody longer,' he said aloud, alluding to his mother's life.

It had got to the point where he was leaving earlier and earlier for work. The journey was approximately twenty-five minutes and as such he didn't have to set off until after eight o'clock. Yet most mornings he was gone for seven thirty. His mother was an early riser and she insisted he sort out her medication and get her breakfast before he left for work. The tedium was destroying him.

As if in defiance of the way he lived, Frank turned up the CD player in the car until Eric Clapton beat at his brains. He lost himself in the music, as was his wont most mornings on his way to the office. It set him up for the day.

As Frank rounded the blind corner, he hardly had time to see the concrete mixer on his side of the road before its sheer weight crushed his lovely Mercedes and him in it beyond recognition. A police spokesman said that the driver of the truck had suffered a fatal heart attack at the wheel, and that Mr Parsons hadn't stood a chance.

Chapter 54

14th July 2001

Eventually giving way to Ellie's unselfishness, Rick spent half a day snorkelling. The shallow, blue sea coupled with the beautiful marine life really exhilarated him. It was as if he lived in one world and was oblivious to another so close by, rarely visited but every bit as real and vibrant as his own. And one without the machinations. He longed to be one of the colourful fish that populated these waters in abundance, with its beauty and freedom unchained by the knowledge which ruined Adam and Eve. The knowledge which threatened to ruin him.

Yet if he took the place of one of these creatures, he would lose the ability to love. The satisfaction of giving, and receiving, at Christmas time would disappear, together with passion, joy, hope and an array of other emotions reserved primarily for human beings. No, the life of the fish here seemed to be unbeatable on the face of it, but in truth it was a poor second best to the gifts bestowed upon him.

As he walked back into the hotel room, he caught Ellie wiping her eyes hurriedly with the back of her hands.

'What's the matter?' he asked.

'Oh, nothing,' she replied.

'You've been crying,' Rick said, pointing out the obvious. He sat beside her on the bed and put an arm around her. 'Come on. A problem shared?'

'Really, it's nothing. It's just me being silly.'

'That's nothing new.'

Ellie smiled, her face still damp with tears.

'I've been thinking about Anna, that's all.'

'Anna? What's reminded you of her?'

'Nothing in particular.'

'Right. Tell me what you've been thinking.'

'Well... it would have been nice if she'd been at the wedding. We were so close as little ones, but as the years went by she changed. She seemed to develop a strange envy and bitterness towards me and I can't work out to this day why.'

'It's hard for me to imagine,' Rick said. 'I always longed for a brother or a sister when I was small, but it took mum and dad nine years to have me. They thought they couldn't have kids. And no more came along. I used to be jealous of other kids at school when they talked about their younger brother or older sister; I'd feel strangely left out, like I had no-one to turn to. My mum and dad were good parents, but it wasn't the same somehow.'

'I feel like that now,' Ellie interrupted. 'But it's worse for me in a way because I actually had, have, a sister but for whatever reason she was wrenched away and she clearly doesn't feel anything towards me. Nothing except jealousy.'

'It's sad, that's true enough.'

'She must hate me, Rick. I hadn't seen her for thirteen years, and within minutes she was threatening me. I just don't understand it. What's more, I might never see her again.'

With that a fresh flood of tears came and Ellie let them run freely, while Rick comforted her.

As he hugged his wife, Rick thought how selfish Ellie's sister must be. He felt a twinge of anger towards her as he imagined the conversation the two women must have had in the café. Ellie would have been elated at seeing her sister after so many years, but Anna extinguished without a care any love showed to her by her sister. Ellie would have regarded their chance meeting as fortuitous, even hoping that they could meet again. Her exuberance would have seen through the surface-Anna sat before her, and hoped of some future between them, but this in turn would have been dashed by the hostile and unloving monster that had swallowed her sister whole years before they met.

This woman, whom he had never met, was responsible for Ellie's sadness now as she cried like a baby on her own honeymoon. As she wept for the love she wished she had from Anna. Rick again felt the anger rise in him, but as it began to take hold of his emotions it was, once again, gone, leaving the familiar warm and tranquil sensation behind. Rick let the feelings wash over him and as he did so he felt a part of them leave him and enter the mind of his wife, lying in his arms. Within moments she discarded her grief, almost unnaturally, and adopted a contented air. She did not question her sudden change of heart, and Rick did not need to ask why she had changed.

Rick secretly wondered about the anger and the calmness. The anger had left him and dissipated. But the serenity he had passed on to Ellie. He hoped there was no more to it than this.

Chapter 55

The MR2 shone in the car-park below, the red paint-work looking at its best in the glorious sunshine.

Anna was late setting off, but she was unconcerned. Not so long ago, she was tied to bus time-tables and unreliable trains to get her from A to B. But not now. The lease car, her very own sports car for now, had given her the ability to lie in a little longer and still meet her appointments on time. This morning, for example, she was in the Sheffield apartment at 9.20, and had to meet Joe at the Roundhay apartment in Leeds at 10 o'clock sharp. She didn't have to crawl out of bed until nine. A ton plus on the short motorway journey between the cities would ensure she was bang on time, if not a little early.

Throwing her handbag loosely over her shoulder, Anna opened the door to the apartment block. She hadn't had chance to walk through it before a man's hand unexpectedly pushed her slight frame back through the doorway and into the hall.

'Mr Warrener,' Anna said, her eyes wide.

'Yes. Mr Warrener,' he repeated in a menacing tone.

'What do you want? I have to go out.'

'Get back into your flat, now.'

'But I…'

'Now,' Warrener said again, this time with venom between gritted teeth.

'And what if I scream the place down?'

Warrener reached into the right pocket of his jacket and raised the jacket. There was something pointed in there, something that looked like a gun.

'OK, OK,' Anna said hurriedly and turned on her heel, making her way up the two flights of carpeted stairs to the apartment.

'What do you want from me?' she said coldly when the pair were inside.

'Because of you, you little bitch, I've lost everything. Fucking everything.'

'What do you mean?'

'What do you mean?' he mimicked her girly voice. 'You had to tell Joe about our little misunderstanding didn't you? Well, since then he's told me there's no more deals between us. He keeps sending threatening mail to my address. I know he's responsible. The wife wants to move, she's shit scared. The kids' lives are being threatened for God's sake.'

'That's not my fault,' she said defiantly.

Anna underestimated the degree of anger in the man. Without warning he let fly with a fist which she was too late to avoid. Feeling like she had been struck with a hammer she flew across the living room, her seven stones no match for the sixteen behind Warrener's punch. Anna thudded against the wall opposite and felt dizzy. The attacker's rantings only half registered in her brain as she fumbled clumsily in her handbag for her pistol.

The cold, hard metal was easy to feel among tissues, make-up and her leather purse. She withdrew the weapon in an instant and pointed it towards the man, who had been advancing on her prior to seeing the wrong side of a gun facing him. Warrener turned and fled quicker than anyone would have thought possible for a man his size.

As he neared the door to the lounge, Anna pulled the trigger and the bang caused her ears to ring. Momentarily, she was deaf. Warrener writhed on the floor, blood flowing freely from his left leg. He tried desperately to plug the gaping hole in his inner thigh, but the task was beyond him.

Anna's head reeled, both from the gunshot and the beating, and she trained the little pistol on her attacker once more.

'Please Claire, please,' he pleaded like a child. 'I'm sorry. Honest to God I'm so sorry. I'll go and I won't say anything to anyone. Don't kill me. Please. Please.' He began to cry.

A feeling of power and control enveloped Anna. Never

317

before had she felt so much in command. Those who had abused her for so many years had felt the power over her. The heroin had that control over her. But now *she* held the reins. This pathetic woman-beater didn't even know her real name, and she held his life in her hands. Just as she would hold Ellie's life. Ellie, the privileged one, would beg and plead with her just as this man was doing now.

She let off a second blast. This one ripped through the man's left cheek, taking half his face off. He fell unconscious, in preparation for death.

Smiling, she aimed the gun again. Her saviour, the little black pistol. It had saved her life and gained her respect. She put the steel to her lips and kissed it. Then she took aim again.

As she looked at the dying man, twitching ridiculously at the other side of the room, an all-encompassing blackness entered her heart and her mind. Suddenly, Anna felt a depression take hold of her with a grip far stronger than any other feeling she had ever experienced. It was if ten years' worth of sadness, melancholy and grief had descended upon her in one unmanageable mass. She became instantly regretful of everything bad she had ever done; every negative thought she had ever had, every ounce of ill-will she had felt towards others gathered together and questioned her ability to face them, here and now.

Tears filled her eyes and streamed down her cheeks, dripping off her chin and her nose. But the sorrow was insufficient to purge the blackness from her soul.

Anna looked at the gun in her hand. She saw it through watery eyes as it turned gradually, as the hole at the barrel-end came within view.

Her hand began to shake as she fought with the feelings within her. But she was unable to halt the progress of the turning pistol. Moments later, the gun faced her, head on. She stared into the black barrel, her finger firmly on the trigger.

'No,' she said. 'I don't want to die.'

But you have to, Anna, a voice in her head answered.

'No. NO,' she shouted.

It's inevitable, the voice warned. Don't fight it.

Every ounce of Anna's strength was taken trying to avert the pistol from her head. She decided not to reason with the voice within any further, but to try to put the gun down. A minute past, two minutes. Still the weapon faced her, its dark eye staring her out, defying her inner wishes.

This is mad, she thought. What's the matter with me? She grappled for a further few moments, but the gun wouldn't budge.

Goodbye, Anna, the voice said dispassionately in her head.

Sweat rolled down her forehead and into her eyes, the salt stinging, as the gun's barrel edged towards her mouth. Anna's lips parted, in spite of her, and the barrel touched the roof of her mouth with intricate delicacy, settling in an almost vertical position.

The confusion written starkly across Anna's face became instantly illegible as the tiny piece of lead rendered her features unrecognisable.

Anna didn't know why she had to die, but it wouldn't prey on her mind now.

Chapter 56

17th July 2001

Josie rapped at the door a second time. She had seen movement in the living room at John and Mary Greening's house as she approached the door, but no-one had answered.

Ever since Josie met Ellie she had been welcomed into her home by Ellie's parents. They had grown close and she loved John and Mary more than her own mum and dad. Her own flesh and blood didn't care sufficiently about her to track her down in over four years since she left home, yet these people had listened to her when she had cried and told how her parents had given all their love to her brother. The day she left without a word was the day when her mum had explained that she didn't want Josie on the family photograph at her brother's graduation ceremony. It was the last straw for her, a blatant indication that she wasn't regarded as one of the family. And she had never heard from any of them since.

Mary Greening, in particular, had listened to her story carefully. Her own daughter, Anna, had left home nine years before Josie arrived on the scene, claiming that Ellie was the only one they loved and that she had been excluded. But that wasn't true. Unbeknown to the Greenings, Anna had begun associating with a boy who took drugs. His circle of friends influenced her way of thinking and she began to baulk against all that her mum and dad had taught her in life. As the months past, Anna became impossibly unreasonable and rows broke out frequently. By the time they realised what was going on it was too late. Anna had begun taking heroin and she refused point blank any help from them. Deep down, Anna had wished she could turn back the clock. She had looked at Ellie with envy as her younger sister tried to ignore the mayhem around her and study for her exams.

When Ellie was praised for her efforts, Anna had interpreted it as a criticism of herself and so it went from bad to worse until the drugs took hold of her completely and she left home in disgrace, knowing in her heart of hearts that only she was to blame for what had happened. But it had been easier for her to cope if she blamed someone else, and that someone was Ellie.

John and Mary knew they had done all they possibly could for their eldest, yet the sense of failure still haunted them, particularly each Christmas when Anna sent a card to them, excluding Ellie's name.

As the years past an unwritten, unmentioned, state of affairs had arisen whereby Josie regarded the Greenings as her surrogate parents, and Mary Greening regarded Josie as a second daughter, a substitute for Anna. Their relationship was never spoken of in these terms, but it was what had happened in their minds. As such, Josie treated their home as hers and visited frequently, even if Ellie wasn't around. Even John Greening had grown used to the arrangement.

Strange, she thought, looking at the glossy red door. She knocked again, this time loudly enough to hurt her knuckles on the hard wood.

John answered the door.

'Yes.'

Josie looked at him, the smile quickly fading from her face as she saw his red eyes and his serious expression.

'What's the matter? Has something happened?'

'You'd better come in, I suppose,' he said.

Josie's appearance at the house had started Mary's wailing afresh.

'Mary, what's happened?' Josie asked, beginning to feel genuinely afraid.

The woman was too grief-stricken to reply.

'Sit down, love,' John said. 'It's Anna, she's… she's…' His throat filled with hurt and he struggled to say the words. 'Dead.'

'Anna's dead! How?'

'She committed suicide,' John said in a matter-of-fact tone.

'When did this happen?'

'Yesterday. The police came to see us.'

Josie wasn't surprised. After everything Ellie had told her about Anna, and after the time she had seen her in person, albeit a fleeting moment, she had realised that Anna was a classic case of self-harm and suicide. Josie spoke to people like her every week as a Samaritan. And very few of those people she tried to help ever came out of the drugs game. Almost all of them spent the majority of their time in police cells and in prison for thieving and burgling and prostitution. Anything to get money for smack. Most of them lost their families in the process, as Anna had, and the inner turmoil caused them such pain that they often slashed their wrists as a cry for help. And after years of abuse and self abuse either their bodies gave up and they died, usually alone whist injecting, or their souls gave way and they took their own lives.

That was how drugs worked. But it didn't make it any easier for those left behind. Those like the Greenings. Nothing anyone could say could relieve them of the guilt. For a long time they would regard themselves as responsible for their daughter's death and nothing could change that in the short term. Only time would change things, as the years brought about a realisation that they had, in truth, done their best.

'I'm so sorry,' Josie said, and she left it at that.

'We all are, love,' John replied, as Mary continued to cry into her tissue.

'Do Ellie and Rick know?'

'No,' John said. 'They haven't rung yet, and they didn't leave a contact number. They're probably having a great time.' He smiled momentarily, but it didn't last long.

'It's not up to me, of course,' Josie said, 'But could I make a suggestion?'

'Course you can,' Mary said. 'You're part of this family.'

'When Ellie rings, don't tell her.'

'But…'

'They have over a week left yet, and although it's something that Ellie *has* to know about, do you think she really needs to know while she's on her honeymoon?'

'She's right, Mary,' John interjected. 'There's nothing the girl can do to help right now. She can find out when she gets home; it'll be bad enough then.'

'OK,' Mary agreed, and she scuttled off into the kitchen to make a brew, simply to occupy herself.

'It may seem silly to you,' John said to Josie. 'All this upset. I mean, we haven't seen her for over thirteen years. Our own daughter.'

'Listen, there's not a day goes by where I don't think of my own family, even though that's four and a half years ago and even though they abandoned me and never bothered to find me. The feelings don't go away just because you don't see one another.'

'You're right there. She shot herself, you know.'

'It's awful, but drug addicts often end their lives, if the drugs don't kill them first. It's a harsh fact of life.'

'Life. She didn't have much of one, did she?'

'And that wasn't down to you or Mary. Heroin, it's an absolute killer, John. Not many people get off it once it gets a grip of them.'

'But we could have helped her, if only she'd let us.'

'Probably not. She would have done anything for a fix, anything at all. Steal from you, even kill. That's what the effect of the drug does. You would have been powerless to help, believe me. All I can say is this; at least now her torment is over, she can rest free of pain.'

'Please, leave the counselling bit out will you?'

Josie put up her hands as a sign of surrender. 'You're right,' she said gently.

'Do you mind if I ask you to leave me and Mary to it? We just want to be alone at the moment.'

'Of course not,' Josie replied. 'And if you want my help in any way at all, please ring me, won't you?'

'Thanks, love.'

'Bye, Mary,' Josie called through to the kitchen.

'Are you going?'

'Yeah. I'll leave you in peace.'

Mary didn't argue.

323

Chapter 57

As the newlyweds enjoyed breakfast, Rick's hopes were at an all time high.

Friday 20th, the day before Ellie's death in the altered timeline, and here they were having breakfast in the Indian Ocean. Things were looking good. Rick reduced days to hours. The time of the shooting had been approximately nine o'clock in the evening on the Saturday. It was ten in the morning as he glanced at his watch now. Just thirty-five hours away. No, he thought, slightly more than that. They were five and a half hours ahead of time in England, so the event was actually a touch over forty hours away.

He sat back and looked at Ellie eating. Was Tal correct when she told him that both Ellie and the killer would be on the quiet country road in Yorkshire at the given time? It was looking pretty unlikely. And if she was wrong about that, then the momentous point in time would pass and Rusak would be foiled. Maybe his extension of the honeymoon would be enough to avert the shooting after all.

'What are you looking at?' Ellie asked suspiciously.

'Can't a man look at his wife now without the third degree?' he joked.

'It depends on the motive,' she replied.

'No hidden intent, honest. I just think you look lovely this morning.'

'Well, that's OK, then.'

'I'm really glad we booked the extra week, are you?' Rick asked.

'Yeah. I've been feeling a bit guilty though.'

'Why?'

'Well, if I'd not been pregnant we'd have done so much more together. You would have had a much better time, but you've spent it looking after me. It seems a waste of a holiday of a lifetime if you ask me.'

'Rubbish, it's been fabulous. I've been able to forget all about the office and I've been with you. That's good enough for me. Anyway, there'll be plenty of time in the future for jet-skiing and all that; our baby's far more important at the moment.'

Ellie smiled at him. It truly was a textbook answer, yet Rick was completely genuine.

'And then there's my mum and dad,' Ellie continued.

'What about them?'

'I haven't rung them yet. I told them I'd ring after a fortnight or so and they seemed happy with that, but I feel a bit mean leaving it so long. I feel even meaner only remembering today that I've got them to ring.'

'Don't be so silly. You've been having a lovely relaxing time; they won't mind.'

'Yes, but I forgot to leave the number of the apartment for them. I've always done that in the past.'

'Ellie, you're fretting over nothing. Go ring them and stop feeling guilty. There's nothing to feel guilty about.'

Ellie nodded in agreement and it wasn't until she'd walked several paces from the breakfast table that she realised that her parents wouldn't appreciate a phone call at half past four in the morning.

'You'd have let me make that call, wouldn't you?' she said, playfully clouting Rick on the back of his head with the palm of her hand.

'Sorry, I was miles away,' he replied.

They spent the rest of the morning on the beach near to the hotel, the grin on Rick's face growing broader as each hour passed by.

As lunch time approached, Ellie felt characteristically tired and she laid on the bed for a nap. Unusually, Rick also felt a little fatigued and he laid beside her.

When he awoke, Ellie was gone.

Rick flew into the bathroom, the door banging onto the wall and cracking one of the boarder tiles. She wasn't there. He flung back the curtains to the balcony expecting to see Ellie sat there. But the balcony was empty.

'No. Please no,' he said aloud in a panicky voice. 'Ellie,' he shouted, but there was no answer.

Without hesitation, Rick ran from the apartment and pressed the button to summon the lift. He pressed it again and again in quick succession as if it would respond more speedily to his impatience. His imagination was running away with him and he abandoned the lift. Rick descended the stairs in threes, almost losing his balance several times on the way down to reception. Still he couldn't see Ellie.

Running outside and back onto the beach his eyes frantically scanned the well- populated sands. In the distance he saw what he thought was Ellie's bikini but as he ran headlong towards the wearer of it he saw that it wasn't her.

Calm down, he said to himself, as he composed his thoughts and stood still on the beach while systematically looking at all areas to find his wife. She wasn't there.

A thorough search of the local supermarket where she enjoyed shopping, and three of the nearby eating places which they used regularly, similarly failed to locate her. It was if Rick had been placed in charge of a two year old, barely able to walk, and had lost the child. He felt irresponsible. All he had to do was keep her close at hand for a few more hours, just a few more bloody hours after all the weeks and months of worry, but he had failed. She was nowhere to be found.

Eventually, despondent and weary with worry, he trudged back to the apartment.

'Where on earth have you been?' Ellie asked, sat on the bed as large as life.

'Ellie. Where have *I* been? I've been looking everywhere for you. I woke up and you were gone. I've been on the beach, I've been…'

'Anna's dead.'

The bald statement stopped him in his tracks. 'What?'

'Anna. She's committed suicide. On Monday.'

'Oh my God,' he said.

'I've been on the phone to mum.'

'How is she?'

'She's absolutely devastated. I was talking to her about our holiday and she seemed a bit distant so I asked her what was wrong. She burst into tears and told me. Hell, she even apologised to me.'

'What about you?' Rick said softly.

'I don't know what to think, I really don't. I was upset about Anna the other day, but I just don't know how I feel now. Part of me feels so bloody angry with her. Selfish to the last. How did she think mum and dad would take it? Me, she hated me, but mum and dad. They're falling apart, Rick.'

'Go and ring them again. Give them some support.'

'Ring them? I'm sorry darling, but I'm gonna have to go home. I can't stay here another week while they're in torment. I simply have to be there for them. You stay if you want, I don't want to ruin your holiday as well.'

Despair hit Rick like a hammer blow. His former optimism was pulled from him as if it were his right arm pulled from its socket. He was totally unprepared for this revelation. His first thought was how stupid he had been questioning Tal's knowledge of events. And how naïve he had been thinking that a simple plan such as extending the honeymoon would be enough to avert the inevitable.

'Please, don't go,' he said weakly, not knowing what else to say or do.

'I have to, don't you see?' Ellie said.

He saw all right.

'Listen,' she continued. 'I've been on the phone for about half an hour, and I've sorted us out with a flight. It leaves at twenty-five to two tomorrow afternoon. They couldn't get us on a sooner one even though I explained the problem. I'm sorry, but family comes before anything else, and we've had two lovely weeks. Like I say, you can cancel your flight if you wish and stay the extra week. I wouldn't mind, honestly.'

'No, we're in it together. And we fly back together.'

Ellie wrapped her arms around her husband and hugged him tightly.

It all fitted perfectly, just as predicted, Rick mused. A flight at around one thirty in the afternoon on Saturday taking approximately eleven hours would get them back in Manchester for around seven in the evening, taking into account the five and a half hours time difference between the continents. A little over an hour home on the M62 takes it to about 8pm, maybe quarter past, then the journey to her mums shortly afterwards. There was no mistake, it had been orchestrated to perfection, and no amount of pleading or attempts at side-tracking the process would work. He had to accept that what Tal had said was incontrovertible. Entirely destined, fixed, unalterable.

Tears rolled down Rick's cheeks as he realised that this could be the very last day he and Ellie ever spend together.

'I love you, so much,' he said to her.

'I know.' Then she noticed his wet face. 'Hey, it's not like you to get so upset. What's the matter?'

'Nothing. I just love you, that's all.'

'I told my mum I'd see her late evening tomorrow.' Ellie had done her sums as well. 'Provided there are no delays, of course.'

'Oh, I think you'll find we won't get delayed,' Rick said.

Chapter 58

'Josie? Josie, is that you?'

'Yes, I can hear you.'

'Hello, it's Mary. Sorry, I can't get used to these daft mobile phones you kids have these days.'

'Mary, is everything OK?'

'Not really love, no. Ellie rang me earlier, and I told her. I didn't intend to but she sensed something was wrong and when she asked me outright I couldn't keep it in. I wish John had been in to answer the phone.'

'Don't worry yourself, what's done is done. What did she say?'

'I feel awful. She insisted on coming home early.'

'Yeah, that's why I thought it might be best not to tell her.'

Mary started crying again. All the emotions washed around her system and it didn't take much to start her off.

'Hey, don't cry, it's not the end of the world. She's had two weeks.'

'I know,' she sobbed.

'Is there anything I can do? Do you want me to come round?'

'Well, I thought it might help if you were here when she arrived, you know.'

'Meet her at the airport?'

'No, not the airport. But if you wouldn't mind been here at my house when she gets back. I think it would help her emotionally, you being best friends. I don't think me or John will be of much use to her.'

'When's she due back?'

'Tomorrow evening. About nine.'

'We're going out with Tom's brother from Birmingham

329

tomorrow night. It's his birthday, but…'

'Oh listen, it doesn't matter then. It was just an idea that's all.'

'I'll see what Tom says.'

'No, forget it, honestly. We'll manage.'

'Well, if I came the next day, would that be of any help?'

'Yes. That would be great. Thanks.'

'All right, Mary, bye.'

'Bye.'

Chapter 59

21ˢᵗ July 2001 – 1.15 pm Local Time, India

As they boarded the plane, Rick's stomach was churning.

Not only had the day he dreaded above all others arrived, but his fear of flying had kicked in as well. It wasn't as though he was new to the game, in fact he had flown fifteen or twenty times before, but it was always the same before he set off. Strangely, being five or six miles above the ground didn't worry him too much in itself. It was taking off and landing that he hated. He knew that most accidents occurred at those moments and he never felt at ease until the thing was well up in the heavens and had levelled off. Then he could relax.

Ellie held his hand tightly as they climbed the steps to the door. He preferred the walk-through corridors where he only had to step onto the plane at the last moment from an enclosed, carpeted gangway. But smaller airports rarely had these facilities. As they ascended the stairway, the rear-mounted engines were already fired up and they hissed loudly, ready for action. Ready for 150 mph plus, along a strip of tarmac. He loathed it. He loathed feeling afraid by it just as much, it made him feel silly and irrational. Ellie had often quoted the statistics that air-travel was by far the safest form of transport, and that he was in more danger travelling to work in his car on a morning. He knew she was right, but it didn't help.

The plane's thrust pushed Rick's head back into his seat as the speed rapidly increased on the runway. 50 mph, 80, 110, 140, 150, 160, all in the space of twenty or thirty seconds. His hands were damp with perspiration and beads of sweat formed on his forehead as he closed his eyes tightly, wishing the seconds away. Then the familiar feeling which accompanied the loss of traction on the rough runway surface. They were almost airborne.

Rick relaxed slightly, but it was premature.

There was a bang, loud and sudden from the rear of the plane and immediately the noise from the engines was reduced. The front wheels, having left the ground, thumped back onto the tarmac with sickly force. The seat belt which Rick always wore tightly only allowed the top half of his body to be thrown forward as the brakes were applied at full force. God knows how much runway we have left, he thought to himself.

Ellie closed her eyes and remained calm, but others around were screaming and shouting. Babies were crying. There was no time for any calming words from the pilot or the crew; they were too busy dealing with whatever had happened and with trying to bring the monster to a halt before it broke up or caught fire or hurtled off the end of the runway.

Rick physically trembled with fright. Every passing second seemed like a minute as he had time to discern the sounds of the screeching wheels on the ground, the banging coming from the damaged engine and the sheer terror of those all around him. As the moments past, the plane seemed to be losing its battle to stop. It just went on and on and on. The skidding, the noise from the rear and the panic, it was incessant. Then the plane began to veer to its left. The runway was left behind as the tons of unstoppable metal crossed a grassed area towards a building which loomed closer and closer as each second went by.

A curious feeling came over Rick and as he opened his eyes he saw a bright light begin to form a few feet ahead of him and near to the ceiling. His panic began to subside as the light grew in intensity. He couldn't work out what it was. As the light became brighter, Rick's fear diminished.

During the last few months he had begun to recognise when things were not as they should be, and this was one of those moments. For a short time, his thoughts cleared. How could this plane crash and get them back to England in time for the predestined event? The plane's collision with the nearby building seemed inevitable, yet that would kill most people on it, and Ellie couldn't die here, today; she was due to die later. None of made sense.

The light's brilliance in front of him grew, and as it did so Rick's interest in living became less and less. He could feel it. As the seconds past the light became more and more attractive to him, and saving Ellie began to be less and less important. Surrendering to the light would have been the easiest thing in the world to do. He just wanted to fall into it, longed for it to envelope him in its beauty. But his mind maintained a stubborn element of doubt, one which put a barrier between him and the light, between life and... death?

That was it! He suddenly knew what was happening. His worst fears were being used to kill him. Sitting on a plane during take-off and that plane heading for a disaster was just about the worst fear Rick could experience. And he had almost fallen into the trap. In fact, he was seconds from death. The light was banishing his fears and beckoning him to abandon himself.

It felt comforting, but he wasn't ready for giving up the ghost yet.

'NOOOOOOO...' he yelled at the top of his voice.

'Rick, for God's sake,' Ellie scolded him. 'You're gonna have to get some counselling for this problem, it's embarrassing.'

The plane lifted gently and smoothly into the air. Apart from his outburst, the passengers were quiet and content. A stewardess unbelted herself and came to speak to Rick, who was sat next to the aisle.

'Is everything all right sir?' she asked.

'Yes. I'm sorry,' Rick replied, looking sheepish.

Chapter 60

21st July 2001 – 7.12 pm BST

There had been a head wind, so the original forecast the pilot made on setting off from Male airport was awry by thirty minutes or so. He had predicted a landing at six thirty five pm but the unexpected wind at high altitude had slowed the plane down and now it was almost quarter past seven.

It didn't come as any surprise to Rick when all four suitcases they had with them appeared on the conveyer before anyone else's, after all the slight delay had to be compensated for somehow. Why couldn't one of the damn things have been lost, like two years ago in Spain? That had held them up for almost two hours.

The traffic on the motorways was light too as the Sheldons made uninterrupted progress towards Leeds. No traffic jams or hold-ups of any kind. The family car pulled up on the driveway at eight twenty seven and Ellie alighted, as if in a rush.

'Listen,' Rick said as he switched off the house alarm. 'Can't I persuade you to ring your mum and tell her you'll see her first thing in the morning? It's been a long day.'

'No way. We're back on time and I'm going to see them. That's final.'

'There's the baby to think about as well, you know?'

'Oh, yes,' Ellie replied sarcastically. 'I hadn't thought of the baby at all, how remiss of me. Rick, I'm not planning on climbing a rock face, I'm going four miles in the car and sitting down on a comfy chair with a cuppa, now lay off.' She seemed agitated.

Rick knew Ellie all too well. There was no chance of him dissuading her, and the more he tried to do so the less chance there was of success. Despair took hold of him, but he kept it hidden, he had to. He felt so powerless.

The time of reckoning had arrived, and with it fear and apprehension.

'Do you fancy a brew before you go?' he called upstairs.

'No, I'm gonna get straight off. The sooner I go, the sooner I'll be back,' she replied.

Rick slumped on to the third stair and put his hands to his face. He had never felt so much pressure in his entire life. The next hour would decide the fate of his family and the whole of humankind, and there was no escaping it. If he remained at home as he had done the first time, Ellie would be shot dead and the detectives would come calling at his door. If he confronted the situation he could fail and the outcome would be the same. It could even mean his own death. Rick exhaled, as if he were about to step into the kick-boxing ring with a man two weights up from his own. He stood and focussed his thoughts.

'I'm coming with you,' he told Ellie as she descended the stairs, having changed into a short summer skirt.

'You're not,' she said flatly. 'You aren't exactly Mr Tactful at the best of times, and I think…'

'I said I'm coming with you,' Rick said assertively, interrupting her.

'Why?' Ellie protested.

'Well thanks very much,' Rick said, as if hurt. 'I've come home with you, haven't I? That's because I love you. Now I'd like to give you some moral support and I think it would be nice for your parents too, us showing our *joint* support for them; we are married now unless that escaped your notice.'

'You big softy,' she said with a smile. 'Come on then, chop chop.'

'OK, OK. I'll just visit the bathroom.'

Rick shot up the stairs as Ellie walked into the lounge. Climbing onto the stool from under the dressing table he reached up to the very back of the top box above his hanging space in the wardrobe, and removed two old jumpers that he no longer wore. In between the two scruffy jumpers was the small, black hand-gun he had confiscated from Frank Parsons' desk. Quickly, he dropped the piece into the right pocket of his light, leather jacket.

The stool replaced, Rick flushed the toilet before descending the stairs and walked coolly into the lounge.

'Are we ready, then?'

'Yeah. And Rick?'

'What?'

'Thanks.'

They headed out to the car.

CHANGING TIMES

Chapter 61

21st July 2001 – 8.32 pm

Keeping his head in a crisis was something Rick thought he had mastered, what with the goings on during the last two and a half months of his life. But he was wrong. His heart beat fast as Ellie drove the car onto the country road leading to her parents' house. Breathing deeply he tried, against the demons inside, to clear his head and stay focussed on the task in hand. At least the next few minutes would end this nightmare one way or another, he thought to himself, but it was scant relief as the butterflies in his stomach churned to such a degree that he thought he would explode. He coughed deeply once or twice and retched slightly, which reminded him of a visit to the dentists he made when he was seven years old. His dad had had to stop the car by the roadside and Rick had been sick. He was almost there again.

Rick told himself that he would not be at his best if he didn't feel this intense worry and anguish. It was the body's way of releasing adrenaline ready for the fight, and of keeping the senses alert and sharp-edged. Several beads of sweat ran down his forehead, one stinging as the droplet entered the corner of his left eye. As if turned on by an invisible tap, his underarms perspired to the point where they were wet and he felt drips of sweat splash onto his side. Without thinking, he loosened his seat belt and removed his jacket, placing it on the rear seat.

'What's the matter?' Ellie asked, 'You look upset.'

'No, no,' he replied. 'Just warm, that's all.'

'I only plan on staying for an hour or so, you know.'

'Yeah, I know,' Rick said, sounding entirely disinterested as he looked furtively all around for any sign of anything or anyone who could start the fearful ball rolling.

Ellie's brow formed a furrow as she mused over her

husband's odd mood.

The houses were now left behind as they progressed into the countryside. As Rick looked ahead and behind there was no sign of life. No cars or pedestrians to be seen anywhere, just the two of them. As they rounded a blind bend Rick saw, maybe two hundred yards ahead, a small vehicle with its hazard warning lights flashing. His hackles stood up on the back of his neck and he instinctively clenched his fists as they neared the vehicle.

'Oh, look,' Ellie exclaimed. 'Some poor soul's broken down here, in the middle of nowhere. Have you got your mobile with you?' She slowed.

The question may as well have been, 'Why don't we stop and die, darling?' Rick was incredulous, as if she had asked the latter.

'Don't stop,' he ordered her in a slightly raised voice, despite trying to keep calm.

'Why ever not? They might need some help calling someone.'

'Just... drive on,' Rick said.

'What the hell's got into you? You've been acting weird ever since we got home.'

'No... it's just...'

'Ha ha ha,' Ellie laughed, her face beaming. 'It's Josie.'

Rick squinted and saw that Ellie was right. It was as if a lead weight had been taken off his shoulders. He couldn't believe his luck; this situation could be tailored to delay them by at least half an hour if he played it right.

'She's damned lucky we came along. Pull in, pull in,' he said hastily.

Again Ellie gave him a puzzled look. 'OK, calm down will you?' she said in a tone which revealed her growing agitation with Rick's demeanour.

Josie peered into the oncoming vehicle's windscreen, her hand shielding her eyes from the sun's rays, lingering low in the sky. She smiled and waved upon seeing Ellie.

Ellie left her car twenty yards or so short of her friend's, and put her own hazards on to alert any other traffic coming up behind of the danger. She and Rick alighted and made their way towards their mutual friend. The bonnet of Josie's car was up.

'I can't believe we've come across you. You've always been a lucky sod,' Ellie joked. 'If it'd been me, I'd have waited for hours for help.' She smiled, glad to see her closest friend again after being away.

'I'm just glad I didn't miss you,' Josie said.

'How do you mean?' Rick asked.

'Well I spoke to Mary on the phone yesterday and she asked me to come over this evening, you know, to give you guys a little moral support.'

Ellie hung her head, having been reminded of her sister again.

'But then I go and break down.'

'What's wrong with it?' Rick asked.

'I don't know. It just died on me as I drove along. Nothing's smoking in the engine or anything, but I can't start it.'

'I'll get the toolbox from the boot of mine and we'll see what we can do,' Rick offered generously.

Ellie looked in Rick's direction as he walked back to their car, a bewildered expression on her face. 'Since when has he known a second thing about car maintenance?' she said, sneering as she faced Josie.

'It seems to me you don't know a good thing when it's staring you in the face,' Josie replied, a serious aspect to her face.

'What?' Ellie said, not sure whether she had heard her friend correctly.

'You do nothing but take the piss out of him. Sometimes I think you don't deserve him.'

Ellie felt herself redden. She didn't know whether to laugh or to slap Josie, whose expression remained fixed.

'If this is some kind of joke, I don't appreciate it; I'm on the way to my mum's because Anna's dead, unless you'd forgotten?'

'Yes, yes. Dear Anna. The druggie.'

Ellie's mouth hung open in disbelief as Rick made his way back towards them, clutching a toolbox. Just as Ellie was about to tell Rick what Josie had said, Josie calmly reached into her handbag, which was still over her shoulder, and pulled out a small pistol which she pointed directly at Ellie. At the same time she took a step or two backwards to put herself beyond Ellie's reach.

Rick was midway between his own car and Josie's as he saw her withdraw the weapon and point it into his wife's face. A feeling of utter dejection washed over him and engulfed him with the force of a tidal wave. Thoughts flashed through his mind at computer speed. He realised first that he had left his own gun in his car, that he was carrying a toolbox and that he was too far from the women to take any action quickly enough to avert the event. It was a body-blow. What surprised him also was that he had felt no hostility from Josie when he and Ellie first went to speak to her. He had relied on this newly-found intuition helping him, but either he had lost the ability or it had somehow been masked by Josie.

There was *no* time to think, no time whatsoever. Within a second Josie would pull the trigger and within a millisecond after that the bullet would do its work and change history to that fashioned by Rusak.

'Why?' he said without shouting. He didn't want to shock or pressure Josie into doing what she had clearly planned to do all along.

'Why?' she said in reply, fixing her gaze solidly on her prospective victim with outstretched arms. 'Why? Because I love you Rick.'

Ellie's face could be read like a book. Utter shock, coupled with fear, was written all over it. Her mouth was slightly open. She was unable to speak or to move, as if being rooted to the spot and dumb would help her cause.

'Do you?' Rick replied, feigning an interest in what Josie had suddenly proclaimed.

'Yes I do,' she said emphatically. 'And you never noticed.'

Rick couldn't think what to say next to continue the conversation. He was afraid of angering Josie and pushing her into pulling the trigger, so he spoke without thinking what would be best.

'I'm sorry. I wish I'd known sooner.'

The words didn't seem to enter Ellie's brain, as she continued to stare at her friend of four years.

'Oh yeah. You're just saying that to stop me.'

'No, honestly,' Rick continued, grasping for a suitable adlib. 'I've always fancied you, right from when I first met you. But other people got in the way.' He swallowed hard.

'Well... that maybe,' Josie said softly. 'But it's too late now, you're FUCKING MARRIED.'

'So, it's only a piece of paper,' Rick said desperately. 'It doesn't have to stop us. But if you pull that trigger, we'll never be together. How could we be, you'd be thrown in jail?'

Tears ran freely down Josie's cheeks. No-one moved a muscle. Rick's mind worked overtime. All those suspects he had in mind; all that trying to eliminate Parsons, Danielle and Sarah from the equation by appeasing them. All a waste of time and effort. It was Josie all along. She had killed Ellie and her plan had worked because a scant few months later she shared Rick's bed, and his life. She had murdered his wife and replaced her.

'I'm right, aren't I?' he ventured, hoping that Josie would train the gun's barrel away from Ellie's head.

'I've always liked you,' Josie continued. 'But since the dream.'

'Dream?' Rick asked.

'Yes, the dream.' The gun pointed implacably at Ellie, who remained transfixed, too scared to move an inch. 'I had a dream, such a vivid one. It seemed to know that I loved you, and it told me that I must have you. It was right, it was what I wanted all along, I just couldn't admit it. I've spent the last three months longing to be with you, longing to hold you and to make love to you.' She appeared entranced by the obsession which had totally taken over her. Her eyes were tearful, yet glazed as she spoke, revealing unashamedly her inner most feelings.

'We *can* be together, Josie,' Rick said in a surprisingly persuasive tone.

'No. You're married to this one,' she said with gritted teeth as she looked into Ellie's eyes. 'And there's the baby. You wouldn't leave the baby. No, it's too late. If *I* can't have you, why should she? She doesn't love you like I do, you know. No-one ever could.'

As Rick frantically tried to think of another sentence to stall Josie he glanced at the gun in her hand. He could see Josie squeezing the trigger. Her forefinger moved steadily backwards and she kept her arms outstretched and the weapon trained accurately at her victim's head.

He had failed. There was no time to prevent the firing of the gun physically, and his best efforts at dissuading Josie had been unsuccessful.

An unimaginably powerful rage gripped Rick, so potent and sudden that he winced with pain and held his head. When he opened his eyes he saw that things had slowed down. A slow-motion scene faced him, as it had done when his anger had grown with Danielle Harper as she lied to his boss in an attempt to get him sacked. But this feeling was incredibly more intense. He concentrated on perpetuating the slowness, and the passage of time obeyed his command. Josie's finger had travelled to its zenith and the trigger rested against the metal bar, her finger curled.

She had taken the shot.

Rick looked at the gun and he saw the bullet emerge from its barrel. The tiny piece of metal and lead, deadly despite its size, moved lethargically through the air, yet purposefully towards its target. Rick mustered all his concentration on the bullet, observing it with every ounce of his strength.

'STOP' he ordered in a quiet yet authoritative voice. The object moved unabated, but as it passed the half-way point between origin and target it lost its momentum and slowed further, eventually stopping four feet or so slightly off centre of Ellie's forehead. Apart from that look originally displayed on Ellie's face, there was no added fear or shock. The bullet would have entered and exited her head prior to her hearing the crack of the pistol or even realising that had been fired.

Time stood still, as Rick had decreed.

Yet he could move within it freely. Quickly, Rick placed the toolbox on the ground and made his way to where Josie stood. To her, his movements would be so swift that she would be dispossessed of the weapon and the bullet pushed off course before she realised what had happened.

As he came within three or four feet of the bullet, hanging motionless in mid-air, Rick fell to the ground, having struck something solid but invisible. The blow physically hurt as it was completely unexpected. He stood and looked ahead of him but could see nothing. He stepped gingerly forward but found that he was unable to move beyond a certain point. And the bullet was out of his reach.

Then he was propelled backwards, falling for a second time on his backside. He instinctively jumped up in a vain attempt to face his attacker. Looking directly ahead of him, the scene was unchanged. Then, almost imperceptibly, he thought he saw a slight shimmering in the air, similar to that visible from a red-hot radiator throwing its heat into an otherwise cold room. A shiver passed along his spine as a gargantuan figure appeared gradually before his eyes.

Rusak.

The professor became clearer over the next twenty seconds until he was there in person, standing a few paces away from the incredulous Rick, who had to crane his neck to look the man in the eyes. Rusak was in excess of ten feet tall and well-built. Rick had no idea of his age, but he appeared to be in the region of sixty. His gold, skin-tight, all-in-one suit accentuated his impressive physique as he peered down at Rick.

Without having spoken a word, Rick heard the giant's thoughts as clearly as if he had spoken them in the Queen's English. 'Sixty? I am two hundred and seven years of age,' he said in Rick's mind. 'Which makes me an impossible adversary for yourself. Now, release time before I have to force you to do so.'

Rick remained silent. A *request*, he thought, albeit one with threats. If he had to ask Rick to do something, then maybe he wasn't able to force him to do it at all. If he were, then this bully would simply have taken from him what he wanted and forced it through without a second thought. But he hadn't.

345

'I *can* force you,' Rusak replied. He had read Rick's mind with worrying accuracy. 'Now do as I say, immediately.'

'If I do that,' Rick said defiantly, 'I lose. I choose to keep things the way they are.'

He peered around the professor's bulk and saw that things were unchanged.

'When you are dead, I will release time and your wife will die. Is that how you wish it?' Not for the first time in the last few months Rick felt pushed around and intimidated to the point where his anger overflowed. He closed his eyes and directed his emotions towards the instigator. When he had felt it leave his body he opened his eyes. The calmness pervaded his senses as the anger left him, and at the same time Rusak staggered backwards, almost falling over in the process. The communication between the two was temporarily broken.

Rusak steadied himself. He smiled malevolently. 'You are spirited for your era, Mr Sheldon,' he said aloud. 'But I am not of your time. Your anger killed your wife's sister and Mr Parsons, but it is not sufficient to scratch the surface with me.'

Rick's mouth gaped open. '*I* killed Anna, and Frank Parsons?' he asked incredulously.

'Distance is not a factor. You felt the anger towards them when you were in India and that was enough to kill them both.'

'Frank Parsons?'

'A road accident. Greening, a suicide. Your doing.'

The shock of this revelation knocked Rick sideways, but he gathered his thoughts and steadied himself. There was a job to be done here, and the past was the past.

'This is all very interesting for you, I am sure. But I have work to do. Release time immediately,' Rusak ordered.

'No,' Rick replied.

Fury and indignation were visible on the professor's face as he eyed Rick. A moment later Rick's head began to burn inside as if someone had inserted a white-hot poker into his brain. He fought it as best he could but the pain intensified exponentially and then he felt himself thrown to the ground. He hit the tarmac with sickening force, as if he had been butted by an angry rhinoceros, and the force of the blow pushed him along the road surface for many yards, the skin peeling off his back as he slid along out of control.

Having stopped, he barely managed to open his eyes. Rusak was stood where had previously been. No tangible blow had struck Rick, it was the power of the professor's mind alone that had injured him. And the hurt was real. His brain felt on fire and as he stood up in ludicrous defiance of this impossible foe he saw blood on the road from his back.

'I said NO,' Rick shouted. He again directed his intense wrath towards Rusak. The pleasure which followed the anger was, this time, hardly recognisable. Rusak's head moved back slightly in response to Rick's attack, the strongest he could muster. But it was followed by a taunting, guttural laugh that chilled Rick to the bone.

The pain from Rusak's previous assault was subsiding, so the onset of even more extreme agony in his head made Rick feel utterly defeated. But he wouldn't release time, no matter how bad it got. 'I suggest you do as I ask, Mr Sheldon,' Rusak said audibly.

'Never,' Rick replied, his teeth gritted and his eyes tightly shut as he endured the growing pain.

'Then it is time to say goodbye. You were... interesting,' Rusak declared.

Rick thought his head would explode as the pain reached new heights. As he gripped his skull with both hands he felt himself lift off the ground and as he opened his eyes ever so slightly he saw that he was being propelled through the air. Then he hit a tree by the roadside. The wind was taken from him entirely. He gasped for air, but seemed unable to take any in.

The pain in his head suddenly ceased, and he took in a lungful of air, though his cracked ribs objected severely. He cried out in pain with every new breath. Rick looked towards Ellie and saw that the scene was still frozen. He wasn't dead yet then. Looking to his right he saw Rusak grasping his own head whilst kneeling on the tarmac. Standing above him was Tal.

Wondering how close to death he had actually been, Rick

watched Tal stood over the professor. From where he was, Rick could see her face. It had a venomous expression as she looked at the man on the ground before her.

'Tal,' he said under his breath. 'Thank God.' Momentarily, Tal's attention was diverted from Rusak to Rick. She looked over to where he laid on the grass verge, but as she did so Rick's face dropped. As though she weighed only a few pounds, her body was lifted from the ground and then slammed into the road before she could regain control of it. Her head struck the unyielding surface with force and she yelled in response to the pain and the sight of the blood which ran freely from her face. Before she could compose herself and redirect her thoughts, Rusak struck again with incredible ferocity. Tal's head hit the tarmac again and again. Rick sensed her thoughts. In amongst them was a communication to Rusak that he could not break the tenets of time by interfering in person. He sensed her fear of death, a feeling that he recognised over and above any other, and a feeling of deep sadness that she had failed in her task as Guardian. The sickening attack continued and, after a few moments, Rick heard in his mind Tal saying goodbye to him.

It looked like a fatal road accident with a difference. Tal lay dead. An eight foot woman, her heart full of goodness and an unfulfilled yearning to achieve her aim, lay motionless in the roadway, her head crushed beyond recognition. Pints and pints of red blood ran in rivulets downhill and Rick could no longer sense any feelings or any emotions from the beautiful, elegant and steadfast woman who had been his rock. She was powerless to help him now.

Rusak stood up. He turned once again to Rick. Rick turned from his gaze. He couldn't bear any more pain and torment. He wished it were all over. He wished Rusak would finish him off and have done with it. At least he would be with Ellie, and his daughter, and to hell with the rest of it.

As Rusak walked towards where Rick laid, racked with pain in his side as he breathed shallowly, Rick felt the tree against which he was leaning for support become insubstantial and soft to the touch. He winced with pain as he turned his head to look at the tree. A strange feeling overcame him, one he could not define or describe in his mind, and then it was gone. It felt as though something had passed right through him. It didn't hurt, it was more of a realisation than a tangible feeling.

The air directly in front of him swirled, and he felt a gentle breeze against his face and his skin. The current wafted around him. It was warm and welcoming. Then it left him and the eddies in the air grew in force.

Formally approaching his injured victim with a sense of urgency, Rusak slowed his pace, then stopped. He looked around him as if he had been disturbed. But that was impossible, Rick thought, time was still in suspense. The bullet occupied the same place as it had a number of minutes earlier. No-one could approach, yet Rusak looked perturbed.

Slowly, by degrees, a figure appeared between Rick and where Rusak had stopped. It was a human figure, about the same size as Rick himself. When fully formed, Rick saw that the figure was about six feet tall. A female, dressed in black attire like a sari, stood there, her long blonde hair flowing down her back, and her feet slightly off the ground.

The woman turned to Rick. She spoke to him in a gentle, soothing voice. 'You are a good man, Rick Sheldon, and you have served your time admirably.'

Rusak's face looked like thunder as he stared directly at the newcomer. The woman looked back at Rusak, and what Rick could only describe as visible electricity flew from Rusak's head towards the woman. She moved her hands gracefully in front of her in a circular motion, entirely unperturbed by Rusak's attack. Sparks flew and the air was filled with a curious multi-coloured infusion of matter, which bounced off the shielding aura she had created in front of her. Quickly, the mysterious woman turned and put her hands together whilst facing Rick. Suddenly he felt warm and protected, as the electrification bounced off the aura that she had formed around him as well as herself.

'You are a disgrace to our kind,' she said to Rusak.

Rusak didn't seem to answer, but the woman spoke again as if he had said something to her in reply.

349

'No, you will honour this person here by communicating in a form that he can understand.'

'Who are you?' Rusak asked. 'And what business have you here?'

'I am Plik. I ask you what business you have coming to this time in contravention of the tenets.'

Rusak released a furious assault on the woman, which met with the same failure as it had previously. He swung out at her with his massive fists, but could not penetrate the protection she had created.

'I never agreed with your plan, Rusak. But I myself was bound by the tenets and you had to be given the opportunity to change the timeline once. But you have broken the rules. Unfortunately for you, you chose this man here, and he proved to be formidable for his time. He truly has surprised us all.' She turned to Rick. 'He is not permitted by the tenets to meet you in person, and when you succeeded in developing your mental abilities so that you were able to foil his plan, he exceeded his authority.'

'So when are you from?' Rick said, clutching his side.

'Oh, many years ahead of the professor. I am a Guardian, like your friend Tal, and I cannot allow this to continue.'

With that, she tipped her head towards the sky and closed her eyes. The ground rumbled and the sky changed colour for a few moments. As this happened, Rusak faded so that Rick could hardly see his features. His protests changed nothing as he slipped away into oblivion. Similarly, Tal's body faded until, together with the lake of blood that had formed around her, it disappeared.

'What have you done to them?' Rick asked in awe.

'Rusak never existed. That is the penalty he has condemned himself and his family to. Tal is dead, but she performed her duties well. Without her considered instruction you would not have been able to achieve what you did.'

'So what happens now?'

'I will place you as you were before Rusak illegally intervened. The rest is for you. I am only permitted to right the wrong, I cannot advise you otherwise.'

'I understand.'

Plik bent down and stroked Rick's side, which instantly healed and he took deep breaths into his lungs. She placed both her hands on top of his head and he felt a warmth and a strength flow through his body. The pain in his head, which had lingered after Rusak's last assault, left him and he felt a tingling in his back as that, too, healed in an instant.

'Goodbye,' Plik said softly.

'Thank you,' Rick said. It was inadequate in the extreme but it was all he could muster.

'Teach your daughter, and your son, your strengths,' she said as she walked away.

'My son,' Rick repeated.

A flash of light flew across Rick's line of vision, and as he blinked he found himself holding the toolbox looking at the bullet motionless in the air near to Ellie's head. Calmly placing the toolbox on the ground, Rick walked over to the scene. He reached out and took hold of the bullet. Between his finger and thumb he changed its path so that it would miss its target. Then he positioned himself about six feet away from the women and took hold of the toolbox once more.

Staring directly at Josie, he willed time to return to its normal course. At first nothing happened, but as he continued his meditation he saw the bullet move slowly through the air. He could see that it was going to miss Ellie and as he relaxed he heard a loud crack. Ellie slammed her hands over her ears and Josie's mouth dropped open in disbelief that she had missed from such a short distance. Rick was ready; he rugby-tacked Josie to the ground before she had chance to compose herself and he wrestled the gun from her grasp.

'Call the police,' he shouted to Ellie.

THE CULMINATION

Chapter 62

18th January 2002

It had taken a great deal of effort convincing Ellie that the visit was necessary, but he had succeeded in winning her over after many weeks of pestering and cajoling.

Ellie didn't really understand, but she couldn't. She only knew half the story.

Rick travelled alone to the secure psychiatric unit to visit Josie, the radio off as he contemplated the last year's events. There would never be another year like it. Life was run at a much slower pace now, and that was how he liked it. Looking after his daughter became a pastime that he loved more than he could ever have imagined. Tom had moved south to live with his brother in Birmingham for a while. He had been torn apart by what Josie had done, and needed time away to recover from the split.

Doctor Phillips had commended Rick for wanting to help with Josie's rehabilitation. He said that facing her fears and her delusions was important in helping her to come to terms with reality and to recognise the difference between what was real and what was fantasy. Despite the reassurances, Rick felt apprehensive at the prospect of speaking to Josie. She had supposedly been hallucinating. She maintained, very loudly, that she had a life with Rick; that they had shared sexual relations and that Ellie was dead. She claimed that she had comforted Rick when Ellie was killed and that they had made a life together. She frequently had nightmares where she dreamed that she was trapped in a dream and she regularly woke half the patients with her screams in the night.

Rick couldn't tell Ellie that the woman had been manipulated; that she was suffering psychosis as an aftermath of what she had been put through. But he could try and help Josie.

After all, she wasn't to blame for any of this, in fact she had been the one to suffer most through no fault of her own.

Rick rang the bell at reception and his stomach turned over. However he was received by Josie, be it with anger or love, it would be awkward. He longed to tell her the truth and the real reasons why she was hurting so badly, but he feared that the tenets of time would be breached and so it simply wasn't an option. He would have to patronise her as discreetly as possible and hope that it would serve to help her and soothe her pain.

Doctor Phillips met Rick personally shortly after he had rung for attention.

'Mr Sheldon, pleased to meet you,' he said cordially.

'You too,' Rick replied. 'How is she?'

'I'm really sorry,' the doctor said, his expression changing in an instant. 'I tried ringing you half an hour ago but you'd already left home. Josie… she took her own life. There was nothing we could do for her.'

Rick flopped into a large material chair behind him, totally dumbfounded by the news. The doctor pulled another chair up and sat beside him.

'Are you OK?' he asked.

'How did she do it?' Rick asked without looking the doctor in the face.

'That's not really important, is it?'

'I said how?' Rick repeated.

'She removed the cord from her track suit bottoms and hanged herself on the back of her bedroom door during the night,' he said. 'She's never displayed any suicidal tendencies in the six months she's been with us. We're all quite shocked.'

'I'm not looking to pin the blame on anyone, Doctor Phillips. I just needed to know how, that's all.'

The doctor reached into his pocket. 'She wrote a note. I was considering withholding it from you because I didn't want you to feel in any way responsible for her death, but I can see you're a strong character and she clearly wanted you to read it.' He passed Rick the note, written in beautiful handwriting on top quality paper.

My darling Rick.

You are not to blame for anything, but I can't live my life without you, so I'll end it here and hope the wait isn't too long before we meet again.

The people here are kind but they don't understand what I'm going through. I've told them over and over that all I want is you, that we should have a life together and that life has been taken off us. I keep having dreams that we are together and that our lives are full and rich. We make fantastic love and share everything. Then it's all ripped away by waking up. I feel that we have a life but that something is stopping us from being together.

When I'm asleep we live, when I wake I die. I feel like I'm living two lives and it's tearing me apart. I believe we have lived together, but I appreciate that you can't understand that. Sometimes I know I'm right, but other times I feel as mad as a hatter.

My love will be with you always.
Josie.

'She was a very confused lady,' Doctor Phillips said as Rick folded the paper.

'You have no idea,' Rick replied, giving the doctor a steely glare.

Chapter 63

2ⁿᵈ October 2039

'Happy birthday, darling,' Rick said, his arms outstretched as Rebecca breezed into the kitchen.

'Thanks, dad,' she replied, giving him a hug.

'So, how's my little girl then?'

'Rick, she's thirty seven, hardly a little girl,' Ellie interjected.

'She'll always be *my* little girl, no matter what anyone says,' he said with a smile.

'Listen, I've some news for you two,' Rebecca said, grinning all over her face. 'I had an interview three weeks ago and I found out by post this morning that I've got the job.'

'What is it?' Ellie asked.

'Well, in a nutshell, it's a research project about diseases of the brain. *You* wouldn't know about it, but there's been a small but growing problem in Chile and other South American countries over the last few years where people have died of unexplained brain disorders. I'm on the research team chosen to look into the problem.'

'And to think you almost decided to leave school at sixteen. Now, an up and coming doctor specialising in neurology,' Ellie beamed with pride for her daughter.

Tears rolled down Rick's cheeks.

'Just look at the softy,' Ellie said, pointing to Rick.

Rebecca gave her dad another cuddle.

It was one of the happiest days of Rick's life. Matthew, his son, visited and the four of them enjoyed a hearty meal sat around the dining table as they had done on so many occasions as the children grew up. It was the first time they had all been together without the children's respective partners for a number of years and it made Rick feel young again. At sixty-eight he

358

didn't feel old, and today's news renewed his faith in destiny and made that year of hell seem worthwhile.

'And how's my number one son?' Rick said to Matthew over a beer in the garden.

'Yeah, fine,' he replied, a contradictory look of anguish on his face. 'I had this incredibly vivid dream last night though…'